Who can tell where love will lead us,
Love the color of a rose—
Love the ever-sounding bell—
Does she summon to a close,
To the bitter of farewell?
To the gorgeous gate of Hell?
Ah, who knows, who knows?

Who can say what love may teach us,
She may teach us how to mourn,
She may teach us laughter fades
And that the Fair, foresworn,
Is not fair in how it trades—
And how eyes may wound like blades—
But, who'll learn, who'll learn?

TANITH LEE
in DAW Books:

THE BIRTHGRAVE
VAZKOR, SON OF VAZKOR
QUEST FOR THE WHITE WITCH
THE STORM LORD
DON'T BITE THE SUN
DRINKING SAPPHIRE WINE
VOLKHAVAAR
NIGHT'S MASTER
DEATH'S MASTER
DELUSION'S MASTER
ELECTRIC FOREST
KILL THE DEAD
SABELLA
DAY BY NIGHT
LYCANTHIA
CYRION
RED AS BLOOD

SUNG
IN
SHADOW

████████████

Tanith Lee

DAW Books, Inc.
Donald A. Wollheim, Publisher
1633 Broadway, New York, N.Y. 10019

AUTHOR'S NOTE

The novel is set in the Renaissance Italy of a parallel world, as certain discrepancies will demonstrate. Correct Italian pronunciation must not, therefore, be applied to the names, which are spelled phonetically, and should be read or spoken as written.

—T.L.

FIRST PRINTING, MAY 1983

 DAW TRADEMARK REGISTERED
U.S. PAT. OFF. MARCA
REGISTRADA, HECHO EN U.S.A.

PRINTED IN U.S.A.

PART ONE:

The Rose

ONE

Who can tell where love will lead us,
Love the color of a rose—
Love the ever-sounding bell—
Does she summon to a close,
To the bitter of farewell?
To the gorgeous gate of Hell?
Ah, who knows, who knows?

"And do you not know, then?"

"Oh, I know. Or I did, once. Before you corrupted me and made me so virtuous."

"Hah! Virtuous. You?"

"I. Do I not sit here, conversing with an enemy? With a foul Montargo, no less. (And who's less than a Montargo?)"

"One of the Estembas, possibly."

"One *only*, then, for the rest of us are saints."

Raising his grey-gold head, Flavian Estemba plucked notes off the mandolin with ringed fingers, and embellished the verse of the song with various asides, in a frivolous yet still very musical voice.

Behind him, over the terrace of the old garden, the sky and the town married with sunset. Everything grew mysterious there, alleys constricting, walls melting into the courts they enclosed. The powderings of dust, which all day rose and fell with the birds at the coming and going of men, sank down like a succession of veils, turning first amber, then apricot, ultimately the shade of ashes. The town also sank downhill to the north and west. In the broad square some three or four streets distant from the garden, the Basilica rested, pale, like a ghost and with its ghostly graveyard at its back. From the square, too, the campanile sounded its own bell as Estemba's verse once more finished. Elsewhere and everywhere, like a forest of daggers, the multitude of towers pointed up,

7

catching the last rays of the sun on their myriad cupolas, carvings and escutcheons.

"Golden Sana Verensa," the second young man said, gazing dreamily at the town, "smoothed by fading light. If only she were as magical in fact as she looks this moment."

"If only anything were true to itself. Oh if only!" cried the singer of the song. He threw the mandolin in the air, snatched it, and leapt suddenly to the top of the low narrow wall that bounded the terrace, beyond which eighty feet of broken brick and creeper tumbled to the thoroughfare beneath.

"Come off the wall, for God's sake. Why break your neck?"

"Ah, do you love me so well?"

"I love you well, you fool. Not well enough to pay for your funeral, and how should poverty-stricken Estemba afford it?"

"Romulan, my good angel, I suppose we would have to steal the money from some hapless one, as Montargo always does."

Flavian Estemba, generally called "Mercurio" by those who knew him, stared toward the street, feigned vertigo; swayed first forward over the drop, next back, and so gracefully and bonelessly fell into the garden, and into the arms of Romulan, who, with a curse, caught him.

Straightening, Mercurio examined the mandolin solicitously.

Romulan turned away, playing anger, almost on the verge of it, and beheld, like his fate, the Montargo Tower, framed between two urns, on the peach-tinted sky. This familiar sight at once absorbed, disturbed him. The tower suggested instantly his father, and that father's father, and thereby all the decades that had gone, both into the construction of its stones, and of Romulan's own atoms: genealogy, lineage. To be nineteen and feel such a weight of time was curious.

The young men, back to back in the garden, had a classical stance. Each was handsome, a handsomeness attractively flawed in Estemba, and in Romulan Montargo unnervingly flawless. His looks approached sheer beauty, which had a fine, almost terrible edge to it. Demon or angel, who could be sure: such a face, endorsed by its mantle of modishly long black hair, its black brows, the black-lashed metallic blueness of the eyes—it seemed capable of any emotion or deed in its savage innocence. And then this savagery was gone, instinctively blurred. The face became merely immature, worldly, eager, bored, for Estemba was saying, "What dangerous adventure do we try this evening?"

Romulan turned back warily. Mercurio was already in the process of leaving the garden. He gave his habitual impression, that he was prepared to leave everything, anyone, unless they hastened to keep up. The impression, in Romulan's case, might be false.

"Danger? You mean the Bhorga, which is currently full of the Ottantas and the Feros?"

"Not to credit the Castas, who are abroad in multitudes. Maybe. Maybe not. Maybe I alluded to entertainments."

"My father says I neglect study. Perhaps you should find me a tutor."

"That I may yet do."

Mercurio swung over the broken shoulder of the terrace, and vanished onto the path below. The notes of the mandolin plincked up in his wake, and the careless, perfect voice:

"Who can tell where love will lead us,

"To the loss of several coins,

"To an ailment of the loins—"

Romulan followed slowly, sullen and melancholy. He could have given no reason for his mood. He expected the friend below on the walk presently to notice, comfort and divert him.

Behind him, three centuries older than he, the Montargo Tower, and all the other towers of Sana Verensa's horizons, were starting to open the lamp-lighted slots of long slim windows. Inexorable vertical eyes of brass and blood fixed on the town, the darkening hills that embraced it. The towers seemed all alive in this moment, like serpents risen on their tails, pitilessly intent. Who, with their antique hatreds, would they venomously bite and devour tonight? Any who dwelled in Verensa were used to the phenomenon, consciously or unconsciously observed. These baleful snakes reared over their heads, which were in reality fortress-palaces sculpted with emblems: Ottanta, Montargo, de Casta, Belmorio, Chenti, Vespelli, Estemba, de Fero. . . . Many more. Many, many, many more. Patrician strongholds, each housing an aristocratic family of profound and unassailable ancestry, proud as eagles, ferocious as bears. Each family fed and armored by its history, its Name, its sigils, its banners, its prejudice, its xenophobia. For each House was a planet, peopled as if by a unique race, mostly contemptuous and in loathing of others.

From such soil feuds, political in origin, growing but too personal with deaths on every side, proliferated, sure as night and day.

The streets leading to the Basilica square were now obscure with shadows. The brown sun had disappeared, delegating formlessness, which blended with the negative dun-colored clothes of the two young men—to sport house colors unattended on the streets after dusk was unwise in the extreme.

The Basilica bell, which prompted some to think of Heaven, or of death, or of nothing, depending on temperament, grew still. As Romulan and Mercurio went across the square, a grey cat sprang from the rim of the public fountain and darted into an alleyway. Nothing else seemed stirring. The ghostly facade of the Basilica loomed over them. Bronze angels above the doors troubled Romulan, as they had always troubled him. He did not understand why; perhaps he had heeded, unaware, some frightening resemblance to himself.

To the west side of the square, a maze of alleys accumulated. The broadest of these, humpbacked and only partially cobbled, was yet here and there lit by the lamps and occasionally unshuttered windows of adjacent houses. The mercantile quarter lay almost directly behind the Basilica, and beyond this (the area to which the broad alley led), the Lower Town, the Bhorgabba.

Down the alley, almost it might appear from force of habit, Estemba and Montargo swung, Mercurio still idly sounding the mandolin. Torches, song, shouts, were not uncommon on this way, nor the slash and ring of blades. The bright hilts of swords were obvious against the nondescript clothing of both adventurers, whenever they passed through a light. Also the masks both had put on as they vacated the square. Mercurio's, a most Satanic devil with gold-spangled lids and leering mouth, covered all his face. Romulan's mask of plain white leather concealed only the upper features. Vanity was less likely the cause of this than the general impatience of Romulan's nature.

It was full dark when a twist in the alley and a variation in the slope and surrounding architecture abruptly revealed one of the more notorious entrances to the Bhorgabba: the old squat wall with its round open arch, torches nakedly flaring in their brackets with a slightly fiendish look of welcome. On the far side of the arch the seethe and teem of life, whose noise had been audible for some minutes, and which made the spot as low in reputation as in geography.

Tonight, however, an impediment to carnal sin had positioned itself before the arch.

Mercurio halted. Romulan did the same.

Striking an avid chord on the mandolin, Mercurio softly and unnecessarily announced:

"Damnable Feros, playing peacocks."

And so they were, the five who blocked the archway. Though masked, they had disdained the courtesy and prudence of disguise, and were arrayed in the colors of the de Fero family—unmistakable as the colors of any House—jet black and flame, and decorated besides with every sort of ornament that was worked with Fero's sigil, the Wolf. Even the masks were wolves' heads. Their swords, last and best clue, were unsheathed, leaning on their knees as they stood or crouched dicing, affecting unnotice of arrivals on the slope above.

"Back, or onward?" said the devil to Romulan.

"On, I suppose, or be ready for pursuit."

"There's clever thinking."

Mercurio strolled forward and down the alley, touching the strings of the mandolin at intervals, Romulan in step with him. As the torches by the gate struck them, the nearest of the de Feros glanced up, and made a parody of surprise. One by one the others reacted, and with a feigned velvety sloth, spread out across the gate, letting the loosely held blades jangle.

"Good evening, sirs," said a de Fero to the left of the arch.

"An excellent, delicious evening," said another to the right.

"Well, well, well," said Mercurio, strolling on into the midst of them. He was so nonchalant, so barely conscious of them, they almost parted in error to let him by. Then a tall one shouted, and stepped directly in his path. The bulk, and the florid complexion visible in the mask holes, gave the giant away as Old Fero's second son.

"I cannot permit you to pass the gate, sir," said Fero Duo, charmingly. "There is a lot of wickedness the other side."

"So I've heard," said Mercurio. "My reason for being here."

"And your noble friend?"

"I have no friends," said Mercurio promptly.

"Enemies, perhaps?"

"A few of those."

"Name them, if you would be so kind."

"Oh, Casta, Lippi, Floria—"

"Fero?"

"*Fero?*" Mercurio was astonished. "Who is Fero?"

"You never heard the name?"

"Indeed I heard it."

"When?"

"Just now, when you spoke."

Fero Duo turned theatrically to his lounging friends and kinsmen.

"We have a wit here, it seems." He lifted the sword, which had black and pink jewels in the pommel. He showed it to Mercurio. "Have you wit enough to say you love and honor the Wolf Tower?"

"I wonder," Mercurio said. He inclined his head toward Romulan. "Do you think I have the wit for that?"

"If you do, then I do not," said Romulan.

A blade left its sheath like red lightning under the torches, and lanced forward with a delicacy and artistry Fero Duo might have envied, had he not been in receipt of it. In three seconds Romulan's sword had scored through the drawstring of Fero's shirt, which now fell apart, revealing a mottled hairy breast and the cameo of a lady on a chain.

Mercurio balanced the mandolin carefully against the convenient wall of a neighboring yard, and moved nearer. He patted Fero's arm.

"My dear, I do trust you were recently shriven. Are you confessed? In a state of grace? Otherwise, my companion will be sending you to a warmer night than this."

Fero Duo thrust him off, fell back a pace, and lugged his sword into the air. It was a dangerous cut, the more so for its raggedness. But where Mercurio had stood was only space. There came a second song of steel lifting from sheath, less couth than the note of a mandolin. Estemba's own blade shot upward in a silken arc and Fero's steel clattered on the intermittent cobbles.

"Name yourself!" Some other Fero, much embroidered, shouted as their big leader scrambled for his weapon.

"*You* name me," invited Mercurio. He fenced like the accomplished dancer he was, every movement choreographed. Someone lunged sideways yelping as the dancer's sword licked his chin, shaving a little line on it. Someone else swore vilely as Romulan thwacked him across the shins with the flat of the blade. Romulan laughed slightly as he did battle, showing teeth as beautiful as the rest of him. He did not analyze what he did, or its mortal potential. Death had seldom suggested itself to him save as an illness to which strangers were sometimes prone. His swordsmanship, fly and glamorous as Mercurio's—Mercurio had indeed taught him some of it—had a playful reckless edge Mercurio's did not. Mercurio Flavian Estemba, who as a boy had seen his own two brothers die on the street in duels such as this, fought neatly and treacherously. Though to fight was second nature to him, he never engaged to fight without apprehension. His one weakness was that he was stimulated by his own fear, enjoyed it, frequently sought it out, as Romulan sought mere action, for its own sake.

"Leave him!" Fero Duo thundered, as the shaved youth, sent raving mad by a nick, careered about Mercurio. "*I* want him for myself, whoever he is."

"You flatter me," said Mercurio. His sword slid almost invisibly through the Fero's lax guard, and bit a second time into injured flesh. As the youth roared, Mercurio's left fist sailed from its elegant sword-dancer's gesturing, and smashed the bloody jaw on its point. The Fero went down and lay motionless. Mercurio, turning, saluted Fero Duo. "At your service, sir."

At his back, he heard a screech of blades, a cry. Another Fero, clutching a bleeding flesh-wound in the side, staggered past and through the Bhorga gate, calling for his servant. Token wounds were normally sufficient, despite the crowing. Murder was less often the outcome than it had been. Mercurio ducked under Fero Duo's blade. The fight was becoming mere ritual, if it had ever been anything else.

Romulan, shoulders to the Bhorga wall, flickered his sword daintily between the two remaining Feros.

His natural impatience, and a sense of boredom, were affecting his judgment. Suddenly there was an oath, a grunt, directly above him. A hand caught at and irresistibly fondled his hair, another ripped the leather mask off his face and dangled it between his eyes. Mirth and invective accompanied the deed. It seemed a Fero servant had climbed the low wall on the inside, and taken it on himself to assist his masters. Romulan cut upward with his sword, losing his temper, reckoning to lose his new assailant a pair of fingers.

The two Feros in the alley smiled at him.

"Romulan Montargo," one said, genuflecting. "An honor."

"Montargo, the sinking ship," said the other. "And tell us, does your father still dally with bitch-dogs?"

Romulan, who hated and loved his father in equal measure, and was sensitive to the mention of him in any context, sprang forward. As he did so he brought a dagger from his belt. He rammed the small blade left-handed into the shoulder of the man who had remarked on dogs. The other got the smart of the sword across his embroidered ribs, slewed and riposted with a speed and virulence that took Romulan unaware.

"Oh Christ, oh sweet God," moaned the stabbed man, sinking between them. "He's killed me. By the Mass, he has."

"Coward and idiot," Romulan snapped. He stepped back, and spat on the man. Up on the wall, the servant was whimpering. The white leather mask lay on the ground, decorated with a little base blood.

Embroidery, who had not pressed his accidental advantage, glanced beyond Romulan, in time to see the Satan-masked fighter kick Fero Duo in the groin, and the inevitable resultant antics of the latter.

Embroidery, now the sole remaining upright Fero, glared at Romulan, panting, trying to see if he had pinked him.

"I'll pay you, Montargo."

Romulan swept him a bow. "If you ever consider yourself able, anyone will direct you to my door."

"Up, Francho." Embroidery bent to tug at his groaning kinsman. "Stop calling on Jesus, and I'll help you home."

Fero Duo rolled through the dark dust, avoided by Mercurio in distaste.

Romulan walked over to him, sheathing the dagger, the sword.

"It's my father now they revile. It used to be my uncle. Bloody Fero."

"Bloody yourself," shouted the embroidered Fero, aiding his kinsman up the alley. "Say your prayers, Montargo."

"Oh, say yours and be damned," Romulan shouted back. He turned abruptly and put his head against the wall. He was shaking with a rage he could neither control nor translate, almost in tears with it, for the fight had stirred but not relieved some powerful passion.

Three Fero servants emerged from the gate and skulked past, one with a slashed palm. Of the flesh-wounded youth who had run in there, there was no current sign.

Mercurio watched these mobile Feros retreat up the slope,

leaving one of their number sound oblivious on the cobbles.
While Fero Duo, having crawled away, was busy vomiting at
a handy interstice, blaspheming between heaves. Estemba set
his hand on Romulan's shoulder.

"Come. We'll find some Castas for you to eat next. Unmasked, you'll be a fine target."

Romulan toed the spoiled mask with his boot.

"It has their stenchful gore on it."

"As you do, my princeling. When will you learn to fight
fastidiously? Next time, go brawling in an apron."

"Next time, go brawling alone."

Mercurio slipped his hand through Romulan's hair, a
caress that swiftly became a hard terrier's grip on the neck.

"I will not have that from you. Save such advice for your
enemies."

Romulan, rigid in his grasp, said fiercely, "Your cousin
killed a Montargo not two years ago, *enemy*."

"And your uncle killed my brother. What odds? Every
tower feuds. You and I do not."

"My father has said—"

"Your wretched father, dear child, is of no concern to
me."

Romulan twisted about. He stared at Mercurio from two
blue conflagrations that must serve as eyes. Estemba regarded
him with elaborate politeness, waiting for this anger to erupt
or go out. When neither happened, Mercurio made one une-
quivocal sign. "—For Montargo. Now kill me for insulting
your precious House."

Romulan stared another moment, then flushed, his eyes
cooling as his color heightened.

"Confound all our Houses. Let's get on where we were going."

Mercurio laughed, took Romulan's head between his hands
and kissed his forehead.

"Let's on indeed. But put up your hood, proud boy, or
we'll not get twenty paces."

Distanced from yet beneath the auspices of Sana Verensa's
multitudinous towers, the Bhorgabba thrummed with its low-
life and its hot lanterns. Smoky radiances flapped from the
apertures of inns; ochre droplets spilled through skew lattices
and shutters. Dull red like dying roses, the open windows of
harlots, here and there a dark silhouette leaning out, white
breasts blooming from a tight bodice, or the breastless torso

of a boy whore, gold-earringed, singing his wares like a flute. Torch-poles at corners, most on fire, or the cook-shop ovens baking their pastries and dubious meats, the odd lamp flowering from a lintel, and now and then some place of business that had nothing to do with the sins of gluttony or lust but inclined to avarice, a leather-workers or house of clerks sitting late over their quills and tomes, lent a pastier light to the carousings, scurryings and fumblings below and about.

A wine-stall nearest the Bhorga arch—three benches piled with clay bottles and corked skins—had provided drink. A sistering doorway had provided an encounter with three Castas, heavily masked and clad in ashy cloaks, but still belligerent: "Enzo, who are these? Shall we bash their noses through their skulls? Say, sirs, how do you like us?" To which Mercurio replied in the friendliest of tones, "I love you as I love my doxies." And to the Casta demand: "Who is your modestly hooded companion?" Mercurio: "A priest, sir, I am showing the seamier side of the town." Enough merriment was caused by this to let them by. Possibly too, Romulan's blood-soaked sleeve deterred their instinct to combat, although at another time it might have operated in reverse, an incitement to further blood-letting.

The blood-soaked sleeve had also become of some interest to Romulan himself. Half a mile into the labyrinth of the Bhorga, making he knew not where at Mercurio's direction, Romulan took another gulp of raw wine, slung the skin to Estemba, walked five or six feet, thrust off his hood, and slumped sideways against a wall, the narrow street, its roofs, yellow lights and the sky between, whirling like a wheel.

Mercurio, having paused to exchange a greeting with some fellow in a doorway, presently came up.

"What, drunk already? The wine must be better than I thought."

Romulan lay back on the wall. He raised his left arm, considered it, smiled with nausea and said, "This blood is mine."

"Let me see." Mercurio drew off the Satan mask the better to observe, dropping it over the stem of the mandolin now on his back. He took Romulan's arm, examining, relinquishing cautiously. "Imbecile," he said quietly. "Why did you not tell me?"

"Imbecile, I did not know."

"Not know? Half-dead and does not know."

Romulan grinned. "They fought so shoddily. The embroidered booby must have sliced me. I wondered how the blood did not dry but only grew wetter." He began to sink down the wall. Seriously, sweetly, he inquired, "Am I half-dead?" It meant nothing to him. He did not believe it any more than Estemba had intended him to.

"Buried," Mercurio said. He plucked Romulan off the wall, drawing the sound right arm across his shoulders, clasping Romulan around the waist. Romulan fell against him, head lolling, laughing, drunk on wine and blood-loss. Through clouds and vortexes they began to move, back the way they had come, Mercurio dragging him, carrying him.

"Where are we going now?" Romulan asked.

"Susina's house."

"One of your jades."

"Susina is two of any man's jades, at least. Also the only shelter I recognize hereabouts. Be thankful."

"Oh, I am thankful. Most thankful. I am ecstatic with thankfulness."

"Hush, child," Mercurio said, with the utmost gentleness.

The sight of his own wound had undone Romulan. Sick nearly to senselessness, yet he derived a peculiar and intense comfort from Estemba's supporting arm, the grey-gold hair against his face, the aura of tenderness and protection.

A house-front loomed up, a door with ornate fitments being vigorously pounded. A shout or so, far off as if on the hills. A gold window burst open, a woman's young and strident voice pierced the eardrums, to be rewarded by Mercurio's most cajoling note.

"Come now, Susina, remember you were always a saint when it came to a handsome face."

"Not when it comes to yours, you demi-demon."

"Ah, Susina. And my charming friend dying at your door."

"I am not the hospital. I do not take the wounded in."

"This once."

"I have patrons and guests. You be circumspect."

"As a monk, dear lady of delights."

"Pah."

A shutter slammed. The door was simultaneously opened. They swung into the light and Romulan out of it.

Mercurio, feeling the dead-weight of unconsciousness, pulled on his devil-mask again, and picked Romulan up in both arms. The girl who had opened the door giggled.

"So you carried me, last month."

"And you carried me another way, I remember."

The girl giggled once more, and lowered painted lids. It

was a game, for she was new and he had never seen her previously, or had her.

"She says you must go through the garden and up the stair."

"Tell her I worship her. If she can procure a doctor she shall be sanctified."

Mercurio passed through the gaudy antechamber at a striding run, Romulan held like an offering before him. The garden spread beyond a door already wide, a square affectation of wildly scented trees, vines, pergolas and absurd statuary in the antique manner. A tangle of apricots stretched up to a balustrade, almost concealing the pitted stair leading to the windows of the brothel's mezzanine floor.

As Estemba took the staircase, he grew aware of a group of three feminine figures, somewhat illuminated, and poised at the balustrade above, seemingly intent on him. A glance gave him Susina, lavish in a true Bhorga whore's gown of lavenders, magentas and hyacinths, that sporadically left bare the two rosy cannon-mouths of her nipples. The other women were ominously clad in sepia, one—and that one a large one—entirely and cumbersomely veiled. The third woman, who was slender, was veiled in dove-grey lace, and in the Eastern fashion, from the lower lids to the chin. Mercurio, even as he negotiated his burden and the stair, looked closely at her. An admirer of female beauty, if not essentially snared by it, he feasted briefly on two smouldering blue coals of eyes, fringed by fans of coal-black lashes. Romulan's eyes, for that matter, and, also for that matter, fixed on Romulan.

Mercurio reached the top step and thus the mezzanine balcony. To get to the chamber Susina allocated sudden guests, he would need to go by the women.

"Susina, can you summon a doctor?"

"Duelling, you devil-beast. Let you both die."

"Ah, Susina. These are not your cherry lips that say it."

"Well, I'm a fool, and will burn in Hell for being one. Go in and I'll do what I can. Sana Vera!" she murmured as he came forward, "but he's beautiful. More beautiful than you, you wretch."

"So he is, and restrain your paws from him. His noble father wishes him kept virgin till the marriage night."

Susina burst into guffaws worthy of the Chitadella barracks. To Mercurio's interest, the fat woman in sepia disguise joined in the laughter as coarsely, her veils billowing.

"Pardon me, lady," he murmured courteously, as the veiling rolled almost over his face, "I will ship oars and sail to leeward of your rigging." At that, the vulgar merriment increased. The little one, however, had nearly shut her sapphire eyes, looking ready to faint too. "Courage, my donna," Mercurio Estemba said softly to her. "He will live."

"Oh," she whispered. "Oh."

Her skin, her voice were extraordinarily young. What was a maiden of good family and no more than fifteen doing in a bawdy-house?

But he was by them now, kicking open the curtain beyond the unclosed window of Susina's private room.

"Thanks, Susina," Estemba shouted. "It's as foul as I recall. Or maybe, a mere touch fouller."

To the melodic accompaniment of her curses, Mercurio laid Romulan on the much-trampled bed, and began to rip his dun cloak to bits for bandaging.

TWO

The bell was striking from the campanile for midnight when the palancina, draped and fringed in the oriental mode, was set down at the edge of the square. A quantity of gauze billowed out like smoke. A sepia bundle of middle-aged womanhood followed. Shaking her skirts, she stingily paid the hired men who, she knew, had grumbled at her weight, then chided the girl who still remained inside.

"Out, my poppy. Are we not late enough? And, God forgive me, we must go in the church and pray before we get to our beds."

The poppy emerged from the palancina, her head bowed under its mantle and its grey lace, face invisible.

"Poor baby, spirits wrung out, and no wonder. Heaven will punish me, I'm sure, for taking you to such a wicked place. But you would go. And can I refuse you anything? Be off," the woman added imperiously to the hired men, who stood snickering. She drew the slight form of the girl into her arm, and swept her away across the square. As she did so, a page boy in crimson bolted from the shadows.

"Pieto, is that you? Were you asleep? Pestful cherub, light the lamp and keep proper order."

Pieto, yawning, obeyed. He had had a long wait among the doorways and courtyard gates, where this great woman had left him. He had been nervous, too, so near lawless streets and arguments everywhere, alone, and dressed in the Chenti House colors.

The lamp evolved like a pink moon, a friendly, soothing glow to see them safe to the Basilica side door, to which the naughty fat hag, his mistress, was wont to traipse after every escapade. Pieto regarded the woman slyly, and her charge more slyly still. Pieto pondered what Lord Chenti and his Lady would say, if any told them their pristine about-to-be-betrothed daughter, Iuletta, had been taken calling at a whorehouse.

Clumping and fumbling up the steps, swerving beneath the angels over the vast doors, Donna Cornelia took her accustomed course, via a plaster cloister, to the thin little dexter door jammed among the carvings. Here she knocked, waiting and puffing, until a grill was raised and an eye appeared. To this eye Cornelia showed a coin. The grill went down, a part of the door was opened. Cornelia, pressing her charge before her, crowded through. The door was shut in Pieto's face. (One day or night, the witch would stick in the door. Like an oliphant of the spice-lands, trumpeting, priest hauling one way, Pieto valiantly pushing the other. But no budging her.) Pieto grinned, and sat on the flagstones by the lamp, for another uneasy wait.

The porter-priest, having accepted his tip, waved the two ladies on into the pillared side chapel, and relapsed in slumber on his bench.

Cornelia bustled, hastening off her veil to reveal blown-rose features of a still-extant prettiness, somewhat resembling the features of the harlot Susina. Which was not very amazing, since they were mother and daughter. Cornelia, tracing before brow and ample bosom the sign of the cross, went over her latest visit with stoical good humor. Though only spoken of in the Chenti Tower as of one deceased, Susina was a lively, charitable daughter, and a wealthy one. On the whole Cornelia, who most of her life had been a wed and apparently respectable servant, did not reckon whoring such a bad trade. For this reason, broad-mindedly, and with a sense of mischief that occasionally had proved her undoing, Cornelia had not balked to take her nurseling with her. Susina behaved reasonably in front of a young aristocratic maiden, and it had given Cornelia a chance to see the girl, and to receive a gift or so—besides exchanging some interesting gossip. Now, however, a vague foreboding was creeping into Cornelia's voluminous and cloudy-sighted heart. Iuletta, who had chattered like a lark on the road to the Bhorgabba, had been intensely silent during the journey home.

"There now, slip off the veil and be modest before God," said Cornelia. Iuletta did as she was told, with graceful, somnabulist motions. From behind the dove-grey lace appeared a hurtfully beautiful face, gone pale as snow. The two sapphire eyes, large and brilliant in the dapple of the candles, looked gloriously blinded. Was the child feverish? Heaven, what now? At this age they were like mad things, one minute light and merry, the next screaming or in tears.

Cornelia plumped down before the chapel altar, and Iuletta Chenti knelt spontaneously beside her. Iuletta's exquisite lips—her whole face and form might have been sculpted by some genius artisan—fluttered around a prayer, and faltered.

Praying earnestly, her mind on other matters and assuming God would not notice, Cornelia worried. It was, for sure, the fault of those two gallants who had come up onto the balcony. One was an absolute Satan in his mask (though a fine figure on him), the other, unmasked and marvelous as a young knight in a stained glass window, stone-white and apparently dead, yet fit for an empress to lay hands on. Moved herself, Cornelia could see the effect this spectacle would have on the impressionable and sheltered virgin. Beg Jesus to put such stirrings out of little Iulet's breast. Thank God, there was a betrothal in the offing, young Belmorio, comely enough to dazzle a girl. (Providing of course the Belmorios and the Chentis did not quarrel again as, until one year ago, they had most murderously done.) So much intrigue, so many battles on the streets and in the forums of Sana Verensa. Shocked, disapproving, immensely thrilled, Donna Cornelia began to pray, half-heartedly, for an end to all feuds. In similar vein, she would presently pray for Susina to repent.

Iuletta meanwhile, worried over but momentarily unwatched, had ceased all attempts at piety. Her eyes wandered about the small chapel, familiar to her and quite comfortable in its sternness, even its glimpses of terror. For, while the right wall of the capella was painted in representations of Heaven, the left depicted Hell. There the flames leapt and the cauldrons seethed. The damned, devoured by serpents, poked with toasting-forks, capered upon by monsters, writhed with sad, despairing faces. In the half-shine of the few candles, the awful scene appeared to quiver and to live, but so Iuletta had beheld it several times. And now she barely heeded. Instead she searched the right wall, among Hell's angelic neighbors. During her earliest childhood, some, in particular Cornelia, had promised her her own personal angel, who would stand always at her shoulder, or hover over her bed when she lay in sleep. A creature, unhuman and sublime, golden-winged, sword drawn and ready—both to smite those who would harm her, and to chastise Iuletta herself should she stray from the virtues of her era and caste. In this angel she had always, to some degree, believed. And now, this night, she had seen him.

Disappointed in the angels on the wall, Iuletta turned precipitately and plucked Cornelia's sleeve. Cornelia started.

"What is it, my catling?"

"His name. I must know it."

"What? Whose name?"

"*His* name. The man the other carried up to the mezzanine balcony. Who *else*?"

"Oh, shush, child. Not here."

"Oh, nurse, how can I bear it? How can I bear to have seen him and not even to know his name? Oh, will he die?"

"Eventually," said Cornelia, and crossed herself. "But not for some years, I would think, being young and strong. And Susina knows a clever physician or two. In her—vocation, that's usually wise."

Iuletta breathed quickly. Her cheeks flamed.

"But his name," she hissed. Her beautiful hand drove all its nails into Cornelia's arm, right through silk and linen.

"Ah! leave go of me, scratcher. How do I know his name? Some fellow brawling in a tavern, some cutthroat or slitpurse, some pimp, some ponce—oh, I beg your pardon, Lord. There now, you make me speak crudely before Christ."

Iuletta put her hand over her face, and looked between her long fingers, on many of which one or two priceless rings guttered or blazed.

"How could he be any of those things you say? He was nobly born. A son of some patrician tower. How could he be anything else and look as he did?"

"Well. That's so. You are probably intelligent, black kitten."

"Then it will be easy to learn his name."

"Perhaps Susina can get it from her Satan friend. And what will you do with it when you have his name?"

"Say it," Iuletta responded with a strange and burning stillness. "Say it over and over, waking or in dreams, until he hears me."

"Hush," said Cornelia automatically. "Not here." Her interest was kindled. (Over the altar, serene and remote, the tortured Jesus concentrated upon the nails of his cross, ignoring the frenetic dialogue going on below.) "But what of handsome Troian, that caught your fancy so, after I contrived to let you see him in the garden with your father?"

"Troian. What's that?"

"Troian Belmorio, you ninny. Your intended-betrothed. Such fine legs. And a glory of hair like a fire."

"He's well enough. I do not want him."

"Not want him? Why, I saw your blushes. I saw you, my miss. If we could have had the priest to you, that afternoon could not have been soon enough. Not want him? I was afraid you would leap from the window upon his neck, like the cat you are."

"Well. But it's past."

"And another you're mad for, now. This will not do, my rose. Fifteen, and due to be wed. You need only one man, I promise you, if he's sound, and good at his business. (May Heaven excuse me.)"

Two rivers of jet-black hair, slightly curling like the petals of thirsty flowers, spilled from Iuletta's hood, running by her neck, over her breasts, falling across her hands, which now were clasped in an attitude of manic prayer. Her eyelids had slammed shut. Failed both by the angels and Cornelia, Iuletta had turned at last to God for what she wanted.

Dubious, Cornelia resumed her own orisons. While, after the warm night, the chill of the capella floor soaked unwelcome into her knees. Cornelia disliked all cold things.

"And let Susina, in due course, amend her ways. For she is at heart a good girl, and does a valuable service for these men, who, as You know having made them that way, are much troubled by the appetites of the flesh. . . ."

Which tower was the nest of that wounded prince now lying in Susina's room? Not a family known to the Chenti household, or Cornelia would have recognized him, being in her way privy to everything. Rank enemy, probably. But then, alliances were made between enemies each day, and fresh enemies gotten. Which House had slain a Chenti last? Malaghela? Strali?

"And God be with us all," Cornelia finished mechanically, crossed herself yet again, and rose up. Not thinking to wait for Iuletta's private speech with God to be concluded, Cornelia lifted the girl to her feet. Iuletta crossed herself listlessly, and allowed herself to be propelled from the chapel.

One street up from the Basilica of San Vera, the geography of the Higher Town commenced. Presently, from the clustered lodges of their lesser kin, and the mounts of their gardens, the towers began to rise. Once purely naked swords, now each was ornamented, and adorned with its palatial facade.

In the hour between midnight and one, few were conspicu-

ously abroad on these pavements. Out of display, lamps
shone from the posts of great closed doorways, and flares in
tubes of succulently stained glass. Isolated high-up windows
let out splinters of light, but tonight Vespelli alone had
pushed a roar of scarlet from her doors. Dogs barked there,
and the vibration of music rang dimly; some banquet or
other show was in progress. Fearing an overflow of guests
into the street, Cornelia puffed into a lolloping trot.

Their destination was, in fact, but five minutes' walk from
the Basilica. Only the colonnaded library and priestly college
intervened, and a grassy walk tented over by trees. Beyond
the walk, the walls of the Chenti orchard rose up, overtopped
by foliage, and above this, the stone pile of the Tower.

A grey ghost on the sky this House by night, a net of stars
fixed round its head, pale gargoyles cranning from its cor-
nices, its winding, ascending stairs and parapets. The topmost
roof, a fair fifty feet from the earth, supported a giant lion-
leopard, plated with hardened gold, that gleamed sonorously
even by dark, and flamed up like a torch by day. The leopard,
pilfered two centuries before from some heathen shrine in the
East, was now the sigil of the Chenti family. It stood for ever
on the roof, soundlessly raging at the town below, motion-
lessly lashing with its tufted tail, and holding up one paw to
rend. There was the usual mythos—that if ever the head of
House Chenti felt himself threatened beyond his means, the
leopard would spring down to the defense of his people. And
too, for the big burnished cat on the rooftop, Chenti had
earned a nickname: Gattapuletta.

Mistress of the side door, Cornelia now unlocked an ivy-
hung access to the orchard, and ushered her charge, her page
and herself into it. A watchman—all entries must be guarded,
no matter how modest—advanced at their arrival, but Cornelia brushed him off like a fly. In this household, Cornelia's
authority among the lesser servants was mighty.

A rapid dash across the orchard, Pieto dismissed en route,
and negotiation of a topiary garden, led to a terrace and a
stair. Here a crenelated box bulked out from the Tower on
broad flying supports of masonry. A long window with a
wrought iron lattice set with panes of red, pink and white
glass, gave on Iuletta's bedchamber.

The lamp depending from an indigo ceiling lit up a narrow
bed, white as virginity, overhung with its crimson Chenti canopy, embroidered in gold with cats and flowers. Lit up chests
that waited about the room, and long stacked cabinets of jew-

elry, and walls which were painted, dark pink on white, with round-topped trees in which rose-red fruit and water-blue birds contested, appeared to be fighting each other, for pride of place. A bolt of smoky lace hung from golden pegs, a gilded lacquered mandolin elsewhere, and a triptych flashing jewels. Little books, commissioned from poets and artists, penned and illustrated by hand and dotted with semi-precious gems, were left lying about as, only a year ago, dolls had been left lying.

How unfamiliar in its familiarity this chamber abruptly seemed to Iulet Chenti, sole daughter of the House of the Polished Cat. All the years of her reason she had known the room, but she re-entered it a stranger. Not till this night had she ever beheld the features of the young man on Susina's balcony, and yet she had known him at once. It was recognition that had twisted like a dagger in her.

Cornelia fussed about the bed-curtains. Through the unshut window came the scents of the orchard: mulberry, pomegranate and damson trees, peaches on a wall. No noises but the papery exchanges of the leaves. Lord Chenti was away on business at Belmorio. The Chenti Tower, wrapped in its age and arrogance, brooded and slumbered. Somewhere over Iuletta's head, her mother also slept, or paced about. Somewhere else, and everywhere else, others snored or lay quietly, or contorted their bodies in those mysterious and sinful acts of love Iuletta imperfectly understood, and fearfully connected with random tensions and scintillations of her own flesh. And he, the nameless one, did he sleep, or die, or commit sin? At the thought the young girl gasped, and hid her face in her hands, beginning to weep.

Cornelia swarmed to her, massive queen bee, protective, far too late. The damage had been done.

"Tell me what I must do in order I may see him. Only once more. But no, more than once," Iuletta cried on the bosom which had suckled her, better identified than the high small mammalia of Lady Chenti. "Tell me what I must do to bring him to me. To—to make him desire me, to woo me. Love me. I cannot live unless he does."

Good hard sense and sheer romance warred in Cornelia's soul. Mischief danced in her brain.

"There now, there now," she muttered, already turning over forbidden things in her mind, scolding herself, feeling her warm power over this fragile pleading sparrow, cast again on her breast.

A distant but resonant bang, a clash and spume of laughter breaking suddenly inside the stones of the Tower provided a momentary distraction.

"And there is your bold cousin coming home," announced Cornelia, with the smugness of (false) ownership. But Iuletta wept more violently. Some unconscious part of her, perhaps, irked by her cousin's male freedom, her own suspected helplessness.

Far from helpless, apparently, Leopardo Chenti, conducting a mock duel in one of the large antechambers overhead, had caused his opponent to upset the bronze bust of an ancestor. The bronze, striking the tessellated floor like a gong, thereupon reduced most of the company to mirth. Leopardo dropped his rapier on the ground with a show of annoyance, and waved his sleepy page forward to refill the wine cups.

"What, no more sword play, 'Pardo? Too tired?"

"Well, if I could find other than sheep to touch blades with—"

"Baaa," two or three elaborated. Others added improvisations of goats, pigs, horses.

Leopardo frowned.

"What, are there Florias in the Chenti Tower? Or would that be a Suvio I hear?"

"Who calls me a Suvio, dies."

Leopardo turned, his long straight eyes finding the speaker immediately. At which the speaker retreated, no longer quite amused.

With Leopardo one could not be certain, even in jest. Louring, frowning, smiling all at once, and those eyes that seldom blinked, always glowed— The curling apricot hair, a cascading halo for face and neck, did nothing to soften or mislead. A leopard's face indeed, fascinating, gorgeous and unkind.

With a swiftness of decision his coterie had expected, yet not particularly looked forward to, Leopardo at last made his move. He flung his wine cup, fully charged, into their midst. Yelling, they scattered.

"Suvios *all*," Leopardo malevolently titled them. "Come kill me, then."

Truly, the leopard from the roof was alive.

Wine trickled from doublets, walls, hangings. But as they floundered, the young men saw total abstraction swoop over

Leopardo's countenance, changing it as if by magic. The feline lids actually blinked.

"Are you not ashamed?" inquired a soft cold voice from the doorway, behind them and facing him, a woman's voice, instantly known. "My Lord is from home, and so you dare to riot in his absence."

Uneasy, entertained, Leopardo's companions watched him blush, the high blood of excitement more than rage or embarrassment.

"Lady Aunt, I beg your pardon."

"Beg my pardon? That is hardly enough. I shall petition my lord when he returns. Must my rest be disturbed? I thought I had been transported to the Bhorgabba."

"Aunt, my donna, I am on my knees. You!" Leopardo made a thrusting gesture at the others. "Take yourselves off, pagans. You offend Lady Chenti."

Possibly relieved, Leopardo's followers slipped out, bowing, through the door, as the woman flowed by them like a snake, into the antechamber.

"They do not offend me. *You* do that. Can you keep no order?"

Leopardo hung his magnificent head.

"If I've angered you, my grief is insupportable."

"Do you still insult me?"

He looked up and straight at her, her white face that was like Iuletta's some fifteen years older and without the beauty, yet with some other element that could make dizzy, that could drown—

"Chastise me," Leopardo said. He went to her. He took in, in one long glance, the pitch-black hair in its golden caul, the plum-dark robe that made her into a stiffly pliant stem, from the prolonged throat to her narrow little feet in their spangled Eastern slippers. Her clear eyes that seemed nevertheless never to have slept, their clarity running into his bones like crystal pins. Then he knelt, then he stretched himself at those feet, face on the floor. "I am a penitent," he said, the high color continuing to beat in his cheeks under the mane of curling hair. "Do what you like. Scourge me, flay me. I am meek."

She drew her spangled feet back from him, as if from a suddenly perceived precipice.

"Your insolence astonishes me," she said, very low.

She turned. The hem of the swarthy robe brushed his mouth. He lay on the tessellations, savoring the taste of its perfume until he heard the door of his uncle's bedchamber thud shut, the length of a passage away. It seemed quite natural to him, as it had for some months, to be inflamed by his father's younger sister.

THREE

On the far side of Susina's house, where by day the market was conducted, geese crackled the air and human voices contested, a troop of whores was passing in procession with bells and tambourines. Romulan, lazily uninvolved in the world, let their sweet shrill mewing sew through his ears like painless needles.

"Love for copper, love for copper. Love for silver. Love for gold—"

The bed was clean, the room hot with sunlight, scented with incenses and herbs. The Fero wound had been nothing, no more than a long, shallow cut, effusive with its dye, yet quickly subdued. Romulan was abashed at it, and at himself. Never hurt before, fainting with horror at his own blood! Yet with a malign pleasure that did not comprehend itself, or wish to, Romulan was glad to have been cared for. Mercurio's solicitude, and the pretty whore, who all the while acted the lady to Romulan, and all the while enticed, inducing in him a swimming concupiscence as enjoyable as it was out of the question. While in the background a phantasmal boy with shadowy skin came and went on errands. Later, again reviving—to a tale of Mercurio's throwing (reportedly), the doctor over the mezzanine balustrade for suggesting the patient should be bled—and to Mercurio himself, who mournfully said, "I'll get word to your illustrious father. That will bring joy to him. His heir a-bed in the stew-house."

Romulan turned on to his face, letting his body soak through the hot rustling pallet. If he slept, his father might be forgotten. . . . The world of which he had ceased to be a part started to ebb away, the market noises, the whores' song, a vocal mallet from some sculptor's yard, wheels, the odor of musk and oranges—

Then Mercurio's unmistakable quicksilver step struck like a flint on the stone outside.

Romulan lay immobile, feigning sleep now, and alert.

The curtain rushed on its rings. Sensed rather than heard, Flavian Estemba was in the room.

"Ah, Master Sloth. I trust I find you well?"

Romulan breathed gently, unmoving.

"Sweet Jesus," said Mercurio, "Montargo Uno is dead. I must fetch the bone-carrier." His approach was silent, but next the voice was at Romulan's ear. "In such heat, the corpse will need to be packed in ice. Such luck I have some here, freshly cut from the cellerage——"

Romulan flung round and off the bed. He stood at bay, naked as a young Jupiter, and scowling like one.

"A second Lazarus," said Mercurio, with satisfaction.

"And where is the ice you'd snow on me?"

"Ice? Oh, melted, my dear."

The precipitate flight had made Romulan giddy, but he determined now not to display it. He began to take up the clothing of the previous night's folly, hesitating unlovingly over the blood-stained shirt.

At which Mercurio tossed a bundle of fresh linen on the bed, along with a clutch of outer garments in the black-blue and summer sky shades of the Montargo family. Romulan did not comment on that, but dressed, dealing with the cut arm roughly, to show he now properly discounted it. Mercurio watched with an intense solemnity that could only cover amusement. He was himself resplendent in the brass and white of Estemba, even the golden Ring-and-Arrow device pinned on his right shoulder with a great topaz glistening in the flight.

"I returned for you," Mercurio said, "with an escort. You must act Estemba for half an hour. Five of our own bravos, and two guardsmen of the Duca's."

"Duke's men? That'll be theater for the Bhorga." Romulan made much of tying sleeves. At length: "And my father?"

"One of my servants insinuated a message to one of yours, who in turn, I believe, weaseled the message to the manservant of your estimable father. Who, being himself not a man but a martyr, no doubt fell down in a fit and foamed at the mouth. Bear up, child, at this rate you'll see him in an early grave."

"I'll see you in one, Mercurio, if you talk of him in that fashion."

"I in a grave and you seeing me—not blind with tears? I'll tie that for you."

"Do not insult my father."

"An old argument. I have no love for your sire. He's vinegar for blood and puts me out of patience. But I beg your pardon for it. Now, let's be going before Susina finishes biting the cash, and comes to ravish you."

"You paid her. I'm in your debt—"

"Yes, yes, and the sun is a vast light, and the world has four corners, and we are all in Lucifer's net. Out of the trap, mouse. The cheese is eaten."

On the street, staring at the broiling sky or the rooftops, ignoring the whorehouse, the two ducal guards sat in their cloth-of-gold finery, embossed by the red sigil of four linked rings, hands to the hilts of swords. The five Estemba men, intimidated by this, were larking and cavorting, getting their horses to dance on their hind limbs, and shouting after the women who periodically reappeared at windows or in alley mouths, and chasing a man who had come from the market with a goose under his arm, hissing and yelling, up the street.

Mercurio's mount, a clove-dark mare, sidled to him, kissing his collarbone anxiously. Stroking her, he called the men to order, then swung up lightly on her back. Romulan took his own seat on a borrowed horse with a balletic violence, disdaining stirrups, reins, and gravity.

"Wounded stars," was Mercurio's response. "Why did I teach you that trick?"

"Did I not learn it well?"

"Very well, for one who desires to hit the moon and sing falsetto on the way."

Romulan laughed. The horses trotted and the walls and overhanging cliffs of the Bhorga, dull ochres by day and curded with dust, jolted backward.

"We will leave you at the Emperor's Monument," one of the guardsmen said.

"At the Basilica if you wish."

"At the Monument. So we were instructed."

"Oh then, the Monument. God forbid I should spoil the lord Duke's dance measure."

"The Duca," said the other man, "is impatient at these combats in the streets."

"My kinsman, the Duca," said Mercurio with delicate emphasis, "has fought on the streets himself, and been notable for his skill."

"In God's Name," said the first guardsman, "every tower is at war here."

"Tradition, dear heart. How else do we eliminate rivals in commerce and love? I presume you are a foreigner to our little country. You must not grudge us our foolish ceremonies. You yourself being quite safe in the Citadel. That tower, once gained, is sacrosanct."

"Death comes soon enough. Why anticipate at your young age?"

Mercurio studied the guardsman in whom Romulan, absorbed by paternal apprehensions, had lost interest.

"Why *not* anticipate? What else have we of free will but anticipation?" Mercurio, arguing for the discussion's sake, questioning nothing, believing very little, mesmerizing the guardsman as a matter of course, smiled gravely at him. "A man, young or old, may go to bed healthy, wake at dawn with a pain like a knife in his side, and be laid in a box by sunset. Or a man may cut his thumb on an awl, a scratch no bigger than a cherry pit, and he may sicken of that, and take that road to a box. Or the earth may shake, as it did here, ten years past, stones fall on your noodle and brain you. Or a plague may breed in the very air. Who can outrun plague? Oh, all roads lead to boxes. It is a chancy business, life. And so, my friend, we kill each other on the streets, the pith of the thing being Surprise! Amazement! My Lady Death, we are before you."

"Death's a woman, then?"

"Love and death, women both. Trust neither."

The grinding, soaring street cry of the whores wafted up again from over the walls. Mercurio, taking it as a bizarre accompaniment, began to sing a courtly love melody of the Higher Town.

"Dance with me while time is yet slow,
Clocks run faster far than you know;
Wear your rose flesh like a glove
For roses wither. Fear it, love."

His voice cut through all like a gold wire, through time, place, dust, heat and faith. A girl on a balcony averted her head from him superstitiously, among the terra-cotta pots of flowers. Romulan looked at him, entranced. None of them had heard a verse sung better, or a love song more like a knell.

Just then they reached one of the Bhorga gates.

With simultaneous precise taps of his heels, Mercurio set the mare bounding, and, as she did so, shot himself up to balance, feet either side the saddle. Ducking beneath the gate, then rising to stand again, Mercurio bowed to their stares as he left them all behind.

The rectangular courtyard at the center of the Montargo Tower contained the sea. At least, the sea in miniature. A basin of yellowish marble ran the length of it, sky blue tiled within, and filled by water. In the midst of the pool rose a ship, a bireme, with one enormous lilting sail that shifted slightly at the persuasions of the breeze, and whose double oar-banks, twenty-five upon twenty-five each side, seemed for ever to pash the water. Figures, one third life-size, as was the ship herself, manned the oars, the decks, the spar of the creaking sail. The Argo, symbol of the Montargo family for five hundred years, a fountain of basalt whose jets played in the basin to simulate reaction to her sweeps, whose sail was once made of the thinnest plates of copper, now verdigris.

Close to the ship, at a table under an awning, Valentius Montargo sat with his secretary over a batch of Levantine documents.

Loitering stupidly among the orange trees, Romulan stood and hated. Hated the black hair of his father, like his own, the patrician face, very handsome in its way, but unlike, hated the stern, shy and brutal honorableness, the imposition of will, the lack of—what? Something so simple as the evidence of affection? Valentius was the Tower. In his presence Romulan shrank, became nine years of age.

Valentius glanced up, as if struck by a thrown pebble of resentment, and beheld his son. As ever, the quite ludicrous beauty perturbed him. Romulan, undeniably masculine, was yet somehow his mother, faithfully reproduced. And there he stood, white as death, glaring, incalculable. Love, which was to Valentius no longer expressible, choked him. Waving the secretary indoors, he became peremptory.

"Come here."

Romulan braced himself at the voice. He went forward, flamboyantly, and looked down on his seated father, sneering, and trembling.

"You are set to disgrace me, then? That is what you most want?"

"Disgrace?" Romulan leered. "Fero's dogs insulted your name, and I sought to defend it."

"In the Bhorgabba."

"In the Bhorgabba."

"You imagine I am proud you go there, that you brawl there? That you spend your nights on the couches of harlots."

"The Feros are the enemies of Montargo."

"Quarrels may be settled in the courts of law. I do not require my son to settle them, inexpertly, with a sword. Nor to sleep off his duels in the brothel."

"You had no word from Flavian Estemba, then, to give you the truth of the matter."

"Flavian Estemba, on whom you lavish so much of your time, is unwelcome here. You mention Fero. Neither is Montargo at peace with Estemba."

"Kindred of the Ducal House," said Romulan proudly, although he did not value such connections a jot.

"The Ducal House is also a rabble."

"Oh God, sir," said Romulan, with spite, "are you not afraid to confide such things to me, worthless disappointment that I am?"

"Disappointment, yes. But not a traitor to me, I trust."

"A test, sir? Maybe I'll run straight to the Chitadella with the news. Hammer on the Duke's gate—"

"Oh, Romulan, be quiet. I've had excess of you."

Romulan snapped his mouth shut. Rebuked, to his acute distress, his eyes stung with tears. He looked away, feigning indifference. He visualized murdering Valentius, nor was it the first such visualization.

His father was saying other things. Romulan held himself in a vise of iron, waiting for the level-toned tirade to end.

"And your neglected studies. Well, there is a remedy for that. If you'll obey me, just once. Will you obey me, Romulan?"

Tight-lipped, fearful of emotion of any sort, Romulan grated: "Your *servant*, sir."

"I think not. But you should serve yourself better than you do. To waste your mind and your energy—"

Romulan riveted the bireme fountain with his eyes. He nailed it to the sky with them.

"—This accomplished man, though a hermit. If you are prepared to abide with the scheme, I have some hope he'll steady you, employ your intellect. What do you say?"

Romulan turned and stared at his father, having barely taken in a word.

"A hermit—" he parroted, hazarding for more.

"His reputation is modest, since he keeps it so. But such a priest has access to a great store of learning, and profound study. Others have benefitted from this Laurus. Pupils of his gain high positions in the colleges. Do you agree to visit him, and to accept his tuition? I do not command you. I ask you, for your own sake."

"You now wish to make a mock of me?" Romulan asked coldly.

Valentius got to his feet. His eyes were weary.

"Be guided, or continue with your own course. If you choose the second method, I'm done with you."

Romulan laughed, melodrama and shock mingling.

"You'd disinherit me."

"No. You're all I have, for my faults, and your further public disgrace would afford me no pleasure. It would be purely my personal resolve, boy, to regard you as my son in name only."

When did you ever regard me in any other way? But Romulan could not bring the words out.

"It rests," his father said, "on your realization of your duty. Not to me, you may be amused to learn, but to the line which made you. And to yourself."

"But, Father," Romulan drawled, "I'm content as I am."

Valentius Montargo moved abruptly from the table under the awning, unnerving Romulan. Generally these frigid interviews ended with a curt dismissal, but this time form had not been observed. Valentius, walking slowly away, seemed suddenly extraordinarily decrepit, about to falter. Romulan gazed at him, appalled. An early grave, Mercurio had said, which seemed, this instant, almost prophecy. Romulan's pulse lurched. Nothing on earth or under it would induce him to pursue that man in his plain dark blue, to court that man, to tell him his son would do as he was bid. Nor could anything, least of all himself, restrain Romulan from obeying his order—inane, not understood, ridiculous, a promise of utter tedium. For to refuse Valentius was to refuse all his forebears, the very mortar of the Tower itself. Such defiance seemed too heavy for Romulan to shoulder, although he ached to do so.

With a string of compensatory oaths, Romulan slumped in his father's chair, and watched the spray of the Argo fountain spot the papers abandoned on the table, until the secretary came back for them.

"This hermit priest," Romulan snarled at the secretary, a little faceless clerk in black, who plainly feared him. "Give me the fool's location, I've forgotten it." Thereby ensuring that Valentius would know his command, despisingly, insolently, had been followed.

When the secretary had informed and pottered off, Romulan strode in the direction of the Montargo stable. Occasionally still cursing aloud, he kicked his heels imperiously in the yard until the black gelding was led out for him.

As the second hour of the afternoon was sounded from the campanile, Romulan rode through Sana Verensa's south gate, where he had left his servant with an offhand: "Get drunk, if you like, but wait about for me."

The road, which ran by a couple of small villages, and thence southward all the way to Padova, was nevertheless an unkempt sprawling thing that blossomed, at every passage, into shawls of dust. Beyond the road the tawny hills, sisters to Verensa's own, made a distant rounded cup to hold the circlet of her walls. And as these walls drew away, the atmosphere of the land swept down tindery aromas to replace the perfumes and stenches of civilization. Against his inclination, which was to be sullen, a sense of enjoyment overtook Romulan. He slowed the gelding to an amble, and looked about him.

Behind him, the town seemed small on its mount in that enduring clasp of the hills. Towers stuck up from within it like sticks, flowerstalks, hazy with dust; unreal.

Somewhere on the left side of the road lay the ancient oratory the hermit had reportedly occupied—invisible. The vista presented merely descending slope on slope of wild bleached grass, tipped with the fire of poppies, out of which rose stone pines, like shade-green parasols. A bird whirled up, fluting, then another and another, a cannonade of birds, shot into the cloudless sky.

Romulan urged his horse off the road, and raced it downslope, through the breakers of the grass and the scarlet flowers. A hare started away before them, and he whooped at it.

Such was freedom, thoughtless, exclusive, and—in a second more—gone. The oratory had appeared, too soon, a cream-washed diptych among the pines, that blocked his way.

Romulan reined in, regarding the sight without memory.

There was some faded paintwork and mosaic glinting vaguely in the sunlight, a weathered mural of Maria Vera, Our Lady of Truth. Below it the door, warped and blackened, stood shut.

The pine tops moved a little in an unfelt breeze, and something glittered amid the savage grass close to the door. The gelding pricked its ears. Leaning forward, concentrating, Romulan too caught a stream of odd metallic sound that lifted, sustained itself, and died. Dismounting to lead the horse, Romulan went forward, clove the grasses and found a wooden post some three feet from the ground. Fixed by a shaft to the post was a battered gilded solar disc with extended writhing rays. The light wind moved again, touched the disc, and it spun vociferously, whistling high and far away, until the wind faded.

Romulan smiled, tolerant of toys, interested despite himself. He took another step and immediately the door of the oratory flew open with a bang, and apparently lacking mortal assistance. A hollow and unhuman voice boomed across the grass.

"Who approaches?"

The gelding shook its head, prancing nervously. Romulan, whose own heart had slammed against his breastbone, angry now, soothed the horse. When the voice resounded once more, and with the same question, he was ready for it.

"I!" he shouted back, clear young man's voice, its tones winging the space easily, and hitting on the walls.

A pause. The voice—of an intelligence, presumably— boomed again.

"Your name?"

"Name who questions me!" yelled Romulan.

"I am the Slave of Fra Laurus."

Pulling the reluctant gelding, Romulan went forward.

"And I am Romulan Montargo." He reached the lightless vertical of the doormouth and said into it, "And no man's slave."

Just within the entrance, a black curtain weighted with polished pebbles cut off any view of the interior. Romulan reached to thrust the curtain aside, and at the same instant, it was dramatically drawn.

Before he could prevent himself, Romulan took a step back, his hand going to the pommel of his dagger.

"No need for violence," said the tall apparition that stood before him. "My apologies for disconcerting you. I do not relish my studies disturbed by idlers or malcontents, and so protect myself as I may. The voice is a device used commonly by the antique peoples of Grechia in their theaters, and by the Egeptsi in their temples."

"I'm most glad for them," said Romulan. He turned to comfort the horse, an excuse to regain his own bearings.

"You are Valentius' son, of House Montargo," said the

priest. "That bough will do for tethering your beast. Then enter."

Romulan did as he was told, acknowledging himself truly outdanced.

The interior of the oratory, thick-walled and cold, was white-washed as without, bare, and made oddly luminous by its glassless pencil lines of windows. No carving and no ornament remained, save the stout serviceable pillars that held up the roof. The altar supported a wooden cross, an ivory Jesus nailed to it. Otherwise, not a bowl or candlebranch. The priest, perhaps unknowingly, dominated this sparseness in his black garment, like a man-sized icon come to life. Though tonsured, the remainder of his hair, richly waving and the color of malt, fell to his shoulders, a parody of fashion. The crucifix which hung on his breast, unlike that set over the altar, was of gold, and complex with small, exquisite jewels. The face and hands which extruded from the holy robe were very pale, as if seldom exposed to sun or any element. The features of the face suggested strangeness, in a manner that owed nothing to their composition, which was quite ordinary. A look of total absorption held the countenance together, an inner absorption, mental, possibly spiritual. It was a clever face, and strong, but its cleverness and strength had nothing to do with the world. This man might walk through beauty or filth, through fire or flood or anguish, and not notice it, or at least not suffer it, for his brain was in constant flight, negotiating some other plain beyond all physical things. It would be facile for him to deny himself almost anything—food, drink, carnality, power, even riches, for the golden emblem of his piety was clearly important solely for its gaudy reminder of duty, not its value. Romulan, staring at Fra Laurus with a mingling of the inevitable respect for his cloth and an equally inevitable impatience, did not miss these signs of the aesthete, but catalogued them too readily as religious devotion. Another might have concluded it was not only God who directed this intellect. Intellect itself had become paramount, and God simply the clue and excuse for its dreams.

On entering, both had saluted the naked altar as a matter of course. Fra Laurus had then moved on, only to reverse himself in the midst of the short nave, looking gravely over Romulan's head. Romulan began to feel the need to progress in some direction, conversational or geographic.

"Well, Father," he said, "I'm here to be schooled. Or so my other father tells me."

Laurus gazed downward, or outward, at him. The impression was, and had been from the beginning, of a man eyeing another from a long way off; and so he was, from some incalculable cerebral distance.

"Youthful gentleman," said Laurus, "we should understand each other. Your father has sent a servant to me, asking that I should take you on in some manner as a student. This is not my function. It does not concern me to be a teacher. Some, by association with my personal studies, those lessons I set myself, have had their own faculties quickened. I will say to you what I have said to others. You may observe, you may assist, if you've a mind. My books and treatises, or a portion of them, you may peruse. You may come and go as and when you choose. Providing you meddle with nothing, disrupt nothing, treating my stores, my library and my privacy with honor, you are your own agent, and, for what it is worth, you can account yourself to your father as my pupil."

Romulan smiled. It was a wicked smile, for he thought himself at an advantage.

"You take a wage for this, I hazard," he said. "And a bribe from me, perhaps, since you suppose you cover for me in my lawless career."

"In actuality, I take no money," said Laurus.

"Then you're unlike most others of your persuasion."

"Quite unlike. Never make the mistake of thinking me like another."

"Oh, *pride*, Father? Is that not a sin?"

"Worse than pride, to scorn the talents God gives."

"You're very talented, no doubt."

"You cannot insult me," said the priest. "It's beyond your means."

Romulan, unsure again, said sweetly in Mercurio's way (learnt verbatim): "And blasphemous to try."

"If you think so, then so it is for you, Romulan Montargo."

Laurus went on, behind the altar, to where a second black curtain and second narrow door were visible. Romulan walked after, striking the pillars idly with his gloves.

"So things are only what we think them?"

On this occasion, Laurus did not reply.

Romulan imagined himself to be winning. "*All* things, Spiritual Father? Sin and virtue, for example? Heaven? Hell? When my debauched road—my father will have mentioned my debauched road—ends in the Pit, I presume that hot irons and the vasts of flame will be illusory."

"I perceive," said Laurus, "you do not credit Purgatory, or the Inferno."

Romulan beamed. He did credit them, but they were far away. His youth, his vitality and his looks assured him he was immortal, invulnerable, and changeless.

"Not to credit them is to miss them, according to your song."

"To disbelieve in anything," said Laurus, "implies belief either formerly, or to come. Who denies the unseen shadow?"

The curtain had been attained and folded fan-wise on its rings. The inner room of the oratory was revealed.

Not meaning to, more by way of exclamation than anything else, Romulan crossed himself.

The chamber was by no measure the retirement of a priest, rather the insularium of a magician.

The area had, apparently, no windows, but a heavy hanging lamp of Eastern design, plus two or three drooling stands of candles, gave light to everything. There were open cabinets of books, more, there were sealed jars of dull glass containing mummified parchments. There were various representations of the Earth as envisioned by her mystics, and as exotic as they were unalike. There was an astrolabium, a clepsydra accurately a-drip. There were charts of the heavens, representing the stars and their houses in weird images of the zodiac. There was a brazen turtle mounted on a pedestal of cloudy jade. There were rows of alembics, crucibles, miniatures braziers, pots, urns, and other vessels in which things grew. There was the athanorus—the alchemist's oven—incapable of disguise, yet put out boldly for all to behold.

In the middle of the room a table, much scorched and disfigured by use. And before everything, guarding it, a terrible stuffed creature that looked to have been alive and animate once, the size of a horse and in every particular a dragon.

"Fear nothing," said the priest. There was neither amusement nor caution in his voice. It was patently a matter of form to pronounce such words.

"*Fear?* By God, does my father know where he sent me?"

In Romulan's voice there were both.

"There's nothing unlawful. I have never performed an unlawful practice." Again, a formula. "Such things are of interest, but merely for speculation. My pursuits are medicine, science, the indulgence of God's disciplines of debate, consideration and inward search."

Romulan's head began to ring ominously like the orb of a bell. Something in the room, indeed most of it, oppressed him. His nature told him here was a joke, a story worth recounting, an anecdote to entertain. Yet a feverish darkness hove suddenly into his awareness, something of the flickering light, the pall of herbs—yet more. He did not identify the lower register of death—although skulls of animals and bones of all sorts lay about, they did not, in the forefront of his senses, name themselves. The miasma attendant on the magician. For, just as disbelief implied belief, so the activities of magic implied the awful and insecure world that had inspired them.

Laurus did not note the effect upon his visitor, or, he was so used to such effects, he paid no heed. His next speech was another automatic response.

"You have seen, and may now depart. Return if you desire it. Or not. As your wish prompts you."

Romulan drew breath to retaliate with some respectful jibe, but the light and dark began to revolve. There was no Mercurio now to take care of him. Romulan turned and walked quickly and drunkenly out of the cell. He was already making excuses for himself—the Fero scratch gone poisonous, the drugs of the Fra-Magio—as he flung one arm around a pillar to support himself and leaned his forehead on the coldly sweating stone. He heard the door of the cell closed softly, as if beneath the sea. And thinking of his father's blunder of judgment, Romulan sourly laughed.

Presently, his head began to clear. He went, almost running, between the pillars and out of the arched door.

Yet one more omen: what had commenced as a zephyr had become a mantle of wind, rolling back and forth among the hills. There were scuddings and frecklings in the sky that had not been there before, causing the grassy shoulders of land to billow and kaleidoscopically to alter their color. As he unlooped the reins of his horse from the pine bough, Romulan saw a comical yet almost dreamlike apparition start to spill down the slope through the fluctuations of sun and wind. At first, still slightly stupefied, he could not make out what it was. Then the parts drew nearer and were translatable.

A vast blowing balloon of crimson vapors was a fat woman, mounted on a little donkey that seemed, with every step, about to crumple. Behind, also donkey-mounted, a crim-

son page with a crimson sunshade to maneuver over the
lady's exuberantly veiled head. Behind these twain, a man on
a grey horse, the single guard common to an important servant's excursion, and maybe needful since House colors were
so bravely in evidence.

Romulan, mindful of his own attire, tried to award the
crimson dye with a tower and a name, but could not call it
up. Which in itself was auspicious, the most ripe of enemies
being instantly memorable. Besides, a woman and her page,
servants at that, should seek no conflict. In addition, their
destination appeared to be the oratory he himself had just
left. Religious council was required, or an impromptu shriv-
ing not to be trusted to the brothers in the Basilica. (Romulan told himself he did not accept Fra Laurus' avowal: I take
no money.) Or could it be the voluminous lady sought other,
less respectable items from a sorcerer-priest?

Now the faintness had passed, Romulan was glad to prove
himself *himself* once more. Leading the gelding, he began to
climb directly toward the descending party. They had already
seen him. The rider on the grey horse had hand to sword hilt,
but that was only show. To draw on an aristocrat would not
be politic. Romulan dressed his face in its most charming and
unpredictable smile, and as the woman rode close enough to
see him fully, he turned it fully on her.

Romulan was not prepared for her answer.

For one breath she gaped at him, her eyes popping as if
she strangled. Then she let out a short shriek, reminiscent of
the fowlyard.

"Oh Jesus and Maria and all the Heavenly Host!" she
squawked.

The guard, the page, Romulan, each was dumbfounded.

"Oh, the villain. The devil! The saint!"

The guard recovered himself. He pulled a lemon-sucking
face.

"Has this gentleman in some way offended or demeaned
you, donna?"

"Ah!"

Romulan, spokesman for the crimson males in their astonishment, said, "Madama, I'll guess you take me for another."

"Not so," she said, patting her bosom as if to scold the pal-
pitating heart. "It's fate, God's grace, so it is. The beauties of
an archangel, who could forget them, the Lord forgive me.
What House are you?"

This was not etiquette at all. Romulan bowed mockingly.

"If you know my colors, then you know my House, madama. I refrain from boasting, save to my peers."

"I'm acquainted with one," said the woman slyly, winking, "your peer, as Eva to Adam. She'd tremble to know."

"I see, gentle lady," said Romulan courteously, "you are a bawd, and crimson is the tint of your comfit-shop."

At which he made the flamboyant actor's leap aboard the black horse that took watchers generally by surprise, and these no less than the rest. As he raced for the hilltop and the Padova-Verensa road, Romulan heard a dim outcry at his back, soon lost. The encounter had cheered him up. He was ready to laugh now properly at all of it, his father, the priest, the glimpsed abyss, since they had been spiced by the outrageous woman on the donkey.

The wind, precursor of a summer storm, hit the dust great blows, driving it to Verensa before him.

FOUR

"Praise Christ! He is a Montargo. And no Montargo has laid murderer's hands on any of your kin for more than seven years."

This recommendation, thrilling from the lips of Cornelia, announced her arrival in Iuletta's bedroom.

"Who is a Montargo?" asked the girl. She was pale and demure in a dark white gown embroidered by a briary of roses. Pearls were braided in her hair, sewn on her under-sleeves, raindropped on her bodice. Cornelia, not having supervised this dressing, looked askance at it.

"Who?" Iuletta repeated, as Cornelia advanced to pluck and twiddle pointlessly and busily at curls, lace, folds.

"Why, he you'd die for. He you cannot live without."

Iuletta's delicate pallor whitened. Her eyes became the shade of the purple core of a peacock's feather. She was extraordinary, and for an instant, Cornelia fell back from her aghast at this unconscionable loveliness.

"How do you know?" whispered Iuletta Chenti. "Have you seen him? Spoken with him? How—"

"Spoken with him, yes, and a saucy rogue. Seen, yes, and a handsome one. I was not twenty paces from Fra Laurus' retreat when I met the wretch."

"Laurus?"

"This Romulan Montargo, dizzy girl."

"Romulan," said Iuletta. She lowered her lids. Tears ran through the black lashes. Even the name had moved her unbearably.

"Now, now," said Cornelia, seeking to divert, "who is coming to the Chenti Tower that you're dressed this way?"

"Belmorio," said Iuletta. Her lids were raised again. In the midst of passion, some previous passion still held some sway, it seemed. "I am to meet him formally. My father wishes it."

"And we talking of another."

45

Iuletta flung about and seized Cornelia's meaty wrist in her strong little cat's paw.

"But did you gain the things we shall need?"

"Yes, yes, God forgive me. And lied to obtain them. And was not believed. That priest, that Laurus. A strange man, though holy, doubtless. Nor a man, for a priest is not a man—But I'd swear he knew what I had in mind, asking for such simples and powders. Heaven preserve me if he should decide I am a witch. But he seems to have no concern, will take no payment, even. We are all part of some plot of his that none of us can devine. Or else no part of it and he takes no care of what we do—we may do anything. For shame, he should have ranted at me, he should. What use is he? But there, I never could make sense of a fellow that will not bed. Unless he will. May God excuse my mouth. But He knows, there are plenty in that line that will. Called a bawd, too. Well, something in that, perhaps," and Cornelia abruptly emitted her atrocious laugh. Jovially she elaborated: "Your knight was with Laurus. It was Laurus gave me his name and House. And you need not trouble for the young man's health, either. He was in fine fettle."

Iulet stood before her glass, tears smoothed away, rearranging the pearl-braided hair that Cornelia had tweaked askew. Iulet was calm as only a person in strong agitation can be.

"Well," she remarked, "if I cannot have one, there is the other to be had." . .

"There's my sensible poppy and my wise rose."

"Or there is death."

This last Cornelia pretended not to hear.

Iuletta, raising her skirts a fraction to clear her silken shoes, floated toward the inner door of her apartment. Her other hand on the door ring, she said, "Did you ever know one who died of love?"

"Indeed," said Cornelia. "It's quite common, they say, in the trade."

Iuletta turned the ring with a vicious grating sound.

"My mother says you are coarse, nurse."

Cornelia, for once circumspect, answered nothing. Lady Electra Chenti, wed at thirteen to a husband three times her own age, and delivered of her first—and only—child one year later, had retained at twenty-nine the figure and skin of a young girl, simply adding to it the resentful acidity of extreme old age.

At as discreet a distance as her tidal crimson allowed, Cornelia dogged her charge along the corridor, across a lobby, and on to the winding stair that led to the eastern courtyard.

It was latest afternoon, the blustery sun positioned westward, shooting the town through every eyelet and loophole with fine red shafts. In the Chenti water-garden fountains jetted from the mouths of green-copper cats. The gusty outer air was warm, flavored by vines which gave off a stormy odor on the enclosing walls, and dazzled with iridescent spray. Above, the sky was a shining haze of blown mellow cloud into which the horizons of the town dissolved. Below, manicured trees staggered heavily and collected themselves. Dense curls were lifted and replaced and the tissues of gowns and mantles shaken.

In an aureole of red light and flame-red hair, handsome face burnished to bronze, elegant figure displayed in a heroic, conceivably natural stance, Troian Belmorio gripped Lord Chenti's palm. Like differentiated subjects in a tableau, Troian, his handful of supporting kindred and their couples of pages, in Belmorio's rich murky green and its liberal slashings of gold. While Chenti red, and the unmatched red of the day's end, surrounded them like a sea of blood. In previous eras, no man of any House would tread inside another family's tower, whatever the pretext, for fear of poison, or a more candid blade in the guts. Belmorio and Chenti, in these softer times, had decided to forget their dead, and join ranks against other Houses whose emnity was fresher—Fero, Malaghela, or Suvio. Wealthy Chenti, besides, was a catch. Belmorio a similar catch, being one of the three or four who had links to the Ducal House—witness the Ring-and-Dove device on Troian's gold chain. (Next to it hung a small portrait, mostly guess-work, but fetching and true in pigments, of Iuletta.)

"And here comes my daughter," said Lord Chenti.

It was to be a show of informality, this formal first meeting between proposed bride and groom. Belmorio had already taken good care to see her—at church, alighting from a litter, and so on. That the girl had seen him was due to the contrivance of her nurse. But that also was not quite unheard of. Initially, both had been elated by what they saw.

Now, however, Belmorio turned, became petrified, gazed as if at first sight of a Madonna wafted from a canvas. In a well-trained, eloquent voice he proclaimed:

"The sun returns! Iuletta is the sun, rising in the east at sunset, to bring me day in night."

There was some chuckling and applause at this prepared ("impromptu") poetry, and Iuletta slowly and radiantly blushed.

Lord Chenti, a hearty devotee of martial arts, still big in chest and thigh, high-colored, quick-tempered, currently playful as a rhinosaur, slapped his young nephew on the shoulder.

" 'Pardo. Lead my timid daughter forward."

Leopardo, whose sculptured nose had been thrust almost into his wine at the blow, straightened, bowed brusquely, and went to offer Iuletta his arm. She placed her hand neatly over the brocade sleeve, but scarcely touching it. Beyond a cursory glance, the cousins did not look at one another. Their dissimilar beauties and gender did not endear either to the other. A lesser branch of Chenti had married the first to produce Iuletta. Leopardo, stranded on the maternal side, father dead, and having to take his Aunt Electra's spouse as substitute father, disliked Iulet also for that. She was a part of Chenti Primo, who incensed him merely by being alive. That she was also a part of Electra, who he so rampantly coveted, seldom occurred to him.

With great courtesy and a slight sneer, Leopardo conveyed Iuletta to within range of the prospective bridegroom. Belmorio, too, he despised. His eagerness to hate had brought Leopardo a certain reputation among swordsmen, and four cruel scars on his smooth body.

Chenti Primo was jovial.

"You act the brother nicely," he said to Leopardo. He clasped Troian Belmorio's hand the harder. "And you, the lover. Excellently done." The big man grabbed for Iuletta's hand. The girl's head was properly bowed now. Lord Chenti approved of modesty in a woman. (Modesty but not chilliness. God knew, he had been saddled with sufficient of that at home.) "Come, look up, maiden."

Iulet dutifully raised her head.

Troian's face, so close, so attractive, instantly fascinated her, and the delight with which it gazed on her—that fascinated, too.

"Well," (Lord Chenti) "do you like what you see?"

The kindred and retainers standing about reacted with approbation to this forthright stance.

"If she will consent to have me," said Belmorio, "I will be her slave."

"Oh, be no woman's slave," said Chenti. "Be her king, and rule her."

"I protest, sir. I'd be the shoe on her foot, the glove on her hand. One of those little pearls in her hair. That would content me."

"And what does my daughter say?"

Iulet, surrounded by a forest of men, young or older, slimly muscular or thickset, but all masculine, all arrogant as lions, turned her head involuntarily, seeking her aloof mother. Electra Chenti, poised by the fountain, stared back at her.

"Well, she looks to you, Wife, for guidance." Chenti was disposed to be lenient. "What do *you* say?" (What indeed, you iceblood fish-souled bitch?)

Electra Chenti smiled. Her eyes did not.

"I say I was well-wed by fifteen. And why should my daughter balk at it."

Iuletta tilted her head and took in all of Troian Belmorio.

If not one, then another. Or why not more than one? Cornelia had murmured, now and then. . . . And this one smiled at her, his white teeth enchanting her, his expression of joy in her, the hint of his arousal—both bodily and acquisitive—making her own heart gallop. Here he was. Chenti was putting her hand into the firm hand that was not related to her, not kin, but which was male.

Iulet sighed faintly. Captivated by everything, Troian watched the sigh. Impetuously, unrehearsed, he leaned to her ear and muttered into the shell of it, "Lady, your beauty makes my head spin, like strong wine."

Chenti, overhearing, guffawed again.

"Well, Iulet. Do I say I betroth you to this gallant or do I not?"

(One could picture his alteration if, in public, she had protested.)

"Yes, sir," said Iulet. She smiled at Belmorio, shyly, surely, glorying in her power over a man which, in that innocent moment, seemed limitless. It was not that she had forgotten Romulan Montargo, rather that by the implication of this conquest, she dreamed of the effect she might have on *him*. The true implications, being young and bound by others to her youngness, she did not see at all.

"Then since she'll have you, sir, I grant you this: you shall kiss her, chastely, on the lips."

So, with Chenti's blessing, they kissed, the betrothed pair, and were clapped by onlookers, as the sun, reaching the horizon's brink, hesitated. And then fell.

The storm did not break that night, although the wind, become many winds, made sallies upon the town. They swirled about the great proud towers as if to whittle them, rushed into alleys and amid garden trees, until the fourth bell of morning. When the blue light began to hollow the sky, the winds sank. They made pretense they were unmalicious, feeble. They scattered from Verensa to gamble with the sheep on the hills.

At seven in the morning, the sun once more glazing everything with films of color and, already, dust, the last vestige of a wind, which had lain sleeping across the threshold of the Basilica Library doors, started up and ran away, throwing in his ecstatic face, as it went, the fierce red hair of Troian Belmorio.

In the Library's vestibule, a few old priests, one with clanking keys at his belt, looked mildly or not at all. An Estemba servant, wrapped in a brass-hued mantle, lay full length and softly snoring on a marble bench. One tall leaf of the doors to the antiquarium gave at a touch. Troian, whose inclination was not for study, walked into the long, wide chamber, and regarded disapprovingly its ancient armors on pegs, its tapestries of the fall of that very city for which he had been named, its multitude of books, most of them padlocked shut. Before the long windows, sprawled lean and couthly, grey-gold head on hand, intent, Flavian Estemba was reading from a tome the breadth of his own shoulders.

"Good day, Estemba Uno."

Flavian Estemba lifted the head from the hand.

"Sir," he answered.

He was nondescriptly clad, unlike Troian, who flaunted Belmorio's color and had left five sigiled Belmorio men on the street, which might be an invitation to others to open hostilities. Partly allied and partly kin, Belmorio and Estemba were not greatly enamored of each other. One did not rise, the other did not go forward.

"I never took you for a scholar," said Troian, eventually.

"You're up early to take me for anything."

"And you've not been to bed at all, I hear, but lurked in the cobwebs of this place. I thought the Bhorgabba was more of your night haunt. Beds, not books."

"Oh, this way and that, I spend my nights between covers."

Belmorio grinned. He was in a wonderful humor, and let the joke touch him.

"Still quick, cousin."

"Not dead, at any rate."

"Nor am I. You may have been told."

"That you were dead?"

"Stars! That I'm to be married."

"I heard some chat blowing about. Strali, is it? They have a daughter, I believe."

"Strali's daughters are geese. This one's a Chenti."

"Not a goose, and rich."

"Rich in more than cash. She's beautiful. Lord Jesus, she's more beautiful than a sunlit rose."

"Save it for the girl."

"Trust me." Troian made a particular gesture.

Estemba nodded dutifully.

"Poor lady, she will be harmed."

They laughed, now prepared to be polite. What came next was no surprise.

"Tonight my father crosses into the Chenti Tower. It's the betrothal feast, food, song, dance and display. Chenti likes the idea of a relative in Belmorio. He courts me as I court the daughter. My father sent to yours to go calling with us, for the appearance of it. But Estemba Primo says he will stay at home. A poor show, Mercurio."

"He's old, my father," Mercurio said. He looked down at the book, tapping the iron clasps of it. "Too old and too weary to provide your ballast. You hardly require everyone of the Ring sigil Houses to go in with you. Who does the Duke send?"

"No one."

"But be sure Chenti still knows your links with the Rocca Tower."

"Oh hang all that. We want a demonstration of unity. You'll come, will you not, Mercurio?"

"Oh, God."

"It'll be a good night. Better than the sordid Bhorga. Than a library."

"It will be tedious. You besotted with your wench. Chenti drunk on high connections. The mother simpering. The maid preening. Heaven defend me."

"And if you will go, you'll take Montargo with you. That looks fair for us, too. Their shipping interests vie with Chenti's own."

"Montargo does not love Estemba."

"One does."

"You mean Romulan. Romulan's in bad grace with his father and is sent off to school with some priest."

"Get him in good grace then. Chenti and Montargo have no recent quarrel. If Valentius dislikes you, he cannot dislike the Duke. Or Belmorio, surely. And Valentius may relish the social policy of this."

"The plan grows more dull with every word you utter. Even the girl, I suspect, is a goose despite your vows. A plain goose."

"Plain goose, eh?" Troian raised himself in his skin. He strode over to Mercurio after all and dangled the lover's portrait before his nose. "Here she is. And this not one hundredth part as stunning as reality."

Mercurio, set to brush the medallion aside, checked.

"So this is she?"

"And not one hundredth—"

"Part as stunning. Yes and yes. But in this kind of mould, this black hair, blue eyes? How old is your betrothed?"

"Fifteen."

"Too young. You'll split the minx."

"Never call her a minx to me," Troian said angrily.

"Why," Mercurio said, coming to his feet lazily, and staring into Belmorio's eyes with his own, which seemed on occasion to englamorize. "Why, the last time I saw her. . . ."

"Be wary, Estemba."

Mercurio smiled. He slapped Troian's shoulder, lightly.

"Was in a dream of the seraphim."

Troian relaxed.

"Then you'll add to our number tonight."

"Why not? For my darling kin, the Belmorios."

Troian frowned, put the frown away, and embraced him.

Mercurio bore the embrace with saintly patience. He was intrigued, inspired. His devilish qualities, not always limited to masks, were awake and stirring.

"Let go of me," he eventually suggested. "Or I'll think I'm mistaken for your loveling. What's her name?"

"Iuletta."

"Iuletta Gattapuletta," Mercurio mused, and slammed shut the book with a thud as of coffin lids flung off. "Yes. I'll visit the House of the Cat with you."

Having recognized, even from the inadequate unveiled likeness of the painting, the notable damsel he had met on

Susina's brothel balcony, little or nothing would have kept him away.

In the snowdrift of her bed, Iuletta Chenti lay on her back and out-stared the crimson canopy above her. She was crying, though she was not unhappy. Her desperation had found a means of focus, an age-old knack: black magic. Its irreligious nature she had not contemplated, and Cornelia had not mentioned unholiness. To Cornelia, prayer and the confessional solved all. Life went on, only returning to God to wash its linen, at fairly frequent, hasty intervals.

After the Belmorio deputation had departed, Iuletta in her nightgown, Cornelia in self-importance, they had burned powders over a dish, spoken certain rhymes, and sewn up a sachet of herbs. Cornelia had bemoaned the lack of hair or nail-clipping, even of blood. A notion that she had been close enough to the delicious boy to get all three—biting a piece out of him, perhaps (God overlook her wickedness), made her effervesce with merriment. Iuletta, flushed by her success as Troian's intended bride, crouched to the witch-work. She lay down at last in her room of pink trees, fruits, birds, the sachet under her pillows, reciting the charm Cornelia had taught her.

The charm had apparently begun to work. In the night, Iuletta had dreamed Romulan came to her. He leaped the wall of the orchard, or flew up over it on angel's wings. Beyond his arrival at her lattice, however, mere imagination would not take her.

Of Belmorio also she frequently also thought. He was a comfort to her, proof of her worth. Every time he had pressed her fingers, looked with longing at her, she had comprehended the gift of herself which she would present to Romulan.

For Romulan could now be drawn to her by sorcery. Irresistibly she could drag him to her sphere.

By the time a maid came to prepare her for the morning rituals of the palace-Tower, Iuletta was keyed to an ascending excitement. It seemed she was eager for this night of her formal betrothal, eager to see Troian once again. Attendants marked her care of herself with knowing winks.

They did not know she expected another—Romulan—to appear at any second, through a door, through a wall, off a roof, out of a tree, out of thin air. But as the day moved on with the new golden clock in the ancient Chenti banquet-hall, so the truth came to her. Since Romulan must come by human means, he would be among the guests at her betrothal.

The perverseness of this did not trouble her. Behind all the dreams, she was glad (without unkindness), Belmorio would be at her side, a foil and a shield.

But, as her hair was washed, and combed with an attar of roses, she knew quite well why, and for whom.

PART TWO:

The Blade

FIVE

The storm broke on a count of twenty after sunset. Thunder, like a clap of enormous wings, the wings of some fabulous giant bird made of metal, smote out impending stars, and crushed the last strawberry colors from the sky. The winds came back, tearing around Sana Verensa like the ruffians they really were: Ah, fine town, we duped you, you thought us tame! A trickle of sound came from the campanile bell, gusts fisting the clapper. (Here and there the ten-year-old earthquake was recalled, and how all the bells had rung by themselves.) Shutters banged, lights were blown out. Young leaves ripped off swirled like bats about the blackened streets. Lightning, a cannon-blast, threw itself on every tower at once, even daring the peak of the Basilica. Rain, all Heaven's emptyings, crashed and sizzled on the roofs, the paving below, and any unfortunates caught between.

Mercurio stood in the rain, water streaming from hair and cloak, and the finery beneath. "I have bathed, Sir," he told the sky. "You may desist."

Half the torches were out, their bearers struggling with blistering curses to rekindle them in the shelter of an overhanging porch. The Estemba musicians cursed as loudly as they attempted protection of strings, reeds and drumskins. Five Estemba and three Montargo houseguards waited stoically, and apart, brass and blue liveries darkening. Two Estemba cousins huddled. All were on foot, all drenched. Romulan, blue-black hair washed into his eyes by water, black-blue clothes a river, put back his head and let nature anoint his skin.

"The rain's warm as milk."

"It is still wet. Come, damn the torches. The Chenti Tower is one street off by my reckoning. We'll run for it."

They ran, in a herd, swords clacking, mantles and smoke streaming, the sodden sheet of the wind in their jaws and their heads down.

57

At the end of the street, on a steep curve, one of the musicians skidded and sat with a mighty oath and ill-omened thump of viola de gamba. Trees poured over walls like jugs. Fresh cannonades of lightning and thunder, a million glasses smashed, lit the way, and hid it.

"Strike Floria!" one of the Estemba kinsmen shouted at the storm, and there was laughter.

The pack, barking blasphemies, hurtled along the second street and collided with the Chentis' tall grey stair-posts. Pink lamps swayed to the wind in their chains. All but masked by weather, the stair, the ghostly Tower, pierced on all floors and at every outcropping by lights, loomed like a lighthouse in the hurricane. Chenti guards blocked the way on the upper landing.

"Let us past in God's name," the second Estemba kinsman pleaded.

"Who are you?"

"We are the drowned."

"Estemba, we are Estemba. And these, Montargo."

"We're unsure of your colors. Your brands are out."

"Swords will be out presently," said Mercurio, stepping to the front. He pointed to the Ring-and-Arrow blazon on his shoulder. "Connected to the fortunate bridegroom. Let us by."

The guards, well-sopped themselves, moved churlishly back, and the Estemba-Montargo party, like an invading army indeed, with bellows of angry mirth, charged the remainder of the stair and against the iron-clasped doors. Fresh water was hurled on them as they buffeted at these, from the banners overhanging the balconies above, gold lion-leopards on crimson, and tonight, for honor, Rings and Doves on sullen green.

The doors were opened. In uproar, twenty-two males exploded into the quite comparable uproar of the house.

A brief lobby gave straight on the Chenti banquet hall, old as the Tower, its ceiling high in the air and stained black with centuries of smokes. From the black overcast, as from its galleries and great stair, the rose-red flags of the House hung down, and high on the walls beneath, the antique swords, the arms and armor, the crested helms of the warlike Cat family. While under all those were flaunted the equally flamboyant signs of peace and prosperity, carved wood and gold inlay, tapestries, wall-hung Eastern carpets, panels paint-

ed by artists of a renown foreign to Verensa. The stone floor
had been camouflaged with mosaic, a complex scene rarely
to be viewed by a guest in its entirety, for when in use the
hall was crammed, as now. These friendly, or passing-for-
friendly Houses had been invited to represent themselves, and
were duly here in the sour cream of Ottanta, the damson and
charcoal of Retzi, and loud d'Ansini purple.

The feast tables stood about the walls, draped with damascine, and already groaning with pastry castles, roccas of
melting ice, pyramids of many-colored fruit. The cost of
candles had been high. Everywhere wax was on fire and drip-
ping. Wax and incense composed the air, on which a thousand scents were overlaid—sandalwood and reseda being this
month's fashion. To that, the steam of wet garments had been
added. Others had been caught in the downpour, it appeared.

Lord Chenti, backed by two wine-bearers in semi-baccha-
nalian garb—vine embroideries, wreaths of crimson grapes—
met the latest arrivals in the door. The solicitous social
approach, as their swordbelts were taken from them with
their cloaks.

"Welcome, young sirs. Chenti is flattered by the visit of Estemba—please not to study our collection of swords, sir. I've
heard your personal collection outshines everyone else's. And
Montargo, welcome. I trust your respected fathers are in
good health?"

Mercurio bowed, a touch too courteously, an edge Chenti,
so quick to speak of swords, quite missed. Romulan, also
bowing, could hardly keep the smile off his face, for he had
abruptly recognized the crimson of the bawdy servant-woman
on the hill.

Cups of wine were handed to Romulan and the Estembas.
They drank their host's health, shaking rain off their long
hair.

The floor was currently solid with Ottantas, Retzis,
d'Ansinis, Chentis, Belmorios, and a sprinkle of intimate servants. Other servants, save Chenti's own, had retreated from
sight. Chenti musicians sat on a gallery in the old mode,
tuning instruments, lutes, viols, mandolins and dulcimer
chembalo, few of which were frequently audible above the
general din.

The room was already growing hot. Outside the thunder
complained, and lightning shot through high-up windows,
unheeded.

"I see you have brought your own musicians, sir," Chenti remarked.

"The rain caught their strings. I fear they'll ring flat."

"A shame. But I suspect one dry mandolin. Strings and blades are your domain, Mercurio. We'll prevail on you for a song."

They had forced a way, nodding and greeting, through the press, and come up against a table-side where a prodigious peacock of colored sugar framed Troian Belmorio, Belmorio Primo, and two or three younger brothers. They had, like most in the hot, scented room, a slightly drunken skittish air, even the old man, who came at Mercurio and clapped him on the back. With a pained look, Mercurio straightened from the blow. "I've been told to sing. Best leave me some ribs if you'd be so kind, my lord. And where is the betrothed maiden?"

"You shall see." Chenti was knowing.

Romulan's hair was already dry, its theatrical blackness somewhat waved by the action of damp and heat. Women of all ages contemplated him. Hardly a woman who saw him did not turn for a second, longer, regard. Such attention Romulan accepted with arrogance, an occasional shyness, a general uninterest. It had always been so. He was more intrigued by Mercurio's reasons for attending this festival, for Mercurio had told him nothing of them, yet hinted broadly at some game or other. Of course, to drink and to dance might be sufficient, and to agitate others, brawls of words if not blades—both were apt enough for that.

Thinking of this, and feeling on him an attention that was neither female nor disposed to liking, Romulan turned his head, and met the long-eyed gaze of Leopardo Chenti. It seemed that across some thirty paces of mosaic, candle wax and human forms, Leopardo had singled him out. The observation was not actually a threat, more a calculation. Romulan, sensing himself weighed, would neither glance away nor move. At risk of dislocation of the neck, he gave Leopardo back watch for watch. The tableau was ended suddenly by a blast of tenor trumpets from the head of the banner-draped stairway.

The guests made suitable sounds, fanned down their noise, and drew aside against tables and walls. The musicians struck up a melody, as an arresting procession commenced its progress down the stairs.

First came girls dressed as moths, gilt masks over their upper faces from which delicate antennae rose, wings of wire and gauze trembling at their backs. Flowers floated from their hands, so they and all who should come after must tread on them, producing a heady fume of roses and mughetto. In the wake of the moths gambolled grasshoppers (tastefully or tactlessly in Belmorio's exact green), their long wings glinting with spangles. The grasshoppers were acrobats, walking on their hands down the stair or catapulting into somersaults, wings cracking like whips. Behind the grasshoppers trod six men dressed as dragonflies, who bore on their shoulders a novel palancina, uncurtained and shaped like a huge whorled snail shell, gleaming the tints of mother-of-pearl. In the snail-shell sat a black-haired girl in a white gown borrowed from Grechian design with a thin gold chain under her breasts, crimson rosebuds and a little tower of gold-wire crown in her hair-dressing, and everywhere the sparkle of jewels. It seemed the betrothed virgin was coming, in the person of the eternally young empress of fairyland—her entrance being thus described by poets. After the snail shell swaggered a final four acrobats, clad as soldierly mice, banging their shields with their grey fur tails.

The crowd of guests applauded, laughing. It was a pretty sight, a concession to the whimsicality of a father who gave away his only daughter. And indeed, Lord Chenti, whimsical, was seldom to be thwarted. Hard and obdurate, his balancing sentiment was lavish, yet implacable. (There was a story he had once used his fist to break the nose of a man who had refused, from pride, a thrown coin in the street.)

Leopardo Chenti was drinking from a crystal cup and had turned from him, and so Romulan glanced at Mercurio. That face had grown ominously demure.

"What is it?" Romulan inquired, casually.

"Do you like the betrothed bride?"

"Do *I* like her? It's if Belmorio likes her, is it not?"

Beyond the guest's duty at such a function, Romulan had no concern for such a girl, already given to someone else. His eyes on her across the distance had seen only symbols, not a face or frame.

The moths, grasshoppers and mice had lined up at the stair foot as the dragonflies lowered the shell with due care.

"By the Mass, if they dropped her," said Mercurio, "there's a thought. Being made apparently of porcelain, she'd shatter. A hundred shards of white perfection. Scrabble, gentlemen, scrabble. See who'll get what."

"*You* like the betrothed bride," said Romulan.

"Somewhat. I like her gadding about mostly."

"Which gadding? Where gadding?"

"One day, child, I'll tell you of a balcony. For now, honor bids me to silence."

Deposited safely, Iuletta Chenti put her hands into the gloved paws of two smiling, genuflecting mice, and allowed herself to be drawn upwards, stepping free of the palancina.

Her fantastical face was for an instant almost maddened; she had a wild and savage expression—these were the seconds in which she searched for the results of magic. Then she faltered, her cheeks turned white, then red, her eyes aswim and enlarged. (A mouse solicitously caught her wrist.) *These* were the seconds in which she beheld the proof, the cunning of the spell she had cast. Beheld Romulan. How lucky that he stood only a foot away from Troian Belmorio, who in his red-haired hauteur and lust, took her aberration as the effect on her of himself. He was not alone in this misconception. Almost all the crowd took it for the same, all that saw it, and were charmed. Troian's younger brothers, envious, poked him viciously with their elbows. Mercurio, mesmerized by sheer pulchritude, had become simply a sponge to receive it. While Romulan, still alert for Leopardo's next move, had turned away at the exact point of Iulet's perceiving him.

But Leopardo had amalgamated with the throng. A pale sunburst of hair intermittently revealed him, an incarnadine leg, but his back was now to the Montargo-Estemba-Belmorio cluster as it hung on the periphery of Troian's second meeting with his betrothed.

Romulan's suspicions were now setting. Mercurio, in his usual humor, intended to make courtly love to another man's intended, before the eyes of both parental families. A faint jealousy, that normally arose in Romulan when any other human thing completely claimed his friend's attention, coupled to a converging desire to be similarly outrageous, now drove Romulan to notice a woman at the far end of the room. She was an almost perfect opposition for the black-haired bride Mercurio fancied, this one, and with *white* roses in her honey hair. Her face was finely made, with ineffable eyes. To improve matters yet further, becoming aware of Romulan's scrutiny, she scorned him, and averted her head to speak to a companion. Romulan, with all the young man's pleasure in challenge and the subsidiary fear of success, recharged his goblet and made the journey over the mosaic toward her.

"My donna," he said, musically, falling easily into one of Mercurio's most charming stances, "the chamber grew dark, but there you were, a lamp to guide me."

The woman, a handful of years his senior, perhaps Mercurio's age, viewed him coldly. Instinctively, by her coldness and by something in her eyes, he knew himself safe; she was a gamester, too.

"I will call my husband, sir, to light you in another direction."

"I will only leave you if you tell me your name."

"Why, pray?"

"Just so. To pray with, for it's sure to be as Heavenly as you are."

"Your bad wit earns you my ugly name."

"Ugly, my donna?"

"Certainly, if it is to be prayed with by you. I am called Rosalena."

"A rose who is called a rose. How could they call you by any other name?"

"And now you may go away."

"How can I leave you? I know you, and am in your power."

Electra Chenti in crimson almost black, a diadem of Grechian influence in her upcombed hair from which unravelled a veil like a golden spider's web, studied her narrow hands and the thirteen rings that gripped her fingers. She cared little for any of them. There was only one she hated—on the marriage finger of her left hand. The scalding room had not tinted her white cheeks at all. Yet she had warmed a fraction. To a perverse, bitter joy that her daughter, too, must suffer marriage.

There was small kindness in Lady Chenti. She had been reared to passionless ritual, sold at thirteen to a high bidder, raped on her marriage night, and thereafter raped on a selection of other occasions, filled, delivered, finally freed to return to the mask of passionless ritual once more. Iuletta meant nothing to her. Iuletta had been a token, and ultimately, when Chenti's further efforts had produced no other child, no desired son and heir, Iuletta had become a symbol of Lady Chenti's unwillingness to cooperate. Chenti had soon left his wife alone. He created other sons in the Tower, bastards he could legalize. Even Leopardo, whom he did not like, might act male heir if commerce, or a boiling up of Versensa's internal strife, demanded it. As for Iuletta, she had shown her only possible worth in alliance-promoting beauty. Electra Chenti had borne the child in considerable agony, had watched the child as she, Electra, was shriven and alotted last rites—it had been for some days quite certain the mother would die—having lived had turned the child over to Cornelia to wetnurse in the aftermath of the woman's own stillbirth, and subsequently to raise. Thereafter, Electra Chenti did not concern herself with Iulet beyond the mother's duty of imposing on her the formats of morality, religion and deportment, those same warmthless things her own mother had taught her. To all intents and purposes, Iulet was simply a pupil to Electra. As long as the pupil did her credit, Electra was satisfied. To see her downfall—the betrothal—pleased Electra as at the fate of some mistrusted stranger.

That Belmorio was young and handsome did not change Electra's opinion. Ostensibly, she was cynically glad the girl had fared better than the mother in this respect. Beneath the gladness, if such it could be called, very deep, the mother added it to her store of wrongs. But otherwise she knew perfectly well that even an idyllic marriage would shortly stabilize into impostment, distress, the horrors of childbearing, and the additional horrors of used uselessness.

The banquet had been in progress some three hours, and was now running down into drinking, music, and a clamor to dance. The remnants of chickens and assorted gamebirds, stuffed with lemons, oranges, grapes, basted with wine and honey, lay in pilfered skeletal form, still in the process of hackery, or being cleared away. Disemboweled pies, pomaded veals in tatters, cakes gutted, pickled and smoked fishes with only their tail fins intact (and not always), peaches padded by sweet mince now unpadded, pastries smashed, candied nuts, lakoums, gelatinas, caramelos, all, all in ruins. And at the center, the saddest casualty, the four-foot-long image of the leopard off the roof, meatloaf with raisins from a mould, and lacquered with saffron so it had shone like gold, lay in pieces, poor thing, to rise no more. (Electra Chenti had not eaten much. She seemed to have no appetite for anything, even sleep.)

While the feast had ruled at the tables, sometimes spilling through on to the central area—mock battle for a pigeon's breast, a swarm of runaway glazed quinces trapped by servants—a variety of diversions had passed down the hall.

Knights of Chentis past, and, naturally, Belmorios, tabarded and exotically mailed, had gone by with banners. A lady on a white horse had ridden through, the horse behorned to resemble a unicorn. Cherubs and satyrs had scattered flowers and vine leaves. Finally Venus appeared, attended by the warriors of Mars, herself lace-veiled but dressed in daring Eastern garb that left free much of her fine skin, and borne in a golden chariot trailing roses. In the traces some fifty odd, mostly white, mewling but well-trained cats. With assistance from the Martian army, the cats hauled Venus past the master table. Level with Belmorio, a Cupid, eyes bandaged in fine gauze, winged and with bow and arrow, tossed a bag into the air and released a cloud of doves to cries and cheers from the assemblage and an externally restrained but irrepressible interest from the dray cats.

Electra Chenti, if any of this excited her, gave no sign. Troian and his sire were plainly tickled—the Dove of Belmorio's emblem having been honored in so appropriate a manner. Iuletta seemed feverish. She gave her attention to Troian as if afraid to look away from him. A young man with ashy golden hair, one long white leg, one long brass-yellow leg, a salt-white doublet and contrary linen dyed to complement the brassy hue, was placed to the Belmorio's right. Brass-and-White had angled himself so he might see Iuletta, and in turn sat with indolent absorption, also watching nothing else, or very little. Chenti himself, big with triumph and goodwill, ordered his stewards, ate and drank, and was now rising, laughing, his face artistically toning with his pleated gown, to call the musicians to order.

Almost all the doves had been recaptured. A quelling of feathers and music was succeeded by a quelling of hubbub. Servants scurried to clear the floor of its bruised flowers.

"My good friends!" Lord Chenti was a drop drunk. (What matter? Not less manly or less in command for that.) "We tidy the floor. We let the musicians breathe. And what more opportune. A prince of singers is among us with his own music-makers." Chenti leaned toward the Estemba placement. "Flavian. You pledged us a song."

Mercurio was bashful. "I?"

The crowd laughed now, and began to harangue the Estembas. They always liked this joke of aristocrats aping entertainers: comedians, clowns, minstrels.

Presently Mercurio rose, smiling to himself, holding out

one hand for peace. It seemed he withheld some secret information, which they might win from him, by and by.

"Well," he said. "What would you have me sing?"

"A song, Mercurio!" someone shouted, one of the Retzi tribe.

"Oh, a song. I do not sing songs."

Mercurio glanced down each of the long tables. The multitude did not daunt him. He knew he could please them, for they were eager to be pleased tonight. Here and there a group was standing up, and in one such the indigo doublet of Romulan Montargo, with its embroidery of ships and combers, was leaning to a woman's arch profile amid white roses.

"If I sing, I ask a favor in return. My minstrel's fee."

The guests liked this, too. Some called, offering items not always wholesome. They were very well-wined. Mercurio waved them down again. This time, he raised his brows at Lord Chenti, who slapped the damascine.

"Sing, Apollo. And ask what you want."

Mercurio gestured to the Estemba page behind his chair. As the boy hurried away to the lobby, Mercurio walked around the tables and between them, out onto the mosaic floor. One could see something of the picture now. It was from myth, the abduction of Proserpina. Mercurio continued until he stood on the heads of Pluto's jet-black horses, on their nostrils blooming ruby chips of fire. As he did so, the boy came back and shyly across to him with the pale fruit of the mandolin. Mercurio, with the composure of one alone in a private chamber, began to tune the instrument. As the boy turned, Mercurio reached out and gently caught his shoulder. "Stay, soul. I'll need you for the descant."

The boy blushed. His voice had recently broken to a true silver tenor, cunning accessory to Mercurio's darker range. He was, besides, in love with Mercurio. Half Verensa had been, was, would be. Filled with terror and joy, the boy waited, trembling.

But it was like Mercurio to have brought four musicians out in the rain with him and to use none of them.

At the announcing chord, the room grew quiet. Quiet enough a second chord, of thunder, but muted, mellowed, as if it too had been drinking wine, strummed through the Tower, the first which had been audible since the eating began.

Then the song flowed in, and gathered like somber petals above the candlelight.

On the quiet, an overlay of quiet. Into which the petals of song fell.

Romulan had lifted his head. It was the song Mercurio had sung in the old garden, he remembered it at once. For some reason, probably that of following events, it disturbed him. The aloof Rosalena at his side had half shut her eyes, gazing through the lashes at Mercurio as he sang.

Iuletta, who knew only one presence in her father's hall, and that presence far off, unreachable, perhaps an illusion, or a ghost, brushed by strange intimations of ecstasy and fear, closed her eyes entirely. The wonderful voice did not soothe her. It penetrated to every artery, pierced, injured her. She surrendered herself to the unfathomable pain of incorporeal things.

And Leopardo, with the clarity of his own drunkenness, leaning on a wall-hung oriental carpet behind Electra Chenti's chair, close enough to brush, with his fingertips, the center of her webby veil, heard the voice and the song with an untranslatable tension, also a scorn of love songs, a loathing of any other man who could express the heat and the irony he felt was inexpressibly blazing within himself.

> *"Who can tell where love will lead us,*
> *Love the color of a rose—*
> *Love the ever-sounding bell—*
> *Does she summon to a close,*
> *To the bitter of farewell?*
> *To the gorgeous gate of Hell?*
> *Ah, who knows, who knows?"*

Like Iuletta, the page brought down his lids, locking himself in candle-printed dark, with only Mercurio's voice to guide him—and introduced the upper line narrow and exquisite as a bird.

> *"Who can say what love may teach us,*
> *She may teach us how to mourn,*
> *She may teach us laughter fades*
> *And that the Fair, foresworn,*
> *Is not fair in how it trades—*
> *And how eyes may wound like blades—*
> *But, who'll learn, who'll learn?"*

The last notes dripped from the mandolin and melted like magic coinage, into nothing. The nothing contained the hall, the limbo that was blind as Cupid, did not breathe, held to its own fancies, its own hidden wants and musings.

The thunder offered plaudits first. Then Chenti's guests, rising and roaring to outdo the thunder.

The Estemba page blinked two long tears of nerves and emotion.

"Clever child." Mercurio, dry-eyed, stroked the boy's hair, once, returned him the mandolin, moved away and left him, going straight through the praise and the cries to place a hand each on the shoulders of grunting affable Chenti and earnest laughing Troian.

"Have I justified a reward?"

"You have," said Chenti. "I'd invite you to sing here every night. The ladies swoon. Come, what's on your mind to have?"

"Let the first dance of the evening be the Turcanda."

"Such energy next after supper. But why not? Granted, Estemba Uno."

"One other thing," said Mercurio.

"Oh, name it, name it."

"Noble lord, noble bridegroom-to-be, the Turcanda, and myself to lead, with Iuletta Chenti."

Chenti scowled. He was, in fact, very drunk. He did not approve of such conduct, sensing jibes, connivings. But Belmorio, also extremely tipsy, flung one arm round Mercurio and with the other lightly pummelled Chenti in the ribs.

"Ah, let the poor man have her for the dance. The measure will part them often enough. And a Mercurio consumed by hopeless love is a rare vision for the rest of us."

It was the league of youth against middle age. Chenti did not care for it, but neither did he care, publically and under these circumstances, to stand in its way. He therefore lifted Iuletta out of her seat and put her hand in Mercurio's, just as he had given it to Belmorio before. She had had no say in the affair, had perhaps not been listening, for she gave the startled impression of one shaken abruptly from sleep.

Chenti was vocalizing fresh orders, the musicians tuning up, guests scrambling for the open floor, others subsiding to glean the litter of the tables.

"Cheer him," said Troian to Iuletta. "For a little, little while, my dearest almost-wife."

Mercurio bowed to Iulet. He kissed her chill and immaculate hand, then drew her on to the mosaic.

As the drums began, the column of dancers formed. They took the five initial steps, Estemba caught Chenti's daughter by the waist and lifted her. She went up lightly as a sawdust doll raised by strings between his hands, pleasing him. Her palms rose and met in the florid clap the dance stipulated. Automatically she was performing, for she still looked dazed.

He let her down, they took a step. In seven further steps he must relinquish her to the man at his back, for the dance was obdurate. Softly, and with great tenderness, Mercurio said to her as they went forward:

"And may I hope to see you again at Susina's brothel?"

As the Turcanda—a dance intended to mimic certain raids and abductions carried out by the Islamite Turci on neighboring lands, and by some considered degenerate—escalated through lifts, leaps, stampings, whirlings, mock fights and quite dangerous running exchanges of partners, individuals, intimidated, fled from the glittering melee, while others, aroused, scurried to replace them.

Electra, watching as her daughter spun through each measure with the brass and white young man, had unwarily taken on the cruel engrossment of Venus' cats when doves were released over their heads. But the solitary finger which touched her shoulder was immediately identified, and immediately evoked response. She turned and stared into the flushed face of her nephew.

"What is it that you want, Leopardo?"

"I want you to match me in the Turcanda."

"Alas, you must go wanting."

"Wanting and burning." Grinning, glorious, he leaned over her. "Why do you torture me in this way? Do you enjoy it?"

"You are drunk," she said, jerking her head aside from the wine fumes which, on his clean young breath, were not remotely offensive.

"Drunk. Drunk on wine. Drunk on—"

"I am tired of your insults."

For a second, her eyes flashed with bright anger.

Leopardo saw the pulse quicken in her throat and longed to seize it. He put his lips to her ear and said, "I'd like to strangle you, my aunt."

One seat away, Chenti, discussing some mercantile interest sluggishly with a sluggish Belmorio Primo, paid no heed, did not notice.

Electra gathered herself into stone.

"You are my flesh and blood," she hissed to Leopardo (both whispered like lovers or murderers together), "therefore I restrain myself. One word to my lord—"

"We'll see." Leopardo raised his voice, leaning across her to catch Chenti's sleeve. "Lordly Uncle? Sir? My lord?"

"What?" Pig-eyed with drink, Chenti bleerily gawped over his shoulder.

"Give me leave to dance with my aunt."

"Oh, take her." Chenti turned back to business.

Leopardo lowered his lips once more to Electra's ear. Her proximity, so easily achieved in the midst of such a crowd, dizzied him. "He says 'yes.' You heard your lord and master. Get up, then, lady, and obey him."

"No." Two narrow fists of bone and rings lay on the table. Leopardo considered them. The urge to take them up and crush them was almost uncontrollable. He swayed against her chair, wanting to fall prostrate on top of her. "No," she said again.

"Lord Uncle? My lord? Sir?"

"Oh, by God, what now?"

"She says she will not. Donna Electra refuses me, and your command."

"Stars of fire. Get up, Electra. Do as you're bid. How does this look to our guests?"

"My lord, please excuse me. I am faint." Never had a woman sounded less near to fainting, her voice a thin steel dagger. It ran through Leopardo like an awl. He knew he could have done the same service for her, there on the strewn table. What, after all, was sin? The body's life.

"Ah," said Chenti. "Do not press her if she's unwell." Solicitous kindness, to impress Belmorio.

Adultery, incest. Leopardo drank more wine. It did not dull the ache of unrelieved lust that gathered in his belly, the sparks in his brain.

Electra, the ice-queen, unlike the ice statues on the tables, unmelted.

She had become aware of her nephew as a man only in the past year. Before that he had been a male child, out of her sphere; a child she heard much of from others, and now and then had unavoidably seen for herself. A nasty unruly thing, who had ridden a horse to death at twelve, beaten his dogs, gone away to the colleges of Padova and been renowned there for brilliant swordplay, drunkenness, orgies with Eastern drugs, arguments with creditors and usurers, and unlawful duels without number. When he had invaded the Tower, an adult just twenty years of age, she had avoided him with allergy, somehow, however, always managing to come on him accidentally. One day, after she had heard Leopardo engaged in a fierce quarrel with Lord Chenti, she had found her nephew in this accidental way, smashing with his sword hilt the faces of statues in the stone garden, and weeping with rage. A strange note had been struck within Electra at the sight. She had lived elsewhere until her marriage, hated all Lord Chenti's property, and had liked to see it defaced—perhaps it was only that. She had set her hand on Leopardo's bowed head and allowed herself a moment with the mass of apricot hair that felt like crisp wild grass to her. Then he had looked at her. Anything might have happened, but Electra elected to withdraw her caress and to say: "What's this? Are you a baby or a man?" And at that he had stood straight, half a foot taller than she, his reddened eyes glaring down at her, and she had known him for a man indeed.

How he angered her, now, and always. She got no peace from him. Night-time disturbances when Chenti was from home, mocking rhymes made and carolled, (disguised, still obviously about herself), gestures dramatic and suspect, the aura of him everywhere. Her anger was like a knot inside her. And when he was by, it became a knot of serpents. She did not know quite yet how she had come to rely, to feed upon this anger, her only appetite.

A crash behind her told her Leopardo had thrown his valuable glass wine cup to the floor.

"Oh, pardon me, lord Uncle. It slipped from my grasp."

Like a spurl of flames he was gone, striding erratically yet powerfully to the next table.

"Donna Rosalena. May I persuade you to the Turcanda?"

Rosalena, one of the lesser kindred of the Chentis, smiled her arch smile at him, framed by white roses.

"The dance is too rough for me, sir. And since no others quit the floor, we'd need to hustle one pair away, or the sets would be out."

"We'll hustle then. Come with me. Who is there to stay for?"

The black-haired youth in unrecognized House colors moved between Leopardo and Rosalena.

"You are superfluous, sir," said Romulan. He, too, smiled, most courteously.

"And you are rude, sir."

"You are rude, sir, insisting a lady dance when she prefers other pastimes."

"You being the pastime?" The third smile, Leopardo's. A pause, both men drunk, smiling, waiting for each other. "And what are you," Leopardo added, "a Master mariner?"

"A *mariner?*"

"I took you for one, covered all over by shipping as you seem to be."

"Shipping, and a mariner? I might as well take you, sir, for an orange."

"And how an orange?"

"By your colors, sir. On your clothes, and on your head."

"Your wit, I fear, limps."

"To keep pace with yours, sir," said Romulan nicely.

Bystanders had gathered. The table, titillated, alert, had in patches risen and drawn closer to overhear.

Leopardo Chenti raised his voice with deliberation.

"Declare your House, sir. Unless you are ashamed of it."

"No shame, I assure you. Montargo."

"Ah, yes. Bloody Montargo, who kills its foes in dark alleyways with the paws of hired murderers. Montargo the House of money lenders, cheats and trulls. No shame at all."

Romulan ceased smiling, and the bystanders tensed. This was too sharp. Rosalena, some noted, had slipped gracefully away from the center of the confrontation.

"You are one of my hosts," said Romulan. "I'll assume you entertain evil friends who misinform you. Or that you have some defect of the ears."

"My ears are sound. My friends are sound, for I have no friend who's a Montargo."

Over the music and cries of the dance, this end of the hall was now extremely still. Lord Chenti was looking in their direction. Lady Chenti had been watching some while. Feeling her eyes like two stings on his back, Leopardo, excited in any number of interconnected ways, made an exaggerated bow to Romulan, whose first name he did not even know, but the measure of whose fires he had already taken.

"Villain," said the bowing Leopardo. "Backstabber. Thief. Dog. Toad. Worm. *True* Montargo. Unless, bloody, backstabbing villain, I wrong you. Unless you are your mother's bastard."

As Leopardo straightened, a hand that was partly a fist caught him in the mouth. Leopardo staggered backward, steadied himself on the table and shook hair from his eyes, and ringing from his skull, grinning. A woman had screamed at the blow. Leopardo knew the sound, the nature of the scream: anticipatory and savage. It lifted him further. He stood up and let his hand fall in the most precise of gestures to the dagger in his belt. Swords had been left off for the occasion, or removed at the door. But daggers, reminder of earlier days when they served for cutlery, had not. The young man in blue who had become his showpiece, a theater for Leopardo's passions, in an irresistible echoing move also set hand to hilt.

Leopardo grinned more delightedly, and whipped his own blade from its sheath. The shadowplay happened again and the blue fellow's dagger was drawn. What price now Chenti's etiquette, Iulet's betrothal auspices? Let them all go hang and be damned. And Electra, the black-eyed insomniac, let her see. She would like it, he knew she would, though never admit she liked it. Disapproving, breathing through parted lips, her little breasts throbbing with her heart—he could, without turning, picture it all.

"A new dance," said Leopardo. "I call it the Deathstep."

Shouting and calling in alarm, the neighboring watchers had already pressed back instinctively to form a ring, as at a cock fight.

Leopardo tossed the dagger in the air, caught it again, prepared lion-like to spring forward—a dart of movement changed his plan. He checked, and found the Montargo's friend, that Estemba with the brass-yellow shirt, who, having leapt straight over the table, stood before him where Montargo should have been.

"Now my dear sir, my best lord of cats," said the Estemba, with the most sweet reasonableness. He blocked each of the fighters from the other with total effect. Leopardo blinked at him, retrieved a name-Flavian, called Mercurio, the singer of songs.

"The business with mandolins is done," said Leopardo. "Move aside. Stay with what you are good at."

Mercurio gazed at him with such innocent gentleness it was a pity to doubt it, but Estemba's eyes were clear almost to transparency, dangerous enough Leopardo did not try for him in that moment.

Montargo had come up on Estemba's left and was attempting to push by him.

"Peace," Mercurio said to him. "This is no Fero you'd be aiming swipes at. This one is the Prince of Swords, they tell me."

"Oh, *humbly thank you* for your praise," Leopardo snarled.

Romulan snarled: "Get out of my way."

Mercurio clicked his tongue, and with the disparagement of an elderly monk rebuked them both: "What sort of behavior is this? Little children should love one another."

Beyond them, the Turcanda had ended in disarray. The musicians were silent, the dancers staring, the rest of the crowd with them. Shambling like a great crimson ox, Lord Chenti was reeling over, thrusting friends and kin violently from his path, intent on putting an end to the brawl.

"You see," Mercurio said to Romulan, looking at Leopardo, not taking his eyes from Leopardo, "he fights to get rid of his nine lives. Kill him but once and he will only be after you again. You would be killing him all evening."

A wink of white light above, then a gigantic blow of thunder seemed to shake the Tower, knocking the last doves from the rafters. A storm without and within. Heads were involuntarily raised and a few women shrieked at the sky-riding thunderbolt—who had not thought to give tongue at the sight of drawn daggers three feet from their noses.

A second, less impressive, thunder was Lord Chenti's incoherent roar, which shook nothing and no one, but which promised that he might. He had reached the second table. He was seizing Leopardo, turning him. One martial hand went up, prepared to strike. And there, in that awful besotted attitude of power, Chenti stayed himself. While Leopardo, before he could prevent it, cringed at the expected impact of a blow which never came.

"*You shame me!*" Chenti bellowed. Spit flew from his lips, striking Leopardo as the hand did not. "You shame *me*, shame yourself, Leopardo. Shame the House of Chenti."

Leopardo had gone yellow. Transfixed in that hated grasp, belittled, helpless at last, and with a sickening awareness of how his impotence must appear, he writhed to his soul, and wished himself revenged and dead.

"My Lord Chenti," Mercurio said brightly, "we beg your tolerance of our foolishness. Come, Romulan, I deduce we are waited for, somewhere or other."

On the mosaic, Iuletta, unable to think what else to do, managed the young girl's trick of semi-fainting, and dropped among Proserpina's poppies.

As women poured around her, and she dimly heard Troian's concerned exclamations, the lover she had drawn to the feast by magic, not having at any point actually seen her as something relevant, walked from her father's Tower.

SIX

"He provoked me."

"You let him provoke you."

"Am I to stand smiling while he insults Montargo?"

"Why not?"

"Would you, if he'd slandered Estemba?"

"He did not."

"*Would* you?"

"Perhaps."

"You would not, bloody liar."

"I was not by."

"No. You were dancing with Chenti's daughter, trying to stir trouble that way."

"And would have done it, too, had I not been interrupted. A beautiful insidious trouble. A subtle trouble. Trouble like a bubble, water and air."

"Mercurio—"

"I am, I confess, enslaved by Iuletta Chenti. Maybe I'll wait till the marriage feast, then carry her off. Help me?"

In a white and flaming rage, Romulan stalked at his side, not to be amused or diverted from his grievance. They had not got far, some three streets from the Chenti Tower. (Around and about loomed other towers, a nighttime forest without boughs or foliage. The rain had slackened, the thunder still rolled and rattled from hill to hill like a huge wagon. Now and then came a lightning, and the tower tops glistened greyly. It was late, most of their lamps were out.) At a suitable distance, the musicians and the pair of kindred Estembas slunk through the puddles. Only four torches had been rekindled, sizzling and guttering. The three Montargo guardsmen, the five Estemba guards, were wary of shadows, walls, overhanging trees, the stairs and doors of buildings. Also, ludicrously, of each other. The breach between these two families, Ring-Arrow and Ship, was bandaged but not healed by friendship, a friendship now evidently strained, on Romulan's side, to the utmost.

Abruptly, he stopped. Mercurio, one step ahead, also stopped, turned, and looked at him. The rest of the party, soaked to the skin, miserable and disgusted with the world, halted and stood kicking its heels, quietly grumbling.

"No man," said Romulan, "shoos me from his house like a chicken."

"And who did that?"

"Leopardo Chenti. Old Chenti. And, dear friend, *you*."

Mercurio's face did not alter.

"Do you think me," said Romulan softly, "so incompetent, so instantly outmatched, such a dolt, such a—"

"I think I'm wet through, that I'd like a jug of decent rough wine, and some music that is not played as a cow is milked. Come and find that with me. Or go home."

"You left a woman behind you in that house you said you liked."

"She'll keep."

"Mine will not."

"Oh, by God, what now?"

"I know which of the Chenti lodges Rosalena occupies. She told me."

"She's well-wed, and you no more likely to get a taste of her than a dog to fly."

"Chenti's daughter would be easier? But then, the wooing is everything, for you."

"I'll settle for what's to be had. Unlike your own over-mounting, earth-shaking, star-toppling and gargantuan lusts, of which we all, my dear, stand in such awe."

This last, said with the enormous respect of devastating sarcasm, finalized the debate.

Romulan swung about, balking only at a great lake of water between the cobbles. As he did so, Mercurio went after him.

"Come," Mercurio said, in the most charming of all his voices, making amends, "let's drink wine and discuss the cruelty of women to us. Women. . . . Never letting us have what we must have."

He placed his hand on Romulan's shoulder and was thrust off. Mercurio's charm became very cold, his diction a razor.

"And so," he said, "for saving you from the Leopard's dagger I must put up with this, must I?"

"Put up with nothing," Romulan answered. "I am going back to Chenti."

"Which is the act of a fool. At least go home, not there."

"Why the surprise I'm a fool, since you already think me one? I'll go to Chenti. And you, Estemba, may go to Hell."

"May I? Thank you. But I'm sure you know the way better than I, having been sent there more often."

Mercurio turned, and with an autocratic gesture that sommoned torches, houseguard and kin, he strode away along the street, into and beyond the curtains of rain.

Romulan, left alone suddenly with a single torch, the three Montargo guards, and a universe of running water, not even the argument to warm him, stopped again and abruptly shuddered.

The thunder took another turn about the sky. In its wake, the tired bell rang from the campanile, the voice of time, or fate. It was two of black morning. And what now? Some cheerless vigil under some pie-dish-hearted woman's lattice. Stupid, stupid. Yet he was sworn to it, that unvowed vow of anger. Sworn not to leave Chenti without some parting shot.

Embarrassed by the sodden Montargo guard, the solitary torch-bearer, Romulan as he went past bade them go home. The disjointed protest flared and was lost, as the torch was lost, in the rainy dark.

There had come to be a lot of noise before the Tower of the Polished Cat. As Romulan stepped onto the street, he heard a sinister burst of it. A moment more, and he beheld Chenti's stairway with its pink-lighted posts and seven or eight torches gusting above and between them. Figures, black on the lights and phantasmagoric with rain, jigged about, reminding him of certain pictures of the Inferno. Fiendish catcalls and laughter augmented the ideas. These were not merely guests going home.

The art of it would be to sidle by without much advertisement. Rosalena's lodge was the far side, but around a small wall-formed alley, secluded, if he could get to it.

Yet Jupiter, that old exiled god of storms, was not it appeared on the side of Montargo tonight.

Almost level with the stairway, looking askance at it, Romulan interpreted the curious scene as one last eccentric drinking party grafted on the packed-up revel of the betrothal banquet. Out in the rain, dice were being thrown, torches whirled about, fifteen men crouching, jumping, cursing, and

assuaging internal dryness. Occasionally a wine cup of heavy
metal would toll down the steps. At this the raucous yells and
quips would increase. Chenti Prima must be dead-drunk and
leaden in his bed to permit such a Bhorgabba riot on his
threshold. The leader of it could be no one but that very one
with whom Romulan had had dealings earlier. It needed no
sixth sense to guess as much. Leopardo's reputation in most
matters was generally known among his peers, even those
who might forget his House or its color. To dice and drink in
the rain was characteristic.

Romulan was almost by, unseen, when luck passed sentence. Firstly, another of the ever-tumbling wine cups
tumbled. Clanging from stair to stair, and over the landing it
came, down the ultimate flight, struck paving, bounced up,
flew, carved through water and rolled, almost to Romulan's
feet.

Immediately, Romulan sprang back into one of the vertical
interstices that pierced the wall behind him. As he did so he
heard the order from the stair: "Ah. Fetch me my cup, Gulio." Delivered slurred yet unmistakable, in the tone of his
most recent enemy.

Down the stair, slouching and hiccuping, came slim, intox-
icated Gulio, talking idly to the air about slavery.

Scat-eyed, he would never, in the usual way, have determined Romulan's atoms from the wall, but as Gulio bent,
picked up the silver cup and drew erect, Lord Jupiter cast his
conclusive vote.

A lightning, vigorous and blankly white, froze the town.
For a second, scarcely a shadow sustained itself, and with the
pale-rimmed glares of amazement and anguish, the Chenti
Gulio and Romulan Montargo regarded each other—frozen
for the duration of the lightning's freezing, and beyond it.

Invocations fluted from the stair.

"Gulio, Gulio!"

"Sweet Ganymede, bring back the cup."

"The levinbolt struck him."

"Oh, Gulio, have you been turned to salt? Come and let us
lick you, it will give us a thirst."

Gulio took command of his voice.

"Hah, 'Pardo! There's a rat in the wall."

Silence grew on the stair and movement ceased. Then Leopardo's voice:

"What kind of rat?"

Gulio, anxious to please, happy to be amid his own, thrilled at his wit, sang out: "A rat off a sinking ship!"

Leopardo, torchlit and like a torch himself, was now obvious on the stair.

"A Montargo. Oh, which?"

"Rosalena's swain."

"She has so many."

Laughter.

"You inquired his name, 'Pardo. Surely you remember?"

"Ah, me. Could it be the baby who came with his Estemba nurse-maid?"

They had begun to come down the stairs now.

There were sixteen, but in the bizarre displacements of fire and water, they looked more. Naked swords were rasping and glinting as they came from their sheaths.

Cold now, with no anger, no audience, a single blade against so many, of whom one was mad Leopardo, Romulan knew an unaccustomed reluctance. Such odds had never been laid on him. And there was no other by to take his part.

The thunder spoke again, closer, galvanic.

Romulan broke from his cover, awarded Gulio a shove that sent him sprawling, and raced for the end of the street. Even as he ran, baying and howling rose at his back, and the slash and slap of feet through puddles. Romulan knew then a hideous elation. It was almost funny to play hare to this pack of dogs. Funny that they might catch, mutilate, even kill him. Eyes wide, Romulan laughed as he ran. He saw his father's figure bent over his corpse, saw Mercurio, could not be sure what Mercurio would do at his death, rejected one image after another, all as he fled.

Re-achieving the street's end, swerving into a side alley, he was all at once floundering in mud. His sword beat on a wall, unbalancing him so he skidded. The pack screamed after him, approaching, not yet arrived. He was no longer thinking. Leaves struck his face, next a bough. Another lightning showed how, heavy with fruit, the arms of trees had come over their wall, hanging level with his head. On the lightning now the thunder, an appalling bang directly above, that trembled the earth at his feet. The rain, revitalized, became an avalanche, blinding him, smiting him. He was all at once sick of everything, of rain, of fight, of flight, of quarrels, of wine. He took handfuls of the tree and leapt. Slithering, dragging and dragged, the sound of rent leaves quite lost in the clash of the deluge, Romulan flung up into the tree, through it, out of it, and fell down into a sea of wet bushes on the in-side of the wall.

Rain fell in his eyes, mouth, nostrils. He moved on to his side and lay panting, crazy, unutterably depressed by every-thing. Around him, denseness tintinnabulating and gushing with water, and giving off the piercing scent of fruit trees in rain and night. An orchard, probably Chenti's own, enclosed him. God's Heart!

Vaguely, like a dream, he heard the welter of Leopardo's mob go by beyond the wall.

Was this safety?

Romulan crawled on to his knees, pushed branches away and stood up. The half-healed Fero sword-cut in his arm had begun to throb and burn. Could it be this foolish hurt that had caused his flight? This absurd intimation of a death which, being young, he did not truly believe in? So slight a wound, which would leave a scar almost finer than a thread. The first scar. As important perhaps as the first woman, if po-ets were at all to be credited.

He took a pace, stumbled, almost fell.

Far before him, a sort of useless beacon, a rosy glimmer, shone into the dark, no larger than his middle finger, some long low window of the house.

And what was Mercurio doing? Was Mercurio to be won back? What had Romulan said? He could not recall, only the friend striding off into distance.

Romulan leaned on one of the trees, rain plastering him to its trunk. He looked at the rose window, unable to decide now whether to go back, go farther, or to linger. And so, lin-gered, until he heard the vague dreamlike din of curses and slitherings renewed about fifty paces off over the wall.

"He's here, where else, impudent brainless wretch? In Chenti's own grounds."

"Give me a shoulder someone. Your hand."

A tree shook. Jeers rang out. Someone splashed down in the mud of the alley. Leopardo's voice came like a knife: "If I take him here, I'll slice him in bits."

Romulan's anger returned because in that moment he was ferociously afraid. For half an instant, he stood, a battle-ground between the frantic wish to stay and meet Leopardo as he came over the wall—as surely he would do—and the renewed inclination to escape. Then he ran.

And, having nowhere in fact to run toward, he chose, with inevitable instinct, the lighted window ahead of him.

They had put her to bed under the crimson canopy. They had pecked and squabbled over her comforts. Lady Chenti, a dark reed, had bowed ("Are you well, now?") pitiless, above her. The question, spoken and favorably replied to, she had gone away. The one person Iuletta had wanted to see—was desperate to see—Cornelia—did not come at all. On the subject of Cornelia's absence, one of the little maids giggled. She reminded Iuletta of the secondary feast the servants had had, the fine cast-offs of the banquet, and half the wine. It was a tradition which Lord Chenti, grudging yet hide-bound, kept up. Cornelia, certainly, had approved. The servants had listened in fascination as Cornelia's conversation grew more and more ribald, less and less shocked at itself. Eventually, roaring drunk as any good madam of the Bhorga, Cornelia had been hoisted up by six male servants and borne, singing her own requiem, to her chamber. No, Cornelia would not be available to comfort and soothe her charge tonight.

And why should Iuletta be in need of comfort? No one was out of patience with her. Even the fainting fit had been deemed maidenly and quite proper. It had shown her of gentle breeding, susceptible. More, it had aided the company over those awkward moments when the Estemba-Montargo contingent had vacated the house, Troian Belmorio had stood biting his thumbnail, and Leopardo and Chenti Primo had fallen back from their vitriolic clinch. Iuletta was approved of, and might now lapse and sleep a sweet angelic slumber, dreaming of the bridegroom she had enchanted, and her virtuous usefulness to her father.

Iuletta did not sleep. When her apartment, lights still burning, had been emptied of all its bustling attendants, she rose. She flung over herself a silk mantle, and began to pace about, for all the world like her insomniac mother.

To begin with, she wept also. But her state was too mixed for a solitary expression, and soon her tears dried. (She flinched at every thunder and lightning.)

The gold-haired man in brass and white, unknown, had yet seemed partly familiar. Something in his movements, and in his voice, only half attended to. . . . Attractive, he had confused her. In her anxious hidden fever (for Romulan was everywhere, yet did not see her, did not come to her) Iuletta was prepared to make a display with this handsome stranger, and was meaning herself, though quite distrait, to shine brilliantly in the dance. Estemba danced as he sang—perfectly, with grace and strength. His touch kindled her oddly, for she was not sure what it wished of her. It was quite unlike the ardent touch of Troian Belmorio, unlike all other brief tactile encounters she had received when dancing. Estemba had smiled at her, looked at her, obviously rapt. And then: "May I hope to see you again at Susina's brothel?"

Before she could snatch her scattered wits, another man had swept her away in the whirlwind of the Turcanda. Turning her head—false movement, the dance decreed the head at this moment should be thrown back—she saw Mercurio sweeping off his own exchanged partner.

When Iuletta was returned to him, her hand was even icier than before. He took it and said, "You're not to be afraid of me. A matter of honor, child-lady. I'll tell no one. But what in Heaven's name were you doing there?"

Her lips parted, she whispered, "Cornelia took me there—visiting."

"*Visiting*? The harlotry? And who's Cornelia?"

"My—my nurse."

"Oh, dear heart, what milk you must have sucked there."

Iuletta blushed, beautifully, almost all she did being beautiful.

Mercurio watched her.

"You ravish me," he said to her. "I adore you. How could I harm one night-colored tress on that exquisite head?"

Misunderstanding, she said, "I'm betrothed."

"So you are. So I perish. No matter. I'll worship you from a distance, as our ancestors worshipped Venus. Am I granted permission to do that?"

Unsure, her heart thudding, she had seen beyond his shoulder then and said in a voice like death, "Oh sweet Jesus—Leopardo has drawn on him—"

"Your cousin draws blade as another man draws breath."

But, "*Romulan*," she said—and found herself abandoned.

And now she felt herself enmeshed in some terrifying masculine sport, she the target at which all took aim. She comprehended nothing, and each seemed her enemy, mocking her. Even Romulan seemed so. What use were her feeble feminine sorceries against the living freedom of a man who came and went as he required? She could never bring him to her, never have him as that willing slave she had fantasized, this prince of men kneeling at her feet—

Her tears began again suddenly, and, as they did so, were cancelled.

Through the interminable violence of the storm, new notes of violence were sounding.

Far, far off had come a shout, several shouts. A slammed door of thunder had intercepted these. But from the very mouth of the thunder something seemed to burst. Something ran through the topiary garden below the Tower, for she heard, in one of the random, soon-ended cessations of the rain, steps beating their way along the paths. Lightning blanched the long rosy window that gave from her room on to the terrace. Distant reflections of branches, angles of the masonry, were flung across the stained glass, disjointed and horrible. For a moment Iuletta retreated from the window, and then some streak of perverse stubbornness changed her. She had been frightened enough. Angry and disillusioned, she ran to the casement, opened it and stared out across the terrace to the storm-contorted garden and the orchard beyond. Whatever was abroad in the awful night she would face it, give it the lie back in its teeth.

The rain, holding off all of half a minute, now resumed. At first she could tell nothing through it, till a sequin of dark reddish light—a smoldering torch—seemed to flicker in the depths of the orchard; then another and another, moving up and down rather than forward or back—as if some search were in progress.

Leopardo! It could be none but he. Some malign mischief he had devised, yet one more male who would scornfully make her days wretched. Trembling with her anger now, she reached to draw the window shut again—and started in fear as a man's voice called softly from the rain and dark and invisibility directly below the terrace.

She stayed quite still a moment then, yet reckoning on her loathly cousin, yet meaning to close the window. But even through the tumult of the weather, something in the voice, which she had never heard until now, stayed her. It was not Leopardo, that was sure. Nor any she recognized.

"Lady," it called again, soft, pitched under the roll of the rain. "My donna."

Bewildered, and in bewilderment strangely impelled, Iuletta raised her mantle to shield also her head, and stepped out on to the terrace. The liquid night tore round her, animate, warm, frenetic. Reaching the balustrade, she looked down. A figure stood among the flowering bushes at the stair base. She could see very little of its character, only hear now the fast breathing of a man who had been running. Having come out, she did not know what she should say, and was dumb. He, too, said nothing. Then there came again a muffled yell from the orchard.

"Lady," said the figure below her, "your kinsmen are in pursuit of me and will probably kill me. If I beg you for mercy, do I get it?"

"Pursuit," she faltered. "What have you done?"

"Incensed Leopardo Chenti."

Her heart stopped, then regained itself with an agonizing rush.

"By what means?" she gasped. Somehow he heard her.

"There was a quarrel at dinner. Perhaps you saw it."

She leaned on the balustrade, not knowing where she was, or anything, save who stood below.

"Lady," he said, "for God's sake take pity—or call Lord Chenti or some guard to stop this. I'm Valentius' son, Montargo's heir. Does this House require another blood-feud on its hands?"

"Come up," she said. The clarity of her voice amazed her. As he dashed toward her up the steps, she moved, puppetlike, to the window, and when he gained the terrace, finding she could not look at him, she hid her face in her mantle and pointed to the colored glass and the room beyond. Propriety and all else had become quite meaningless. "Go in there."

He obeyed her gladly. She followed him, shut the casement, and almost fell against it, aghast, her back to him.

Romulan stood facing into the exotic bedchamber, not yet having seen it, coughing for breath, with water falling from his garments to form a series of seas and isthmuses with the tessellated floor.

In the last instants of his flight, he had been brought to panic. That and lack of breath, not prudence, had subdued his voice. The panic shamed him, enraged him, as this new predicament did. Hearing him blundering through the garden, some light woman of the house, immodest and inquisitive, had come out on her balcony to spy. He had seen nothing of her but a shape in the storm. But he had begged refuge with her, and now was trapped. Between self-consciousness and dislike, he could not bring himself to glance at her, and so said, with heavy irony, "Your generosity is much appreciated, madama. To let a desperate man into your room at such an hour. Please be assured, you have nothing to fear from me. Your honor is safe." (No doubt much to your disappointment.)

Iuletta had reversed her position. She leaned still against
the window, but facing into the room—as if she did not
mean him now to escape from her, all her slight flesh, all the
fragile panes to prevent him. The silk mantle, top-heavy with
water, had slipped off her hair, her shoulders, and she
clutched it across her breasts, not feeling it, or anything at
all. She had become simply a pair of eyes and a heartbeat, incapable of speech or motion.

Getting only silence in return for cynical politeness, Romulan guessed uneasily that he must after all turn and confront
the probably voracious creature who had let him in. Appre-
hensive, a very little excited, he moved about and stared
straight at her. So he saw Iuletta Chenti for the first time, not
ten feet away. Rose silk, white skin, a stream of black hair
crystalled by rain. Two eyes like blue glass, leaded with black
lashes. Fifteen. Beautiful. And, in feminine form, his double.

There ensued a long, long hiatus.

Each was riveted by a stupefied recognition. Their faces
had become almost blank, and their eyes, either seeing only
the other inhabitant of the room, almost sightless.

Presently, however, through Romulan's first astonishment
there drove another, more mundane and more imperative.
Like a song never listened to, yet suddenly remembered, the
identity of this person had established itself.

"You're Chenti's daughter," he said. His voice was rough
and sounded ridiculous to him.

Unable to vocalize at all, the girl nodded.

Taking himself by surprise, Romulan laughed, one staccato
shout. It was absurd. Chenti's daughter. And to have seen her
all evening, yet not seen her—how could he not have seen
her, when she was—Puzzled, unnerved, struggling, he
frowned at her, then quickly rid himself of the frown. In
truth, she must be terrified. (Why then let him in, a strange
man, to this regal apartment of pink trees and little jewelry
books?) Loftily he nodded in turn to her, and took command
of his voice.

"Lady, by Christ I swear I will not harm you. You've done
me a wonderful kindness."

Her reaction was unprophesied.

"You!" she cried, her own voice regained in fierceness as
she had not been able to gather it in humility. "You, Romulan Montargo—how dared you come to this window? *My*
window—how *dared* you?"

Amazed again, he shook his head.

"I did not know it was yours, my donna—"

"You did. I insist that you did. You do this to make a jest of me. Perhaps you schemed it with 'Pardo."

"Oh, *trust* me, nothing further—"

"Or with your friend. Oh, it is some game." Childish, breathtaking, she threw her hands before her face and began to cry bitterly. Unheeded, the silk slid down her body, leaving her in her lace-trimmed linen shift. Through this, as through smoke or cloudy glass, the form of her was indefinitely visible, the sculptured stem, the highlights and the shaded, always-curving lines. Her naivety, her loveliness, the heart-stopping sensuality of the very young girl—the virgin—caught him by the throat. No other sort of woman could have moved him in such a way. In a single instant he desired her, pitied her, admired her, longed both to mar and to magnify, and to protect—most of all to protect her—from the longings she herself had conjured. So he went to her, drew up the fallen mantle and wrapped it around her, leaving only the rain-sopped end to trail upon the ground. And then, because to touch her pleased him, he left his arms about her, holding her lightly between his hands.

"You utterly misjudge me," he said to her. "I was in fear for my life. No one but God guided me here." Recklessly, growing drunk all over again, he added: "I'll never cease to thank Him that He did."

At that, she raised her head. Water beaded her lashes now, as her hair, but no ugliness had come with weeping. It seemed she could never be ugly. And again he laughed, at her, in sheer delight, which was in that second like Mercurio's delight in her, aesthetic and humane.

And then again the wondering extraordinary recognition overtook each of them. Their resemblance to each other, a thing not everyone would see, but which they, perforce students of themselves, saw and were lost in. They were surely like brother and sister. More, they were each other. And what formed between them now, though narcissistic, was yet innocent and vital, and quite irresistible.

They gazed. And then, like the Trump of Doom, from the garden below there came a cacophony of brutal noises. Leopardo's army of fifteen, having reached the base of the Tower and cheated of a quarry, giving tongue to frustration.

The grisly din had an immediate effect on Iulet. She cast herself against Romulan, against drowned clothing and the firm musculature beneath, and clasped him resolutely.

"They shall not take you," she muttered. Her voice was primitive, and he felt her surprising strength. She would protect *him*. Touched, and set ablaze by her action, he found he was no longer concerned with Leopardo, indeed scarcely credited his existence in a universe that comprised, for this minute, only himself and Iulet.

"Let them take me. How should I care? Heaven is here, and you an angel in Heaven. If they kill me they will only send me back to you. I should die happy—"

"Hush," she said. "If you die, then I must die, too."

The veracity that seemed to underlie her words stunned them both. He had often spoken as now he did, she never. And by the gleam of her honesty, he seemed to glimpse, though without acknowledgment or admission, his own. So once more they stared, guiltily, caught out. And as they did so, they heard phrases stabbing out of the hubbub below.

"He's gone, was never here. 'Pardo, we misjudged him."

"Yes. How should he run into Chenti's own orchard?"

"He was ahead of us in the alley, gave us the slip."

"I'm weary, 'Pardo. Let's to bed, for God's sake."

"Or go in and drink some more, 'Pardo. Eh, 'Pardo?"

And at last Leopardo's voice, rising like a vicious bird from the cellars of the darkness.

"Or maybe he's secreted with my chaste cousin. Ho, Iuletta! Iuletta! Who warms your bed tonight?"

The yowls amalgamated in improvisations on this theme and pluvious mirth. They were worn and wet, sobering and therefore dulled. None believed, least of all Leopardo himself, that the white fool, his uncle's brat, who left her candles burning from fear of shadows, would have the life in her to lure a man into her bedroom. As they roiled into the house, Leopardo played with one fond visualization, that of catching the silly girl *in flagrante,* and plunging a sword through both her and a Montargo lover. He went in grinning, not recalling Mercurio's song, how eyes could wound, as well as blades.

With the illogical suddenness of nature, the storm had dissipated, flowed away beyond Sana Verensa, away over the hills, away from the world. A stillness bloomed, and stars began to shine from every quarter of the sky.

"The cat-pack has gone," Romulan said at last.

"Be sure, my love," she said, "before you risk yourself."

"Your love," he said. "Am I your love?"

She lowered her eyes. The black fringe of her lashes lay on her cheeks.

"No," she said.

"Who then? Tell me, I'll seek and kill him."

She looked up and laughed at him, finding the humor of what he said before he knew it himself. He began to laugh, too, the third laughter, and the most real.

"Well," he said, "I think you like me."

"No, I do not like you at all."

"It must be more than liking, then."

"Or less."

"Perhaps love is less than liking."

"Oh," she said, "never tell me so." Then she glanced away and murmured, "Cornelia would say I am wicked and wanton." And then again the sapphire eyes blazed up at his. "Cornelia went to Laurus' cell in the old chapel by the Padova road, and fetched herbs from him. I worked a witchcraft on you. Oh, I have ensorcelled you. Forgive me, forgive me, I brought you here and bound you to me!"

Her evident horror amused him, and also filled him with heat. He drew her back to him, against him, every line of her body pressed to his, and the flame engulfed him.

"And now I bind you. That's fair."

"I should have died if you had not come to me," she said.

"I am here."

She lay on him, her head tilted back, her eyes closed. There was no other law on earth but that he must kiss her, and so he did. The kiss perpetuated itself. It seemed to have no end. Somehow they breathed, their mouths never parting from each other, or perhaps they did not need to breathe, drawing breath from the elements of each other, as fish did from oceans.

Finally, with the expression of one drugged, Iuletta removed herself from his embrace. She stepped back, and said seriously to him:

"You must not ask any more of me."

Unsatisfied, wanting, yet he was light-headedly exhilarated both by her intimation that he might think to seduce her and the fact that she trusted him to abstain.

"I will not. Though it grieves me."

"You must go," she said. "Sweet love, you must go before the first light comes."

He went to the glass door and opened it, and saw the storm had vanished, and the mosaic of stars appeared.

She, coming after him, looked first at the garden, the orchard, determining its emptiness. The watchmen of all the gates would be sheltered still from the rain, and possibly asleep. The villainous cousin and his crew had certainly not disturbed them. Said cousin and crew were now themselves indoors.

"It's safe," she said. "Go now, Romulan, at once." And flung her arms about him, securing him to the spot.

Again their bodies and their mouths met. Again they were submerged.

In the orchard, alarming them so they fell once more apart, a nightingale began its melody, a harp which had waited out the storm.

"Will you think of me today?" she asked him.

"Of nothing else."

"Shall we meet again?"

"How not? My life is nothing without you."

"You will forget me when the sun rises."

"I will forget the sun and think it is you, walking toward me from the east."

The words were enough like Troian's greeting in the water garden that she shivered and became afraid, for this love she had willed so hard to have was complex in achievement. Romulan took her hands, kissing them.

"Swear you'll not forget me," she said.

"I could more easily forget myself."

"Swear it."

"I swear it. And will you pray for me, angel?"

"Yes."

He left her abruptly, as if knowing fascination with her would otherwise delay him. But on the third step he paused, looking back at her, her whiteness side-lit by the glowing room against the serene embers of night, accompanied by the chirruping of the nightingale.

"Pray for me, Iuletta," he said again. And then, throwing back his head to take in the sky, "But who would need to pray? The sky is prayer enough, so full of stars—"

And springing down the stair, into the close-drawn shades below, he was gone without a backward glance.

SEVEN

Framed by the morning doorway, Valentius Montargo had stood perfectly immobile some five or six minutes, regarding his sleeping son.

Outside and beyond the door, the pillared veranda and the courtyard below were very quiet, save for the rustling noises of the huge fountain-ship. On the roofs, doves purred and fanned their wings. The sky was blue as the tiles of the pool, flecked with only the faintest and most iridescent clouds, the heat of the day already imminent. By contrast, the room inside the door was cool, its shutters folded closed. On the surface of the bed, uncovered and naked, Romulan lay asleep, left arm flung out (unbound, marred by its incipient scar), head turned toward the right shoulder, legs quiescent, unconscious and still as death.

And death was what Valentius saw on him, like a fine glaze. Not merely through the classic pose, like that of some expired young hero or god sprawled on a tomb, nor the undersea quality of the skin in the dimness. No, death as a mathematical deduction. The mother had died when the boy was six years of age, without any true cause, being unexposed to danger of any sort, protected, cherished, but all at once putting her hand to her head, saying there was a sound in her ears like bees, falling, carried indoors, lifeless inside seven days. Valentius and Valentina—how odd their names had been almost one, just as their affections. A love match, and seven years of love, and seven days of agony, and thirteen years of emptiness. Death had been love's price. He had been nineteen when he wed her, twenty-six when he lost her. Twenty-six and afraid, Valentius had withdrawn his love from the boy, and so surreptitiously withheld it from the adolescent, who, as he gained years, gained more and more of the mother's translated image, and less and less of her tranquility. Romulan ran toward death, courted disaster. It had been simple enough for that dark angel to kill the protected

91

woman. But how much easier to slay the son, who offered himself to every sword, every lightning bolt of malice and savagery.

When word had come to Montargo—as word would always come of such events—*your son has taken a de Fero sword in the arm,* Valentius, who prayed now only out of courtesy to God (prayer as a tool had failed when Valentina died), had spent the sleepless night at his papers, seeing none of them, nor the room, seeing only one dead son. But when Romulan came back to him alive, having been preceded by a messenger from Estemba (guarded, the feud) Valentius had been unable to convey one iota of his innermost feelings. All he had conveyed was disapproval, the stone spine of the Montargo Tower. Ah yes, feuds, House with House, but this feud father with son, Montargo at war with itself.

Valentius stirred stiffly at his vigil. He had come determined to speak of the matter in hand, for usually the boy was up, had even quit the house by midmorning. Now Valentius, distressed at this moribund slumber, determined instead to go away. Even as he straightened, however, the figure on the bed moved, flinging out its other arm, (the pose of crucifixion), then woke. The right arm was once more lifted, but now languid as a swimmer's, to shield the eyes from the sunlit door. The eyes themselves drifted open, closed, open, and the face, turned slowly to Valentius, smiled at him. It was a smile of marvellous sweetness, like a child's, trusting and happy and at peace, for Romulan was clearly not yet fully aware. The father received the smile with a deep personal sadness, already assured it was not for him.

"I am sorry to wake you," Valentius said. It did not surprise him that this mild sentence, meant as a politeness, was interpreted as criticism.

Romulan, forcing himself alert, sat up, managing as he did so to contort his body, ensuring that his genitals were now concealed. The gesture struck Valentius not only as evidence that Romulan found his father's eyes on his nakedness an embarrassment, as the eyes of servants and friends were not, but as an instinctual protection in the face of an enemy.

"My apologies, sir. I was out drinking most of the night."

This kind of boast—it was clearly that—no longer moved Valentius either to amusement or displeasure. It was a symptom, not the illness.

"I had a mind to discuss something with you. Perhaps you'd be good enough to visit me when you've breakfasted."

Romulan lowered his head. Morosely: "Yes. Very well. If you wish it."

"You have, obviously, another more pressing engagement."

Romulan said nothing, sitting there, waiting for the intruder to leave him alone.

"Well," Valentius said, "since you have so little time, we will discuss it now."

"*Now*, Father?"

"Now. It's soon said. I fear I misjudged in the matter of the priest."

"Which priest?" Romulan stared almost comically. Valentius could not be sure if the slumbrous confusion was an act or not.

"Laurus, the hermit-friar I suggested you accept as tutor."

"*Ordered* me to accept as tutor," Romulan snapped back. An act, then.

"It seems he is unsuitable. A clever man, a man of unusual intellect and skill, but as a teacher—things have come to my ears."

"He's an alchemist," said Romulan. "Do you mean that? Probably a magus, a sorcerer. The place is packed with stuffed dragons and giant brazen tortoises. I saw no bones of small children, or flayed hides of virgins. Hidden perhaps."

"Perhaps. I think there's no vileness in the man. An experimenter. But too eccentric for our purpose."

"And I am so infinitely corruptible."

"Since you know yourself so well, you'll be glad of the alternative I have discovered."

"Oh, more schooling. I'm not to escape."

"There is a college conducted on the classical formula, in Manta Sebastia. I'm sending you there."

"*What?*" Forgetful of everything, Romulan leapt off the bed. "To *Manta*! That's in Lombardhia—"

"Across the Duke's borders."

"Is that how you seek to separate me from my friends? I did not realize, sir, you hated Estemba, and the Duca, so much."

"Verensa is rife with quarrels, and in the summer becomes a beast-pit. Be glad to get away from it."

"I am not glad. Do you command me to go?"

"I trust it will not come to that. That your duty will command you."

Romulan flung himself about the room, striking the bedposts, the wall, with the flats of his hands. The sunlight patterned him as he moved, a statue come to life.

"Why to Manta Sebastia? Why?"

"Because you have collected too many enemies here."

Romulan froze. With his back to Valentius, he said, "Your reference?"

"I had word of your party and the Chentis in argument at a banquet."

"My God, your spies are all about us, Father."

"You do not deny you and Leopardo Chenti were at daggers drawn."

"I do not deny it."

"Leopardo has a name for rash deeds. He is besides an excellent swordsman."

"He is besides a fool."

"And you are a fool, Romulan, if you suppose you can match him, blade for blade. It's no mark of cowardice to give way to a madman."

"Let him give way to me."

Valentius checked a surge of rage at Romulan's own raging lack of self-concern. Cold as iron, Valentius said,

"We have had our discussion, then. In five days' time everything will be ready for your departure. I'll trust you to make it. By winter, when you return, perhaps I may find I have a son, and not a spoilt and senseless baby."

Romulan turned. For the first time, Valentius saw, without a hint of camouflage, all the hatred Romulan felt for him, a wall of it, overtopping both of them.

"If any other man but you, sir, so tilted me, I'd kill him."

"Yes, you would doubtless try to kill him. And if you failed, he would kill you. I hope that you become aware of such possibilities, Romulan, before they are on your neck like dogs."

Valentius turned and walked out into the sunlight, which blinded him no more cruelly than the look on his son's face.

The old garden, rising above the town three or four streets distant from the Basilica of Sana Vera, flickering with the activity of grasshoppers, its terraces, already parched, palisaded by equally parched stone balustrades, urns, fragmentary marble figures, had once been the property of a House brought low in an earthquake and now generally forgotten. A curious arching facade, with nothing to stand behind it, marked the ancient building that had previously dominated the garden. That, a few random bricks, and a beautiful cistern with a fluted cupola and nymphs in green velvet robes of moss.

Romulan, leaning his arms on the rail, stared down into the stagnant water far below, seeing his own miniaturized countenance, hypnotized by it.

"And so he gazed forever, and pined away, and became a plant that eternally mirrored itself in the stream."

Romulan, whirling about at the first word, eyed with unease Mercurio who, silent as a shadow, had come up to within a few feet of him.

"I sought you at Estemba," Romulan said.

"What, sought me on earth, having sent me to Hell? I'm returned, as you see."

"Forgive my foul temper. I was drunk."

"Can it be you are apologizing?"

"On my knees."

"Then I may overlook the matter. Perhaps. Though you are not on your knees."

"My soul is on its knees. In five days my father means to exile me to Manta Sebastia."

"For insulting me?"

"No, fool. For living. For drawing breath. For saying 'I like you not' to Leopardo Chenti."

"Your father's wise. Manta is a pretty place. Palaces, churches—"

"To go be schooled at some college till winter."

"Winter?"

"Winter."

"Ah."

"I'm aged past schooling, Mercurio."

"No man is that, would you say?"

"What am I to do?"

"Go. What else."

"Damn my father."

"Oh, now it comes out."

"Damn him for treating me like a child."

"Well, child," Mercurio said, walking about the nymphs, fondling them with a gentle lewdness that was quite respectful, "for once I think your vinegar father has been clever. To get you out of the Mad Cat's range till he sheathes his claws."

Romulan seated himself on the curb of the cistern. He

stared across the garden and said, "There's another good reason to be gone."

"Which is?"

"Last night, after we—parted—"

"Last night after we parted?"

"I made a stupid promise to a girl. One she believed."

"Promised to do what? Bed her? Wed her?"

"Neither. Worse. I hardly know."

"Rosalena?"

"Rosalena is snow. I wish it had been Rosalena."

"A girl not snow but fire. Who could that be?"

Romulan, flushed, stood up again and turned away. Sternly he said, "What does Chenti's daughter mean to you?"

Mercurio, not to be evaded, put his hands on Romulan's shoulders and moved him round again.

"Now I *am* intrigued. You went wooing Rosalena and ended under Iuletta's window."

"In her bedchamber."

Mercurio, horridly aghast, fell back swooning and crossing himself, so Romulan burst out laughing.

"Well," Mercurio said, "I doubt you vilely dishonored the poor maiden. Being yourself of a noble disposition."

"I never saw a girl so beautiful."

"Nor I. And for looks could be your sister. Munch on that."

Romulan, confused by this aspect which unconsciously had so moved him and yet which, at the forefront of his awareness had not registered at all, shook his head wildly.

"I think I made some idiot's vow."

"But not of marriage, you say. You're safe."

"And you? You spoke of her for two streets' length."

"I am outnumbered. Unless we can find a priest to join her to the three of us, yourself, Belmorio, and I. Perhaps weird Laurus?"

"Oh, everything is the play to you. You love no one."

Mercurio looked sideways at him, slightly smiling.

"Do I not?"

"Save one. Yourself."

Mercurio awarded him the swordsman's salute.

"A hit, sir. However. Self-love saves me your predicament. Afraid of some vow you swore to a lady, and unable to think of anything but said vow, and sent away to Lombardhia, which is to say another planet. By winter, Iulet will be in Belmorio's Tower, clad in wet green like these nymphs round the

basin, and with the result of Troian's energies swelling beneath her girdle."

"I'd rather you would not speak of her in that way. You
make her sound like one of your jades."

"Not quite."

"Well, but I'd rather you did not."

"When you woke today," said Mercurio, "were you
happy?"

Romulan, surprised by this divination, stared.

"Yes—till my father turned his cannon on me."

"And then, recalling this mighty vow to Iuletta Chenti—"

"It's a fine afternoon for riding," Romulan broke in.

"So it is. Or for hunting, or hawking, or sleeping or gaming or drinking. Or something or other."

"Damn Manta Sebastia," said Romulan.

"Damn this, damn that. So much profligate damning. Hell
will be busy. How do you mean to see her again?"

"See who?"

"See who. I wonder who."

"God knows."

"Some difficulty over approaching Chenti's Tower. Chenti
Primo's pique, Leopardo's wrath—"

"You've not heard the half of that—nor will I tell it
now—How then do I see her again?"

"Disguised as a beggar, lie down at the threshold. Turn
into a bird. Fly in through her window. Ask her to put you in
a cage."

"Mercurio, I'll break your neck."

"So have said many now sadly deceased."

"Mercurio—"

"You require a go-between."

"You?"

"I decline. Someone you know who has favor at Chenti,
and can be coerced or persuaded or bought."

"No one—*I've only five days more in Verensa.*"

"Some servant perhaps. . . ."

Romulan struck the fluted canopy of the cistern with his
hand. Little stars of moss and stucco separated and went
down into the black water below. A metaphysical perspective
came to him, and he glared after them, seeing how an instant
of mortal anguish could dislodge what had stood peacefully
crumbling for decades. Thus must it be with men, subject to
the sudden rage of God—What was it the alchemist-priest
had said—"If you think so, then so it is for you."

And Iuletta had said, "Cornelia went to Laurus' cell . . . and got herbs from him."

And the Chenti-crimson woman, billowing on the donkey among the poppies above the oratory, had said, "I'm acquainted with one, your peer, as Eva to Adam."

"Wait," Romulan said. "There's a fat woman, looks like a bawd-mistress. Named Cornelia, I think—"

"Cornelia is Iulet's nurse. Or was when she needed nursing. I think I saw Cornelia, on a balcony once, a great-rigged quinquireme indeed. Oh, infinitely buyable, my dear. Your luck's in."

"Only if I can contrive to meet the woman."

"Where does she go about?"

"To Laurus' hermitage. Or I saw her there once."

Romulan turned toward the terrace's edge, striding, almost running. Mercurio leaned on the nymphs intimately.

"Are you going alone, or in company?"

Romulan turned again, impatient, obliquely guilty. Diffidently he said, "Alone. The priest partly expects me. Two of us might make him awkward."

"Go carefully then, my child."

Romulan nodded, started down the uneven steps.

"Child?"

With blatant impatience now, Romulan stopped a second time. The quarter-formed plan, amorphous and with only vague hopes of a logical progression, still buoyed him up, rushed him forward. Five days left no margin for anything. And then again, he did not even know whether he wished to have success—"What now?"

"This other thing you mentioned, with Leopardo Chenti. Yes, now."

"He and a pack of his gave chase to me. They were sixteen and it seemed incautious to pause for them. I escaped him in the Chenti orchard, and Iulet gave me sanctuary."

"He was so hot to argue with you."

"To cut me up piece-meal. Now, sir, may I leave you?"

"Fly, bird."

The bird obliged.

Mercurio strolled up and down the terrace of the cistern for some while. A singular but abstract emotion had possessed him. That it sprang from other emotions and impulses, of which he was quite sure, did not dispel its sense of mystery and foreboding. Mercurio was at times given to the darkest of dark reveries, cloaking them, masking them even from himself, with songs and tricks, or displays of mocking and mostly controlled lunacy. Now, walking up and down arm in arm with this new dark mood, he began to see what showed itself to him as a strange whirling center of events—Leopardo's shaming in the banquet-hall, Romulan's sudden obsession with Chenti's daughter, the incident at Susina's brothel, the ribaldry of the nurse, the recounted peculiarity of the priest. And from this whirlpool, filaments spread sticky as spider-flax, a web, a trap. In all this treacherous pattern, only by thinking of Iuletta Chenti did his thoughts come to rest, lightening as they did so.

Iuletta had surely enraptured him by her physical marvel. He was delighted by the girl, enthralled, as a man might be with a rare jewel or flower, or with one of those exquisite cats brought with the spice-caravans out of Persia. That Romulan fancied himself in love with such an artwork seemed only fitting. The notion amused and charmed Mercurio, for, with those he himself loved, he could be kind and generous, and—unusual talent—disinterested. There was no rivalry, no desire to sour the innocent infatuation. Though it would probably exhaust itself in the face of the Belmorio betrothal and the miles between here and Manta.

Descending the terraces of the garden, Mercurio Flavian Estemba beheld three of the Vespelli clan in their black and white wasp stripes, trotting horses around the lower paths.

Mercurio's clove-colored mare, tethered to a damson tree, stood in their way. The young page, Benevolo, (who had sung descant to Mercurio's song the night before), was standing beside her, acting groom, and now displaying haughty nervousness as the Vespellis drew level in a cluster. The Vespellis, seeing Estemba's colors on the boy and the mare's trappings, reined in. The Wasp House normally had a quarrel with everyone.

"Well, well, what a shoddy animal."

"What a shoddy little boy in charge of her."

"Tut. Do you not know who you're insulting? This adolescent is no servant. No indeed. This is a Montargo bastard, playing cuckoo in Old Estemba's nest."

Benevolo held his ground. He was no bastard, having been conceived in wedlock, fruit of a secret marriage—one of the collection that now and then took place between lovers whose Houses were actively engaged in feuding. Valentius Montargo's brother and the sister of Estemba Primo had created Benevolo between them in sanctified ardor. But the Mon-

targo, having thereafter slain Estemba Primo's (then) oldest
son in a duel, had been sent into exile in Lombardhia. A
month after, plague had lifted its never-quite-dormant, ugly
head in that province, and Valentius' brother died of it. Estemba Primo's sister, weakened by bad news, perished in
childbirth. The child, Benevolo, nephew to Valentius Montargo and Old Estemba both, the cousin of both Mercurio
and Romulan, (Estemba by adoption, Montargo by name),
had not knit the two Houses together, for presently another
cousin of Mercurio's had fatally stabbed another of the Montargos, perpetuating the breach indefinitely. Even the friendship of the heirs of the Ring-Arrow and the Ship had not
solved matters, though it was expected to do so on the two
fathers' deaths. Assuming, of course, both heirs had lived that
long.

Mercurio stepped onto the path as the youngest Vespelli,
black-haired to match his clothes, was sidling his horse over
against the tethered mare, and Benevolo, white as washed
linen, setting himself between.

The Vespellis, seeing who had now arrived, drew back, but
did not ride away. They watched as Mercurio, apparently
quite unaware of them, untied the horse and mounted her.

"Who is this?" they finally began to ask each other.

None laid hand to sword. In the upper walks of the town it
was not merely unlawful but also usually considered base
practice.

Mercurio turned the mare, and as he did so the boy at his
stirrup demanded of him clearly, "Cousin, do I accept then
that they call me bastard?"

Mercurio glanced down. Benevolo's face was a wound
growing cold.

"Cousin," Mercurio said back to him, as clearly, stressing
the family title so Benevolo should know the Vespellis heard
him reckoned, "these gentlemen must be excused. They do
not understand that to say a man's a bastard is to insult him,
for the Vespelli Tower is founded on bastardies."

With his shoulder to them, Mercurio listened while the
Vespellis grew still. With a fixed gaze of adoration, satisfaction and sheer worry, the boy studied the ground. A voice
spoke to Mercurio's spine.

"Sir. Will you be so gracious as to repeat what you said?"

Mercurio did not turn at all.

"Why repeat it when you heard?"

"You maligned the Vespelli Tower."

It was the youngest black-haired Vespelli again who spoke, and who again urged his horse to move forward, but another man caught his arm.

"Wait, Saffiro. That is Flavian Estemba. Let him alone."

"What do I care who he is? He who insults my House—"

"Be quiet, Saffiro."

It was sufficiently reminiscent of the Leopardo-Romulan-Mercurio confrontation that Mercurio smiled a little as he waited for the Vespellis to decide on retreat. That he kept his unguarded back to them all the while was perhaps the most potent insult of all. And soon enough there was yelled at this back:

"All Estembas are fools. Who marks the utterance of a fool?"

A flurry of hooves and rattle of accoutrements followed and they were gone. The dust powdered the sky.

"They feared you," Benevolo said with pride.

"They feared a breach of etiquette."

"They guessed if you drew, they'd die."

"Ah, reputation."

EIGHT

The afternoon, as on the previous occasion, was hot, the sky blue. The landscape was still contained by its distant horizon of hills. The town as ever withdrew up its slope, the Padova road, a river of dust, fell away and fumed about him. And the bleached grassland went down, tipped and stippled by flowers, among the parasols of the stone pines, toward the invisible oratory. Even the scents were unaltered. A bird, even, was catapulted into flight as he breasted the tall grasses, just as before.

And yet, all was changed in some subtle, faintly inauspicious way.

He did not ride now, but had come on foot. Could the lowered perspective be responsible? Or was it due to some vagary of the weather or the light impossible for the mortal eye to interpret?

Or was it that a great deal was no longer as it had been? The emotional perspective and weather unlike that of the first such excursion, unadmitted or misunderstood as it might be, still re-coloring everything.

Or was it the memory of fear, face to face with the insecure world, that had beset him before in Laurus' retreat?

The faded diptych of building stood totally silent as he came to it. The black old door stayed shut, and no phantasmal voice boomed out to demand his business and his name. Such things compounded the sense of difference.

In among the poppies the gilded sun-wheel, windless, did not move. So he put his hand on it and spun it round to catch its metallic sound.

He waited awhile, considering the place, wordlessly reiterating that he had no need for timidity. This hermit, despite his avowal, took money (how else the curios of the cell, the undoubted magical experiments?). Probably the rotund Cornelia had often come for eccentric preparations of various sorts, since amateur witches abounded and were never long unbusy.

Romulan went forward, struck the door with his fist, and raised his brows at it as it opened. Beyond, the dark curtain was already drawn back. The chapel lay bare and remote before him.

He went in, absently genuflected to the Christ on the wood cross, and looked toward that second curtained door which gave on the cell.

Five days, then exile. What could be accomplished anyway, in so short a time? Well, he could lie with her, if she would let him. At the thought, his whole body, even skin and bone, seemed to engorge. He felt a violent pleasure and a curious nameless quickening of the spirit, which he named at once as Urgency.

Before he knew what he did, he found himself at the second door, pushing the rough curtain aside, next pushing at the timbers—no longer an attempt to knock. This door opened just as the first had done. And once more he peered into that extraordinary space, the cell of the Fra-Magio.

This, too, was changed. What inevitably he noted at once was a totality of darkness; next that the totality was in one spot pierced by a muted ellipse of light. As he gazed at it, the voice of the priest—a most ordinary voice, neither harsh nor musical, yet for some reason entirely remembered—spoke to him from somewhere in the core of the chamber.

"Welcome, Romulan of House Montargo. If you wish, enter. That done, please close the door at your back. Move gently. Something is in progress."

Even at the words the pallid ellipse seemed to move, to rise, and to elongate, curving inward at its lower edges by infinitesimal degrees, also swelling fractionally in size and brightness, unless this were some deception of the eyes. Surprised and reluctant, yet attentive, Romulan did as instructed. He closed the door in particular with great care, as if to avoid the blowing out of a candle.

But the light in the room's center (all else, the priest included, was hidden) was certainly no candle. It did not flicker or tremble, and now, as Romulan leaned on the door, nonchalantly, crossing one ankle over the other, thumbs hooked in belt, an idler's pose he displayed but did not feel, now the bow of light most definitely was strengthening.

In color, it was the purest and most translucent white, but as it intensified, the white shade came to resemble silver. In size the shape looked to be the width of his own shoulders, but he could not be sure in the dark how far or near it was. Also it was now most surely rising, and growing greater as it rose. When it lifted to its completeness, he saw it was in fact a crescent, the two diminishing cusps pointing directly down, the broad curve of its back forming the apex. By this descriptive means, Romulan came to realize that some other object of an impenetrable blackness, partly intervened, and that the moonlike crescent had ascended behind it.

In another moment this conclusion was borne out, as a second light began to evolve, some distance below the silver one. The second light, of a milky rose, itself commenced by forming a crescent shape with up-pointing cusps, but swiftly revealed itself as a being both smaller and more fiercely lit than the ghost above. As more and more appeared of it around the lightless base of the intervening object, the second light demonstrated itself as a whole disc, and its color metamorphosed from rose to copper and so to incandescent gold, from which Romulan was inclined to shield his eyes, but which, in actuality, seemed not to effect them at all.

As the disc passed free of the intervening darkness spokes or rays were hurled upward from it. Most expended themselves and went out, but the longest fired itself across the center of the silver crescent, and a melding and a stasis followed. A bizarre cross now hung in the blackness before Romulan. A golden upright streaming from a golden disc, the horizontal of silver with two down-curving arms.

Until this instant, there had been no sound Romulan had heard beyond his own breathing. Now, however, a turgid popping noise, like that described as being about the hot mud attendant to a volcano, was abruptly audible.

At the juncture of ray and crescent there began to be a sullen glow. Initially red, it pulsed in a few seconds to a ruby brilliance. The light of it extended, filling the area, catching things as the glow of the earlier lights had not. Yet nothing was distinct, a crystal net hung all about, like ice dashed with drops of blood . . . Inside the ruby furnace, which now looked the size of a man's hand, Romulan discerned, or imagined, a most uncanny picture, made up of variations in the fire itself. Shadowy towers seemed to go up, and long vistas of streets, and a square, and skeletal staircases, while behind all else a sun of palest crimson burned in the Hellish sky—for yes, this was a vision of Lucifer's domain, Hell in little.

"Do not approach any nearer."

The priest's voice startled Romulan, that he had moved at all startled him further. With dismay, he perceived he had begun to walk toward the tiny Hell.

A second after the priest had spoken there came the ferocious crack and skinkling of breaking glass.

The icy glints, the glints like blood, went out. The unholy gold and silver cross faded like smoke and in the quarter of a minute was no more. The vision of Hell was similarly gone, though a reddish smoulder, dying and shrinking by degrees, remained awhile on the air.

A fresh light dazzled up. Romulan, stepping quickly back from it, beheld the silhouette of the priest now at the mundane task of lighting a stand of candles.

Romulan assumed a patronizing smile. He was in awe.

"I came at the right time, then, Father, to see some magic. It was very pretty."

"You were witness, Romulan Montargo, to a most strange phenomenon, which is called The Marriage of Apollo and Selena."

"Sun and Moon? Yes, excellent. What does it do?"

"It produces this."

Laurus emerged from silhouette, one burning taper in his grasp, while at his breast the rich cross gleamed. A white hand pointed.

On the worktable had been mounted a peculiar acrobatic pyramid of crucibles, alembics and similar distillery apparatus, much of which was of cloudy glass. The noise of breakage was now explained, for the center of this arrangement had given way, presumably due to extreme heat. Left behind amid the crystal smashings a clay dish on a tripod held a heap of cooling embers—the red Hell Romulan had conjured for himself. And on these embers, no longer than the nail of his smallest finger, nestled a phoenix egg.

"*Gold?*" he blurted before he could contain it.

"No," Laurus replied. His eyes, gazing from their faraway heights were, for a moment, almost compassionate. "The appearance of gold. Which appearance will soon vanish as the metal grows cold." The unweathered hands folded. The remarkable, remarkably ordinary features composed themselves. "Like most human passion, deprived of heat."

"So, you're no magus after all. I'd thought at least you could turn lead to orichalcum."

"It has been done. But not by myself. I am more interested in the attendant phenomena such experiments entail."

"But since you cannot make gold by sorcery," said Romulan, enjoying his own self-command, "perhaps you'd care to make it another way. By doing me one very small service."

To provide the man with a pause to brood, Romulan glanced round the cell. Given illumination, the tortoise-turtle of brass had come back, the bones and books and scrolls and astrolabes, the charts, the mystic ciphers. The hive of the athanorus stood like an odd headless animal on its little legs. The stuffed dragon had been moved and seemed to sulk in a corner. There were three hideous fishes he had not noticed before, with terrible pointed teeth. He had a desire to steal one, attach it to some fellow's line as he slept by a pond, tug the line, observe the reaction as such a beast was drawn forth—

Romulan became aware he had given the priest a great deal of space, and gotten no response. Looking away from the fanged fishes, Romulan observed Fra Laurus had gone to the table and commenced systematically to tidy it.

"Well, Father," said Romulan briskly, beginning to be doubtful, "what do you say?"

"I do not take money," said the priest. "As I have already explained to you."

"Oh, you wish it in barter, do you?" A hint of desperation now: "Very well. What would you require?"

The priest went on tidying, gathering the broken glass.

Romulan strode over to the jars of parchments. He was uncomfortable and angry. He lifted a jar at random, opened it, pulled free one of the brown leaves on its gilded rollers; held it toward the priest. Romulan disliked the idea of a threat, of dishonorably and unjustly saying to this wretched man: See, I can destroy this and this. And then, before he could open his mouth, a strange sensation in the hand holding the reed-paper caused him to look down. Romulan swore and almost dropped the scroll, for something took place on it. Beside a chill tingling in his palm and fingers, a line of symbol-writing was appearing on the papyrus chiefly composed of eyes, with, in the midst of these, the green figure of a man, kilted, collared, and with an Eastern diadem on his head.

The priest had turned about and come quickly to Romulan. Laurus plucked the papyrus away deftly and gently, and bore it without a word back to its jar. Inserted therein and

the stopper replaced, the figure and the hieroglyphs demateri-
alized.

"You should not," said Laurus, "meddle in this room without my advice."

Romulan flexed his hand, stubbornly refusing to question.

"A mild alchemical," said Laurus, "which answers human
tissue. Harmless. The pictures on the scroll appear from the
same cause. It is a portion of the Osiraeum, the Egeptsi Book
of the Dead. Faithfully copied and extremely old."

"So you're a necromancer as well?"

The priest had returned to his labors at the table, as if
nothing at all had occurred.

"Calling up of spirits. Traffic with demons of light. The
Duca," said Romulan, "might be disturbed by what I've
learned here today."

"These attempted threats, these attempted bribes, they are
all one and all nothing to me. Only your rashness attracts my
attention. Perhaps you should tell me what it is you wish of
me."

"Why? Would you do it?"

"If it seems to me in accordance with the balance of this
place and time, fitting to the character and essence of this
moment, then yes. Providing it does not contravene any basic
law. I am," said Laurus, "an instrument of God's design. It is
my practice to flow with such streams as I'm directed must
carry me."

"*I'll* direct you, then. The woman Cornelia, who serves the
Chentis."

"Who is this?"

"You deny her visits to you?" demanded Romulan haughtily.

"I merely ask a description."

Romulan described Cornelia at some length, and most un-
flatteringly.

"She came for herbs. You purveyed her witchcraft."

"No danger there. She will never make a witch. Her will is
vapid, she is too much of the body. I recollect her now."

"When will she come again?"

"I cannot say."

"Oh *say*," Romulan implored sarcastically. "I need her to
bear a message for me."

"Still I cannot say. A message to whom?"

"One in the Chenti House, where I'm not welcome."

"A girl perhaps."

"Perhaps, perhaps." Romulan struck an attitude, feeling at a loss. (Some part of him now declared: You have tried and failed. Who can hold to a vow under such circumstances? You are free of her. And at the thought he was glad, and sorry, relieved and desolate.) "What if," Romulan said, "you go visit the fat madama in the role of shriver. They'd not turn a priest from the door."

"I am not your messenger," said Fra Laurus, with neither reproach nor any hint of arrogance.

Romulan balefully regarded the stuffed dragon, not seeing it.

"If *you* will not go, and *she* does not come here, then *I* must get into Chenti again, by some means. And probably will be set on and cut to bits there. How will you like my death on your conscience, Father?"

Laurus looked at him. The beautiful young masculine face, so vivid in its theatre and its inner turmoil, its complexity of wanting and not wanting, might have evoked response in any other. But the priest, far beyond the world, concerned only with his balances of time and space and era, his alembics bubbling with human dreams and the guiding force of God, seemed impervious.

Then he moved about, crossing the chamber. He reached up and unshuttered a single narrow window, which till that instant Romulan had never been aware of, set as it was between charts and cartographies, and partially masked by a tall clepsydra fashioned as Noah's Ark.

Judging himself—final humiliation—ignored, Romulan turned for the door.

"Wait," said Laurus, as a blue slot of sky appeared between his hands like a spell.

"Wait, but for what?"

"For your messenger."

Romulan halted. He was now beyond himself, at his wits' end, unsure whether to curse, or giggle like a child. So he waited, and watched as the priest took a small set of Panpipes from a shelf, blew off the dust, and brought them to his lips.

No melody issued from the instrument, but a series of sweet notes, thin as pins. Romulan discerned no phraseology, or even repetition, yet he guessed the purpose. Sure enough, a portion of sky flew suddenly in at the window, and a blue-grey dove perched, with a flirting contrivance of its tail, on the Ark rooftop of the water-clock.

The priest set down the pipes and took up the bird, which sat tranquil in his palm.

"You shall have ink and paper. A brief message, to fit the size of its bearer."

Romulan, unwilling now, or skeptical—or both—said, "How will it find the way from here to the Chenti Tower?"

"A simple matter. Such birds are wise, when trained. I will remind her of the scent of those herbs I gave your Cornelia. I recall the woman's mention of a young maiden, her charge. Maiden and nurse will have made up a sachet, for this is what such herbs are culled for. Sister dove, here, returns to her nest at sunset, among the towers of Sana Verensa. She will search carefully this evening until she finds a place where the herbs are recently kept. She is tame, as you see, and will render her message to the proper hand, for these herbs leave also a faint residue for many days. Either girl or nurse will do, since they are in collusion."

"The plan sounds far-fetched and has holes like a sieve—"

Having seen the ink-horn, Romulan was already reaching for it.

The day, drawn up in a shower of gold, galloped away with, cast in its wake, a flaming sky. Every basking stone of the town was honey-colored, every upper vista limned with red-amber, and the plume-topped trees, that stood like oriental fans on the light, were black as ebony. Not a glass window that did not catch ablaze, not a fleck of gilding. And the air itself, shirred with birds, and harp-strung with the up-rising chimes of the campanile, was a great bath of transparent blushing clouds, swimming westward like dolphin.

Through this splendor on her articulate wings, flew the dove. Air and earth were the same to her. The sensational power of flight, after which thinking man craned and yearned —a thing of no moment or particular excitement. Her loveliness she had never enjoyed, or been told of; to the glory of the sunset she paid no heed. Nor did she know, poor innocent dove, happy ignorant dove, that she, as in some antique ritual, was to be the first sacrifice.

NINE

Leopardo, balancing in one hand the corpse of the dove (whose neck he had just broken), was uneasily surprised, as frequently, at his own viciousness. With Gulio and a couple of others, he had been aiming stones at a mark in the topiary garden. Chips and shards were hurled through the honey light, and when the target, a small bell fixed to one of the sculptured hedges, shook and sang, a crude cheer would go up. But half the satisfaction was in missing the bell, hitting instead the bush and spoiling thereby its shape.

Tonight, Lord Chenti was again from home. He had ridden south at sunrise to inspect an area of Chenti land located five miles from Padova, and would be away some two to three nights. There had also been, between bell-strikings, some discussion of this venture. It was well-known Chenti Primo kept two women at Padova, and a bet had even been laid as to which one he visited on this occasion. How to prove the bet was solved by the notion of watching the lordly gentleman on his return. In Leopardo's phrase: "If he is leaning over to the left, it is Bianca. If walking or anxious to dismount, then we know it is the other wench, of whom I've heard strange tales."

The absence of Chenti invariably produced in Leopardo a fierce physical exuberance, and a mental quickening. At such times he was aware of moving at great speed, an awareness which excited and now and then astonished him. The prospects for havoc were always increased. In some disregarded corner of his brain, Leopardo recognized that he would eventually outstrip all bounds and bring the roof crashing upon his head. He looked forward to this hour blindly, with an insane crowing delight that possibly was the disguise of doubt. In the interim, he had been shamed by Chenti at the betrothal dinner, and before all the guests. This shame Leopardo had harbored, not referring to it—nor did any other dare to—not even considering it, yet unforgetting. Someone

110

was in Leopardo's debt for that shame, and since Chenti was
inaccessible (save in elaborate, bloody dreams), the Montargo, Romulan, had become the debtor. Again Leopardo,
having expended such energy on the chase and failing to
catch his quarry, had sunk back into apparent indifference.
But Leopardo was seldom indifferent to anything that had
once touched him in any way. His goals, of whatever type,
were obsessive. He had, for two months in Padova, bowed
and beamed at a fellow student he had come to hate, until
one night, when they sat drinking together, Leopardo had begun the poisonous banter he had long been preparing which
finally persuaded the youth into drawing on him before
witnesses. Leopardo killed him and escaped the law, though
sent home to Verensa in disapproval. A peacock, a leopard, a
prince—he saw himself through a shining haze. Others could
only pierce that haze and reach him by processes of rage or
insult or rivalry or some deep and personal intrusion. He was
perverse and knew it and gloried in it. Others feared him for
his madnesses. Others fearfully admired him. Perhaps he himself was one of these.

A handful of silver stars had been thrown out on the sunset sky, and with them a dove. It circled above the crennela-
tions of the Chenti Tower, the gardens and the orchard,
eventually flying over the topiary, back and forth, as if questing, confused as a hound on an elusive scent.

Gulio saw the dove. He called it "love-bird." Leopardo
said, "Let us show Love we love him not. See who can bring
it down."

Stones flew. The dove, unhurt, sped frantically toward the
lower masonry of the Tower. The young men, howling, gave
ground pursuit. Where the stairway lifted to the balustraded
terrace, the dove seemed in two minds, beating back and
forth. As it alighted on the balustrade before the stained-glass
door of his cousin's apartment, Leopardo took aim and flung
his stone. Missing the dove, the stone might well have
cracked Iuletta's pretty glass (Oh! A thousand pities!) but the
shot was true, striking the delicately ringed neck, and snapping it. A limp blue carcass, the dove, no longer a thing of
air and grace, flopped clumsily off the balustrade on to the
terrace. Leopardo ran up the stair, lifted the prize and waved
it at his companions below.

Then, feeling the soft warmth of the dove dying like a coal
in his palm, and the rapid stiffening of its tiny anatomy, he
looked down at it and knew a sudden horror. Racing at such

speed ahead of himself, not thinking to, he had set out to kill something, and had killed it. It was a fact, he had slain men with more composure; he had planned their deaths and believed them essential. Now he remembered a foaming horse stumbling under him, and how he had dug his spurs into it screaming, wishing it to get back life like a second wind.

In revulsion, he was about to cast the dead dove over the balustrade, when he beheld the scrap of parchment tied to its leg.

"What is it, 'Pardo?" demanded the idiots below, as he turned his back to them and bowed his apricot head.

"Quiet!" he shouted. "I'm praying for my victim."

They laughed and fell still. Even Leopardo's jokes were normally obeyed. One ran to pull the bell off the hedge, and tolled it.

Leopardo, dove in one hand, paper in the other, read.

My Lady Kitten. The sun rose today but gave me no light. Come to pray at Sana Vera tomorrow morning at nine, and at nine the sun will rise a second time, and everyone will cry: A miracle! R.M.

Leopardo raised his head and stared at Iuletta's door of colored glass and, as it seemed to him, straight through it. So. *So.* Unbelievable as it was—that white fool had after all given sanctuary to Leopardo's enemy. For who else but the Old Cat's daughter would receive this touching whimsy of a title—Kitten? And who but the enemy would sign himself R.M.? (There were others who might have done, Roderigo Malaghela, Rufio de Mirrani. Leopardo chose to forget these appropriate names.) Such a messenger as the dove must somehow have been arranged between the two lovers. It had appeared at the last to know its destination. Now the curled head was thrown back. Leopardo guffawed lunatically. "What is it?" called the idiots in the garden and got no reply. Leopardo was so tickled by this fiendish bit of fortune, he did not know what to do with it. Any number of unorthodox reactions were presenting themselves to him, not least the glorious idea of himself keeping Iuletta's tryst with the Montargo at the Basilica. That would be an impediment to passion and no mistake.

Leopardo turned. Now immune to his self-disgust he tossed the corpse of the dove at Gulio, who, dodging it, fell down aggrieved on his vari-color hose.

"Scatter, flies," Leopardo said. "I'm tired of you."

"Oh, tired of *us*, 'Pardo?"

"Tired. Sick to vomiting. Go, you vermin, you two-legged plagues."

Grumbling, coaxing him, but as always relaxed to be leaving him, they went toward the water garden, thence doubtless into the house and out of it. (Gulio smoothed his rose, gold and vermilion legs as he went, hopping like a stork.)

Leopardo waited, then hammered violently on the glass window-door.

"Iuletta! Iuletta! Darling Cousin! Best girl!"

Someone had said the fool was a-bed, the women's weakness, or some such excuse for lounging. Well, let her get up and endure a slice of real trouble.

"Iulet-violet. Rose of roses. Kitty-kitty-kitty!"

A window was opened, but not the one whereat he knocked. Looking up and a short distance along the dexter jut of the Tower beyond the supported box where Iuletta was housed, he soon spied the narrow opening and the narrow figure poised in it.

"What is this noise?"

Leopardo composed his face to a sinister politeness.

"Dearest Aunt. What noise?"

"The noise you make. Were you at your cousin's door?"

"Just so. I had a gift I—"

"You are mannerless. To behave in such a way by a young girl's chamber. Do you think her one of your women from the Bhorga?"

"I have no women in the Bhorga," said Leopardo. He had begun to shiver slightly with tension. "I find I cannot—But I'm sure you comprehend me, donna."

She was gone. The shutter slammed.

Leopardo stood smiling, ready to race straight up the side of the building and to force the window—but it would be better to employ the stairs. The scintillating mood of Chenti's absence and Iulet's stupidity and all it entailed now refocused. As ever, Electra put other matters from his mind, or else all other matters were complementary to her. Even the dove, broken and bruised afresh by its fall onto the walk below, now had a use.

Dashing up inside the spine of the house, he knew himself to be an agent of the Devil. And knew she waited for that agency, that deviltry, to come to her.

That time in the stone garden, when Electra happened on

him in the tears of his rage, he had found himself confronted at length by a worthy adversary, one who was not afraid of him and who would play his game to the full, as he saw it. No one before or since had been capable of this. His hated uncle strove to crush him, and all others avoided, placated, ranted—or merely ran. But Electra, by her one caress, and by her everlastingly bitter tongue, her cold, cold icy blaze, would raise sword against sword on each occasion. Allies, too, against the old man—though neither would admit it, in their separate obscure ways they grasped as much. All this, more than any other thing, more than the lust by which he named it, magnetized him to her. In fact sex, at twenty-one, had already begun to bore Leopardo. He had forced his first girl at eleven years of age, and with her, as with all the numerous others he had had since then, it had been an unexploratory, snatching, selfish process, whereby he had denied himself, unknowing, the almost unendurable ecstasies dependent on physical involvement. Love songs were his mock mainly because sexual love, to him, was a myth. Inside him, cheated, the well-springs of his excellently made, beautifully coordinated, strong, young and sensitive body, lay in wait for him like demons, and perhaps had augmented those other demons which drove him.

He reached the lobby that gave on the apartments of his uncle, and stopped, for there she stood. It appeared she had been supervising the re-hanging of a tapestry, which now hung crookedly enough. Servants had been sent away. Yes, she had expected him, though of course she said, "What do you want?"

"Your good opinion," he said. "As ever."

"At the banquet, you spoke of strangling me. By saying such things and by acting as you do, you make me suppose you demented."

She turned to the tapestry and began to tug, with sadistic elegant little motions, at its lopsidedness.

He walked up to her and thrust the dead dove over her shoulder, almost in her face.

"Look what I found in the gardens."

She did not flinch. She merely moved away from him.

"You revolt me," she said. He knew she did not care what he did, so long as it provided the excuse to berate him.

"You would not dance with me. You have made me cruel."

"Go away," she said. "Go with your companions to the Bhorgabba. That is where you are happy."

"No. I've begged every madam in the district to find me a trull with a thin white body, little squeezed lemons of breasts, black hair, black graveyard eyes . . ." (He noticed dimly, becoming partly delirious, that her gown was of a greyish-pink—it must be her jibe to wear pastel.) ". . . but no luck. And until there's one like that, the itch remains unscratched. I burn, my donna. I fry and bake and scald. Oh!" cried Leopardo to the roof, "who'll put out these fires?"

"Even your soul is filthy!" she shouted. "As your filthy words. You'd defile me with them. I will not listen."

She had raised her voice. It was the first time she had ever done so with him. He sensed some barrier giving way and braced himself automatically, as if she might rush at him, attack him—braced himself with great willingness. But it seemed the barrier, smashed, revealed only another palisade behind itself. She stood panting, but she was quiet again. In that moment he had almost felt her flesh fastened on his.

"You will not listen. Yet you stay to listen," he said.

"I will stand no more of this from you."

"Ah, lady. I am the one who stands."

She caught the lewd meaning as if she herself had devised it for his lips to say. Her face seemed to retract, her pale mouth sewn together, but her eyes enlarging. Like his own, these eyes would seldom blink. She walked toward him now, neither fast nor slowly. It came to him that when she was sufficiently close he would take hold of her. But one of the narrow hands reached him first. She slapped him across the left cheek, and as his head swung at the impact, across the right cheek also, weird parody of Christian ethics. The blows were hard, steely enough they numbed his flesh, so for some minutes he did not feel the smart where one of her rings had cut his cheekbone.

He stepped back involuntarily, and her hand fell.

"Insult me again," she said, "and I will set others to lesson you who can do so better than I."

"No one," he said, "can lesson me better." His hands shook, his wrists and arms, his legs, but from strength, not weakness.

"We shall see."

"So we shall."

"Go," she said. "Get from my sight. Or I'll call your uncle's men."

"Such terror overcomes me." He skipped away, twirling
the dead bird. "I'll tell them you're a sorceress who has be-
witched me. I am so virtuous, who will trust your word
against mine?"

When he had danced from her sight, Electra Chenti raised
her own hand, which had struck him, and studied it.
Presently, she put it to her lips, laid her mouth against it,
held it to her.

Notes from a lacquered mandolin and a thread of voice
drifted like zephyrs about the room. The turquoise afterglow,
filtered by strawberry glass and milky glass, spread its panes
of pink-blue and blue-green and violet and lavender over the
floor.

> *Dance with me while time is yet slow,*
> *Clocks run faster far than you know;*
> *Wear your rose flesh like a glove*
> *For roses wither. Fear it, love.*

> *Sing no more your dragonfly song,*
> *All things are mortal, life is not long:*
> *There is an ending to all that's begun.*

> *So, my love, you shall not repent*
> *Sweet wine spilled, warm kisses spent.*
> *Night is close to end our day,*
> *There is no sin, love, but to delay—*

> *There is no sin, my love, but to delay.*

Iuletta played adequately if not brilliantly. Her voice was
neither strong nor peerless, yet had a fragile clear quality
which could charm. Linked to her beauty of appearance the
effect was fey and frankly marvelous. Tonight, however, the
clarity of her tone was lacking, for as she slowly sang, she
slowly wept. She had lain in her bed all day, weeping, and
her complexion was temporarily flawed, though neither lids
nor chiseled nose had swollen. The reddening of her eyes had
only made them, if at all possible, bluer.

Her condition of insoluble despair had finally sought relief in song. She felt, with the intensity only fifteen could
know. And it was a true and dreadful intensity, no less to be
credited because one found her wracked in the throes of it. It

seemed to her she could not live if she were not loved, if she might not exist in the scope of the loved one. Before she had spoken to him, before he had held her, embraced her, made such vows to her as he had made, before all that, there had been some measure of an option left to her. But no longer. She knew herself as a part of him. She knew herself, in separation, mortally severed and bleeding to death. A year ago last night he had promised not to forget her. Yet he had forgotten. If he had remembered, somehow, by any means— mundane or extraordinary—he would have got word to her. But no, no word, no sign. He had lit her like his candle. The cold airs of truth had blown her out.

She had eaten nothing all day. Her youth assured her she might starve herself to death, might simply lie still and quiet and perish, her consciousness, her life, dropping from her like petals. The pangs of her hunger she welcomed, like a kind, releasing poison. How long would it take her to die? Would he be sorry at all when he was told of it? (She pictured his stricken face. Then, the cynicism of insecurity besetting her, she watched him shrug.) Her tears flowed. She was an inexhaustible fount of them. Wherever did such gallons of water come from in this small and slender body? Surely her blood had become the salt sea. Perhaps, like the woman in the legend, she would dissolve in tears like a pearl in vinegar.

The inner door of her apartment was suddenly thrown open—Iuletta had no means of protecting her damaged heart by lock and key. Cornelia, raucously robed, a vast sad bladder, blew into the room.

The nurse too, in other than dress, was pale and drear, but her trouble had come from the wine-pots of the previous evening, a condition not quite exorcised. Her head throbbed, her stomach writhed, and under such punishment her Godless behavior among the servants had returned to torment her. Dear Heaven, what had she said? What had she *not* said? And, hoisted up the stairs, had she not laid an improper hand on Pieto's cousin, the fellow who saw to Lord Chenti's dogs, declaring nostalgia for such lacings? Cornelia gave a melancholy cackle, held her brow and upbraided herself.

In her wake came a girl with soup, wine and bread. Cornelia waved the provisions to a resting-place, ordered candles ignited, then sent the girl away, closing the door on her.

Cornelia sighed. Her world was not complex, or she would not permit it to be. Taking in Iulet the Waterfall, Cornelia's affection steered the obvious course, which was to bully. To weep and starve was not good for her charge. Therefore she must be forced to smile and feed. To such frustrations as these, Iuletta owed much of her basic spiritual strength, for her fifteen years had been spent in combating Cornelia, outwitting her, utilizing her, dominating her. Now, in true grief, Iuletta must fight to retain the solace of her misery.

"Come," Cornelia invited, bearing down on the mandolin player, soup and wine in her arms.

"I want nothing."

"Indeed you do."

"Oh, you are worse trouble than 'Pardo."

"Your cousin is a fine young man."

Cornelia approved of Leopardo. Unapprised of most of his deeds, going on rumor, she respected what she saw as reckless valor and thrilled to the dashing figure she supposed he cut. And one or two other things. It was only proper. What women wished to bed with a clerk? And he was a pretty hero, too. His insanity she mistook for a sort of genius, in which mistake she was partially correct.

"He beat on my door, shouting," said Iuletta.

"Well. Maybe that was concern."

"He is a beast."

Cornelia, not after all to be led aside, brought a silver ladle, brimming with soup, to Iuletta's lips.

"Sup and swallow."

"No." A turn of the head.

"Do as you're bid, you wayward child."

"You cannot make me."

Cornelia sighed again. She put down the soup which had become too heavy for her. In a rash and vulnerable moment, Iuletta had already confided the doings of the prior night, causing the nurse doleful agitation.

"I am a wicked woman. This is all my fault. Magics and meddlings. God will chastise me—you to bring in a *man*."

"Oh," said Iuletta. The candle glare offended her. She let the mandolin fall on the bed, rose, walked toward the glass window-door as if to pass straight through it. "Oh how can one so wondrous to look on be so false, so vile, so—"

"Praise Jesus it was only the door he got by. You slander him, you do. A young man alone in a girl's bedchamber, and to offer her no harm. A perfect saint he must be. Or a eunuch. Which I doubt, God pardon me."

"If I had not let him in, Leopardo would have killed him."

"Some misunderstanding. They drew on each other at the

feast, I heard." Cornelia's face blossomed into a little color at this heady thought, but the color faded as her resolve came back. "I've been lax with you, and you as naughty as you might for it. We are to go to the Basilica chapel. Now, this minute. I have your mother's permission. We will not be shriven—thank Christ she does not know why it is needed. I'll not have all this on my head, which head complains so. Perhaps the Lord will calm my belly. It's a chastisement. No doubt."

"I will not go," said Iuletta. There was almost panic in her tear-roughened voice, and her eyes were wide.

"God help me—what have you to confess that's so wicked? You did *not*—"

"No, no! Would I had. He might then have loved me."

"For sure he would not. Once fed, a lion sleeps."

"I will not go to the chapel," said Iuletta. She had recalled kneeling there, searching for Romulan, whose name then she did not know, among the angels on the wall. She could not bear to return, having met him, having failed, her dream in ashes. (She had wished him to be her slave—this had been her fear, to wish so. Now she would gladly be a slave to him, if she might only be near him, see him—)

Cornelia waxed belligerent. She was anxious to wash out her soul, but Iuletta's soul, too, weighed on her conscience. Unless Iuletta was also washed clean, Cornelia was sure God would give her no peace. (When she imagined Romulan Montargo allowed into this room at three in the morning, and the wild love-scene which followed, she had only praise for him and scolding for Iulet.)

Iuletta rested on the glass door. She was all at once too tired to weep, almost too tired to struggle. She allowed herself to slip down the colored crystal to her knees. The light of day beyond the door was all gone, the light of love gone with it, unmoved by sorrow.

Some part of her had crazily visualized that her pain, like her sorcery, might call him, but he was deaf to both.

Oh, let me die, let me die, her heart said. I do not want my life.

"For shame," said Cornelia, "to be downcast when you have another wooer just as handsome and as bold, courting you, betrothed to you. Best think of Belmorio, my minx."

But Iulet was alone on a benighted planet whose only inhabitants were Romulan and herself. And he had left her in the dark.

Registering her charge now lay prone on the ground, Cornelia swooped. Pulling Iuletta aside, in an attempt to revive her, Cornelia thrust open the glass door.

The light of the room now fell out on to the night as the light of evening had formerly fallen into the room, in a tangel of panes and patternings where the shadows of plants and the bodies of the two women dismembered it.

Caught in one such dismembering, a dead bird, also much broken, lay like an offering three paces from Iuletta's threshold.

Clad in vague grey, Romulan had been patrolling the town since an hour before sunset, searching half-heartedly for Mercurio Estemba, or for any acquaintance intimate enough that he might boast to them. The boast, which concerned dealings with a magus and lawless wooings of a girl, was in turn the outer show of inner misgiving. Having come on no one to whom he could unburden himself, his intensity of doubt had grown heavier.

At first, wending back to the Montargo Tower, he had been inclined to laugh at the antics of Fra Laurus. The notion of doves trained like hounds was patently absurd. The bird would fly about the pastures and the hills, or round the roofs of Verensa, on its own business, until the parchment scrap, ruined by weather, fell from it into some midden. And yet, if he reckoned the priest's plan of such small value, why had he written on the paper at all? And why signed the initials of name and House? Having entered Montargo, found garments suitable for the Bhorgabba, managing the while to avoid his father, he strolled out again into the streets. Here his mood changed to a mad certainty that the priest's dove would find the Chenti nurse, or Chenti's daughter. The message would be delivered and the girl would shriek with triumph—the thought did not appeal to him. Somehow, in his search for companions thereafter, his steps led him toward the very Basilica which he had stipulated for tomorrow's assignation. Some guess that Mercurio might be secreted in the antiquarium of the Basilica Library was, ostensibly, the reason for his coming in this direction. But, halting at the edge of the square in the thickening peacock-blueness of the dusk, Romulan eyed the terrain with a disfavor born of regret.

It was quite common for lovers to make trysts, using the capella of Sana Vera as the excuse. Girls went out to be shriven or to seek holy consolation, and young men arrived simultaneously at adjacent pillars. A discreet tip generally dissuaded brothers-of-the-cloth from intruding. Under those painted warnings of Hell, so many sinful pledges and mutterings had gone on it was a wonder the place had not long ago been consumed by a thunderbolt. Romulan himself, not a year before, had flirted with a girl, one of Suvio's daughters, in just such a spot. After three meetings they had grown bored, the girl sobbing on a reflex at losing so handsome a suitor—and soon comforted; Romulan attempting a poor song on the fruitlessness of love, composed early in the morning, blind drunk, in the Bhorga.

Yet this meeting, if truly the message had been received and was accepted, this meeting was not like that other, or like any other. Wrapped in his gray mantle, staring through the dusk, Romulan felt the jaws of the trap closing upon him. Even the great figure of the Basilica seemed ominous and louring, its star-shaped window, its angels of bronze faintly and gloomily shining, as if drowned in water. On the rim of the public fountain in the square, a grey cat was picking its way. It seemed to him he had seen the cat before, sleek, smoky creature, now in mimicry of his garments. The cat, too, was an omen.

Well, then. He would not keep faith tomorrow. He would ungallantly be absent. None would strike from the campanile, and he would be a-bed, or out riding, or anything and anywhere save here. If she came, she would be peeved. She would curse him, hate him, and flounce home to marry idiotic red-haired Troian, who wanted her. And in five—no, in *four* days now—Romulan would be in anathemous Manta Sebastia. Romulan swore, and the grey cat turned to gaze at him with eyes like two green flames. (Perhaps a cat had eaten the dove?)

The cat leapt free of the fountain and away as Romulan strode across the square.

When he reached the Basilica steps, rather than turn uphill toward the colonnades of the Library, Romulan fell prey to an abrupt and stupid fancy. The fancy was to enter the capella now, and to pray for forgiveness. For it seemed to him, in the gathering dark, that he did not really know himself, or what he wanted, or where he should go. Seemed too, that he had harmed that beautiful silly girl by playing the love-game with her, and that he must ask some other to protect her from such as himself.

At the top of the stair, irresolute even in this, he once

more paused. There he began to examine, unhappily, his religion, and perceived that he reckoned God was like his father, and that to pray to a vaster and more immutable Valentius would not do.

Some time had ebbed. The sky was black and starry. Behind the Basilica, the death trees of the graveyard murmured. With another oath, now blasphemous—his defiance to the masonry and garden of God—he was about to go down the steps again, when he beheld one more oddly familiar sight.

Downhill toward the square came a large and billowing woman, escorted by a page who illumined her with a pink lantern on a pole, and a man walking five or six paces behind, hand to sword hilt. As the lamp moved behind obstacles or through dense shadows, the group vanishing and reappearing, Romulan stood transfixed, half believing the party a mirage. But his heart began to thunder inside him.

In the mosaic of light and shade, dwarfed and enfolded by Cornelia and her clothing, they were almost to the foot of the steps before he realized Iuletta was a part of the group.

In a surge, like blood leaving his brain, Romulan felt every wit he had desert him. Mindless, he drew back and leaned on the carven facade of the Basilica, unable to do anything else, save to exist. Dressed as he was, the big doors closed and emitting no gleam, and carved animals and men all about him, it did not occur to him he had become virtually invisible and might be overlooked. That he made no move toward the arrivals or away from them was simply because at the moment his reasoning had entirely failed.

Like one paralyzed or turned to stone, he gazed as they came up the stair, Cornelia grunting and puffing, the page scowling, lamp swinging, the guard matter-of-fact. The girl's head, with a flimsy veil thrown over it, was bowed, her face unseeable. All wore the Chenti crimson.

Reaching the top of the stair, everyone hesitated for Cornelia, grampus-like, to catch her breath.

Romulan, directly facing them over three yards' distance, waited to be found.

"Ah," said Cornelia. "Ah. Oh."

Iuletta's head remained bowed. The pink light started sequins on her veil, and he remembered the rain spangling her hair. She looked so very small, so slight, as if born of another race than that from which Cornelia had lumbered forth.

"Why," said Cornelia, "must the House of God be placed on top of a mountain? Oh, my head. Come on."

The party began to move again. They advanced, and the lamp-glow passed over Romulan's face, but none looked or saw him, not even the supercilious houseguard. They went directly by him and around the side of the building.

Romulan stood dumbfounded. Was escape, after all, to be so easy? And this girl, this damsel who had called him "love," who had seen him somewhere or other and determined to witch him to her, was she now so oblivious of him that she would sail straight by, proud little toy ship with a spangled flag?

Foolishly incensed, still unreasoning, curious, intrigued, bemused, Romulan turned after them.

In the plaster colonnade, a pink-lit flutter of mantles, and suddenly the Chenti guard was in his way, drawn sword foremost.

"Well, sir," said the guard, "and who are you?"

"I did not think you saw me," said Romulan, ridiculously.

"No, I saw that, too. Skulkers must answer. Do you mean these ladies insult?"

"I—no."

"Your House?"

Romulan came back to himself in the same surge as that wherein he had lost himself, and lost patience instead.

"Montargo, damn your bones." He pushed the weapon upwards and away. "Refrain from waving that at me, unless you want my own blade through your neck."

The guard lowered the sword, but did not sheathe it.

"You are a gentleman, sir, and if a Montargo, you have no quarrel with us."

"Nor do I. Yet."

Romulan looked past the man, waiting for one of the group to own him. Looked straight into the face of Iuletta.

That face, which he had recollected as the epitome of tenderness and innocence, was like a blow.

It was not her beauty, this time, which stunned him, though she was more beautiful even than he remembered. Her eyes were level and terrible, made of blue steel. One might have seen Electra in her at that instant, but all the young man saw was the astonishing stamina that underlay her delicacy. This look was not superficial, it came from the depths of her. Had she been a man, Romulan would already have reached for sword or dagger.

Was it that the message had come to her, and she, regretting her words to him as much as he had regretted his to herself, was now furious at his insolence? (Had he regretted those words? Had *she?* In what manner had he been waiting, then, that in retrospect she had not liked him?)

Forgetting the guard, Romulan walked by him. When the hand came on his arm he thrust it off angrily, and then Iuletta spoke.

"Let him by."

The guard complied. Cornelia made clucking noises, but grew silent, alert to listen. Romulan, stopping a few feet from the two women, bowed with stiff formality to the nurse, knowing she would enjoy it, be impressed, give him room. To Iulet he did not bow, but with her own coldness said to her:

"What have I done to earn such a glare, lady?"

"You have done nothing. And so you have earned it."

His own anger bothered him. How could she anger him, this slim dark reed that he could snap in his hands?

"Then, what have I omitted to do?"

"Oh," she said. Suddenly her eyes faltered, she gave ground. The shine of the swinging lamp—the page was also agog—touched her cheeks, and Romulan saw the faint impression of roughness on her skin, the bruising of the lower lids, things which marred her, made her human, showed she had been crying a very long while. With remorse?

"If I offend you," he said, "I'll take my leave."

"You have offended me," she said, and her voice broke, "because I thought that you would send some word to me, and having no word—"

"I sent you word," he said. Before he meant to he stepped close to her and took her hands—long-fingered, slender, cold, ringed with cold jewels—"I *sent* you word."

"I did not receive word. I think you lie."

She would not look at him now, her warrior's stare having failed her. All those tears had been for him, then. From wanting him.

"No lie." He glanced at Cornelia, embarrassed by the audience, and said, in apparent rage, "You did not, then, madame, pass her my message? I'd have repaid you for the service, you might have trusted me for that."

"I?" Drawn in, Cornelia—was it conceivable?—*swelled.* "I got no message, you saucy boy. And for shame, to send messages to a high-born girl—" He could see she loved the notion. (The page was grinning, damnable brat.)

"Donna Cornelia," Romulan said. He dropped one of Iulet's hands and grabbed up one of Cornelia's. "Let me take her into the chapel. Privacy, for the love of God. I mean nothing dishonorable."

Cornelia smirked.

Was he supposed to bribe her, in full sight of her servant and the guard? She seemed to catch his mental drift, and half shook her head at him. The bribe must be awarded later, then.

"I will follow you," she said. Seeing his displeasure, she protested, "You must allow me that, sir. She's in my charge."

Which must be for the watchers. Inside then, the bribery. Or did she insist on being their witness?

He looked at the guard sternly, and thankfully found Cornelia doing the same. The man, expressionless, turned his back, looking away along the colonnade.

Romulan placed his arm about Iuletta. An indistinct but wonderful perfume rose from her hair or skin, like no aroma he had ever scented. Would she now refuse?

But she said nothing, and let him draw her toward the dexter door of the chapel, the nurse trundling in their wake.

A moment or so to tip the porter-priest, and they passed through.

Inside the chapel entrance, Romulan rounded on Cornelia and put a gold coin in her hand. Cornelia jumped in her fat. Her fingers curled fast about the gold.

"No, sir. Truly."

"Truly, yes."

"You are a noble gentleman," she said. "I can trust you with my girl. You were with her before and never did her wrong. You celibate, you," she added, winking.

His renewed embarrassment was all at once offset by seeing the kindness that underpinned her greedy smile. Startled, he could only turn and seize Iuletta's arm— unchivalrous gesture to which she responded by pulling away—so he seized her hand again instead and dragged her along the chapel, as far as the altar. Here the ranks of pillars hid Cornelia.

Romulan and Iuletta, hands falling apart, regarded each other.

"Well," he said, "you think me a rogue, an imbecile and a liar, to say one thing and do another."

"I think you a man, therefore faithless and cruel."

It was flattery of a subtle clever sort. She did not even know she flattered, nor he that he was flattered.

Romulan walked to the altar and laid his palm on it.

"I swear by this, I sent you word to meet me here——" a second inspiration, he lifted his hand——"this evening. When you came, I concluded you'd come in answer to that request."

Haughtily she said, "Had I had such a message I would certainly not have come."

All about, angels, devils, the blessed and the damned looked on. An audience persisted. Romulan walked from the altar to the girl. He took her head between his hands. The veil sank, the ocean of her hair filled his fingers. He leaned to her mouth and kissed her, before God and Hell, and felt her yield to him, give way to him, melt into his body. He drew back at length, and said breathlessly to her closed lids, "*Now* say you would not."

Her eyes opened, swimming as if after a faint.

"Is it true——you sent——"

"How not?"

"*How?*"

"By my lady Venus, how else. A dove."

He sought her mouth again, but she stayed him, her fingers, now warm, pressed to his lips.

"What?" he said.

"A dove was lying by my window, its neck broken——poor messenger——"

"And a paper tied to its leg."

"No."

The implication was too obvious to voice. After a moment, recalling as if from a century ago the riot of knocking on the glass door, Iuletta said,

"*Leopardo.*"

Romulan paled. It was not fear, but sheer horror that Leopardo had read his florid phrases.

Iuletta misinterpreting, herself afraid, tried to push him from her.

"Go swiftly. He is not yet here——something has delayed him——"

"Oh no," Romulan said, "it's tomorrow morning that the cat will be in wait at the mouse-hole. Perhaps the mouse will surprise him."

"Tomorrow——but——"

"I confess one lie. Our assignation was for tomorrow, but on finding you here——"

"Oh, my beloved and my only love," she said. She laid her head on his breast. "Leopardo is a madman. If he has set his heart on harming you, he'll strive and strive—Go from Verensa. Run. Fly."

"Run, fly? Do you love cowardice, Iuletta?"

"I would love the living not the dead."

"Then you wish me gone to see me no more."

She lifted her head again at the laughter in his voice.

"Do not mock me. To save you death, I'd die."

The capella was cold, and abruptly the cold grew absolute.

"Do not," he said. He could say nothing else. He gazed at her and knew, as before, that what she said was truth, and now at last the shadow of death's wings spread over him as over all men. He beheld death, a new tinting, which had mingled with the color of everything about him, and only she, this woman—this child—stood bravely between him and the abyss. And in some strange and unreasonable manner he trusted her to save him.

It was only a moment. Then gone. But like all wounds, it left its scar behind it.

Now and utterly, the facts reared before him, the everyday facts, every impediment, desired or otherwise. Now, in the wake of that other thing, mightier than all. And, "Iuletta," he said, "in four days I must go to Lombardhia. Until the winter. My father's command."

"Lombardhia," she said, her voice far away at least as Lombardhia. "Till winter?" Her hands slipped from him. Her eyes on his, she said, "I shall be married when you return."

"Long married," he said. "A beautiful, celebrated wife, the glory of the Belmorio Tower."

"And you will be safe," she said. "Even Leopardo could not hold one spite so long. He will have some other quarrel by then. Yes, go. I'm glad you will go."

"If they had not betrothed you," Romulan said.

"I care nothing for Troian," she said, softly now, with ludicrous, admirable dignity. "I was born to love you."

"How can I leave you when you say these things?"

"Then I'll tell you I abhor you, hate you."

Romulan remembered how he had visualized her seduction. But death had brushed him, the knowledge of death. He could not use her or profane her, this mirror image of his life.

"If there were some way," he said.

"There is no way. Go now."

A dreadful thing had happened also to Iuletta. She had seen herself just as he had seen her, his only hope of safety. There was no logic in the sight, nor her sudden total awareness of her cousin's enmity, she only knew she must display no sign which could detain Romulan. An hour ago she would have wept, swooned, torn at herself, gone mad—anything to keep him with her. But not now. At fifteen she had assumed all the frightful responsibility of love; at fifteen she had grown old.

There were twelve inches of space between them, and the gap was wider than infinity. They no longer tried to touch each other, for it would have been hopeless, across infinity, to touch.

He turned and left her without any further ornament, but with her image carried before him all the way into the night.

Outside, he looked about and saw enormous stars, and the tall forest of towers above the square, starred with their windows. He could not recall the passage through the chapel, the colonnade, down the steps. If he had gone by the porter-priest, or Cornelia, he did not know. The lamp-boy and the guard he might have walked through.

He went at a heavy pace, like one drugged, to the public fountain where he had noted the grey cat.

He leaned there a long time, and eventually he saw the pink light bob down the Basilica stair and the incoherent group surrounding it like moths. But he could not see her, not to be sure, only glimpses—a sequin's flash like a firefly, the hint of her body moving like a ghost.

When he saw her again she would be Troian Belmorio's wife.

"My felicitations," he said to himself aloud, and in Mercurio's tones. "You have got away."

There was an ache in him somewhere he could not trace or name.

The square was empty, though maybe not for long. He should seek friendly company, or go home.

The moon was rising, rosy yellow as a peach, and not far off a dulcimer began to mourn some poet's imaginings. Romulan's sight and hearing attended these familiar things with a bizarre sense of novelty. The smell of vines from some garden, conifers and lilies from another. The silken plash of the fountain. . . . Like symptoms of some wondrous illness, the figments of the earth overpowered him.

Having sent him away to live, she would cry for him all night. And how many nights hereafter? Troian could never comfort her. Only he, Romulan, lying at her side or in her arms, could do that. Only he.

TEN

The tall trees which sometimes brushed the half-closed window had their own intrinsic sound. This was unlike the sharp and irritating rattle which had now happened thrice. Such a noise, however, belonged some three or four years in the past. They had been boys then and Romulan, arriving unlawfully in the Estemba grounds at dawn, would hurl stones with dread accuracy at Mercurio's shutters, producing hideous rattlings on the slats, rousing the sleeper to cursing, elegantly nauseated wakefulness.

The Estemba Tower, one of the most ancient of the town, older even than Rocca and Chitadella, was in portions ruined. It had always been untaxing to get in at the broken wall when once Mercurio had shown the way. The Montargo-Estemba feud had been cooling in those days, but still warm enough to make such traffic hazardous, therefore doubly acceptable.

But now. Why now? For sure the Estemba porter, elderly Marchello, would be snoring, but a lusty thump or two on the doors would have raised him—and few others, Estemba being now as it was. Mercurio, who had been miles from sleep, discerned in this choice of approach some search for reassuring adolescence. Alerted, he crossed to the shutter, pushed it, and snatched back his hand as another stone shot by, actually clinking on the metal of a ring.

"Oh, God," called Mercurio, voice exactly pitched to carry without loudness, "my nose is broken by a careless pebble. Blinded in one eye, my looks wrecked. What decent girl will wed me now?" And was rewarded by wild muffled laughter from the walk twenty feet below. "Dear Heaven," said Mercurio, leaning out, "a lunatic is in the garden."

"A lunatic is also in the house," Romulan called back at the same quiet carrying pitch. "Shall we compare delusions?"

"It is, by my reckoning, past midnight."

"Sorcery! My misfortuned friend has been witched into a clock. Do I come up, or rent here all night?"

"It's late."

"Late enough to be early. And when did you concern yourself with the lateness of an hour?"

"I see I'll get no peace. Come up then."

"How?"

"In the old way, I imagine, employing the creeper. If it will bear you, great strapping giant that you've become."

"We'll see."

Romulan took a flying leap at the black lion's mane of plant which mantled the ancient wall, and began to draw himself up it, with much tearing of foliage and tearing of the air with curses. Mercurio leaned in the embrasure, occasionally making an unfavorable comment on method. When Romulan had drawn near enough, Mercurio deigned to offer him a hand. Romulan negotiated the window and swung into the room.

Mercurio's apartment, located in the northern quarter of the Estemba Tower, was masculine yet beautiful. White-walled and patternless, it was hung in many places with antique swords of bronze and iron, historic prizes most Houses retained for their banquet-halls. There were also two down-hanging Persian carpets, and a strange commissioned painting of the Adoration of the Magi which, among other marvels, depicted a pure blue oliphant with gold-tipped tusks and wing-like ears, and a serpent for a nose. There was something of the Grechian fashion to the room, the bed of which was broad yet low and lean, finely yet sparsely draped, the corners of which held no clutter of any sort. A wooden panel in the tall chest showed the god Mars, youthfully and nakedly asleep amid a shoal of armor. Two books, old as the Tower, rested together on the chest. On a table stood a beaker of wine and a cup. The mandolin, that element of Flavian Estemba's soul, sat on the bed like a peg dog of unorthodox shape, awaiting her master.

Romulan observed the room with detached interest. Here, they had talked, argued, drunk, sung, discussed Plato, Virgil and Petronius, and remade the world, on several nights, in seven minutes. Romulan had not visited in it for more than a year, yet it was barely altered from the era of their boyhood. It came to him to wonder, though only for a second, why mercurial Mercurio kept about him such a symbol of order and changelessness.

"Wine?" Mercurio inquired.

"Thanks, no. Yes. No. I need no wine."

"Something has confused you. Can it be you've met with Iulet?"

"The weird hermit sent her my message. Which message the cat-cousin intercepted."

"Leopardo?"

"Who but. He means to keep tryst with me, I suppose, at nine tomorrow by the Basilica."

"How disappointing for him you'll be absent."

"I may not be absent."

"Be absent. Oh, be absent."

"Well, but I'm not here to discuss that orange gentleman."

Mercurio laughed, liking the title, poured wine and passed the cup to Romulan. Despite his protestations, Romulan drank thirstily.

"Then why, child, are you here?"

Romulan set down the empty cup and walked away from Mercurio to inspect the oliphant picture minutely.

"As it turned out, I met her by chance, at Sana Vera. I told her," he said, "I was to go to Manta."

"And she bawled and begged you to remain."

"She allowed I should go."

"So soon bored? Ah, Woman. So young, so fickle—"

"To save me from Leopardo, who she dreads almost as much as you do."

Mercurio poured wine for himself.

"Creditable Iuletta."

"Mercurio," Romulan said, "I told her I'd make no claim on her and I left her in the chapel. But Mercurio—she's with me still."

Mercurio drank. His face, which Romulan deliberately could not see, was enigmatic and unreadable. At such moments, Mercurio was at his most transparent, for enigma was his mask, as was frivolity. One might look closely and perceive trouble somewhere in the eyes, and some conceit of age. He was twenty-two, his spirit far older. And this spirit, with a sure psychic awareness, had now tensed within him. Aloud, he said nothing. When Romulan, emerging from his self-consciousness in the heat of self-revelation, should be ready to turn and face him, Mercurio was ready to meet him with the open wicked regard collusion might desire.

"I find I want her," Romulan told the oliphant sternly. "I

mean to have her. It cannot be helped." He turned then, and Mercurio's face sent away its inner self. Mercurio smiled.

"I take it, by wanting and having, you intend to assay such deeds without disgracing her."

"She's not to be harmed through me. Through anyone."

"Well. There's this little business with Troian."

"She cares nothing for Troian."

"She told you so."

"In words. In how she looked at me. The touch of her——" Romulan glanced away again, again confounded by his own body and its emotions.

"You could do this: Be gone, come back when she's wed. Wait till she's truly sick of Troian, then woo her again. If you're circumspect there need be——"

"*No!*"

"No?"

"No, by God and Lucifer and all the fiends of the Pit. No."

"She must not have him then."

"Only me."

"Only you. Then you have no other course than to marry her yourself."

"That I knew."

"But do you know your own mind on this?" Mercurio said. "Yes, she's gloriously fair, she puts out the eyes. Yes, your blood drums and your head roars and Adam's Rod grows large as a tree and draws you after it like a goat on a tether. Yes, yes. Marriages are made on less than all this. But will *you* marry on it? God joins and death sunders. Once in the water you must swim till you go down."

Flushed and angry and hardly pausing to take note of either state, Romulan said:

"I'll wed her. There's no other prospect, except she weds Troian and dies of grief."

"Oh, she'll not die of grief, even for you, dear angel."

"Or I'll go mad," Romulan said, distressed by his vehemence, not believing it, unable to avoid the words. "Truly, I think of her with him and I could take a sword and kill him, and myself after. I must have her. Lawfully and before God. Mercurio, I *must*."

"Then, my dear, you must."

"You'll help me."

"You won't manage such an intrigue alone." Mercurio, appearing now brilliant and demoniacal, took a turn about his room, raising his hand and patting Romulan on the head, lightly, as he went by. "Point one, the ruined Belmorio match. Belmorio can be paid, and will need to be, to prevent a feud. Will your stony father take on that?"

"By Christ, I do not know—"

"He may. He may be charmed his idiot son is bound to a girl of noble family, become responsible and lead-heavy like himself. I think, at his most sullen, your father has thought you whore's meat only and due to be ruined as such. Well, but if he will not pay the dark green family, I might. Belmorio and your damned father settled, point two (or three) is Chenti. Chenti Primo will gripe and growl. Montargo's equal to Belmorio in trade and ships—your connections in the Levant are worth the girl's dowry alone. But you've no blood-tie with the Rocca Tower. Old Chenti will bellyache over that, you may be sure. Still, you and I are comrades, and Estemba has its own links with the Duke. Maybe we can mist the red fool's eyes a little. Now, child. Do not grow agitated. These things must be considered. Or do you want to straddle your girl atop a hill of corpses?"

"No, but for the sake of God—"

"Point three (or four) being the marriage. In time-honored tradition, it must be a secret one. Do you agree? Wed first and, the damage done, declare yourselves to both your families. You'll need witnesses."

"Can you provide—"

"I can. I think."

"Mercurio—"

"I can. I can. Now, not merely a secret match, but a swift one."

"Tomorrow?"

"By stars and whirling comets. He is in earnest."

"Never more so." Romulan caught him by the shoulder and held him still.

"You look like death," Mercurio said. "Trust me. If you wish it, we'll get it done. Someone must take word to the maid. And you're disqualified from the work. Old Chenti is from home with some doxy, a useful departure. I'll play my name then, act messenger, while sweet Leopardo is out at the Basilica mousehole. There's a winning notion. And she'll say 'yes' to all this, will she, your Iuletta?"

Romulan's face tightened on its bones, as suddenly as he saw the gulf before her feet, knowing she would throw herself into it for him. He said, very low, "I have no right to ask it of her."

But, "Every right," Mercurio said gently, placing one arm around his shoulders. "All rights. Love's rights. But, good lover, stay away yourself from the Basilica and the orange cat-gentleman. You must live, to love."

The moon withered like a pale yellow flower and the last windows of the Higher Town faded in darkness. A great white owl circled the campanile like a ghost in love with the voice of the bell. In the Bhorga, blood-red lights sank into dead scarlet; sad cries of pleasure or despair fell from slits of windows. Music turned from ribaldry and dance to songs of dead lovers, and the night turned toward the morning to be comforted.

Beyond the town, the hills waited for the sun to climb them, striking their tops with solar winds and rays.

The stars dried to opacity, like tears.

The sky opened, one enormous window.

The towers began to harden on the dawn, their crenelations, slopes, angles, balconies, overhangs, ornaments, emblems, banners. Those terrible towers, the quills of a porcupine, the spines of a dragon—

Birds flew out of the sun into the town, and off the roofs of Verensa into the sun, passing each other with contemptuous cries: *This* way is the better way. Until the heat of the morning quelled them. And in the Chenti orchard Cornelia's page, Pieto, had tossed one dead bird, a dove, under a peach tree to manure the soil.

At a fraction after nine, Cornelia, pummeling through the orchard, trod on the corpse and crossed herself.

She had not slept, not a wink. She was worn by the memory that, had she not scandalously taken Iuletta with her to daughter Susina's house, Iuletta would not have had thrust before her the heartless youth who now caused so much upheaval. It was true, Cornelia had been unable to pry from her nurseling—at the Basilica unweeping and abruptly adamant in her privacy—what had passed between the two in the capella. But Cornelia herself had beheld the young man leaving with a hard marble face (like Iuletta's own). No joy had come of the interview, so much was evident. Cornelia took this slight on her charge personally. Was not Iuletta a gem, a rose, a Venus? (And had she perhaps supped some of this radiance from the nourishing nipple of Cornelia, who at

Iulet's age had been well-manned three years and more and pretty as could be? Cold Electra had no looks at all, thin stick that she was.) How dared the fellow make light of all this loveliness of Iulet's? Poor girl. Yes, indeed, Cornelia knew what it was to suffer from the faithlessness of the bold and carefree male. How did the song go? You might break a maid's chink but once, her heart a thousand times. Tut, for shame to think of that, and the poor baby crying hour by hour all night, those tears she would no longer shed before the nurse. And opening the bed-chamber door, what an icy little tune had issued from the bed: "Go out, nurse. I am well." Like Electra herself, who had never dropped a tear that Cornelia could recall, and as few loving words. But: "How can I think you well, when you lie crying like a hare in a trap all night?" had protested Cornelia. "You can think me well since I tell you that I am." "And am I to suppose day is night if I'm told so?" Victory? No. Back came the little tune, remorseful now, but still unbreached: "Kind nurse, be kind and leave me. I'll be better tomorrow."

Cornelia, the expected tantrum, the wails, the torrent, withheld from her, had gone away perplexed. Like many who tend and worship a child, thriving on the beneficent power this function gifts them, she saw the onset of the adult with misgiving. Partly for this reason the recurring corpse of the dove, sigil of destroyed innocence, unnerved her. It reminded her too, that in the excitement, she herself had never prayed; nor, she suspected, had Iuletta.

"Donna Cornelia," a boy's voice yelped.

Life-giving annoyance. Cornelia recognized the vocality of her page. A moment more and the cherubic pest had sprung out on her from a stand of mulberries.

"Donna!"

"Do not bark at me, you hound. What's to do?"

"In the house is a gentleman who asks for you."

"Is it that spice-merchant again?"

"Not at all." Pieto was disposed to tantalize.

Cornelia, generally indisposed, boxed his ears.

"Did I not instruct you to bury that dove?"

"Indeed—I gave it Christian burial," muttered Pieto, sourly. "A cat must have dug it up."

"Such lies. You nasty fragment. What a monster you'll be when you're a man, Lord bless us."

"It's a prince of Estemba Tower," said Pieto hastily, now earnest to distract. Cornelia was distracted.

"Who Estemba?" she demanded, as if she knew them all.

"The one they call Mercurio. He that sang at the banquet and danced with Lady Iuletta and whose friend drew dagger on Leopardo and—"

"What a gossip! As if you'd seen it with your own eyes, and you in the kitchen making yourself sick on comfits the whole while." Mightily curious, Cornelia was already swirling toward the house. Pieto, long-practiced, skidaddled from her path. (I on comfits, you on *wine,* massive madama.) Pieto, boxed ears and all, was not out of sorts. The glamorous Mercurio had bribed him with coins in the lobby to do this service of Cornelia-getting. Though what any man could want with this vast puffing pudding—

The visitor had been let into a tiny antechamber off the entrance lobby, whose only virtue was the white glass of its windows. This he was apparently admiring.

Cornelia, bustling in, looked at the fellow's back shrewdly. Yes, she recalled this one, from the brief perambulation of the betrothal banquet she had been allowed to make. And, more to the point, this was the devil-masked devil who had first carried Romulan Montargo into her young lady's sight. Cornelia recognized the body in its fashionable closeness of garments, and certainly it would be a pity, with so many young men of such excellent shape, if the fashion should be altered. . . . Cheered by his style, she almost forgave him. Then he turned, swept her a bow as if she were an empress, strode over, calmly took her hand and kissed it.

"Most beautiful Donna Cornelia," said Mercurio, in a voice like a caress, "I come to you in jeopardy, anxiety and great puzzlement. Only you can help me. Will you take pity?"

"Go on with you, you wretch," said Cornelia. "Give me back my hand."

"Not till you answer with a charitable 'yes' or a killing 'no'."

"I'll promise nothing till I know what you want."

"Beautiful lady—"

"Who is beautiful? Is your sight to blame, or your lying tongue?"

"Why," said Mercurio seriously, looking at her with great attention, "I would call you beautiful. Lustrous eyes, a skin like a pale pink rose, a fine full figure to delight any man who likes to travel in comfort—"

"Oh! You villain, you!" shrieked Cornelia and burst into

ear-splitting merriment, radiating joy in this game to the ex-
tremes of her person.

Mercurio, laughing at her laughter, waited till she had
stopped, gazed at him, and so restarted, holding her ribs.
When her mirth ran out, leaving her beaming and beaming,
and wiping her eyes, (which were indeed as estimable as he
had described them), Mercurio regained her hand and
vowed: "I take you prisoner, lady, till I'm answered."

"You demon. You've no business here at all. Be thankful
Lord Chenti is away. And our fiery Leopardo, too."

"Why else am I here at this hour?"

"Hah. Well, speak up."

"Do I at least get a favorable hearing, fair lady?"

Cornelia grinned importantly. She had forgiven him everything.

Meeting each other's eyes in that instant, both of them
were suddenly aware of a streak of pure niceness running
through the characteristic flesh of the other, like a backbone.

"I'm predisposed," said Cornelia. "But I'm not the mistress
here. I assume you want time with my young Iuletta."

"Time indeed, but for another than myself. All the time
there is."

"What's this? Can it be red-headed Belmorio sent you?"

"No. Black-haired Montargo sent *me*."

"Oh God!" cried Cornelia, clapping her hands to her
bosom, smitten (vicariously) to the heart by the words as she
knew Iuletta would be. "What for? What does he want of
her, having almost slain her with liking and grief."

"To slay her all over again with love. In a bed."

"Oh Jesus and Maria!"

"A lawful bed."

"Oh, my stars."

"He wishes to marry her, madama."

Cornelia tottered. Mercurio supported her. With pleasure
in the acting, she courteously did not throw her weight upon
him, he courteously pretended she was weightless. They were
confederates.

"Your friend is belated," Cornelia said at length. "He
should have spoken before Belmorio did."

"My friend had not seen her then."

"Nor she your friend. Oh my. What is to be done?"

"Let them wed in secret and then declare the match. Montargo is a noble House, and very rich. Belmorio can be persuaded to lie quiet if it has no choice."

"Yes, Red-Hair lusts for her, but it's the fathers arranged it. He'll find another. And if Romulan Montargo pines for her as she for him—"

"Oh, nearly dead, I assure you."

"Then." Cornelia sank in romance until it reached her chin. All but her sense was submerged.

"Then, it rests with you."

"Me, sir?"

"You tell Lady Chenti you will accompany her daughter to seek further consolation from the priests. Girls betrothed suffer humors—some holy father must reassure her. Embroider. The larger the excuse for a delayed return the better. Does her mother know anything bad yet of Fra Laurus, the sorcerer-priest?"

"No, the Donna concerns herself with nothing."

"Then tell her Iulet goes to visit him, outside the walls. Some account him a sage, kissed by the saints."

"So I tell a pack of lies. What then?"

"Take Iuletta, and a couple of her maids only, and bring them to the south gate. We'll meet you there, on the Padova road. There's a priest in Marivero can cope with a marriage."

"A village not fit to keep hens?"

"What else? Would you have trumpets and a bridal procession and the bridegroom butchered on the Basilica steps? Can you be on the road today?"

"Mercy, no."

"Sunset, then?"

"Why, what a thought—"

"It must be done while her lordly father's from home. If they wed this evening, we can let them have at least one night to imagine themselves in Paradise, before the walls of Montargo and Chenti come smashing round their poor little ears and they know themselves in Hell instead. Consider, if Iulet is missed that night and her father home, he'll have his household and his men out searching before midnight. Are you with me now, wise Cornelia?"

"With you, you spicy ruffian? We shall burn together, no doubt."

"Let's earn burning, then. An hour before sunset, by the south gate."

"A secret marriage," said Cornelia. "I dare not tell her. She'll die of love and happiness." Romance had now closed over Cornelia's head.

Mercurio took her hand again. As Romulan had, Mercurio

pressed gold into it. As with Romulan, "No," she said, shutting her fist on the money.

Mercurio, extravagantly not noting this, was shocked.

"But you must. For luck."

"Oh," she said. "Get off then. I'll do what I can. I'll swear you're a fine dancer, with such legs. I would I had *my* fifteenth year back again."

"To me," said Mercurio in the doorway, "you are perfection now. We'll dance at their wedding."

Cornelia hastened in the opposite direction. She massively bolted, in a wallow of gown and poundage, to the inner door of Iuletta's apartment. As she threw the door open, some shadowy idea of subtlety suggested itself. But Cornelia had no time for this shady character. Circumstances had given her back power over her darling.

Iuletta lay on the bed. Her face was blank and she looked dead, but the nurse felt no premonition and no need for caution.

"Wake, catling," she said. She pushed shut the door with a thud and came to the bedside. "Such news I have for you."

Iuletta's eyes opened. They were a thousand years of age. She spoke serenely, almost sympathetically. "What is it?"

In some two or three ecstatic sentences, Cornelia told her what it was.

The nurse was prepared for almost any reaction, save the reaction which was the reward of her efforts.

Iuletta leapt from the bed and away. In a wilderness of hair, she backed to the very wall, and pressed herself to the pink trees on it. Her hands were clenched, her eyes insane. She screamed: "No! No! No!"

At some twenty minutes past the hour of nine o'clock, the Leopard, lying in wait in the Basilica cloister, raised his apricot head with a soft growl of satisfaction.

Iulet he had obviously scared, and he had begun to think she had somehow got word of danger to her dove-sending Montargo lover, or else the lover had grown tired of her—possibilities which had been a source of frustration to Leopardo. However, he had just perceived the sunlit funnel of the cloister's entrance broken by the shape of a slim dark youth swathed in black-blue, which apparition now strode boldly on into the colonnade.

Leopardo reclined in concealment on a pillar, listening and smiling while the brave and swinging steps approached. As the long shadow of Romulan Montargo fell before him into Leopardo's sight, the Chenti sprang out, slapped first at a glimpse of appalled countenance, and next offered a mighty shove which sent the slim body sprawling backward on the paving. Over this prone and gasping form Leopardo now leaned with a friendly: "Good *morning,* sweet love—" To meet the aggrieved and horrified glare transfixing the face of Saffiro Vespelli.

"Ah!" Leopardo shouted, and jumping away, burst into furious hilarity.

The error was not illogical. The very black hair, the cloak—now also visible as black, not blue, and plainly marked on the shoulders with the Vespelli Wasp badge—plus the correct impression of good looks. Leopardo was prepared to enjoy the joke even while he abhorred the disappointment. But faint scrambling noises caused him to desist, and mockingly solicitous, to aid Saffiro to his feet.

"A thousand pardons, gentle sir. I reckoned you another."

"God help him then," muttered Saffiro.

"God has helped him indeed. God has kept him out of my way."

Saffiro, nonplussed, vaguely touched at his sword hilt, and thought better of it. If his blood had been up he would have fought, as he would have fought that damned Estemba, in the garden yesterday. Saffiro's brothers had prevented him then, and cooling, he too had thought somewhat differently on the affair, for Estemba Uno had a reputation as a swordsman that in some ways rivalled mad Leopardo Chenti's. Nevertheless, since the quarrel in the garden, Saffiro had become obsessed with Estemba Uno—who was called Flavian or Mercurio, depending on who spoke. All last night, indeed, Saffiro had been dreaming of Flavian or Mercurio, and of a prolonged and curiously stimulating duel, which neither won, and during which both displayed great skill, while an increasing fascination and respect grew between them, to the point of their exchanging poetic couplets or cunning puns over the snick and glitter of the blades.

Saffiro did not wish for a new disagreement to muddy the odd interest the first had afforded him. In fact, he had elected to patrol this area of the town with some random notion of coming on Estemba, who apparently frequented the Basilica Library, and therefore, conceivably, the chapel.

Besides all this, Leopardo Chenti alarmed Saffiro in a way Estemba had not. (One of Leopardo's trademarks was his knack for instilling such alarm.) The idea of combat with Estemba was exciting, a challenge. But combat with Leopardo. . . . Another item altogether. And in any case the shock of being so abruptly felled had dislocated Saffiro's spirits. He was shaken and disturbed, and wished on the whole to escape.

"I do trust I did not hurt you," cajoled Leopardo, obviously determined to make a banquet of someone's discomfort, patting and smoothing, dusting off, and even combing out Saffiro's black hair with his fingers.

Saffiro stepped aside.

"I accept your explanation that you sought another than myself. I'm not offended."

"Oh, not offended? *Not? Truly* not? Be calm then, my heart. I was in such agitation this warlike prince might ask recompense with sharp steel—" Grinning accommodatingly, Leopardo slunk toward Saffiro who, handsome face falling, and unknowing he did so, backed away. Leopardo screamed with laughter, literally screamed, in a maniacal sunburst of hair.

"Who—" Saffiro attempted to divert, "who was it you—"

"Who was it I took you for? Romulan of the Montargo tribe."

"Montargo," said Saffiro. Romulan Montargo had been the friend of Flavian Estemba since boyhood. How strange he, Saffiro, had been mistaken for that Romulan—"I myself," Saffiro said proudly, "have something to settle with that fellow Mercurio, who consorts with the Montargo."

"Perhaps," said Leopardo, "we should make an alliance. Vespelli and Chenti against Montargo and Estemba. What a pity we've no more Chenti Primo daughters you could wed. You'll have to wed me, Saffiro," said Leopardo.

Flinching, becoming angry and panicked, Saffiro turned to walk away.

"Be careful of Estemba," said Leopardo.

Feeling he should be stung by this, Saffiro now spun round again, reluctantly once more setting his hand to sword-hilt.

"Do you say I'm unequal to him?"

"You? Why, your prowess is renowned. Particularly when you're in company with seven or eight of your brothers."

Saffiro whitened and the sword began to lift. Leopardo, aware he could kill this one in two heartbeats, without fire, not wanting him, yawned.

At a loss, frankly stupefied, Saffiro let the sword drop back in its sheath with a clank.

"Did you know, dear Saffiro," said Leopardo, "Mercurio Estemba collects all manner of antique swords, one of which, anointed centuries ago with the blood of a fiend, unerringly contaminates all that he even scratched thereby. Oh, beware of that awful sword, dearest wasp."

Guessing, if not completely understanding how, he remained the butt of Leopardo's joke, Saffiro nodded stiffly and stalked out of the colonnade.

Antique swords—yes, he had heard of that collection of Mercurio's. Saffiro himself had once appropriated a Grechian sword of incised bronze from the Vespelli vaults—

Coming around to the head of the Basilica steps, Saffiro stopped.

Across the edge of the square, a man in brass and white was riding a clove-dark mare. Seeing Saffiro, he drew rein.

Instinctively, Saffiro had it all. Mercurio too had mistaken him, or else paused to be sure not to mistake him, for Romulan. Saffiro found himself, before he quite predicted his own actions, running down the steps and straight at the rider.

"You, sir," Saffiro shouted, as Mercurio neatly sidestepped his horse from the path of Saffiro's advance. "You owe me something."

"Do I?" Mercurio Estemba was at his most bland.

"You insulted the Vespelli Tower."

"Then I beg its pardon."

The mare was already being guided away. Saffiro caught at the bridle.

"Mercurio, that's not good enough."

Mercurio Estemba leaned from the saddle. As he did so, the early blaze of the sun ran over his hair like golden water. Quite unroughly, he plucked the hand off the bridle and returned it to its owner.

"You have," said Mercurio, "my most sincere and enduring protestations of love and honor for the Wasps' Nest. And I, my friend, have no time to linger."

The horse galloped away.

When the dust had settled, Saffiro, at his own pace, went after. He was not sure of his errand, merely sure he would not be fobbed off from whatever ritual of retribution or acquaintance had yet to be completed. Having reached the Estemba Tower, inspected its banners and its decadent walls,

Saffiro loitered and presently encountered an Estemba servant, unhappy and thus susceptible to bribes.

Mercurio had come and gone. The servant had a message to take to Montargo and was nervous to deliver it for the sake of the feud. Eventually a portion of the message was disclosed. It concerned the hour before sunset, and the south gate, and the track which left the Padova road for the village of Marivero.

ELEVEN

It was, perhaps, a bride's privilege to be late.

In the clear yet coppery light of ultimate afternoon, a small group of mounted men were to be seen by the roadside, about two hundred paces from Verensa's south gate. They had been there, in various stages of stasis or motion, for almost an hour. In scarcely more than half an hour, the sun would begin to go down. Already the walls of the town had blushed to a terracotta shade, already the westerly ripples of clouds were drinking in the sun's color as if porous. That eccentric clarity of vision was in progress, special to the climate and time of day, a clarity which seemed to intensify even as the light thickened and the haze of dust resting on the land became a blur like powdered ginger, as if what should obscure, did obscure, yet made the air incongruously more luminous and penetrable. The slightest nuance of movement was seemingly discernible for miles, which made the absence of human movement out of the adjacent gate all the more provoking.

Romulan, who had been trotting his horse up and down, making it act his own nervous inability to keep still, now rode over to Mercurio and said, "So much for your precious Cornelia, the bitch. She took our coins and stayed dumb. I'll ride to Chenti's Tower and get his daughter for myself, before they shut the town gate for the night."

Mercurio shrugged. "My Cornelia, as you term her, liked the idea of an illicit marriage more than she liked the gold."

"Or did you fail me?" Romulan demanded. Then frowned, caught Mercurio's arm and said, "Forgive me that. You did not, I know. But Oh God, damn this delay."

All the group were nondescriptly mantled. The nondescript, serious young man beside Mercurio leaned over to Romulan and said encouragingly, "The maid will be timid, perhaps. It may have been difficult to get away. This has

145

been done often enough, but is still no small adventure to take on."

Romulan, not the only prospective bridegroom to look as if he were on his way to his execution, thanked the young man tersely for his concern, begged his indulgence, and rode the horse at a canter fifty feet toward the gate, swerved, rode back, swerved, returned gateward—During this second maneuver, two palancinas with drawn curtains of fawn brocade were born out of the gateway.

"Hell's fiery angels," said Mercurio mildly. "I'd hoped she would have the wit to get the girl a mount."

"Would that be seemly?" asked the serious young man.

"No, dear Chesarius, probably not. But this way we'll be marching dead slow as in a funeral cortege, all night. Now do you suppose," he added, "you can guess which of those curtained boxes has our Donna Cornelia in it?"

The second palancina was supported by four men, but the foremost by six, who seemed to be making somewhat heavy weather of the task.

Benevolo Montargo D'Estemba, seated astride the grey younger sister of Mercurio's mare, laughed. (He was perhaps the most lighthearted of the party, and with least cause to be. This secret wedding might, quite likely, have stirred thoughts of his parents' similar and ill-omened match.)

Mercurio's servant and Chesarius' man sat side by side, discussing the price of saddle leather, which seemed to be a point of great concern to them. A remote half-cousin of Romulan's—one official Montargo witness had been deemed necessary—kept moodily apart under a hazel tree on a fierce yellow horse of uncertain temper. This Montargo, Luca, by name, mistrusted the Estembas and felt it encumbent upon him so to demonstrate. Romulan had not divulged the purpose of their outing until the youth was through the gate with him, whereat an altercation had ensued. Mercurio parted the combatants. Luca, automatically presenting Tower unity against The Enemy, was now obliged to go along with Romulan's wishes.

The foremost palancina had halted in response to energetic commands from within, and the gesticulations of a boneless female hand through the curtains.

Romulan rode up to the conveyance and drew rein.

The serious young man, Chesarius, noted Romulan's pallor and stark tension, and glanced away, too polite to dwell on it. What he thought of the matter was kept to himself, his slight, uninvolved objections had already been voiced to Mercurio, and answered. (As Chesarius moved, a slice of gold cut through by scarlet appeared under the edge of his tabby mantle. Chesarius was from the Rocca Tower, fifth and youngest brother to the Duca: in such circumstances, the very best companion and witness to be had.)

The curtains of Cornelia's palancina, now set on the road, opened again and the lady herself thrust forth head and shoulders. She, too, was plainly dressed, yet as ever veiled like a fully-rigged man-of-war.

"What trouble I've had," Cornelia announced to Romulan. "Was there ever such a silly miss? You offer her marriage out of the generosity of your noble heart, and she—she shrieks she will not have it."

Romulan turned to stone.

"She's not with you," Romulan finally said.

"Oh, yes, good and generous sir. She's with me here. But you'd think I was bringing her to her death bed rather than yours. By God's huge all-seeing Eyes—Heaven excuse the oath—any other maid would have run all the way to Marivero in bare feet over briars, flints and upturned nails, so she would."

"She does not want me, then," said Romulan. His face grew cruel and terrible and blind. He did not know what to do, and was about to wrench his horse's head away from the litter.

But, "Yes, yes," cried Cornelia, flapping up at him from among the curtains. "Want you? She's very nearly dead of wanting you. Dismount, noble gentleman, and speak to her, for Heaven's sake."

Romulan complied almost involuntarily, flinging himself off the black horse. Striding around the litter to its far side, and dragging back the curtain, he stared down, and found Iuletta less than a foot away from him in a nest of gleaming and colorless silk.

"Well, girl," he said. "Do you or do you not?"

She would not look up at him, but twisted a rose—white, Cornelia's conceit, maybe—in her fingers. Abruptly he dropped to one knee and caught Iuletta's wrist. The urge to pull her head about by its black hair and slap her face had warned him to a restraint that never in his life before, perhaps, had he exercised.

"I've spent the night and the day," he said, "getting this arranged. Against my family, and against yours. Involving my friends, setting three or four Houses in uproar. And now you say this. Am I to be shamed and made a laughing-stock?"

"You did not ask me," she said. Her voice was colorless as the silk mantle.

"*Ask* you? I thought you swore yourself born to love only me."

"You left me," she said. She looked merely at the rose, still endlessly twisting it, so he felt the flex of her wrist against his fingers. "You left me, and I knew I must bear it, so you should be safe. If you do this, you do it out of pity, because stupidly I revealed I loved you. I had a dream," she said in a whisper. "I dreamed you died and I was to blame. I do not want you to die. I told you this."

A silver bead, manifested, like magic dew, upon the rose.

Cornelia bulked beyond, patting her heart. The hired men stood about, down the road the wedding party waited on its fate, mostly watching the palancina. Romulan lifted the curtain of Iuletta's hair very gently, and very gently drew her face upward and toward him, and unremembered who watched.

"On every occasion that we meet," he said, "you shed tears. That hardly augers well. What is all this foolishness about dreams?"

"Dreams are not foolish. I—"

"If I say they're foolish, they are. You must obey me, if you marry me, must you not?"

They looked at each other, until everything else became distant and faintly unreal.

Cornelia, closest to both of them, felt an almost indescribable pang, somewhere between arousal and astonishment, envy, compassion, and sorrow. Their combined aura was such that to be near them was both fatally desirable and unendurable to a spectator. Like two blazing candles, catching fire and melting into each other, the composite heat and brilliance might scorch anyone in the vicinity.

Romulan said, "Put on your veil, Iuletta, and get out. I'll put you up on the horse with me. He's docile and you weigh nothing."

Cornelia objected feebly. "That's not proper, sir—"

Neither of them took any notice. She did not expect them to.

When he lifted Iuletta up on to the black gelding, she sat above him a moment, her head raised, her features misted by the flimsy Eastern half-veil, like a princess in some legend.

He did not entirely believe in her in that moment, but all his doubts were gone. Afraid, yet no longer afraid of being afraid, she waited for him, and when he swung back into the saddle behind her, bringing his arms around her to take the reins, their bodies pressed together as if in imitation of those several fevered embraces they had shared, the more feverish embraces which were now to come. Some absurd emblem of perfection seemed to have occurred. No one who saw could quite ignore it.

Chesarius, his attention having returned to the lovers despite his will, remarked: "There is no lord like unto love," misquoting slightly.

"Ah, my dear Chesarius," said Mercurio softly, "can it be even your gravity collapses at the onslaught of sentiment?"

Benevolo, with a ribald cheer, threw his cap in the air and caught it. Luca Montargo's horse sidled as he stared. The man-servants had stopped discussing leather prices.

Romulan and Iulet, black-haired on the black horse, flew down the road toward the group, and right past it.

With a whoop, Benevolo was in pursuit, and Luca Montargo pelted after, more at the will of the startled yellow horse than his own. The hired men were hoisting Cornelia's litter and the palancina with Iuletta's maids, where two little veiled girl-faces were peering out.

"Best stay with the baggage," Mercurio said to his servant, indicating the litters. Chesarius nodded to his own man.

The two servants fell behind to serve as out-riders. Mercurio and the Duke's brother galloped after the rest through the luminous dust.

The path which led to Marivero lay a mile down the Padova road. The track itself, little better than an indentation made and permanently renewed by soles, hooves and wheels of diverse sorts, passed east of the road. Even on foot, it was a journey of no more than half an hour.

The sun was settling into its dust-scarves of ginger and cinnamon, and bright smoke, as if from a burning city, flooded the horizon and drowned the hills. Something of the beauty of this westering glare rode with all of them, though mostly they were unaware of it as a source of their pleasure. Only Mercurio, turning once in the saddle to glance back toward the town, consciously responded to the kiss of the sunlight and its warmth, receiving from it the impression of some earlier time, perhaps a thousand years before his birth, with a strange and bittersweet nostalgia.

Soaked in the sunset, Marivero gathered at the foot of a
hill. Small, intrinsic to itself, unwalled, baked together by its
summers and frozen into the roots of the earth by its winters,
it boasted a marketplace, a pile of houses leaning on each
other, an inn, a church. For a modest wedding it had, therefore, all that was required. (Indeed, the houses and the
market might have been dispensed with.) Some whim of
nature and the hour had also made Marivero attractive to the
eye. Dark green trees crowded around it and closed in the
edges of the track as it descended the hill, barring it with a
fallen colonnade of shadows. The village, when it came in
view, showed henna-red in the last glow of the sun. A white
star stood ornamentally in the sky directly over the belltower
of the church.

Looking down into the piazza, one saw a public cistern,
the ranks of doors and alleymouths, the shut portals of the
church. No human thing seemed abroad.

The pace had slowed on the track, to permit the two litters
to regain ground. Romulan and the girl were still at the head
of the caravan, but once or twice he had shouted some comment or quip over his shoulder to Mercurio, and gotten there-
from a suitable reply. Now Estemba and Chesarius drew level
with the black gelding, and all three men gazed at the village
some twenty paces down the track. Behind them the palancinas lunged to catch up, and Benevolo and Luca, having
dropped back, rode side by side, ignoring each other.

Chesarius said, "So quiet. Can it be someone warned these
people to stay indoors?"

"Where's the danger to them in a marriage?" said Romulan.

"Oh, some danger," said Mercurio, "if frenzied kindred are
liable to descend, mouths a-foam and blades a-flop, to stop
it."

He had moved about to regard Iuletta who, resting against
Romulan, unspeaking and large-eyed, watched the village
also, her head turned on her exquisite throat with a play of
curved angles, soft shadings, which made the stance like that
in some ethereal painting.

"Or perhaps," said Mercurio, "they fear to be struck
sightless by such beauty, and are indoors blindfold under the
bedding."

Iuletta looked at him. He beheld something in her face,
which was changed subtly, yet for all time, behind the wisp

of veiling. How to name this alteration? Surely, not love alone. "There's no trouble here," he said to her. "Marivero is safe for this as that star is safe in the sky. And I was here some six hours ago, or less, and made arrangements with the priest. Come on, my children. Come and get wed." He urged the mare by them, and trotted her down the track, riding first into the apparently deserted piazza.

As the rest of them followed, he was already off his horse. Leaving the mare to admire her reflection in the cistern, Mercurio hammered on the church doors, singing out: "Plague! Fire! Famine, war and earthquake! Open for the love of God."

Despite the promise of such extreme disaster, one door was very promptly drawn inward, and the dark interior of the church gaped from the sunset facade.

A little fat priest with a kindly chicken's face came forth and smiled upon Mercurio.

"If you heard a cry of earthquake, Father," said Chesarius, riding up and warming to the proceedings, "you must blame our winged messenger here."

"There has been an earthquake all along the road," said Mercurio. "We've been nearly shaken to pieces by the thudding hearts of the bride and groom. To marry them swiftly would be a charitable act. Not to say prudent."

"Enter the church," said the priest, nodding, smiling, and stepped aside.

There was a brief furor as Luca Montargo, thundering round and round the cistern, (unintentionally), vowed not to give his horse into the custody of an Estemba servant. This was resolved by Chesarius' grimly pointing out his own man. Luca scowled but did not dare refuse the Ducal Tower. Somehow, he then dismounted, against the contrivance of the horse. The hired men, the empty palancinas, the seven beasts and the two servants went off towards the inn.

The western face of the town was losing its hot color; the door no longer gaped so black, so like a premature mouth into the night.

They walked in, and found the dark not dark at all, the narrow unglassed windows deepening, but candles burning on their spikes, many candles, an extravagance of them. By this light, as if entering into some banquet hall, the guests of God threw off their mantles. Each was revealed, a gaudy beautiful doll, in his true colors.

Luca Montargo, zebra-like on indigo and blue-striped legs,

stared indignantly at Benevolo in brass silk, a blue ship worked on one shoulder, its timbers shot clean through by the Estemba Arrow—Benevolo was sometimes given to puns. Chesarius was sheer gold, the four scarlet rings linked to form a bizarre cross, and embroidered along every hem. Next to him was Mercurio in white with a dull-brass pineapple motif. Romulan's suit of clothes might have been cut out of a morning sky.

The two little maids were in Chenti crimson; by contrast, Cornelia wore a very sober pink. Iuletta emerging from her mantle was clad defiantly in a gown of crimson lace over a camisola of pleated cream silk. The priest looked at this splendid regalia in silence. Maybe he guessed she had donned it in an angry fear, which in some ghostly way was still apparent about her, even though she herself seemed to have put it from her mind, forgotten her fear.

They had all saluted the altar and all immediately turned from it to each other, except for the priest. He, having eyed the crimson lace, and next the ducal colors on Chesarius, pattered to the altar and kneeled down there. (The priest, too, wore the colors of his House—God's: faded vestments, and the magenta stola proper to the ceremony.)

Waiting for him, the rest became uneasy. Lacking most of the general forms of such an event—which forms, as aristocrats, they all knew well, they were at a loss in some odd, purely habitual way. Romulan, clasping Iuletta's hands in his, was speaking softly to her. They resembled solemn children hovering in an antechamber for some festival to begin.

"The girl will miss the show she might have had," Chesarius murmured, "if this had been done openly."

"Hmmm." Mercurio leaned on the stone wall, watching his two protégés intently. "They might be," he said quietly, "a hundred miles off, might they not? And they make me age to see them. A year for every mile."

"Ah yes," said Chesarius. "There never was anything more aging than another man's love affair. And you. When will you wed, Mercurio?"

"Oh, I'd wed Mercurio tomorrow, but he will not have me."

"I mean take a wife."

"Oh you mean take a wife. When I must, and not one quarter second before."

"I thought so. And does Estemba Primo never press you to marry and get sons, solitary heir that you are?"

"No. He's too wise for that. He knows I know how matters stand with Estemba."

"And you'd find it dull, besides."

"For certain I would. What?"

"Getting sons. A lawful mattress."

Mercurio glanced at him.

"Save your carving for the joint, dear Chesarius, I'll not be dissected. And in the church; do you not blush?"

The priest was rising, turning about, and he had been transfigured by his swift communion with God. His face was sure and aesthetic. He beckoned with his hands, gracefully and powerfully, as if summoning spirits of great waters.

Romulan broke off his inconsequent speeches to Iuletta. His need had been to soothe her, keep her safe, her thoughts fixed only on him. To protect her had been virtually his most initial feeling for her, protection immutably mixed with a hunger to overwhelm. And now, focusing her observation upon him, holding her so, so he held his own attention, and no sudden misgiving could come near him. Yet, looking over at the beckoning priest, his face religiously ennobled, a comparative image of Laurus intervened, like a phantom. Harbinger of truth. No, Romulan at this moment could not and would not have sworn that to marry Iuletta Chenti was what he wished or what he required. And yet, the deed was like a mirage, it did not concern him. It was a way and a means only, and as such he would take it, for the truth also was that he could not let her go. And then, looking from the priest to Iulet, he became at once glad to wed her, for she seemed to flame up like the candles on the altar. If this would make her happy, why then he could be happy in it too, and he started forward to the priest, leading her eagerly.

Iuletta, seeing the transformation in the priest, had become conscious, as if for the first time, that she was about to be married, and her heart sprang into her throat. She grew both elated and afraid as Romulan drew her forward, and the priest and the altar came close. And as, in accordance with the priest's mimed directions, she and her lover kneeled on the dry unliving floor to be blessed, she seemed to flow away from herself, out of her body, remaining totally aware of it, yet able to visualize its condition—not by sight, but in some other, more perceptive way. And even as the holy father began to speak over them the phrases that would bind her for ever, flesh and brain and soul, she who from her childhood had been taught that marriage, and the rites and vows of marriage, were of supremest value to her, discounted them all. She knew in this instant that he and she had no need of such auspices. That their liaison itself was valid, transcending everything. And that, had Romulan asked her, she would have gone with him in mortal sin to any pit or depth of earth of Hell, caring for nothing else but that she might comfort him.

So, as the priest invoked God and law to join them, the young man acknowledged he could be happy in another's happiness, the young girl comprehended the same of herself. These words were not spoken aloud, as were others of duty, honor and endurance.

While, as the ancient ritual moved on, intimately involved and yet beyond it, the lovers forgot that they had momentarily found such selflessness in themselves.

"It is done. You are man and wife."

The priest's voice came from far off, but, accustomed now to obeying it, they turned and gazed at each other in awe, Adam and Eva in a dark and candlelit garden, and knew it to be so.

Romulan sought in his mind for something courtly to say to her, some poetic prose. Nothing was there to be said.

"Are you sorry, now?" he inquired of her dazedly.

She laughed silently, her eyes shining so he saw their blueness like day sky left behind in the night.

"No. Nothing can harm you. I was foolish, as you said."

"You mean I've got a fool for a wife?"

"Oh," she said, lowering her lashes, "she is a fool, for she will kill you with love."

He kissed her and she returned his kiss, both with a kind of stillness. Their kisses had been a curious sort of proof of something, which now was proven. And in a very little while. . . . As if his thoughts ran also in her skull, her hand was tense and trembling in his. Yet warmly trembling, consenting. Some part of him had dreaded this symbolic first union a man must fashion with his wife. But from the contact of her hand, a chord sounded within him. His entire body waited on the brink of its own self-knowledge, fiercely and without reticence. As her trust made him gentle with her, her worship had made him strong.

They had walked, almost without noticing, to the church doors. Which were abruptly opened. Light dashed against them in a wave, and they stopped to face it, hands gripped, unafraid.

Nor was there cause to fear. The village piazza, having lost the redness of sunset, had now gained the new redness of torches. And this red lit up faces which smiled and grinned. Most of the village, in hiding on their arrival, had now manifested before the church. That the village knew what had taken place was evident.

The scent of burning pitch, together with the fragrance of Marivero's surrounding trees, poured about the church doors. And now music started up, tabors, tambourines and lutes, and the crowd clapped and shook its brands. A small angelic-looking boy-child about seven or eight, a devilish black-eyed little girl of the same age, the former clad in blue, the latter in pink, came into the door, and held up garlands for the bride and groom, almost purple roses, the marriage color, like the stola of the priest, and wound between with vine-leaves, and myrtle the plant of Venus, which flourished wild on the hill.

Amused, embarrassed, Romulan accepted the garland like a king from the angelic boy, who stared at him in wonder. The musicians were too good for the village, the garlands too diligently woven to have been made gratis.

"Oh God, Mercurio. You've been busy here."

Mercurio, innocently amazed, waved the accusation aside.

Romulan watched Iuletta bend like a flower-stalk herself to receive her garland from the little girl. For a second it seemed to him they had passed into their future, that these children were their own. Such notions took him by surprise, as Iuletta's beauty, burnished now by the torch-fire, took his breath away.

This additional ceremony pleased her, she touched the garland with reverence, and once more he was glad since she was glad.

"Some show after all," said Chesarius, turning startled but not displeased to accept himself a garland of leaves and blue corn-daisies from a buxom girl rather older than the child in pink.

"Simply an escort to the inn," remarked Mercurio. He bent his own golden head for a garland to be placed on it, kissing the girl on her summery cheek.

Through the doorway they had by now vacated there walked the priest, still lambent with his dignity, lifting his hands so the crowd fell quiet. From behind him, moving out

on to the piazza, came two beaming men, bearing on their
shoulders a miniature Virgin two feet tall, veiled and robed in
white, with a face of delicately painted wood.

The priest rendered his blessing to the crowd, the pretty
Madonna presided. Countless hands rose and fell in a motion
like birds' wings, describing the cross before breast and brow.

Preceded by the Virgin and the priest, and by small children who threw flowers and yet more flowers, so they stepped
on a carpet through the perfumed and gilded darkness of the
narrow streets, the friends and witnesses coming after, and
the whole unwinding streamer of the crowd, to the gleeful,
part-oriental rhythms of the musicians, wed like Christians,
garlanded like pagans, the lovers walked toward the inn.

And at the inn, the gate to the courtyard standing open,
saw geese baked with apples and cakes rouged with sugars,
and veritable urns of wine gleaming in the yellow lamplight.

Cornelia, scenting goose, remembered her own wedding
day to Iuletta's maids, who were not listening, one of whom
indeed was making eyes at Benevolo, while he, lofty and self-
conscious, encouraged her.

A nightingale in a cage hung on the pergola, sang madly,
to free its voice if not itself from prison.

Iuletta said, "Do you recall the nightingale in the orchard?
And how I said you would forget me."

"You note, I quite forgot you."

"I thought I should not see you again. Oh unthinkable
thought. And then to Manta Sebastia—"

"I cannot, I divine, be sent off to Lombardhia now."

They discovered themselves seated under a starily flowering hedge.

Fountains of wine cascaded into cups. Beyond Mercurio's
shoulder, Luca Montargo was earnestly telling Chesarius the
virtues of his ghastly horse.

Like the hedge, the sky had flowered in stars.

TWELVE

The room was very small and the bed large, with high black posts, round which flowers had been twined. Flowers and stars looked through the slender window, whose shutters stood open. Aromas of flowers and night, wood and wine, and irregular dim bursts of noise from the courtyard, came in at this window, and presently the pale moon would pass there, and eventually the dawn. But not yet.

Mercurio, by turning the feast into a bacchanal, had allowed the married lovers space and means to escape, unfollowed, or scarcely—Romulan's last sight of his friend had shown Mercurio herding a drunken Luca and a giggling village maiden from the stair with the threat: "Keep your place, sir, or I'll feed you to your horse." The priest, too, had been drinking and eating at the tables, and waxed merry. Cornelia had taken a fancy to him, unexpectedly, and hung on his every word. "Such learning!" she would cry, and the priest would bashfully lower his eyes. The others—Romulan had lost sight of them. They had become golden shadows, swirling at the periphery of his thought and feeling. Iuletta, the center of his awareness, appeared to have worked some spell on him indeed. Each movement that she made, slight as it might be, communicated to his senses. She raised a goblet to her lips, he seemed to feel the cup against his own, and next, like the cup, he felt the pressure of her mouth drinking from his. The black hyacinth hair slid across the point of her shoulder where the gown left it pure and nacreously bare, and he experienced the smoothness of her skin beneath his fingertips, as if they and not the curl had brushed it; and next he knew how that hair of hers would feel to him as it ran across his own body, and the scent of it as he buried his face in its depths. It became an effort of will not to grab at her, to fondle her, caress her before the whole crowd, and this he would not do, having seen something of the sort go on at other men's weddings. But to stop looking at her was impos-

sible, and she, though she hardly looked at him once, was, he
knew, acting out these things for him, making her world only
to enrapture him, drawing breath to pleasure only him.

At length, when the food had ceased to taste and the wine
had carried him to a plain where he would soon have lifted
her in his arms and run out of the courtyard with her, (a
barbaric tradition several might have applauded), Mercurio
had somehow drawn the assemblage into some mad game or
other, nodding as he did so, a nod perceptible only to Romulan. So he and she had got up and gone away, and now they
had come into this sweet-smelling room, warm as a dove and
fresh with the darkness, and with only a pair of tawny
candles to give light.

But their hands had parted, and the bed had now come between them. He gazed at her across the bed, and suddenly a
kind of nervousness after all did get hold of him—that she
might be timid, that he, with this passion on him, might dismay her. A thousand Bhorga jests seemed capable of springing up like rank plants about the room, and the strange ethic,
that put carnality to war with love, beset him. Even as he
foundered, however, she lifted her eyes to his, eyes that
blazed and faltered and went quickly down again. And then,
her cheeks dark with blushing in the candlelight, her fingers
unsteady but determined and quick, she began to pluck asun-
der the ties of her lace gown, and when it slipped away, of
the camisola, and cast it also aside. Astonished, he beheld her
again only in an almost transparent shift, and that cloud of
her hair, and the room beat with his blood, dulling and
brightening, dulling and brightening. And in the brightness
she kneeled on the bed, reached, caught his wrist and pulled
him mutely toward her.

He did this mute bidding and found himself beside her,
and as swiftly covering her, the shift dismissed and all of
her glowing pulsing slimness contained beneath his body. And as
he discovered her then, with his lips, his hands, every inch of
his flesh, all this exquisite feminine country now his by right,
her own hands worked their way in through his garments,
and like two warm creatures separately live, also found him
out. Oh, she was not afraid. Her abandon was beautiful and
frantic, like that of some nymph in legend coupling with a
god. In fact, he must ask her to let go of him, slip free of
her, laughing, to get rid of his own clothing. Then returning
to her embrace and so into an extraordinary unspeaking desperate whirlpool that each appeared to gain solely through the

medium of the other. Barely hampered by virginity or un-
practice, their bodies seemed to know each other as their
souls had seemed to. And this ecstasy, though quite new,
was yet simple, unavoidable, essential, as necessary to them
as the air. So that in their innocence, it was as if they had in-
vented both the condition and the act of love, and performed
it here, beautifully and surely, for the first time in the history
of mankind.

On the grassy slope above the inn, where the myrtles grew,
Flavian Estemba sat like a piece of classic statuary, watching
the last lights fade away from the apertures of the building
below. He had turned the festivities into a riot. There had
been a juggling contest, which he himself, whirling five
wooden cups and a razor-edged dagger in the air, had won.
There had been some Moorish dancing. The musicians had
become as tipsy as most of the dancers and the dancing had
ended. The priest had been helped home. Cornelia had
laughed till she swooned and been revived with goose liver. It
was noticed the bridal pair had absconded and certain ribald
jokes were hurled at random shutters of the inn. Grave Chesarius, uproariously drunk and crowing like a cockerel, had
shinned up some ivy and arrived to make a commotion at the
wrong window—the innkeeper's wife had spilled forth and almost brained him with a chamber pot. There had been a
horse race, of which Luca Montargo had been the victor, and
of which he continued the victor, since the yellow horse refused to stop. (They came back much later.) Benevolo and
the Chenti maid had flirted and challenged each other very
nearly into bed, at which point both became affrighted and
drew back in terror, the girl to hide behind Cornelia, the boy
to get more wine from the kitchen, and sink to sleep over the
table there. The second Chenti maid had primly fallen to
reading a book. Chesarius' manservant, having a woman in
the village, had gone off with her. Mercurio's man had found
friendly company in a cornfield. (Nothing was so stimulating
as the proximity of true lovers.)

Mercurio, having seen them all out like candles, Mercurio,
sardonically beneficent, had come eventually away up the
slope, kindled the mandolin and offered some slow embers of
music to the gods of the hill, before laying the instrument
aside and growing still, still to his very spirit, as the moon
went out and the heart of the night gathered around him like
a mantle.

Not that, despite his stillness, he was unaware of the nature of the environ, of the conversations of foliage, the black zephyrs of the dark hunting through the grass. Once or twice the silver-wire chirrups of the caged nightingale in the courtyard came to him. But mostly he had begun to listen to the stealthy whispering a couple of booted legs were making as they stole up through the myrtles toward him.

When the figure edged about and loomed suddenly before him, Mercurio's muscles loosened and his stance subtly altered, yet he made no move.

"I'll declare myself," said the figure, a little blacker in silhouette than the night. "I am Saffiro Vespelli. Do you remember me? We spoke this morning. And yesterday."

"I remember you."

"You're not amazed."

"The innkeeper told me there had been a wasp buzzing about."

"Buzzing?"

"Buzz, buzz, my dear. You bribed one of Estemba's servants, I presume to learn my destination. Then came here and sat on a wall till you knew our business."

"Something of that, more or less. But a secret marriage. By Jesus, you'll have the Gattapuletta cat-pack after you for this. And the Montargos may wake up their grievances with Estemba as well. How do you like that?"

"Oh, I like it," said Mercurio. "Where would we be without our delicious feuds."

"And you also have," said Saffiro, "a feud with me. Or did you forget it?" His voice quivered; it had the harp-strung note to it that belongs to some intense emotion of which the victim is himself uncertain, or at which he is in disorder. But it was a voice that meant to demand blood.

"A feud with you? Surely not," said Mercurio.

"Surely," said Vespelli. He paused, and made a gracious gesture over the stars. "It's a pity. I heard you were better friend than enemy."

Mercurio's voice also had changed. It had grown silken, and impenetrable. A shield had been raised within the dark.

"Who told you that?"

"I can judge for myself. I see how you've befriended Romulan Montargo, who never gave you anything in payment."

"Oh, alas. Is my friendship then to be bought?"

"I meant—I meant he uses you as the vine leans on the

stock. And like the vine, when ready, the grapes will go elsewhere."

"Ah," said Mercurio. The silk was now fine steel, but it was doubtful if Saffiro, taut as that too-tightened harp string, registered this further change. "I see you have been reading old romances and got the pith of the matter wrong."

"Not wrong. You treat him as a brother, he uses you, and now you're in trouble up to your ears."

"My ears shall be valiant and not mind it."

"You're in error, Mercurio."

"And you are here, like the good little sacristan you are, to set me right."

Saffiro walked over the grass and came up within two paces of the seated figure.

"Your leave to sit."

"The hillside is as much yours as mine, sir."

"Damn you then, I'll sit."

"It's hardly needful you should send me to Hell for that. But then, you have another way in mind."

Saffiro stretched his long legs on the turf.

"They also told me I'm no match for your sword. It's not likely you will get in Hell's gate from my blade."

Mercurio laughed, soft as a cat's paw in the blackness.

"By the Christ. A genius with the double phrase."

Saffiro seemed in difficulties and hard-pressed. He thrust a wineskin, carried with care up the hill, into Mercurio's relaxed hands.

"What's this? Do you think I've not quaffed enough?"

"Red wine from the Bhorga. You prefer it, do you not?"

"So I do. It's the only vintage can make me drunk. Ah, Saffiro, profit by the example of my dissolute life."

"Drink it."

"How urgent you are. Is it envenomed?"

"*No.*"

"A gift, then? Ah, yes, I see. I'm touched by your generosity. I call you bastard and you bring me wine. I note I've handled my acquaintances unwisely. Cur and idiot, I must say to a man, who will then award me half his fortune."

"Mercurio," Saffiro snarled, "do not, I beg you, mock me."

"Do not, I beg you, beg me not. I mock everyone. Mock, mock, mock. An unhappy trait. Either you must endure it, or you must go home."

Saffiro sprawled into the grass and the myrtle.

After a moment, Mercurio uncorked the skin and drank, his head tilted back, his eyes closed.

"Thank God," he said at length, "for a corrupt grape. Who have you told, by the by," he added, "that you would come here?"

"No one."

"We love you for that, then, the Montargos and I."

Saffiro stirred the grass with his long, ringed fingers, looking at the stars. He was himself fairly drunk, having kept pace somewhat with the revelers from beyond the inn gate.

"Speaking of blades," he said finally, "I have one antique blade of the Vespelli Tower—I brought it with me."

"Indeed, indeed." Mercurio's profound graveness tottered on the brink of extreme uncontrolled hilarity.

Irritated, Saffiro snapped: "I heard you were an authority. It's bronze."

"Ah. Bronze."

"Yes, *bronze,* by the heaving stars. Oh, have it all, then. I thought I wronged you in that garden, spoke out of turn. I came to beg your pardon, but you make it difficult for me."

"So I do," Mercurio said very low.

"My brothers are fools," Saffiro muttered hotly. "Your brothers are dead. Where do I go for instruction? So. I'd care to juggle wine cups and daggers as you do, ride as you do, dance, fence, sing . . . as you, may Hell devour you, do."

"I see, I see. You perceive in me a tutor."

"I perceive in you the enemy I would not take you for."

Mercurio began to laugh. It was not the usual musical and dangerous laughter. He coughed and cawed and rolled on the ground, bent double as if in pain—he might have been weeping. And somewhere in his soul, possibly he was.

Ultimately, in an abysm of humiliation and rage, Saffiro rose. But in the midst of his farst retreating stride, Mercurio spoke to him, and at Mercurio's first word, Saffiro halted.

"Forgive me. You see I'm ill-company. Better ride home, brother wasp."

"I am," said Saffiro mournfully, "too drunk and too weary to ride home and spend an hour bribing the town guards to open the gate for me. Do you have any sort of chamber here? Can I share it? Or I'll sleep on a bench in the yard."

Mercurio, too, had risen to his feet. Tilting the wine skin once more, he once more drank.

"I've a room. You've paid for a share of it in wine. Here,

drink yourself. Why be half-sozzled when you might be pickled as a fish?"

Saffiro took the skin and drank wine.

"A fish am I," cried Saffiro, "the earth is my ocean."

He careered in a circle. Mercurio caught him before he toppled down the hill. They began to aid each other solicitously toward the inn.

"Well, dear fish," said Mercurio, "this is a fine thing. The blind leading the sighted."

Saffiro, who was elated, made no attempt to object to this statement, or to fathom it.

A close yet not unpleasant warmth lay on the Higher Town of Sana Verensa, as if the night had wrapped it in velvet sheets. The moon which had ascended from among the towers, now went down among them, streaking their edges with a wet pale shine. Wet, too, was the glittering water of the Chenti fountains, spat from the mouths of the green copper cats. Leopardo lay full length in one of the shallow basins, the tepid bath up to the lobes of his ears, satin and linen soaked, hair soaked, face dappled by the downfalling spray. Lying there alone, he had conceived the notion the stars were showering from the sky on him, stars that were water-drops. How many, what an endless supply of them. Would there be any left in heaven by the time he vacated the fountain?

He had been to the Bhorga, to a hovel he knew where the sweet bluish hemp of Inde was available, with other oriental candies. To go to such a place too often would have bored him. The sensations such drugs produced were, for Leopardo, valuable only in their uniqueness. He had no dependence on them, and not a great deal of joy at their prospect. He had been in a raddled humor all day, ever since the mistake at the Basilica that morning. The Chenti Tower was a further irritant, being full of female fussings over Iuletta's forthcoming marriage to Belmorio, and the fool herself gone off to bleat to some hermit priest. (Lady Chenti was secreted in her apartment, perhaps mourning, though he doubted it, the absence of her spouse.) The town itself had oddly emptied of life. Seeking Romulan Montargo here and there, Leopardo had continually not found him. It had been oppressively hot. The Bhorga had begun to stink. Leopardo, striving very hard to pick fights with all his companions and unable to do so— for they were canny and fearful, and knew him in a most hazardous mood—as each eluded him grew more vicious and

more prone to aggression. Having had a woman, roughly and
unthrillingly (as ever, the itch haphazardly scratched, made
worse), having drunk and sobered, having eventually sought
the smoky rat hole of the apothecary, he had ultimately woven a way home, his violence lifted to some soaring and insidious elevation, where every emotion mingled, unsatisfied
yet fabulous.

"Sir," a hesitant voice stole over the basin.

Leopardo looked through the fountain's rain and beheld a
servant. Leopardo stared at him, and the fellow made nervous placatory gesticulations, unaware of them.

"Sir, there's some trouble."

Leopardo stared on from his glowing leopardine eyes
which, curiously, did seem almost luminous in the dark.

"Sir, the Lady Iuletta has not returned, and my lady, your
aunt—"

"It is past two in the morning, and as you see, Caspa, I'm
at my bath."

"Sir, I've been asked to summon you to the Lady Electra."

Hazily Leopardo, on his back, let the thought of that swim
over him with the water.

"Caspa. Return to my darling aunt. Tell her, yesterday evening I was cut on the face by a poisoned ring. Tell her I'm
now languishing, and far too sick to go to her."

"Sir—please—"

Leopardo raised himself suddenly on one elbow, his face
horribly reminiscent of that of the gold liopard on the Chenti
roof.

"Do you *argue* with me?"

The servant moved away, waved his arms, sighed, and fled
across the courtyard.

Leopardo lay down again on his back and visualized the
resulting scene within doors. Fascinated, he felt his body,
lapped by the milklike water, begin to respond even to this
fancy. The woman in the Bhorga had been as nothing. He
might have done as much for himself. In a while, one part of
him, at least, was eager to return inside the Tower, and had
already started in the prescribed direction.

"You are, my donna," he said aloud, "the lodestone to my
compass point," and hurled himself out of the fountain in a
detonation of spray.

He passed up through the house, which seemed quite silent,
no great outcry over Iuletta's absence. He himself scarcely
considered it. Reaching the door to the anteroom of his

uncle's bedchamber, he found it open. There was the servant mumbling, and—just from his sight around a screen of carven wood—*she* sat, for he felt her to be there, as one might be aware of the light of a fire thrown up beyond its enclosure. Cold fire.

"Well, well," said Leopardo loudly. "But I'm here after all."

The servant started and gazed at him, poor Caspa, all bowed over. Leopardo, soaked to the skin and the water plopping in a heavy glass fringe from his clothes to mirror his image on the floor, jerked his thumb imperiously at the doorway. The servant, not waiting for Electra's command, hurried by and out. Leopardo looked interestedly at the water he had brought in with him. (Just so had Romulan, chased from the rain storm, stood in Iuletta's room, if Leopardo had seen it.) But Electra did not emerge from her screen, or speak. Leopardo splashed to the doors and closed them with a crash, next removed his boots, emptied the water and slung them skidding across the floor. Prompted to sneeze, he did so vociferously. It was all done to anger her, and so apparently it did. Her voice came slicing around the screen: "This is no hour for your jokes. Come here."

"So you can beat and poison me again?" He touched the quarter inch thread of wound on his cheek where her ring had cut into the flesh as she struck him. "I'm afraid of you, my lady. Truly, I deserve punishment, and entreated it. But you do not play fair with me."

Behind the screen, he heard her stand up, the rustle of her garments as she did so.

"My lord, your uncle, is away," she said. "It devolves on you, Leopardo, to act as protector to this House and to your female kindred."

Leopardo walked water across the floor. He moved to the wooden screen and rapped it here and there with his knuckles.

"The Tower is haunted. A piece of wood which speaks. And with such a shrewish voice."

He came around the screen and looked in at her on its other side. She was robed for bed, surprising him in white, a white over-gown clasped with a crimson jewel under her high breasts. Her hair was loose, the first time he had ever seen it so. The downpour of blackness made her look young in a way he had also never before seen, and like a sorceress of some kind. He pursued this mythical allusion, putting it in words halfway through.

"Lady Medea. She cut up her little nephew in bits and strewed him on the sea. Would you like to cut me up in choice joints, Aunt Medea?"

"It was her brother," Electra said. "If you must rant, have at least your facts in order."

"Oh," he made big unblinking eyes at her, "my donna, what a scholar you are. What a wise and educated—"

"Be quiet," she said. "Listen to me. Iuletta went out in the late afternoon to visit the hermit priest on the Padova road. She's not returned. The gates are shut at sunset. What are we to think?"

"To think? Why, think anything. Let her sleep in the grass or on the hermit's knees. Bloody Iuletta. Let her be lost."

"*Fool,*" Electra rasped. "Chenti will go mad if the Belmorio bargain fails him. Do you think either of us will escape his wrath if Iuletta is harmed?"

"Oh, I blanch and quail. Oh, Heaven have mercy! Let him but lay one touch on me," Leopardo said, "and I'll break off the hand and feed him it."

"One touch? He has touched you."

"So he has, and I've borne enough of that old bullock's roaring and mouthing. Does he reckon himself a match for me? And you, you think him so, do you?"

"Is your cousin," said Electra, "with a man tonight?"

Leopardo paused, and grinned.

"God's starry Genitalia. How should I know what that ninny does?"

"You are in half Verensa's dirt up to your crown," she said, sharp as a whip, "I thought you might have arranged it. Is it Estemba?"

"Estemba? You mean Mercurio-who-is-Flavian?" Leopardo laughed. "I think not. And am I a pimp now, my donna, in your eyes, that you suppose I'd sell my beloved little cousin to the highest bidder?"

"I do not know what you would do."

"You do know. You know me very well."

"I know nothing of you, save you're mad and I may not rely on you."

"You may rely on me to do two things. If Iulet were with some fellow and I came on them, I'd take the old privilege of the *flagrante,* and skewer both of them to their love-couch with my sword's point. That is the first thing. The second, this: I will one day kill Lord Chenti your husband, and give you the flayed skin to hang up in your dragon's cave, Madama Medea."

Electra stared at him with her black eyes. It began to seem to him he could gauge the depths of them. He became hypnotized, and felt himself about to fall forward. He liked the notion of tumbling eons down into those darknesses and the crashing, stunning collision when he reached their floor. The apothecary's drugs still worked in him. He wondered she could not feel his own sensations, and began to believe that possibly she did.

(All her words were an excuse. He knew she did not care about Chenti or the stupid daughter. But she would go on with any argument or debate to keep him here, the fountain water streaming from his clothes as if he had come to her from the primordial ocean, some sea-demon, who would soon carry her back with him, and drown her there.)

"If she's unlawfully with a man, you must call Chenti's guard and go to find her," said Electra.

"*Must* I? How should I know where she'd be?"

Romulan Montargo, Leopardo thought vaguely, and flung back his head as if to laugh, but did not laugh, merely poised there in a sort of trance, gazing at the ceiling of the antechamber, the muscles of his neck complaining, the room spinning, all of him ready at a second's notice to drop straight backward on the floor.

Wavering fragments went over his mind, with equally wavering ideas that maybe he had been duped—misleading messages tied to doves, persons not where they might be expected to be but elsewhere. The fat hag, whore-mothering Cornelia, (who loved him so well, as her offspring plummy Susina did, amid that expensive house of boys and girls), had waddled off too, according to women in the Chenti Tower who had been looking for her. Cornelia was the pimp, maybe. Pretty Romulan and pretty Iulet playing see-saw in the Bhorgabba? Leopardo, at these suggestions, knew a fiendish delight. Honorable Chenti's daughter in a brothel, and that treacle-faced sput Belmorio father to a babe not his—

Electra's hands, like two narrow vices, fastened on Leopardo's arms. She attempted to shake him, and her strength excelled her physique, for shake him she did. His body was palpitated inside the sticky damp wrappings of his clothes, and his head was shaken down again that he might look at her. From this vantage, he watched, and allowed her to go on rocking him, wobbling back and forth, her image wobbling similarly, until she exhausted her stamina and let him go, breathing very fast, her face almost as white as her bed-gown. (Even her mouth was white, but a different white, a sultry, parched color, thirsty for warmth or blood—the mouth of a succubus.)

"Will you do *nothing?*" she raged at him coldly, her repressed fury almost daunting him, making him shiver at this wonderful alchemy which permitted him, who had no fear of anything save those things so deeply buried he must never confront them or know them if he had, permitted him a second of childish fear, unreal, theatrical, restorative.

"We are such enemies," she said, "that even in this, you will not help me."

"I'd help you where you would not go."

"Get out then. Go back to your vices and your filth, back to the stye, like the hog you are."

Leopardo sinuously pivoted, at his most graceful, and grunted melodiously: "Oinc, oinc, oinc!"

"Yes, you are mad. Insane and corrupt, both. I could pity you."

"Oh do pity me. Though," he smiled, "I have found a solution to my problem—the problem I mentioned to you. The problem of my reticence in the matter of women—"

"Out!" she cried. Her voice had risen.

The blood sang through his head and limbs as he saw he could goad her once more to that screaming fury he had witnessed yesterday.

"A barrrel of ice," he said. "I asked for that and they brought it to me. I judged your measure, lady, and made a hole in that ice, and then—"

"Get from my chamber!"

"—And then I lay with it. With that cold ice. And was satisfied, for you see I made believe that it was you."

He had never said, until that instant, anything quite so outrageous to her.

Even as he spoke, he staggered slightly, as if she had already struck at him with the entire force of her malevolence. But this time she made no move. Her face had not altered at all. He wondered if he had finally shocked her. He waited for something from her, and nothing came. The dilation in his loins had by now become painful to him, a pain to which he was accustomed, and which angered him and made him hate her, and with the hate desire closeness with her all the more.

In a burning roiling dream that was only the air of the room, he walked toward her, took hold of her white over-gown at the shoulders, and tore it apart. The jewel, dislodged, rang on the floor a mile away. He had not meant to do this but now he did not care, for she, as if she had attended some cue, began to fight him with all her strength.

Her terrible thin blades of hands slashed at his face, his breast. He avoided them, trying to catch them, but they were independent of her, no longer motivated by her reason, but by their own lust to tear at him. So, he seized her narrow face between his hands, squeezing at her skull through the cushioning fall of hair till her eyes elongated like those of an oriental, a metamorphosis that intrigued him, for such he had only seen as slaves. As he observed the phenomenon, the wild hands, not heeding the fate of the head, started to tweak and twist at his flesh, excruciating pinches of idiotically unbearable agony. In fury, he took his own hands from her face, and ripped open the bodice of the undergown. Her breasts, the upper stem of her body thus displayed, were so exactly as he had pictured them that he cursed her. (His fantasy, coming true, was almost intolerable.) High, shallow breasts, but perfectly formed, like those of a virgin of fifteen or sixteen years, and the ribcage pointing through the pearlized skin and the waist narrow as a bone, and over it all a stream of the inky hair—

"You bitch," he said, "you're only a woman. Flesh and blood, you skinny harlot. Is this what my kind uncle takes to bed with him? Does he never think it's a skeleton lying by his side?"

She screamed something at him, he did not hear the words, and her claws went into his neck. He pushed her from him involuntarily, and losing her balance—the floor was slick with fountain water—she fell. He watched her go down and as she hit the tessellations, again involuntarily, he cast himself over on top of her. This was part of the fantasy, too, to pin her writhing beneath him. She sprawled so, her hands pulling uselessly at the ground and at his shirt sleeves and the shoulders of his doublet, and he held her in position sheerly by his own superior weight. As she struggled then, each contact massaging the surfaces of his body, chest, loins and legs, he slipped into a type of delirium, content to lie over her and let her own violence go to work for him, making no move himself to violate her further. Presently he became aware of his mouth pressed to the cool floor, lips fixed open in a rictus, his eyes

blind and not quite shut—she had ended her struggle and lay
still beneath him, the exquisite bruising movements withheld.
He had subdued her, and she had been the victor. The duel
was over.

Trembling so he could hardly stand, he raised himself off
her and gained legs that had no feeling in them. The pressure
in his groin flamed and gnawed, and sank to a dull red coal
of pain. His brain thundered in his head, and turning, he
thrust at the carved screen which had been her shelter, so it
went over with a terrifying clap of noise.

"So, good night," he said. "Good night, virtuous witch."

He moved slowly, step by sluggish step, toward the closed
door of the antechamber. At the third step he heard a strange
misty susurration of material behind him, and next her fingers bit into his arm. He stopped, and turned his head. Then
turned about altogether, staring at her, his mouth ajar.

She had emerged from the broken gown and stood there
naked, girlish, serpentine, and mesmerizingly pallid, and with
that devilish blackness of her hair reproduced in the black female triangle between her thighs. Her face was as frigid as
ever, but the pale mouth said to him: "You say you want me.
You must defile me. Over and over you have said it. Come
here then."

Leopardo caught his breath and laughed—"*What?*"

"You heard very well. I said if you'll have me, I am here.
Come to the bed. You shall take me as he does, your uncle.
On his fine sheets, under his velvet canopy. Your head on his
pillow. Come, then. You vaunt and you jeer, you strut and
boast. Sheathe yourself in me, if you are so urgent."

"You—" he said. Sweat trickled down his back amid the
water. "You'd cheat me—"

"I will not."

"Yes, you trull, you'd—"

"No. I have said. Must I swear it? You've your dagger
there, the metal one. You can force me if you've a mind, if I
go back on what I say."

His eyes were dazzling, the room rising up and swimming
down. He did not quite see her as she came to him. Again
those hands fastened on him, now on the drawn pleats of his
shirt, and with a vandalistic strength that vied with his own,
suddenly she had done that same service for him as he had
done for her, rending the linen, stripping him to the waist,
save for the sleeves. And as he stood there, still not thinking,
stunned, her hands which had battled with him began to slide

and snake about his body, as if to model the amber skin, the statuary quality of the muscles, the three visible greyish scars awarded him by the blades of others, the points of his breast which at her touch seemed to turn to blades and pierce him afresh.

She led him from the antechamber through the bedchamber beyond, quietly, steadily, as one would lead a child.

Seeing the bed, the crimson and ebony and golden canopy looped up over it, the covers spilled about, and her whiteness glowing against them as she approached, Leopardo knew a moment's utter and uncomprehending horror. For, all the while he had played this game with her, some part of him had trusted her to put him off, prevent him. . . .

"Here," she said. And she lay down, dragging him toward her, so he almost fell across her, he white-faced now as she was. The touches of her hands flared up all about him, and he seemed to be buried in the nakedness of her flesh, breathing only the scent which rose from her hair and skin, the pits of her arms and the deeper pit of her thighs. And so, unable now to prevent himself, parting her legs with a desperate combing motion of his own, himself desperately ripping himself free of the last impediments, he did indeed bury himself within her.

At that first thrust, she gave a tiny indrawn cry. He had no regard for her anticipation, had never troubled with such niceties, and now, his lust almost murderous, he had no margin or wish to learn. But she, who had been raped and used and left to freeze for so many years, had found in these courtships of words and blows the stimulus no rough and no cunning caress could provide. Leopardo was food to her, food, drink, religion, life. At the first surge of his body into hers, her own body surged and came to quickness. Touching him, clasping him, feeling the quivering tension that ran through and through and through him, her own flesh was educated, copying his. Her response was so great that, his attention crazily attracted, he raised his head, gasping, to look at her. And so for the first time in his selfish impoverished existence, beheld the essential duality of eroticism under him, twisting and straining and striving as he himself twisted and strained and strove. And seeing this, his eyes blackened and his heart engulfed him and he fell down on her into the great explosion of ecstasy, vaguely astonished to hear his voice cry out just as hers did. Only as the spasms of pleasure withered and he came back to himself did he grasp the inevitable significance of it. Explicit sin was sweeter than mere carnality.

Drained, he would have rolled away from her immediately, but she held him and would not leave go. Leadenly he sank down on her again, his face in Chenti's pillow, his body slack, weakened as never before, in a deathlike speechless aftermath where thought ran all too free.

But he was young and in health. His strength came back to him. The next occasion that he stirred to leave her, he thrust off her hands. For a few moments a novel and a silent fray took place between them, different from all the others. At length, she pushed him away herself. With contempt, in the familiar icy little voice, she said,

"What, brave knight, are you afraid now?"

"Well," he said, "we've sinned."

"Oh, sin. But that was what you demanded."

He knelt over her. It was true, there was some emotion on him now that could be fear if he gave it space to make itself known to him. He had that urge to slaughter her which had so frequently visited him. A slight nausea was growing in him at the sight of her pale body which had shared with his the throes of lust.

He smiled, showing his teeth, his eyes darkened, troubled, for once the eyes of a boy.

"I must get shriven," he said. "Confess my sin of incest and how I yielded to the seduction of my sorceress aunt. How will you like that, when I go tell it all to some twitching priest in the Basilica? He'll need a good fat bribe to keep him quiet, will he not?"

"Do as you please," she said. Her head was turned.

Irresistibly he reached and took her slim throat in his hand. It was a fatal gesture, for it permitted their bodies to regain contact. And she, too, this demoness beneath him, knew as much. Before he could snatch away, her hands were back upon him, and even in his aversion, his sickness, the fires began to rise up in him again. Her hands on his skin were very sure, very clever. It was not that she had ever taken a lover, nor had she learnt to play that tuneless instrument, her husband, in such ways. She must have dreamed of touching Leopardo often in this manner, though she had never consciously remembered the dreams.

And he, as he squeezed her throat, bent his head and kissed her. As with no other woman he had ever had, he began in turn to explore her, not meaning to, but magnetized, all at once fascinated by her response to each caress.

"Sin," he said into her mouth, to her breasts, her belly. "Sin, sin. This is sin."

She said nothing, but before he moved to do it, she was already crushing him inside her. Her palms and fingers closed on his buttocks, forcing him against her, through her, even as he thrust to obey. He had a vision of Hell as he rode her now. Hell was Electra, not a punishment of horror, but of pleasure which *was* horror. (And yet he dimly sensed the specter at his shoulder, waiting for him to be done so it might speak with him once more.) Panting curses at her, blaspheming God, sobbing, he spent himself on the tumult of her body, and felt the tides go from him away into her, as if he bled to death.

THIRTEEN

Night-black in the flood of morning, a devilish cock stood
on the inn-yard wall, cawing at his seraglio in the court below. The hens pecked eagerly around the legs of the deserted
tables, and around the feet of Luca Montargo who, yellow as
his horse, leaned by the open gate. The remnants of the
bridal dinner and the follies which concluded it had long
since been cleared by the bustling innkeeper's wife. Benevolo
had been ousted from the kitchen, and now sat (surprisingly
fresh, gnawing a bread crust and intermittently twanging a
small lute), on the brink of the well. Cornelia and the Chenti
maids were notable only by their absence; the lovers, not
amazingly, by theirs. Chesarius, strolling into the yard tidy
and gravely self-satisfied, without a trace of the previous
night's debauch to mar either demeanor of countenance,
seated himself on a table, and instantly a boy ran out to him
from the kitchen with a pot of wine, a platter of bread, meat
and apples. Chesarius began to make a hasty, thorough
breakfast. (Luca glanced at him, almost succumbed to unconsciousness, and averted his eyes.)

All this Flavian Estemba beheld, as he paused in the
shadow of the inn doorway.

Like Chesarius, he too was apparently unmarked by the
emblems of riot. Unlike Chesarius, however, Mercurio evinced
neither gravity nor satisfaction. Unobserved at that moment,
Mercurio's enigmatic, faintly cynical expression conveyed
mostly cruelty, a strange cruelty directed at no one in
particular, unless perhaps inward, at himself. One might
think of a crippled miser, peering from some hole in the
masonry at the morning world going by beyond his confinement. That was the curious undercurrent of the look on Mercurio's young and inordinately attractive face. A kind of
resentment, jealousy, coupled to a wish to remain in isolation,
more than a wish, indeed, a contemptuous burning lust to remain so.

Then Chesarius, glancing up, caught sight of early sun glinting on gold.

"This cold goose is excellent, Mercurio. And there's some fine veal, too."

Luca made an offensive noise between mock retching and retching in earnest.

"I've breakfasted," said Mercurio, coming out into the yard. "Our companion, it seems, has not. Ah, poor Luca. A heavy head and a light character."

Luca, incensed at this familiar address and revitalized by outrage, strode from the yard.

"We should be on the road to Verensa shortly, should we not?" Chesarius inquired.

"So we should. We wait for the bride and groom, now breakfasting at the inn-mother's sentimental behest, in their chamber. Which may lead to further delay."

Chesarius smiled, and downed his wine. Glancing again at Mercurio's sword-belt, he remarked, "That sits oddly this morning."

"That? What?"

"This." Chesarius rose, tapping the girdle and hilt of his own armament.

"Oh God," said Mercurio, dismissing him. "No bloody jests for the love of—"

"I'm in earnest."

"Oh, I am *certain* you are."

"Are you sure you have on the right blade, Mercurio—"

Mercurio, taking up an apple, slung it at him. Chesarius dodged heavily but accurately, and the apple flew into the well, missing Benevolo by the breadth of an ear. Benevolo shouted laughing indignation.

"Your pardon, gentlemen," Mercurio said, "but no more jokes, if you please, concerning blades sitting right or left or up or down of God knows what else. The marriage bawdy night is done. This morning we have the hard fact to contend with. Montargo and Gattapuletta. Acid Valentius and choleric Chenti. Enough work for any man."

"True. How is it to be managed?"

"Romulan will tell Iulet—if Venus allows him memory—that she's to go home and plead Verensa's sunset shutting of the gates for her excuse of unreturn. Kindly Laurus lent her some cot in the oratory, and with Cornelia as chaperone, that will go off well enough. To consolidate this rouse our party and the litters take separate routes. Then, when Chenti Primo blunders home this evening from his enamorata, Romulan—hopefully with his daddy's blessing—will ride up amid the Montargo host and claim the girl as his wife. Then comes the earthquake, Mount Chenti in eruption. Presently a frantic messenger is dispatched to the Rocca Tower, hollooing for your witness."

"I'll keep ready."

"If you'd be so good."

"Hazardous business, as I mentioned once or twenty times."

"Life is the hazard," Mercurio said. His face gave nothing away, but his eyes, which Chesarius did not comprehend, were old and angry. "Who can tell," Mercurio said softly, "where love will lead us." And he took the dregs of Chesarius' wine from him, and drained them. "It seems to me I knew another morning like this morning," Mercurio murmured. "A hundred years ago, maybe."

"Oh, you subscribe to the pagan beliefs of Inde. The rebirth of the soul in flesh."

"Do I so? Perhaps. A new body, and gender immaterial. Sweet Jesus. Think what it must be to be made a woman. Nothing to do but preen and keep still in an arbor. Nothing to do but wait."

"God save us. A woman. Few men ever wished for that."

"Nor does this one, Christ forbid."

Chesarius was suddenly staring intently at the doorway. Mercurio turned and saw how, embarrassed, diffident, radiant and beautiful, the two wedded lovers had emerged self-consciously into the sunshine.

Mercurio also watched them for a moment, watched them as they gained their bearings like two persons who, for a great while, had lived nocturnally, and grown unused to the light of day. Then he crossed to them, swept them a flourish, and said:

"Children, the horses and the litters are about to arrive. You must prepare yourselves to part. Nearly a whole day from each other's company. How will you bear the sorrow of it?"

Romulan found his voice.

"To part will be sweet, since we do so only to meet again."

It was a courtly phrase. He raised the girl's hand and kissed it; that was courtly too. Yet these dramatics burnished rather than dulled the ardor that was evident in him, an ardor not burnt out, but increased by the night. And she? She had a secretive faintly wicked inner brilliance to her. As if she had partaken of some mystery. But of course, she had. And both their faces, similar as plants of one genus: brother and sister.

"Well," Mercurio said lightly from beneath his illegible eyes. "As author of your sanguinity, may I at least claim a single kiss from your wife?"

Romulan smiled at him, unassailable, so sure as to be almost indifferent. The girl, also, met Estemba's gaze with serene clarity. Her regard was knowing, now. Or was it only that all her pretenses were momentarily dispensed with? She had not trusted Mercurio Estemba; indeed, after he had lead her in the Turcanda at the Chenti feast, speaking of brothels and subterfuge, she had had small motive to trust him. Yet it was a fact, he had brought her together with her hopes. And did she trust him now, this gold-haired Mercury? Or, like Romulan, did she merely fancy herself invulnerable?

"One kiss," Romulan allowed, rather as Troian Belmorio had allowed Mercurio the one dance measure.

"With the lady's leave, then," Mercurio said. And leaning forward, took the pale flower of her face, the black hyacinth flowers of her hair, between his ringed hands, and placed his lips against hers. It was a decorous kiss, yet unhurried, and plainly very much a lover's. Within herself, Iulet experienced the smallest flutter of surprise, pleasure and consternation, all mingled, for it had not occurred to her that any other touch of lips would speak to her beyond her lover's, and she had been wrong. Yet it was not simply liking or sensuality that this kiss evoked. And when he drew back, still gently clasping her exquisite face between his fingers, all at once she fathomed his eyes and felt some awesome darkness stirring there within them. Quietly, and tenderly he said to her, so soft even Romulan perhaps did not hear it: "You taste prettily of apples, my donna. And perhaps that is what love should taste of. The sweetness of the Fall. Be happy, beautiful girl."

Even as he stepped away, instinctively she would have caught him back, for her spirit, energized by fulfillment, quickened to a wild and desolate and unlooked-for concern. But Flavian had already turned from her, and abruptly the yard gate was blocked by horses, and Cornelia's strident complaints trumpeted through the inn.

Then, as Romulan drew her to him again, finding herself as it seemed in the pressure of his body, she was afraid, a new and voiceless fear, as if she had offered battle to unseen

and supernatural forces, tempting them to rebuke her in her
joy.

Some ten minutes later, seated in the litter with Cornelia
(wine-logged, irritable and benevolent by fits and starts, and
saucy by others, with such queries as whether or not her
charge would rather recline to ease the twinges of deflower-
ment), Iuletta Montargo de Chenti had not lost her superstitious fear, sinking deeper and deeper into it the farther the
journey carried her from her lover, as if each mile of separation were a mile downward into some pit.

"There now. Rest, rest and be at ease," said Cornelia,
recognizing, she supposed, the uncanny post-amorous depression a young wife might be prone to. "Lie against the
cushion. There's a brave kitten. And what a fine man you've
gotten for yourself. Why, I'll be bound you could scarcely
rise from bed without a groan."

But truth to tell, Cornelia, the wine lodged in her skull like
an axe, also knew foreboding. It had finally occurred to her,
all that might yet go wrong. And how she, dependent servant
that she was, had enmeshed herself in the venture, up to her
brows. And she had Lady Chenti yet to face with bold lies.

As the day began to blister and fume beyond the curtains
and the palancinas were borne toward that town of towers,
both women grew silent, brooding with eyes downcast.

In Lord Chenti's bedchamber, still draped and shuttered
and closed altogether like a coffin-lid against a night two-
hours departed, the name and the nature of Iuletta had been
mislaid. If one of the carved creatures which crowded the
screens and chests had leaned over and bawled *Iulet! Iulet!*
the room's two occupants might have raised their heads in
bitter shock, startled, but uninterested.

"Where are you going?" Electra said.

She lay on the crushed and tumbled pillows. She was now
an extraordinary compendium of opposites. Her mouth,
reddened and bruised, her eyes hollowed, her hair tangled
and randomly curled, her skin printed over, the peaks of her
breasts darkened and swollen—and yet her look, her movements, her stance, even her recumbent posture, and certainly
her stealthy little voice—apparently unflawed; still cold.

"Will you not answer me?" this voice said at length.

Leopardo, dressing himself at the foot of his uncle's bed,
his shoulder turned to her, his head bowed over the fastenings

of his doublet and concealed in his cat's mane of hair, replied sluggishly,

"I told you once. To find a priest."

"You fool."

"Fool with trull. Well-matched." He lifted his face and shot a glance at her. He, too, bore evidence of their violent lovemaking, but on Leopardo such garb was not quite unfamiliar. Only a sullen almost sodden quality lurking behind the appearance told this night had been unlike all others. Untidily but effectively dressed, he now moved around to her, and said, "And you can lie a-bed, lady, and picture to yourself how I'll regale the holy father. Some monk's pot will bubble this morning."

"Am I to suppose you serious?"

"Follow me down the street in your bedgown and you'll see I am."

"You are a fool indeed, then. Do you think so much of your stupid petty conscience you must spill it out like vomit?"

"Vomit? Aptly put. Vomit you forth, delightful aunt. Spew you from me, sorceress."

"You are so much consumed by guilt. Shall I number the times you had me? Go to your priest. Go tell him all you did. And then come back to me and repeat the exercise."

"By Christ! You can smolder in your own syrup from now till Doomsday, you'll get nothing more from me."

"Will I not."

She uncoiled herself from the bed as she spoke, and he stepped away from her. A horrible grin now made his face very ugly.

"Burn, witch," he said. He swung round and half ran across the room to the door into the antechamber, where he turned again, and bowed to her. "Listen for a crash like cannon. That will be God striking me dead in the nave of the Basilica." He awarded her a sign of the Bhorga gutters, before darting through the door.

Electra's countenance closed, as if to retain her thoughts. Her eyes were motionless as those of a lizard, and she made no further move to call him back. She knew he would return.

But Leopardo, walking along the corridors and down the stairways of the Chenti Tower, no longer knew anything for certain. Save he had spent the night with a succubus, a vampire, who drained his life. Not that he was fatigued, rather fantastically alert, feeling he must hit out at things—the hang-

ings, the walls—must mutter oaths, grind his teeth, all as if
to prove to himself he had kept some contact with the
material world and with his own body. Beneath this frenzy a
corrupting self-amazement had begun, and a sense of challenge and of dare. For he had dared God, had he not, dared
God to smite him? And now, if Leopardo were to confess to a
priest, that was not an act of repentance, but only a provision, that God could not overlook his fault. *See what sin I
have committed,* he would cry. *See and hear. And so, slay
me, if You are able.* But whether he really regretted anything
was moot. He *suffered* no regret, no horror, and yet he suffered something, some incoherent abstract crawling of the
flesh and shuddering of the intellect. As if the woman had begun to devour him alive. Or as if he himself, discovering in
himself some hidden vault, had opened the door and let forth
monsters.

In this frame of mind he crossed the banquet hall, stepping
on Proserpina's mosaic face with sudden awareness and loathing. A servant, caught dallying, he sent for wine with a
curse and a blow. And when the wine came, Leopardo drank
it, rinsing his mouth of the taste of the woman, yet still not
rid of her.

And was he to visit the priests? Was he to get himself
shriven? Why not?

He reeled out into the morning, staggering through the air,
(gold and heavy as some new element basting the town), and
as he poured himself out from the Tower of the Cat, down
its stair, beneath the liopard on the roof and into the street, a
barely containable unpremeditated urge to shout and roar
came over him. He did not know where to fly to be free of
himself. And so he fled toward God, at a swaggering stride,
sword on hip, mouth clamped tight, full of a dreadful inex-
plicable emotion that would not let him be.

God would either punish or forgive. In the latter case, God
too would be shown unreliable. Aside from God, however,
this ghastly pilgrimage toward retribution was a terminal
point, a frightful summit of all the profanities and boasts of
Leopardo's existence. For as he hurried, mocking and writhing, afraid and in terror and in pride, to slap the cheek of
God, Leopardo was displaying, in its ultimate crisis, that most
incurable and terrible of all man's ills, his rage at being alive.

Entering the Basilica square, mounting the steps, advanc-
ing, on this occasion through the main doors above which the
bronze angels gathered with their swords and tablets, Leo-

pardo did not pause. Only when he reached the wide flagged inner well of the edifice, cool, gloomy, immeasurably solid, the lacework windows burning their brands into the ground and across his breast, the heavy pillars marching towards the distant altar, only then, dwarfed by architecture and design, did he falter. No one and nothing moved, beyond the vague gustings of candle-smoke, the husk of a dead flower trembling like a damaged insect at his feet.

Then the great and intolerable shout gained mastery of him, breaking out of him, deafening and numbing him— where before he would have shouted at random, uncaring what forces possessed him since he reckoned them to be his own.

"A priest!" he thundered, filling the whole echoing casket with noise. "Come and shrive me! I demand a priest! A priest!"

And when the thunder faded, he rested his forehead on one of the cold clammy columns, smiling, or yawning with nervousness, and waited.

"Mercurio, you idiot—"

"Oh, let him alone. He's in one of his maniac moods."

Having ridden back from Marivero over pasture land and so through the standing crops that lay in on Verensa's eastern flanks—aiming for a lesser-used eastern gate, further subterfuge, perhaps pedantic, the palancinas having returned through the southern portal—they had now come into a derelict vineyard, and thence a wild orchard. Mercurio, leaping upright on the back of his running horse, was plucking hard fruit off the trees and throwing it to his companions. Even Luca had received a rock-like apple—and very nearly a blackened eye.

"Oh God, Flavian, enough," shouted Chesarius.

Angelically, Mercurio resumed his seat on the mare. He trotted her back to them. Luca having tossed the dangerous apple aside, Mercurio leaned perilously to retrieve it. He stationed the mare across the path of the yellow horse and fed the apple into the snarling yellow mouth, which began to eat. Luca, unable to control his mount, sat glaring, ignoring both his horse and Mercurio, pretending to scan Verensa's sunburned walls, which were now visible at three slopes' distance.

"You should feed your animal, Luca," Mercurio said. "See

how starved the poor beast is. A little kindliness might work wonders."

Luca began, apparently, to count Verensa's host of towers.

Romulan, allowing the black gelding to crop the proud turf, gazed almost idly in the same direction. He seemed to have forgotten the urgency of return, the mission before him, or to wish to forget. The yellow horse, apple finished, began to eat Mercurio's glove. Withdrawing it, Mercurio rode across to Romulan.

"I wonder what," said Mercurio pleasantly, "Valentius is doing this morning."

"Oh, God, do not," said Romulan.

"Well, but we know what he will be doing in an hour more. Flaming, foaming, calling for horse-whips—"

"Mercurio—"

"Calling for a notary and procedures of disinheritance. At best, a lecture on his disappointment."

Romulan grimaced.

"When did he ever do anything else, my father?"

Faint and sheer, the notes of the campanile bell wafted unexpectedly toward them out of the distant town.

"It's struck eight," Chesarius said.

"My thanks on my knees, Chesarius," Mercurio kissed a hand at him. "One day you must teach me, also, how to count."

Benevolo laughed.

Romulan persuaded the gelding to raise its head. Luca, disdaining them, somehow coerced the yellow horse into cantering out of the orchard.

"Well, child," Mercurio said, "take heart. Your father may only kill you."

They rode headlong up the last slopes at the walls, splashing through the high dry blue waters of cornflowers, and straight in the slender gate.

The town was all at once about them, in the form of an old marketplace crowded round with houses of the lesser sort, for they were in the lower streets. From here, by a winding path, the Bhorgabba was not inaccessible, but a broader way cut through to the Basilica square, and thence to the upper thoroughfares—and revelation.

The heat, finely tuned in the countryside, grew darker and more oppressive here between the enclosure of walls. A shadow made of the very light seemed to come down on them. The smell of the Lower Town came also, every interstice an oven, and promising to be foul by noontime.

As they rode up between the windings and in-pressings of brickwork and plaster, they found the road blocked before them. A funeral cortege of the meanest type was propelling itself from an alley of hovels, a pale drab priest of some minor order coming bell-clanking before. Seeing the riders, the priest raised his hand.

"Take another street, good gentlemen. We have the Summer Sickness here."

Luca swore, jerking the yellow horse backward and aside. Chesarius frowned. He called to the priest, the frightened mourners: "Has this been reported to the Duca?"

"Yes, sir. There are several cases. Go around, if you please."

They turned their horses' heads and broke for a side street.

"Damnation," Chesarius said, automatically and inappropriately crossing himself, as the bell resumed its tinny clank behind them. "I thought we'd miss it this year. Summer Sickness, by God's Heart."

"A euphemism to sugar the unsugarable," Mercurio said.

The hooves rattled now on cobbles.

"It was contained before," Chesarius mused. His duties as ducal relative were plainly crowding in on him. "Such priests as that one performed miracles, the Franchescans in particular. While the brothers of the Basilica sat on their fat stubs and trembled."

"Plague is plague."

"Yes, by Heaven. Flavian, Romulan Montargo, pardon me if I make on straight away to the Rocca Tower."

They exchanged courtesies and Chesarius galloped for home. Luca had already precipitately vanished.

Romulan's face was dark and still.

Half an eye on Mercurio, Benevolo, catching something of his idol's thoughts, had begun to strum the little lute and to sing, sweet and weightless, riding his grey horse behind the gelding and the mare. Mercurio turned and nodded at him, and Benevolo would remember ever after, that nod, the light catching on the hair and brows, firing, and then fading, as some shadow came between them and the sun.

FOURTEEN

"A bad omen," Romulan presently said.

"Only if you credit omens."

"Who said, 'The price of love is death'?"

"Some impotent who hoped for long life."

"I come back wed, and walk into a plague-burial."

"Your father's the only plague you need fear. A plague of Valentius. Ah, deliver us from such."

"My father would make six of yours," Romulan bantered absently.

"True. You would require six of Valentius to make one of Estemba Primo. Where, by the by, is Luca?"

Benevolo broke his song to say: "The Bhorga."

"Excellent. So he'll not be home ahead of anyone to babble."

The street, after a quarter of a mile, gave way to another, and trotting up it they passed between two garden walls and so emerged on the edge of the Basilica square.

Driven indoors by hot weather or rumor of sickness, no one was about. Like an edifice of flour, the great white building loomed across the space. On the public cistern the light fell in blades, running the water through to the bottom. Birds like papers blew into an opaque sky.

Benevolo concluded the tracery of the lute.

"Someone is signaling to you from the Basilica steps."

Mercurio glanced up the stair to the facade. Yesterday, from that same direction, Saffiro Vespelli had come rushing, flawed alter-image of Romulan, to intercept him.

"Crimson," said Mercurio. "A pair of Chentis. It charms me we're to greet the Montargos' new kindred so rapidly. But perhaps it would be ill-advised."

"What?" Romulan drew rein. "Run away from the cat-pack again? Can I not stay and make peace with them?"

"You can stay. I doubt you can make peace."

Mercurio rode on, but Romulan did not, and Benevolo

halted beside him. After a moment, Mercurio, too, eased the
clove-colored mare to a standstill. He looked back, and then
across the square. One figure remained on the Basilica steps.
The other, a pink and mauve bouquet, hurried toward them.

"By the legs, Gulio, I think."

"Gulio," said Romulan. His mind moved backward,
through trees and rain and doorways, to a lightning flash, and
Gulio's surprised and eager face, and the shouted words that
had betrayed: *'Pardo—there's a rat in the wall!* Because of
that betrayal, Romulan had sprung into an orchard, rushed
toward a window of rosy glass, and so met the power and
puissance of love in the form of Iulet. To settle the score
with Gulio now meant to deny the marriage that had followed.

Deny the marriage—*I have come back wed. . . .*

He was changed. The town, the world were changed. Only
habit was familiar.

Gulio, smiling and waving, came to rest between their
horses' mouths, bowing, genuflecting; harbinger of habit and
familiarity.

"Good morning."

"Oh good morning, good morning," Romulan and Mercurio soared into ecstasies of greeting.

"Dulcet Romulan Montargo," Gulio said.

"Oh, dulcet yourself, indeed."

"I've a message for you."

"From a bawd, no doubt," said Romulan, and felt ineffably
cheered.

"From my kinsman, Leopardo Chenti."

"From a bawd. You said," Mercurio congratulated Romulan.

Gulio sneered, eyes narrowing.

"Would you say it to his face, Estemba?"

"Certainly not."

"Coward then."

"No, peacemaker. Save, we're not making much peace."

Romulan laughed. "Make peace with us, Gulio."

Gulio menacingly put hand to sword hilt and was greeted
by cheering and gesticulatory applause.

Gulio knew himself, though did not care to admit it, small
fry. Nor was he in a joyous humor. Iuletta, that girl-crea-
ture, had been out all night attending some priest (she *said*)
and on her coming home not half an hour ago, Gulio had
been dispatched to inform Leopardo who, the story went, was

loitering at the Basilica. Gulio had sought Leopardo there, and come on him at length in the graveyard, hanging on some House mausoleum, (Suvio's by the armorial markers), and spewing violently. Gulio, vaguely pleased to see the liopard so helpless, and also unnerved, stood by mumbling and somewhat in distaste. Eventually, Leopardo, death-faced, choking and with the eyes of insanity, straightened, looked about, and saw his witness. With an oath fit to rouse the buried ones all around, he struck Gulio a blow across the head that would have been murderous had there been any strength in it. As it was, Gulio tumbled against a tree, smudging the flesh on his bones. Thereafter, sulking and perturbed, he followed Leopardo's weaving course among the tombs, and so to the cloistered colonnade that gave on the capella. Here Leopardo lay upright on the wall, his face in its carving.

"An interesting night?" Gulio had at last inquired.

"Blast you with poxes, be quiet."

"Ah," said Gulio, and fell to studying Leopardo's brocade shoulders.

In a while, Leopardo said into the wall,

"I was with a whore. The most accomplished and best of her sisterhood. And this sin I confessed." At which he suddenly doubled over and lay curled against the stonework, making the most terrible sounds of unproductive nausea. Gulio, offended, gave ground. When the dreadful spasms ceased, Leopardo called to him. "Find me some wine, damn you."

"Wine? I'd say you—"

"You'd say nothing. Go do it."

The horrified Gulio had bolted to the nearest wine sellers. He had been in two minds whether or not to return, but ultimately fear of Leopardo had forced him to do so. Regaining the spot, Leopardo, however, was not to be found. Gulio searched indifferently, then himself leaned on the wall to sample the wine. In this method he was interrupted by the Cat, who crept up on him, seized the wine receptacle and drained it.

This done, Leopardo stood grinning evilly.

"I came on a cure for my ills," said Leopardo. "I've been drinking holy water from the font."

Gulio was shocked, and disbelieving. Nevertheless, prudently he smiled in response.

"What does it taste of, then?"

"Brimstone."

Leopardo's unblinking eyes swam slightly, and he swaggered from pillar to pillar, so Gulio must follow him all over again.

"I'll tell you another thing."

Gulio waited apprehensively.

"My aunt, Lady Chenti, Donna Electra, my uncle Chenti's wife—" Leopardo broke off, so Gulio must prompt him with:

"Yes, 'Pardo?"

"Had a man in her bed last night. And my poor uncle from home, trustingly fornicating with his Bianca."

Gulio did not like this idea, for it boded a unique trouble. But Leopardo turned and watched him until Gulio was forced to say:

"You know as much?"

"I know, beloved Gulio."

Gulio, confounded, muttered, "What will you do?"

"Why, draw my sword, my darling, and skewer her. Skewer her to the length of my blade, forthwith." At which he burst into frantic laughter, staggering with it, his eyes like colored flaming ice. In this way he pranced and stumbled out and around to the front of the Basilica, falling from carving to carving, beneath the bronze angels, sick, drunk, and maddened, beyond anything Gulio had ever beheld before. Then, to Gulio's total stupefaction, Leopardo had flung himself against one of the huge opened doors, clinging there and striking his head against it. In the midst of this, three horses had come up into the square from the direction of the Lower Town. Nondescript mantles had been cast aside in the heat, and Gulio saw at once the colors of Estemba and Montargo—enemies Leopardo might be pleased to attack in preference to the delicate person of Gulio himself.

"Here come the shipwrights and the Duke's fletcher."

"What?" Leopardo said.

"Montargos and Estembas."

"Montembas and Estargos, ho!"

"Looking for a brawl, no doubt."

"I desire only Romulan, Valentius' son. He owes me my cousin's honor. Unless the musician is with them. I'll tune his mandolin for him, see how he'll dance to that."

"Both, 'Pardo. Romulan and Flavian Estemba together. And that half bastard, Benvolio or Benevolo or how he's called."

Leopardo unhung himself from the door. He strolled to the edge of the stair, drawing in long breaths, steadying himself.

His cruel eyes grew clear and unpleasingly intelligent; he seemed to sober, fantastically, between one heartbeat and the next.

"God's instrument," said Leopardo.

Gulio took this for a sexual blasphemy, and laughed. Leopardo did not look at him.

"Will you try for me then, Sir Christ?" Leopardo said. "Gulio." Gulio started. "Approach them and invite them to meet me."

"I?"

"They will not bite you, gentle maiden. They'll save their teeth for me."

"And meet you where?"

"Here. Where but? The foot of God's staircase."

Gulio prevaricated. Leopardo reached and squeezed his shoulder, an agonizing pressure that showed the cat had his strength again, and all his appalling awareness.

Gulio set out across the square, through the birds and the dust and the pollination of the daylight. He felt Leopardo's presence behind him as he moved, thrusting him on. And so he came up to Estemba and Montargo, one of whom had the score of betrayal to settle, the other of whom had a swordsman's reputation to rival 'Pardo's.

Having got through the preliminary bout of effusions and insults without delivering the 'message,' and with no sign of either party dismounting, Gulio, hand unhappily to sword hilt, found himself at a loss.

To his dislike then, Romulan, leaning from the horse, said charmingly to him, "Why not pretend, Gulio, you're my kinsman."

Incensed, Gulio glared. The glint of mockery was in the Montargo's eyes for sure, yet his tone had been offendingly sincere. Mercurio Estemba, on the other hand, was invoking God.

"We have no feud, you and I," said Romulan, smiling adorably. "Nor I with Leopardo, come to that, if he would see it."

"He says otherwise. That you dealt lightly with his cousin."

Romulan lowered his lid-fringes of jet-black lashes, seemed to consider, looked at Gulio and began: "Rather than deal lightly I—"

At which Estemba broke in.

"*No*. Not yet for that."

Romulan appeared uneasy. Gulio was intrigued. Something

else went on that might be interesting, being harmful only to others.

"Not yet for what?" said Gulio, and was himself broken in on by a fearsome yell that crossed the square, hitting him amid the shoulders like a javelin: his own name garnished with invective.

"Leopardo," said Gulio hastily, "would meet you over there, by the steps."

"If he'd meet us," said Romulan, "let him come over here."

"Or better still," said Mercurio, "let him stay where he is. An urgent appointment, Gulio, bids us hence, else we could not bear to prise ourselves from your company."

"Afraid to confront him then."

"Bones water, the heart of a mouse," said Mercurio.

Romulan, staring now at Leopardo on the steps, small as a figurine, said, "Why should I run? He'll think for sure I dishonored her."

"Let him think it. He can eat his thoughts tomorrow, gristle, beak and all. Leave it be."

Romulan flushed slowly with an indecisive anger, noting his hands shook on the reins. Himself, he could not have said what was directing him. Everything had seemed all at once to have moved too swiftly and in too variable a sequence of ways. He was wed, he had lain with her. And through these primitive and innocent acts he had made a tangle of his life. Only the habit, the familiarity of the quarrel, the brawl, remained recognizable, easing. Though not to be considered any longer, for now her future rested upon his. He dared not play this game again, and yet, how the game drew him, the alluring perversity of foolishness.

He turned, presumably for guidance or to be ruled, toward Mercurio, and so was astonished yet again. For rather than the relaxed and lethal face of Mercurio's judgment and caution, or the innocuous face of his play-acting, or the ironic beautiful face of enigma, Romulan beheld a new face, or in fact the inner face which he had never somehow surprised before. Mercurio had let fall the mask, abruptly too tired or too exasperated to maintain the rigid control that was necessary to keep it in place. Some part of him was, it seemed, disgusted by the childishness he found in Romulan. Stung, Romulan recoiled. It was a misinterpretation, but inevitable. The countenance of disapproval reminded him of his father. In the way of one often hurt by censure, (from infancy, he

had seldom thought himself free of it), all criticism led him
to effect immediate retreat.

Not properly reasoning what he did, Romulan urged the
gelding forward and across the square, toward Leopardo
Chenti.

And Mercurio, for his part, sat and simply watched him
go.

The sunlight blazed and Romulan rode through it, shining.
Mercurio Flavian Estemba observed, as if the scene meant
nothing at all to him. Within himself, the unavoidable hiatus
had presented itself. He had attempted to miss looking into
the depths of himself this morning, but helplessly, gradually,
he had been persuaded to do so. These bottomless darkening
spaces overwhelmed him, and the young man riding away
toward another, the young bridegroom in his blue clothing,
seemed at length no one that Mercurio remotely knew.

In the early hours of the morning, a little before dawn
came over the inn at Marivero in a silent, extraordinary tide,
Flavian Estemba had dreamed that he was damned. It had
been a savage and unlikely dream for a man who did not,
generally or seriously, deal in such terms, and who could not
in his intellect credit any such fancy as Hell, or Lucifer. Yet,
Lucifer he had seen, tall as a tower, a blackish cloud, staring
at him eyelessly though inescapably, until at length the face
became that of a very old woman, whose eyes were the im-
probable Tyrian blue of Romulan's, or Iuletta's, and from
this awful stare, more than from the cloudy visage of the
Fiend, Mercurio could read his condemnation and his sentence as if they had been written large therein. For what,
then, had he been damned? For sin? For a guilt and religious
sensibility that his waking mind rejected? Or was it love that
had damned him?

In the shade of these curious metaphysics, the daytime
world seemed meaningless, his life also, meaningless, for all
at once the external impression of codes and practices, which
he despised and which amused him, had caught him up, revealing themselves in the long term as inexorable. So he sat
his horse, and disdained it all. The dream, the threat, the day,
Leopardo, the companion who, turning his back, plunged
toward misadventure—what did any of these items matter in
such a world, whose unpatterned and senseless and unfor-
givable tenses drew it upon him and would, ultimately, allow
no refusal.

And even as he sat there, so disdaining these things, these

unanswerable, inexorable things, it is possible that at some
nadir of his unconscious he became aware, nor perhaps for
the first time, of the clever solution of his own death.

Dimly then, like someone half-asleep and wholly uninvolved, he beheld Romulan dismount below the Basilica stair,
beheld Leopardo moving down the steps toward him in paro-
died courtesy. But did not hear what was said, nor feel it
needful.

"Mercurio," said Benevolo urgently. *"Mercurio."*

"What?"

"Will you let them fight? Leopardo will settle for no less.
Romulan's just wed, and she's the Leopard's cousin."

"It had slipped my mind."

Mercurio yawned. It was not an affectation, but that strange
convulsion of airlessness connected to malaise or anguish.
Misunderstanding, as Romulan had, Benevolo grew partly
frantic.

Gulio had trotted back to the stair and lurked there,
watching the dialogue of the two adversaries.

Leopardo waved his arms like a madman, some threat or
mock at a threat. His face was ghastly, drained—yet every
other aspect indicated wild energy.

Dust rose like a swarm.

Flavian Estemba glanced, and saw Benevolo hurtling his
little horse across the square, calling. With raised eyebrows,
Leopardo and Romulan had turned to look at who was about
what. Benevolo rode straight at them. He waved his arms just
as Leopardo had done. In a minute, one or other of the Montargos would give the marriage away. But what did that matter either? (As the boy drew nearer, the two young men
discounted him, and resumed their confrontation.)

Flavian Estemba became aware of his divorce from reality,
but could not seem to recall himself to the world of the Basilica square. An image of his enfeebled father, a ruin like the
Estemba Tower, had ludicrously intervened. Mercurio studied
his father objectively, conscious objectivity was a shield
against hurt. And then, in his turn, Mercurio remembered
Saffiro, drunkenly and exhaustedly sprawled across the inn
mattress, his black hair spilled, asleep. Suppose, not the
mattress but the street, not sleep but death. Not Saffiro but
Romulan.

Romulan stepped back as Leopardo swung his hand out to
shove at him, and Romulan noted, with sartorial silliness, that
Leopardo's sleeve was inadequately tied. The hand, deprived

of force, flapped on his chest. Romulan, pushed beyond endurance, said, "I only restrain myself for her sake. I would not sprinkle her name with your foul blood."

"But you'd part her, cleave her, clog her," said Leopardo. "Or was it some other poet she trysted with last night and—let me see—*made the sun rise a second time?*"

"You do not know my intention to her."

"Do I not? Ram and board, shipmaster."

"If you would shut your mouth, I would tell you—"

Benevolo had reached them, but was again ignored. He broke out:

"Romulan, go home."

"Yes," said Leopardo. "Good advice. Go home before I send you there in portions."

Until this instant neither, (unlike Gulio), had set hand to hilt.

Even in fury and in habit, Romulan had so far kept his head. But now it was oddly borne in upon him that Chenti, too, kept his. Chenti who was mad, and clearly never more a lunatic than now. This revelation, perceived all at once, checked Romulan, and Benevolo also—virtually in the same moment. Each stared at the sickly face of the Chenti in perplexity, and Benevolo, swinging off the grey horse and sending her aside with a mild tap, opened his mouth to speak again, when Leopardo, with a skull-like grin, hauled steel from scabbard.

The reason, which the two before him had not yet noticed, was that the selected opponent, Estemba, had also dismounted, and leaving the mare untethered, was walking toward them.

And Leopardo began, of course, to yell, to scream.

"You will not draw, sir? Afraid, sir? Content to skulk by walls, to get over into orchards, to clamber up on a girl's belly. No use for your hands but to tickle, no use for your legs but to kick. Eh, sir? Come, let me show you a new way to couple."

"I think," said Mercurio's bright, caressive voice, suddenly come close, "you are too busy."

Leopardo, aware of Estemba to the hollows of his arteries and the roots of his hair, paid no apparent attention. He advanced his sword, touching Romulan delicately on the shoulder, the breast.

"I long to fight you," Leopardo said now softly. "I long to

see the color of your blood. Is it the nice watery tint of the lily?"

Romulan put his hand to the hilt of his sword, slowly.

"At least it's blood. Not the leakage of a dog's bladder, which I shall see, and smell the stench of, when I cut *you*."

As the sword started to lift under his hand, another hand came down on top of his, cramming metal and flesh joltingly back against the scabbard. Romulan cursed at the insulting pain of a bruised palm; he had been braced for the bite of steel.

Mercurio said beside him, in a voice no longer caressive or bright but leaden, folded flat, "What are you doing? Does it all mean so little, then, you'll throw it away because a cat meows at you on the street?"

"I—" said Romulan. But he had come to his senses again very hard, as if cast from a high window. He beheld, as never before, the tiresome vapidity of all this, this clowning which could end in a grave. Romulan took his bruised hand from his sword hilt, and looked at Leopardo Chenti levelly. "There's no dispute," Romulan said. "I'm not your mirror. I apologize I led you to believe I'd duel with you. For I will not."

Leopardo snapped up his head.

He looked at Estemba, now, and Leopardo's eyes, gleaming like the sword he still poised over Romulan's breast, stayed static as the flickering blade did not. To Mercurio and not to Romulan at all, he said: "If he will not draw and match with me, I'll thrust this through his back. I'll thrust it through so he'll die choking in blood on the ground, here, by your feet and God's. Oh, believe me, sweet fletcher, sweet minstrel. I'll do it."

Mercurio said, in the flat toneless voice, "Do it, and you will get the same service from me." Hearing that voice, you would never credit he could sing a note. Hearing that voice you would think him sick to death.

"Do me the service now, then," Leopardo said.

The face under Estemba's gilded hair was the same, the eyes, gilded by their lashes, were wide and still. But there seemed no color to Mercurio suddenly, even the gilding was ashen, and on his doublet the pineapple design stood raucous as a shout. So ghosts would look. On the verge of speech, Romulan only fell silent. But that, utterly, because—not glancing at him—Flavian Estemba said to him, "Keep quiet and step away. It's me he wants and me he can have."

"*Have* you? You're too generous, my *dear*," said Leopardo. But he danced back, the sword now a glimmering wheel on the air from which spokes of water seemed to fly off. And Romulan thought randomly of the golden wheel that spun on the post by the magician's oratory, in the wild grass.

Mercurio now drew in his turn, neatly. There was a gracious economy in the gesture which suddenly faltered. For an instant Mercurio, not looking at the blade he had released, seemed to take its measure, as if he came to it for the first. Then his fingers closed intimately on the hilt of it, and the stance became warningly explicit.

Gulio, gone greenish, scampered from the edge of the stair. He turned to look up the street in the hidden direction of the Chenti Tower, then round again. He went no farther, back or forth, held fascinated and afraid.

There were only the five men in the square of the Basilica, below the steps Cornelia had tilted a mountain. The town lay all about, rich and ripe with heat and garden fruit and sickness. Nothing stirred now but the dust, the distant fountain, and one solitary banner of cloud crossing the sky above almost as imperceptibly as the sun. Five men. Leopardo exercising the sword like another limb on the bottom step, Gulio stuck as if unwillingly, in glue. Benevolo among the untethered horses, Mercurio's, Romulan's, his own, holding their reins. Romulan retreating, his face white and empty and the pulse rocking like another life trying to escape his temples. Mercurio who, blond and white and gilt, was the palest object to be seen in the square save for the Basilica itself.

There was also a sixth presence. Something else, dominant enough to be felt by each of them, as they would have felt the presence of another man. Death, perhaps. Or truth, black and uncompromising truth, for which their town of towers had been named.

Leopardo's sword had stopped wheeling now. He flexed it. He whispered without words and moved.

As he moved, Mercurio, unerring partner in the dance, moved too behind his newly measured sword. It was a nondescript step, almost casual. It took him aside from Leopardo's feint and past Leopardo's realizing sweep and up against Leopardo's open side. The Estemba blade made a small motion, like that of a sleepy snake, and came out with the smoking hiss of hot metal whose edge has been seethed in liquid.

Leopardo Chenti shrieked. Not in hurt, he had not felt it

yet, but in a kind of awful triumphant affront. A stain like that of berries or wine blushed under his arm, along his ribs. It could have been a killing stroke, but either the balance of the blade had been curiously misjudged, or it had turned, or Mercurio, about whose intention no verdict could now be given, had not aimed for murder.

"You pierce as gently as they say you do," Leopardo sang out. "All those that love you, Mercurio, and write your name on the walls. All manner of insects—"

Mercurio moved now in the old way, assuming the familiar beautiful fighter's rhythm, evading, pivoting, so that Cat's sword missed him—then springing over as if from a hinge to nail his own sword once more into Chenti's flesh—but this time blocked, cast off, evaded in turn.

Leopardo fell back, mincing, whispering. He murmured as he fought, wordless, as if demons woke in him and susurrated as they looked through his parted lips at those he slew.

A streak of blond hair, intensified by sweat, lay like a vein of dark light across Estemba's forehead. The colors seemed coming back into him. His arm rose, effortless mobile sculpture, and his blade met Chenti's in a clanging kiss.

Something unbelievable happened.

Leopardo's blade, continuing its stroke, carved down in a blur toward the ground with, slung before it, most of Mercurio's sword.

Off-balance, expecting to be caught steel on steel and to fight for the unlocking, instead flung forward on unresistant nothingness, Leopardo almost crashed against his opponent. Righting himself he propelled his whole body away and hesitated, staring. Mercurio, still as glass, moved only one arm and extended to him the blade, which Leopardo had sheared about half a foot below the hilt, with the difficulty of smiting through butter.

"A cookery sword," said Leopardo. He spoke in words, conveying a momentary breach in the fighting. "Is it pastry, or marzipan?"

"Bronze," Mercurio said. His voice sounded quite normal, even recognizable. He lifted the dregs of the weapon and looked at the hilt. "An antique blade. A sly surreptitious gift, I think for my celebrated collection. From the Vespelli Tower." Then his voice changed. It turned into something none of them translated, but which might have been laughter or a sheer and trembling rage. "A bloody keepsake. *Remember me.*" He turned sharply and slung the broken sword

across the square. It landed in the dust far away with an in-
audible, visible splash, as if in deep water.

Benevolo reacted to Flavian Estemba's face and flinched,
as if someone had kicked him in the side as he lay sleeping.

But then Mercurio, bowing his head, only murmured
courteously to Leopardo, "This is too bad, sir, to keep you
waiting about like this. Do I have your leave to borrow a
weapon from a friend?"

"Is there some reason for it?" Leopardo asked. "You'll not
take my life, I suppose, with any sword you can get?"

"One of your lives perhaps, prince pussycat."

Leopardo tilted his head again. He spoke to the slothful
banner of cloud in the sky.

"Do you heed him, Sir Christ? Whatever he says he'll not
help you. But then, I doubt you'd place your business with
an acrobat from the cities of the plain."

Mercurio's eyes ran up on him then like knives, and looking into them Leopardo shuddered.

"Borrow your sword," said Leopardo politely, and licked
his lips. With feverish comedy he completely dropped his own
sword, pretending not to know its use, and walked harmless,
hands loose at his sides. Down one of which the blood, rather
richer than the Chenti crimson doublet, stole in long unravelling threads.

Mercurio walked toward Romulan.

Romulan already had his blade concisely from the sheath.
But he too now saw Mercurio's face fully, as he had not
since that former revelation, misinterpreted, had so stung
him. This second revelation for a moment stopped him
breathing. For it was not at all to be interpreted, rightly or
wrongly. It had no parallel, exact or false, in Romulan's experience. But the colors of life had returned, the vivid hair,
the chiaroscuro of the skin. It was not the quality of a ghost
any more. Rather it was a kind of disappearance. As if the
flesh remained, untarnished and actual, while the soul was
gone.

As he hesitated, Mercurio said calmly, "Give me your
sword."

And as Romulan stared at him, his attention riveted, Leopardo ran abruptly toward them, toward Romulan's face,
Mercurio's back, and Romulan moved swiftly, unevenly, to
look instead at him. Leopardo shouted hoarsely, and with im-
measurable excitement:

"Strike the Montargo *now*, Gulio!"

So that lastly Romulan dashed his vision away from both of them to seek pretty pink Gulio, who was about to raid him from the side. And as he did so, Romulan lifted the weapon, extending it in a strong defensive grip, his weight and his brain behind it.

And in the second that Romulan saw Gulio, ten yards away, motionless, unarmed and gawping, Leopardo seized Mercurio firmly by both arms and thrust him forward and down, onto the hard held blade of Romulan's sword.

The steel passed, pure as light through crystal, straight through Flavian Estemba's body. The rib cage seemed to shift to accommodate its passage. Neither muscle nor bone nor sinew, and least of all the glowing spirit, seemed able to stop it. The point drove out ruby-red from a little below the left shoulder blade, and then retracted, or seemed to, sawing backwards as Leopardo dragged Estemba free.

He held him a moment, as he would often hold things he had destroyed, marvelling, bewildered. Leopardo smiled still, but his eyes were dull. He rested them on Romulan who stood with the red sword dropping out of his hand; and then Leopardo also let go of his burden, and walked backward, softly, through the sunlight, away from them.

As you do not, at first, believe in the promise of death, so you do not usually believe in the arrival of death, when it lies in front of you.

Romulan did not move, it was Benevolo who ran and who kneeled, and caught Mercurio against him, trying to support the golden head which lolled aside, its cheek in the dust.

Romulan did kneel then. He put out his hand, and straightened the head on Benevolo's arm and thigh. And Benevolo, already weeping, turned his own head away so his tears should not fall on Mercurio's face. Blood was running from under Mercurio's body to assuage the thirst of the dust. It ran through his clothes, and the young cousin's, through to Benevolo's skin. The blood was warm.

"Mercurio," Romulan said. It was reflexive, for, while not believing it, he still supposed Mercurio already dead.

This was not so. The lids drifted up, and stayed half-open and half-closed, the eyes peculiarly lambent, like far-off and unreachable water.

"Now I know," Mercurio said. "The bell, the gate. It seems I'm going, after all, where you sent me."

Romulan did not decipher this, could not or would not. He

discovered himself, as if he had no sensible volition, leaning forward and taking hold of Mercurio's shoulders.

Mercurio was real in his grasp. The strong musculature, the graceful hands, the arched throat (with no discernible pulse), the tasselling bullion of hair. But the silence was there to be felt, the ending, the crumbling away. Here was the known companion, the god of the revel, the dancer, the swordsman, the singer of songs, the man he had ridden over hills, through vineyards and orchards with this morning. And here, too, he was not. And all this had been evidence in his face in the minutes before the sword ran through him, plain to be read, unreadable.

"My fault, then," Romulan said. Afterward, he did not recall having said it, but knew he had said something like it for he retained the answer his words provoked.

"Not," Mercurio said. And then he paused for breath, and breathed, and said, "I'm dead of a plague." He closed his eyes then. It was probably out of a macabre decency that no one else should have, presently, to do it for him. He said: "A plague of Houses," and breathed quietly outwards, and did not breathe in again.

Benevolo continued to hold him, but Benevolo no longer turned away. He put down his face into Mercurio's hair and wept with low, desperate cries, violently shaking, so the corpse of Flavian Estemba shook with him. If it had lived, it would most surely have stretched out a hand or an arm to comfort. But such a thing is not possible to the dead. They must go away into their silences, no matter how much loud grief is left behind.

It was a woman, screaming again and again, who caused Romulan at last to get to his feet, and looking up to see her.

She stood at the top of the Basilica steps, a merchant's wife, he thought, over-dressed and bloomed with veiling, her little page behind her with her parasol, and a girl at her side with paniers ready for the Bhorgabba market. After she had screamed for a while, she grew faint, and was aided back into the building. The work had been done, however. Shutters opened on the square. Figures appeared at the edges of it. A priest, emerging now from the Basilica, peered down and then hurried away. Already some would be running to the Rocca, hammering on the gates for ducal horsemen.

Romulan noticed Leopardo also had turned to look up at the woman. As she withdrew, he commiserated. To the priest, he bowed. Blood-stained and beautiful, he was a Hellish sight. He returned his gaze to Romulan, and said, "What now?"

Benevolo made a different sound as he wept in Mercurio's hair. It was incoherent and wordless. Only in Romulan's ears did the words seem to be spoken: *Is he to live?*

Romulan bent to pick up the blood-red sword. As he straightened, a tide of his own blood, inner and contained, went over his eyes, darkening them, so he staggered for a moment and, not meaning to, caught the shoulder of the dead to steady himself. The body of Mercurio had begun, already, subtly to change. It no longer had the feel, that shoulder in its silk, of anything which could lend support.

Holding the sword point down in the dust, Romulan began to walk toward Leopardo. As he did so, the other, Gulio, fled with a shriek, bolting away toward the safety of Chenti's vertical stones.

But Leopardo, his livid face seeming to burn, awaited Romulan with every appurtenance of civility, his own sword lightly held in one palm and gently at rest across the other.

Romulan reached him and raised his blade. He offered a very professional feint, followed by a slanting sidelong cut. Leopardo's sword woke in his hand, and stalled the stroke. The two blades formed a random silver cross, spitting and slithering free.

(Romulan saw Mercurio at the center of the Chenti feast, singing, all eyes upon him, faultless and excellent, at ease as if alone in some private chamber.)

Leopardo's sword bit low and Romulan sprang away from it, crouched as he came down, as he had been shown to do by Mercurio, and trickled his blade under Leopardo's guard—almost, but not quite, catching him. They dropped away like flung vessels, then plunged together again. And again the steel rang barrenly, and in a haze of sparks.

(He saw Mercurio seated on the table in the Bhorga, inventing flawless stanzas with flawless obscene rhymes, while the room clattered with laughter and slapped itself for joy. He saw Mercurio on a holy day, walking behind his father, draped in snow and brass, his nobility a sudden amazement. That had been two years ago.)

Leopardo kicked one of his legs from under him. Romulan, rather than fall, threw himself sideways and lurched upward even as his knee touched the ground. He stayed Leopardo's sword, this time, with arm upraised as he surged

desperately from the dust. And found the Chenti's left hand,
unemployed before, had suddenly a dagger in it. Romulan
angled his body, while fisting the fingers with the smaller
blade away and scraping out from under the longer one. As
they disengaged, he spat in Leopardo's face.

(The first time he ever saw Mercurio, the latter had been
hanging upside down from a wayside fruit tree. Flavian Estemba, seventeen then, perhaps. Romulan, a haughty bystander, black-haired and blackly scowling, fresh from some
war with his father. The fool in the tree was but another of
the day's irritants, yet, intrigued despite himself, he waited
with two or three others, to behold the fool drop on his face.
But the fool dislodged himself, spun and landed upright, quite
in command, his hands filled by plums. One of which, seeing
two immensely blue, widely open eyes on him, he had thrown
to Romulan. Romulan snatched the plum out of the air as it
went by. The friendship, it seemed, came as simply. But
maybe not so simply for Mercurio, who every day of his life
and night of his solitude thereafter had dwelled as two persons in one skin. From the commencement, Mercurio had
owned his personal darkness. He protected his charge, therefore, not only from others, but scrupulously from himself.)

Romulan knew nothing of this, or did not know it with
his mind, even now. He saw images, but asked no questions
of them. He revisited the countless warrens of the Bhorga,
the room in the Estemba Tower with its arcane swords and
the picture of the oliphant. He saw the streets, the broad
marble-ice chambers of great Houses. Mercurio was in each,
suitable and couth in whatever altitude, high or low. Romulan saw stars colliding, blowing out, and felt the arm which
held him. He heard Mercurio say: "It seems I'm going, after
all, where you sent me."

Leopardo had dallied away, wiping his cheek on his inac-
curately tied sleeve. He drew a line of fire over the sky with
the sword as he did so. Romulan's eyes followed it irresistibly, and almost missed the incoming thrust—

("Now," Mercurio said, "kill me for insulting your precious House.")

—Which tore through the fabric of his wedding clothes.
Romulan riposted, this time aiming for the dagger. But the
thing was gone, plucked from range, and the Cat leapt with
it, grinning.

("My Lady Death, we are before you.")

Romulan pursued him. His arm was heavier now. Leo-

pardo, who bled, seemed to have grown lighter, made
weightless and fey by the catharsis of mortal liquors. As Romulan turned, clapping sword once more to sword, he beheld
faces streaming by. A small crowd had blossomed by the alleyway that led down into the Bhorgabba. How long before
the Duca sent his men?

("There has been an earthquake all along the road," Mercurio said. "We've been nearly shaken to pieces by the thudding hearts of the bride and groom.")

Iuletta. Romulan, his wrist singed by the maniac's sword,
swung back and felt the earth crack under him. *Iuletta*.

"Do you recall the nightingale?" she said to him. Her hair
fell soft as scented water across his cheeks as he clung to her,
his head on her breast, and wept.)

The swords struck each other, slewed, came away. Romulan
staggered as he had when he rose from Mercurio's side. And
Chenti crowed, mocking him. All life, now, was the square.
The taste of life was dust and bitter sunlight. The walls of
life were watching avid faces.

("A single kiss from your wife?" Mercurio said. He lifted
his head from her lips, and was thrust forward to the length
of the hard held sword until it came from his back. "I am going where you sent me.")

Romulan cried out. The cry sounded loudly to him, in fact
it was muted, nearly restrained. Gasping, and blinded by the
tears that burst now from his eyes, seeming to shatter them,
he stumbled, groaned, clutched at air, at reason, and relinquished them.

Then, because he could not see him, he ran at Leopardo
blind. And, because he did not care what Leopardo might
bring against him now, knife or fist or sword, he beat through
the Chenti's guard, no longer with finesse or wisdom or any
of the swordsman's trained and beautiful symmetry—which
Mercurio had so rigorously taught him—but hammering,
hacking, clawing, and screaming, a long soulless masculine
breaking scream of pain and hunger.

Leopardo had paved the road to this. If he had wished to
receive death at the end of it was uncertain, but now for sure
he faced death, and he knew it. Whatever had been his urge,
his motivation, the horror of the thrashing sword, mindless
and already basted in another's blood, appalled him. Romulan's tears struck his cheek as he gave ground. Leopardo
snarled, blocking off the butcher's blows automatically but
with an increasing weakness. Romulan sought to kill him, de-

termined to kill him. Romulan, now, would rip his way through wood, through metal and through fire to come at him. This Leopardo understood. A man unmoved by such a passion, particularly one who lost blood for every feint and weave and twist he made, could not long resist this advance. While men who fought as Romulan now fought would fight on with their death-wound already deeply written in their flesh. They would tear, if the sword were gone, with hands and teeth. They would trample and gouge and rend, until only the silence under them released them from the spell of blood-lust. This, also, Leopardo understood. And Romulan, though he did not, had become the proof that such things were possible.

Slammed back against the Basilica steps, Leopardo lost footing suddenly. Now, he, too, stumbled. The dagger left him, skittered from his reach, and barely saving himself, his skill and his fighter's appetite failed him for the first time, and utterly. It was not quite fear, not quite anything that was namable, that made the Leopard in that moment turn and run. As he did so, trailing his sword, up the incline of the street that led by the trees, the colonnades, to the Chenti Tower, he laughed raucously, and felt the blood erupt from his side. His legs, as when he had courted the woman who had brought him to this hour, were nerveless. Each racing step threatened to bring him down under the blade that rushed blue and black and ceaselessly calling, a cry like a starving beast's, behind him.

No one was in the way of this side of the square. The lawns of the college and Basilica Library swirled past. Already, already, the slope of the home tower was visible, with its golden Cat upon the pinnacle.

Leopardo ran. His eyes were peeled open, and his mouth. He still laughed, when he found the breath for it.

He had reached, under the heavy boughs, the side-door that led into the orchard, when Romulan caught him.

The sword whipped across Leopardo's back, shearing through everything but solid bone. He sprawled on his face, his lips blotted by dust, his own sword gone. And there, he attempted to crawl away, and a hand came and dragged him over. He lay on his wounded spine then, and on the carpet of his blood, gazing up. Romulan's face, a thing of incredible ugliness in its physical jewelry, swam and roiled against the canopied trees. Otherwise there was only the sun-splashed sword, lifted, about to come down. Leopardo swallowed dust and salt blood, and said quickly, "Iulet—I lessoned her, too. Thank me? Against a wall, beneath a bush. I had her in her juices before you—" And stopped as the sword broke in the shell of his throat.

The possession was ended; the hunger had been fed.

Romulan let go of the sword a second time, not concerned with it anymore. Turning, he set his hand against the wall, and dimly recollected this was *her* wall, and this the orchard of her kindred, through which he had been hunted into her arms. He walked a short distance beside it, and then dropped to his knees, the corpse of what he had killed not far behind him. The wall, hot from the sun, was so ordinary. It cradled his shoulder and balanced him against itself kindly. The leaves crisped over each other. His weeping now was like Benevolo's, so strong it seemed to disintegrate him. He could scarcely breathe for weeping, certainly could not think for it. In some strange way, even the cause was lost.

And over the wall, she was. He could have gone to her. She would have held him, more sweetly than the wall, her hair, her voice, more subtle than the leaves. In all the world, there was only Iulétta now who could rescue him. And yet, even so soon he knew, he would never see her again.

Eventually, the great growing noise in the square below reached him, and then reached through to him. He got up then, slowly, and as he did so, the bell of the campanile began to toll, dulled iron strokes, and each passed through him and after it another passed.

When, in their expected turn, he heard fierce hoofbeats on the cobbles, he waited, mastering himself as best he could, which was no man's best, and finally looked up to see the gold and scarlet of the Duca, the drawn blades and austere faces come to take him, and stood there witlessly because rather than these, Benevolo was on the street below the Tower of the Chentis. Benevolo mounted on his grey horse, the black Montargo gelding pulled with them by its reins.

"Romulan?" White-faced Benevolo, the first to smash, had now commanded himself as Romulan, now, could not.

"What?" Romulan said.

"The Duke is in the square, and the Estembas have been sent for. Chesarius took his body from me," said Benevolo. He frowned, clenching his face and next his fists to keep from crying again. "Here's your horse. Get from the town. The fools—" he stopped and stared at Romulan in a sort of terror. "They think you killed Mercurio. They would not listen to me."

"I killed him? Yes—"

"No. *No*, Romulan. That bitch on the stair—she saw your sword had red on it, and Leopardo's none, and Mercurio—" Benevolo suddenly arched his back, flung up his head and shouted at the sky a chain of blasphemies, clear as the notes of a bird, clear as when he had sung at the feast the descant to Mercurio's song.

(Who can tell where love will lead us—I know. The bell, the gate. It seems, after all, I shall be going where you sent me.)

The bell of the campanile ground out Benevolo's voice. Benevolo looked down again.

"Take the horse," he said.

Romulan turned and put his face against the wall, and his hands against his face to hold the two substances, flesh and stone, together. Just so had Leopardo lain against the carving of the Basilica, if Romulan had seen it.

Benevolo looked aside and saw Leopardo's corpse under the sprinkled shadow of the orchard trees. At length one noted the marks of him were not all shadows. Benevolo smiled, though partly the sight made him wish to vomit. Then, turning back, Benevolo leaned from his horse, took Romulan's long hair in his hand and wrenched at it. The head was forced back from the shelter of the wall, excruciatingly, cursing, not desiring to be separated.

"He did not want you dead," Benevolo said, "and that was how he came to die. So live, now, Montargo. *Live.* Or it was for nothing."

"Live to love," Romulan said.

Weeping still, he went from the wall and pulled himself, with a helpless discounting grace, on to the horse, and sat there, his head hanging.

"Where, where on God's earth am I to go?"

Benevolo studied his reins.

"Do you ask me? I'll tell you, then. Go to the one above and beyond the law. The crazy priest in the field."

Below in the square, the hubbub gathered itself. They had forgotten the plague. Conceivably the congregation of so many men would spread it. Everything, perhaps, was to be overturned.

"Laurus," Romulan said.

"He, if so you call him. Go on, for the love of Jesus. *Go.* I'll get word to Valentius."

Romulan did not answer. He huddled on the horse. He sobbed now, his head in his hands, loudly and hoarsely, hating the sounds he made.

"You," Benevolo suddenly said. "So much grief. But what did you ever give him, save your steel through his heart?" And heard the sobbing choke on itself, and stop. The blue eyes, like two raw sapphires in the reddened rims, came up and struck on his. Benevolo whispered, "But he asked you for nothing, did he? Go, Romulan. Go to the priest. I'll tell Valentius and no other where you'll be found."

The bell tolled.

Romulan, straightening suddenly, wheeled the horse. Mount and rider galloped away and Benevolo ceased to watch them. Instead, he watched Leopardo's corpse, watched and watched it, as if it might try to rise. The sword, Romulan's, which lay beside the ill-tied sleeve, Benevolo did not see.

PART THREE:

The Bell

FIFTEEN

Since the shutters had been opened, the sunlight was dippered upon the polished mirror and on the polished face reflected in it. One of Electra's maids, who feared her, dusted the face with powdered rice scented with the rind of oranges. Another, who feared her almost equally, brushed down and down the rope of hair, a spillage like black oil, and began to plait, to elevate and to pin with garnets, and next to torture out, with hot tongs spiced by ambergris, three spirals before each ear.

In Electra's face no change was visible. In the body, the changes had shrunk and faded swiftly, altering as inevitably as the moon altered, from the full to the narrow crescent. Now, nothing gave her away. Her hands were frigid, her eyes hard. Only the gown she had elected to wear, a costly robe of oriental silk, crimson merely where one could find it under the dragonflies of lilac and golden thread, was oddly festive. But then, her husband would return this evening. It might be a mark of her respect for him, to dress in this exquisite gift he had given her, years before. The present was allotted publicly, at a feast in the hall below. Whimsicality had again prevailed. The material was laid between boards of cedar-wood, like a book, which had perfumed it as the incense had also perfumed it in which it had been steeped, bolts of fabric stacked for weeks in the smoke of burners of musk and frankincense in some shed of the spice-lands. This assemblage had been brought to her by masked and spangled demi-gods with wings, to the sound of pipes, amid a deluge of roses. The guests had applauded. Later that night, Lord Chenti had mounted her for the last time, the very last. The gown was made and put away, worn on a handful of occasions, when he had demanded it. By the night of the betrothal feast, Chenti had forgotten it entirely.

Now as she rose, a bone knife in a sheath of colors, glitters and faded, dully dazzling aromas, she heard the bell begin to toll from the campanile, not the ninth hour of the morning, but the advent of death.

The two maids, one after the other, crossed themselves. Their eyes were large, for death was a dreadful commonplace, and only a truly dreadful death, notable and of significance, was so sounded for.

Electra Chenti did not mark herself with the cross.

She said, "Someone is to be buried today?"

"No, my donna. No one."

"Then someone," said Electra, "is newly dead."

The maid who had spoken moved to the open window. She stood there, not looking out, but listening. Her face grew very still.

"There's shouting somewhere, lady. From the Basilica square, I think."

The other maid, the powder bowl in her hands, paled to rival the rice.

"Someone slain," she said. "Oh God grant mercy."

A month before, two of Suvio's servants had mortally stabbed her brother. The bell had not rung for Gianotto, yet her brush with the shadow was near. She began to cry, hiding herself from Electra.

The three women in the room did not otherwise move for some moments, and then the girl at the window said, "I hear horses." And then again, after a little while, "I think the shouting is closer. Madama, shall I send one to ask what has happened?"

"Yes," Electra said, her small voice like a needle.

The two girls both ran gladly out and left her, and she turned to look at the opened bed beneath its thunderous canopy. *Listen for a crash like cannon,* he had said to her. She had lain and watched him leave her, knowing he must and would come back.

She did not move again for some minutes, but stood there, attendant. She heard the billowing noise the crowd made now, over and about the endless groan of the bell. Next she heard a banging of doors and a muffled shouting below her, in the house. For some reason then, briefly, her thought turned to Iuletta. Electra's daughter, arriving whey-faced and fragile after her unseemly absence, beside a Cornelia flushed and puffing with anxiety, had been sent to her chamber and ordered to remain there. Cornelia's account then taken—the priest's holy benison delaying them, the night spent in the or-

atory in a cell kept for visitors, Electra had accepted as tire-
somely adequate. Nevertheless, she berated the woman, in
three or four succinct and vicious verbal carvings, which in-
cidentally stripped from the nurse most of her self-esteem and
left her puffing anew in necessarily inexpressible rage, and a
frustration near to tears. Iuletta's personal chastisement was
to be saved for sunset, when the threat of the father's blood-
shot wrath might also be added. This cruelty was Electra's ef-
ficiency rather than her pleasure. The lamb might not stray,
so the law of this House ran, and so she would keep it. Thus
Electra had been trained. That she herself had broken free of
all contemporary morality in one long night, with the golden
body of Leopardo's youth nailed to her own, made the surface of her ethic, inevitably, the more rigid.

But as the notion of her daughter melted away, Electra
felt, as it were, the edge of a knife against her nerves. She
could not have said what it was, she had seldom debated with
herself. Nor did she, even in the teeth of it, admit her premonition. Yet she turned again sharply, the oriental silk sizzling
over the floor, and as she did so a terrible wail shocked
through the house, a noise so horrible and so real that half
the Chenti dogs began to bark and howl.

Across Electra's face, then, something sprang. It was a wild
and unconscionable anger.

Even as she stepped toward the antechamber and the outer
door, hands beat on the panels and she heard the female
voices summoning her.

When she appeared the woman fell back, sobbing in alarm
and distress, not daring to speak to her, and not needing to.
At last, the words came from elsewhere, borne up the staircase in shrieks, and in a sort of mortal terror that had nothing to do with sorrow: "Leopardo Chenti is dead!"

Flat-backed, her ringed hands clasped under her high bodice, unspeaking, unquestioning, Electra descended through the
Tower. She came, at every lobby and landing and passage-
way into a storm of disturbance and noise that fell dumb at
her advance. And then she came into the heart of the disturbance, which also fell dumb, and stole aside to let her see.

They had brought him, like a feast, into the banquet-hall.

He lay on a heap of cloaks, over the mosaic chariot of
Pluto, the god of death, so inadvertently apposite was their
placing of him.

A cloak had also been flung across his body, covering him
from the calves to the lips.

Electra stopped. Clearly, like a handful of coins striking the floor, she said,

"Remove the cloak."

A servant at her elbow said, "Madama, he's sorely hacked. Best not to look at him before someone has seen to it."

A few then began to report to her the sequence of events, as they knew them. Gulio Chenti, it appeared, had rushed into the house not long before. His information, imparted to the houseguards at the door—that Leopardo was embattled—brought slight response. Gulio was integral but inconsequent to the Tower, and the Cat's reputation well known, both as a brawler and as a swordsman. Lazy in Lord Chenti's absence, the guard had no mind to stir and to be trounced by the antic nephew for their pains. Gulio had run then in search of other cousins, but they had gone hunting in a pack, no one was there to help him. He himself had no wish to return to the square. He had seen enough and hysterically foretold the rest, and so he ran lastly to his chamber and sat there, eating quantities of sweetmeats from a dish, and nervously sniveling.

The guard at the garden door, though he did not admit it, had been asleep under a pomegranate tree. He was perhaps thirty feet from Leopardo when he was cut down, though separated by bushes, and a wall, and all the hills of unconsciousness. What ultimately roused the man was a vague argument that seemed in progress in the alley under the wall. He made no sense of it, but coming alert, he had diligently resumed his proper post. A set of hooves rode off while he was doing this, and not long after, another set. He was well aware of the tolling bell and the shouting from the Basilica by then, and had duly crossed himself. But it was curiosity that at last impelled him to open the door and peer out. So he saw the broken doll in the alley, crimson clothing, crimson wounds, a pool of blood mingling in the pool of pale orange hair. The guard began to shout. When others came, they found also the sword, under its rank red of whippy long-bladed steel, with a ship, oared and sailed, incised both in hilt and blade.

"Remove the cloak," Electra said again.

After a moment, cautiously, someone obeyed.

There was another noise in the hall, swiftly smothered. They looked to see what Electra would do. That she and her nephew had disliked each other was well known, nor was Leopardo in scarcely any instance liked, only feared, and in

some cases worshipped, as a god who required bloody sacrifice. Save now he was his own. And Lady Chenti, whose
veins were plainly filled by water cool enough for eels to
swim in, what would she do? For hate him if she had, the
boy was still her closest natural kin, the nearest she had
gotten to the possession of a son.

Electra moved forward. She neither caught her breath nor
exclaimed. She gave no evidence of being on the verge of
tears or swooning. Like adamant she stared down at him, and
some were certain they beheld her abhorrence of him now,
naked as swords in her gaze, as if she might kill him all over
again.

His eyes were open but ungleaming, dull as fish scales dry-
ing in the sun. His lips were parted also, but only a little way,
and from the left corner of his lips one black thread of blood
had issued. His throat was hideous, the sliced and withering
membrane and debris of sinews and discoloring flesh wel-
tered in blood. Blood bearded his doublet, overwhelming the
other, slighter wound he had taken in the side. The wound in
his back was concealed. All this she looked at, all this she
comprehended. She saw, too, the blood in his hair, and his
amber skin, disclosed by blood and torn brocade. She saw the
expression of his face which, though gradually sinking in the
general sluggishness of death, yet retained for now its elements of terror, violence and ghastly mockery. While on his
right cheekbone she saw the tiny healing scratch where her
ring had cut him, one further wound.

What would she do? They did not know. They did not
know she would surprise them.

Electra Chanti, whose flesh was ice and whose ichors were
water, threw herself to her knees. Her thin fingers ripped and
tore the flimsy fabric of her costly gown, so in a shattered
tinsel of dragonflies she leaned above him, tearing now at her
hair, her cheeks. Her mouth was a square rictus, like that of
an antique tragic mask, the kind sometimes set into walls to
pour fountains. Electra's distorted mouth poured loud hoarse
cries that burst against the walls of gold and wood and pictures and weapons, and were cast away into the rafters overhead where once the frightened doves of Venus had perched.
Amid the streamers of her falling hair, she wordlessly, ceaselessly railed. She was watched with horror, yet some noticed
that while her mouth screamed, the rest of her face stayed
cold, stayed to hate him, cursing him with its rational stone

eyes as she rocked, a madwoman, above his body. It was doubtful if any of them, her husband's retainers, his guards, her own abject retinue, could divine the particular agony that was the root of her display. For this was not the outcry of love, but of one at last, and utterly, and forever, cheated.

A few minutes after her confinement in the room of pink-painted trees, a cordial had been brought to Iuletta's door. Cornelia, greatly bothered for her young bride, her kitten, properly deflowered but now with all the day to linger and fret, had had prepared a drink—honey, cloves, wine, the pulped sweetness of peaches—in the heart of which lay one dark dose of poppy juice. While Cornelia faced Electra's barbed tongue strangely with a bombastic silence, a comically and pathetically cringing ebullience firmly stoppered like effervescence in a bottle, Iuletta had taken the cordial and drunk it for its pleasant taste. Then, straying to her slender maiden's bed no longer suitable for flesh or spirit, she lay down there. A while she stared at the canopy with its flowers and cats. She played with one of the little jeweled books, a poem of Phoebus Apollo's hapless son, Phaethon. The representation of Phaethon had somewhat evoked Romulan for her, for blue-eyed and black hair, in ornate and only mildly Grechian garments of sky-blue, he whipped the golden horses of the sun toward the west, heedless as all the exotic creatures of the Zodiac rushed in alarm from his path, and the world, catching alight, smoked under him.

So she, Romulan's world, had flamed. Nor had she, in the bawdy tradition of the bride, slept on her marriage night. Between the several meetings of their desire, tumbled and consumed in the joy of her lover, while he slipped soundlessly asleep in her arms, she, in another lonelier ecstasy of finding and possession clasped and caressed him, wept for her love of him, could not slumber, would not waste a second of the precious night when, awake, she might know him with her. So, the drugged drink, in a short space, dislodged her awareness. She fell asleep with Phaethon and the galloping steeds, they with their feet of fire, he with feet of clay, under her hand. The coming of horror and clamor into the Tower did not rouse her, not even the howling of her mother in the banquet hall. All this, Iuletta was spared.

But in the end it was her very savior, Cornelia, coming heavily as wet washing, soaked in tears to her door, who ended the pace of sleep and mind.

The nurse had little subtlety, for in her sphere it could avail nothing. Her husband was long dead, her living daughter a whore, and herself a servant in an opulent House that allowed her rights mostly out of inertia. These things were facts; they were not subtle. And all the delights of Cornelia's life, simple, often brutal things, old couplings, more recent fumblings, current filthy jests, good food, red wine, a soft mattress to bed on (even if now alone), in these she took a grateful happiness, knowing all she liked was a sin, and begging pardon for it dutifully at frequent intervals, her only provision against the toils of Purgatory and the coals of Hell. Even though, in her heart's soul, she doubtless believed she would not be forgiven. For so life was, and so death would most probably be, another fact, harsh and definite. And maybe, in Hell's very jaw, between roastings Cornelia, who would wrest her pleasures where she might, would tell jokes and admire the legs of the male victims, to her eternal, damnable, admirable credit.

One other happiness she had, however, which could not be a sin: her domineering love of Iulet. The love was quite selfish, for through it Cornelia gained her only taste of temporal power, and through it too Cornelia lived again her youth. These things the nurse had not fathomed, nor needed to. She loved, and she provided love. There had been no sin, till now. Now when she had allowed, with ready connivance, the innocent girl to bind herself to a murderer.

Cornelia, having shut the door of the bedchamber, came to Iuletta and called her, and next laid on heavy ungentle hands, not meaning to be rough, and full of compassion. So Iuletta woke startled, her heart already racing, and met the raining eyes and the mouth loose with grief, and herself screamed: "Nurse! What has happened? Oh my love, my love—is he dead?"

"You mean your husband, young Montargo. He's not dead," said Cornelia. "Better he were, better he had died before ever you saw him."

"He lives?" Iuletta's eyes were full of flames, not tears. "Why then weep? Why then speak such abominable things?"

"He is damned. He's cursed. He'll die for what he's done, and well-deserved."

Iuletta gave a shriek thinner than the note of a reed. Her hands rose as if to rip and rend, and Cornelia lumbered away. Covering her face and its wetness with a square of pink linen, she moaned.

"How dare you wallow there like a great stranded whale?" Iuletta cried, pitiless in terror. "Tell me what he has done."

And so, through moans and linen, Cornelia told. The story was only one of many that were circling, ridiculous, insane, and therefore carrying in its wake such intimations of chaos that all Iuletta's life seemed to perish within her.

"Your Romulan quarreled with his friend, that fair honest lovely young man, Flavian Estemba, and drawing his sword, your Romulan ran him through. And all that fine body wasted. And then, not content, Montargo picks up the quarrel with your cousin, with our Leopardo, the jewel of the Chenti Tower. And how he does it I know not, the Leopard being the Prince of Swords, but your husband kills him. Kills! Hacks him in bits! I saw the remains. God save us all, horrible to see. So much blood. I never would have known a man had so much blood in him to spill. Leopardo, that noble excellent creature, the hope of this House. All dead, all bloody. And this your husband did. You wedded a lunatic. You bedded a fiend. And I am to blame."

Iuletta sat like a statue, her blue marble eyes quite blind, and she said, "Is he taken?"

"No. He ran, as a dog will run. The Duke's men search him up and down. He will have flown from Verensa."

Iulet whispered something. The nurse heard her. It was a prayer of thanks.

"For shame," said Cornelia. But she came back to her charge and said, "It's a tragedy. But a few hours his wife—to bring you this sorrow. He must be—is—mad."

A pale blue lightning ran through Iuletta's eyes. She saw, but only her future.

"He cannot claim me now," she cried out suddenly. "What will become of me?"

"Poor rose, poor baby," cried Cornelia in turn, and reached to comfort her. But the person on the bed, grey-white as ash, in mood between a panic-stricken child and a demon, pushed the paddling hands aside.

"Go away," said Iuletta. "Leave me, go."

"You fear I'll betray you?" Cornelia said. "I'll catch those maids of yours and see they keep their mouths shut, too. You must say nothing of what has been done. You must forget this marriage, which has ruined us."

"There were other witnesses," Iuletta said, but absently. Her mind was not on betrayal or its implication. Her mind was nowhere, dashed through space like a falling stone.

"God aid us! A Montargo witness, the blue fool with the yellow nag. And the boy Benevolo, who is also an Estemba. And the Duca's very brother—Ah! Maria protect harmless women led into the garden of briers by the deeds of men."

"He will send word to me," Iuletta said. Her voice was far away, it too fell through space.

"Who? The wretch of a murderer? He will be well-gone and you'll get no word. Men are our masters, child. They break us where they cannot bend. Dear Jesus—your father—"

"He will send word to me," repeated Iulet. "He will not abandon me."

"Even if he would, how might he? If the Duke's men take him, he's dead."

Iuletta left the bed. The jeweled book, unheeded, dropped to the ground. Iuletta walked to the window of colored glass. Blood and roses, the sunlight came in through the panes, touching her face with a color it did not have.

"And you've lain with him, may be with child," said Cornelia. She broke into orisons, and then abruptly ceased. Seizing facts by their throats she, who had learned to make the best of very little and sometimes of nothing at all, announced, "But we're safe. You are to marry Belmorio. That will cover all."

At the window, Iuletta caught her breath. Falling, she had now struck the earth. The blow of reality dazed her. Automatically she said, "Let me alone. I must be alone."

Cornelia held her side, out of breath with events as if with running.

"You'll do nothing unwise to yourself?"

Not comprehending, the black hair was shaken with the sculptured head. Like the child she was, fallen hard as she had, she was as yet too stunned to lament.

"Your mother's gone mad with sorrow," said Cornelia. "A wonder you did not hear her shrieks. Horrible to listen to." In the center of this evil, something of its drama now began to support Cornelia. "And the poor young man, so thick with blood."

"*Go!*" Iuletta shouted, all her fingers, one still ill-advisedly clad in its marriage ring, spread on the window. "Let me alone for the love and pity of Christ."

Cornelia, her eyes flooding once again, suffering rejection, assured at last of her loss, crept like a huge pink mouse from the chamber.

Through the corridor and into the lobby Cornelia crept, and in the lobby, by the stair that led to the eastern courtyard with its old copper cats and fountains, Cornelia herself became a fountain. Her grief, unbuoyed by drama after all, brought her presently to sit on a carved bench. Here, holding the remnant of her kerchief, pink string like seaweed, before her, she cried in earnest, her sadness stretching them beyond today's despair into her dark yesterday, into her cold tomorrow. She wept for all of them, and for herself, and scarcely knew it.

And here, in this way, her page Pieto found her. Not that he had been looking for her, the fat monster he served and mocked at, and who boxed his ears, and about whom he concocted rude rhymes. Rather, threatened by the nightmare whirlpool the Chenti Tower had suddenly become at the tolling of the bell, Pieto had been seeking refuge.

Happening on my Donna Pudding then, Pieto halted, and stared. He had never thought of it but, however reviled, she was one of the mainstays of his world. To see the mainstay crack and totter filled him with fear and doubt.

Clutching her seaweed, drowned in her sea of salt water, Cornelia became aware of an insistent tugging at her sleeve. Looking up at last, she saw the child at her side, his own face now coursed by frantic tears, and his voice saying over and over, "Donna Cornelia, please stop crying, please stop, please, please—" and in another moment he had dived into her arms like a minnow, and clung to her. And, "There now, hush now," Cornelia said, through her unending tears. And so they clung together and wept as one.

The Duca, who had begun in a fury, had ended in silence. The small but well-appointed chamber in the Chitadella, with its murals of the wise and foolish virgins, its fine window-glass and its scarlet velvet chairs with knuckles and knees of gold and the linked sigil Rings worked in gold on their backs, had unfortunately overlooked many scenes of familial discord. This, less vitriolic than others, was also less easily dispatched. The fundamental stumbling block had been that the Duke, who did not grieve, vociferously acted grief, the cause of the act his genuine rage at the death of close kindred to the Ducal House. Chesarius' grief, on the other hand, was unevidenced yet profound.

Having listened to a tirade against both the Chenti and the

Montargo Towers, and the unqualified verdict of Romulan Montargo as the murderer of Flavian Estemba, Chesarius had finally found room to broach his own views, and next the formula of his previous evening's business. His brother, a black-browed barrel of a man, capable equally of cunning and of precipitation, listened in his turn. The Duke was some fifteen years the elder. But, at his most considered and cerebral, Chesarius was the more mature.

"So, you are in this midden up to your brows?" snapped the Duke at length. "A secret wedding. By pagan Jupiter. What possessed you?"

"I was asked to act witness by Mercurio. Who, as you stress, my lord, is near kin to us both. Was near kin. It might have ended well enough, if 'Pardo Chenti had not been abroad."

"That Hellspawn. Always the master of misrule. He came home here with half Padova in cry behind him."

"No doubt, sir. But you will see, I think, that Romulan Montargo is unlikely to step sweet from his marriage night to kill without reason the girl's very cousin on the streets of the Higher Town. Nor to run a blade through Mercurio, who was his friend in this, as in everything else. Those two held no feud between them."

"You credit the boy's story, then?"

"Benevolo D'Estemba? Yes."

"But he has the Montargo blood, has he not? He'd lie for Romulan's sake."

"Not if Romulan had harmed Mercurio, he'd not. Flavian was his god. No, it's a vile tale, and vile enough to match the whims of Leopardo Chenti, to thrust a man, unarmed, on the sword of his friend."

"The other has a different song."

"Gulio? He ran away."

"To fetch help, at Leopardo's request, Romulan being incensed and crazy."

"Oh, my lord brother," said Chesarius, "do you visualize Leopardo squealing for help in a duel?"

"He, too, ran for home. They found him at the orchard gate, I hear," said the Duca, "cut up like one of the fruits for stewing."

"His crime was foul, and at the end he knew he'd get no mercy. Having killed him, and avenged us all, Romulan rode for his life, knowing how the matter would appear."

"What will his hussy do now? She can hardly expect her lover to go calling after this. Montargo and Chenti will be at feud."

"Unless Lord Chenti can be persuaded of the truth." Chesarius looked calmly at his brother. "Chenti had no love for his nephew. Probably, he had some fears for himself with such a devil in the house. I think he could be bought."

"And who will buy him?" the Duke demanded.

"I, if you allow me."

"Ah? You'd do so much for Romulan Montargo? I'll begin to suppose you have Flavian's tastes in friends. Or are you hot for the young wife, this Gulia."

"Iuletta. I'm troubled by her misfortune, yes. And by the knowledge that, if this breach goes unhealed, she may be forced, unlawfully, to marry Troian Belmorio, when already wed to another."

"I see where we drift," said the Duke. "You mean she may lack courage to admit her secret."

"She may. And if she does, at a risk to my immortal soul, I'll not be the one to unmask her."

"Unmasking, eh? And where, Chesarius, is Romulan masking himself?"

"I have no knowledge, my lord."

"But some happy guesswork, perhaps. Let that go. I myself am unanxious for trouble. God has already sent me another plague to deal with. I need no more. If Leopardo Chenti was the cause of our kin Estemba's death, then he's payed the required price for it, and we have Romulan Montargo to thank for the safeguarding of our honor. That is one way, and works only if the Chentis will lie quiet. In which case I'm willing to cajole and you are willing to pay. (What will they want, do you think? Land, I hazard.) The story can then be breezed about till Sana Verensa swallows it. At which time we'll invite Montargo home, and he can claim his mistress."

"My own hope, sir. I thank you."

"Yet, little brother, there is the other road. I want no skirmish either between the Rocca and that choleric tribe of Gettapuletta cats. If they refuse to take their bribe, if they make any public noise, my hand is forced. Then the story is that Romulan slew both their kin and ours, turning on bystander and friend alike, as a mad dog will. And in that chance, we must hunt the Montargo down, and when we have him, rather than circle his neck with the pale hands of his lady, it will be done with the noose of the garotta. His death releases, by the by, your Gulietta from her inconvenient vows. And your precious snowy soul, Chesarius, remains unspotted."

SIXTEEN

The second time he came to the place, it was the same, yet altered. The third time it was not even the same.

Having ridden fast, and sightless, through town and through gate, and down the road and among the dust, and off the road and amid the poppies and the grass and the pines, suddenly he came to the spot where the oratory would stand and memory checked him, and he reined in the horse. And saw before him only the parasols of the trees, and the white grass where the grasshoppers drizzled in the heat. The oratory was gone.

Romulan sat and stared, and then he dismounted from the gelding, shaking, and leaned against it, shaking still.

"Mother of God," he said, and seemed to feel the earth opening before him. Here he had fled for sanctuary, and here—did not exist.

And then, something blew, something rippled, like water. Arrested, puzzled, awed even in the midst of his life's tumult, Romulan went forward, tardily, leading the horse. A curious eccentric disguise had been affected by the genius of the magus. Great banners of cloth had been attached in some way to the top of the oratory's diptych, and permitted to float down across the building's face. Bluish above, like the sky, pallid below, like the grass, and all over flecked and banded by shadings that suggested the burden of trees, the banners blended the retreat into the land, and hid it. Indeed, to one who did not know and drew no closer, it would most probably have remained invisible.

Even as he saw this, his foot struck the post in the ground with the sun-wheel fixed on it. Romulan looked down, but the wheel did not revolve. He remembered Leopardo's whirling sword, which had reminded him of this very thing, and a flat dull nausea opened in his body, from the groin to the throat. But it passed, and he went on.

He was almost at the area where the door must be, already

reaching out to come at it through the coarse material of the camouflage, when the trick voice thundered at him.

"Who approaches?"

"Romulan Montargo," he said, fumbling, finding the door, which this time opened slowly.

"Enter," the voice said.

He left the horse, untethered, stupidly forgetting it, and went in through the clinging door curtain.

The oratory was bare as ever, but for the picked bone of Christ on his wooden crucifix. Outside the heat, within the chill of the stone. Romulan began to shiver as he walked to the second door behind the altar, and as he beat on it the blows seemed to pass through his own body. As the notes of the bell had done.

"Father," he said, "Father, let me in, for God's love."

No answer came and the second door did not open itself and was not opened.

Turning then, leaning on the door, Romulan looked at the back of the crucifix with his blue eyes, savaged by crying and dust. The Christ seemed to call to him, sternly, and soon, like a child, he went to the stone altar and kneeled before it on the icy floor.

"I have sinned," he said. "I have sinned. I'm damned. I have sinned."

Then he only kneeled there, half lying against the altar, his face pressed to its coldness. He neither entreated nor prayed. Outside, the grasshoppers sang, and he heard his own heart heavily beating, but no other sounds. He saw Iuletta dressed in mourning, following Leopardo's bier. He had killed flesh of her flesh. And then he saw Mercurio's eyes as they closed, and then he saw the sword shear through Leopardo's neck. And Iuletta as she clasped him, her head tilted back in ecstasy. So, my love, you shall not repent sweet wine spilled, warm kisses spent. Night is close to end our day, there is no sin, love, but to delay . . . dance with me. And he saw the dance of death.

Time had moved over him, like water on a beach, but how much time he did not know or care, when he heard the pebbles that weighted the door-curtain brush the floor, and then the door was shut.

"Romulan, Valentius' son, of House Montargo," the voice said. It was the voice of the priest, and he remembered it.

Romulan shifted a little, but did not get to his feet. He felt, but did not hear, the priest come toward him.

"Stand up, Romulan Montargo." The voice was imbued neither by particular sympathy or condolence, yet had a wonderful, almost an oceanic serenity.

The body, if not the brain of Romulan noted it, and responded to it. He rose, and faced the priest. Facing him, he found himself able to say:

"Father, I've killed two men and I'm hunted, no doubt. Will you shelter me, or shall I go at once?"

The strange man looked out of the windows of his eyes at the shapes of the mutable earth. One of which was the young man before him, wrung into whiteness, trembling, and partly dehumanized.

"I will shelter you," Laurus said.

His unweathered hands held baskets in which lay the roots and herbs he had been out gathering. The cross blazed on his breast and the long hair seemed but newly combed.

Romulan coughed.

"I remember," he said, his mouth stretching, so one realized the cough had been a sort of laugh, "if it accords with the balance of place and time, true to the essence of the moment, then you will do it. Does it then, Father, accord, to keep me from justice?"

"Come," said Laurus, and went away toward the second door. He touched it and the door, formerly immovable, opened.

Romulan followed him into the insularium. The little window was wide, the window through which the dove had come to be his messenger, and to die. Laurus, having set down the simples, began to go about, waking the candles, and next, letting down the lamp on its chain, ignited that too. Up, in the curdled light, sprang the brazed turtle on its pedestal of jade, up sprang the dragon, the alembics, pestles, scrolls, and fanged fishes, the zodiacs and worlds and crucibles and scales and skulls. Romulan saw and recalled them, known, it seemed, as if from infancy. And seeing them, he flung his arm across his face, and standing at the brink of the cell, he wept again, beyond everything.

The hermit did not go to him or speak to him. He went on with his work among the lights, and when the lights were seen to, began to sort the growing things he had gathered.

After a while Romulan's pain receded, as it was apt to do, rising and falling in his consciousness as breath rose and fell in his body. Then, he sat down on a stool beside the scarred old table.

"Must I tell you?" he asked.

"No," Laurus said.

"I should confess my faults to you," Romulan said. He laid his arm on the table and his head on the arm. "I should be shriven."

"I will not," said Fra Laurus, "shrive you."

"False priest," Romulan said. He closed his eyes, wearily, as Mercurio had done in death.

After a while he sensed Laurus standing near him.

"Something is here," Laurus said. Then he was gone, and then again returned. Perhaps minutes had passed in the interim, perhaps seconds. On the table he placed a wooden beaker. "You will drink this."

"Give me poison," Romulan said.

"You are poisoned enough," the priest said. "Drink."

Romulan watched his own hand reach to take the beaker, and bring it to his mouth. The fluid had a taste of hot and unsavory spices.

"I've tethered your horse," Laurus said. "Presently someone will come."

"My enemies," Romulan said. He put back his head on to his arm. "Can you raise ghosts with the magic scroll? Mercurio will come and laugh at you." He did not finish the disgusting elixir. The room sank down like a dying fire, and he slept.

Something woke him; he did not know what it was. The room was quite unchanged, cool, smoky from its candles. Yet the sky in the unshuttered window blazed, an almost colorless gold; the day was ripening and would soon be plucked from the bough.

Romulan's arm had grown numb, so he must drag it off the table like a dead thing, and massage the muscles of it to restore life. This he did, looking about him unrefreshed, yet with a kind of deadly calm on him now, which the sleep seemed to have brought, or maybe the unfinished cordial in the wooden cup. The magician was no longer in the cell. Tiredly and with no interest at all, Romulan left the table and went to the door. And so found the priest, who knelt to pray, straight-backed before the altar. There was no murmur, no click of beads, and, at the sudden conclusion, the brief holy salutation was performed without flourish. Rising, Fra Laurus turned, and came toward him.

"You must be ready to ride," the priest said.

"To ride? To ride where?"

Laurus went by him and back into the cell, and as before perforce Romulan followed him.

"To Lombardhia, I would think."

A dim sound of pouring came in the shadows. Laurus, moving from shadow to light, again presented him with a cup, this one of pottery.

"More medicine?"

"Only wine," said the priest.

Romulan drank from the cup. The wine was fruity and sweet, a flavor he knew. During the wedding, there had been a wine like this. He drank a little more, and could not bring himself to take the rest. The sweet and nourishing taste stayed in his mouth, and he folded his arms about himself tighter than cords, until the joints in his shoulders cracked, to keep from weeping again.

"Lombardhia," he said at last. "Is that your plan?"

"Go to the outer door," said Laurus, "and see whose plan it is."

Romulan hesitated, then turning swiftly stepped into the body of the oratory and so to the outer door. Opening it, he noticed at once the banners of concealment had been let down on ropes to the ground. The cream walls stood clear in the blistering light, and the faded painting of Maria Vera, Our Lady of Truth, waited above once more for the sun, the rain and the air to wipe her away. Nearby the black gelding, tied to a tree, ate the grass unhurriedly. The sky was so bright as if it burned from edge to edge, at first he missed the movement on the slope. Yet something kept him standing in the arched doormouth, kept his eyes on the downward combers of the hills that flowed from the road toward him. Abruptly, as if he himself had conjured them, he saw a small mobile patch, objects which moved. The land was dark at its rim against the sky. Only as the moving things descended into the place where the pallor of the grass came visible, and the red powderings of the flowers, only then did he tell what they were: two men whose mounts breasted the poppies like ships, with, led behind them, a pack-horse, minimally laden.

Dressed dun, the riders might be any, friend or foe, coincidental visitors. Then one pointed, the arm describing first the oratory, next the black horse cropping there. And in that moment the second rider spurred his mount, and came galloping at Romulan, the plants breaking like flaming foam before him.

Down this slope Cornelia had cumbersomely wafted, with her page and the out-riding guard. Unbearable memory was everywhere, even in this, even as he waited here perhaps to be cut down by a Chenti sword, some vengeful cousin, or an Estemba that did not hearken to Benevolo.

Then, when the rider had come among the trees and out of them, Romulan saw the features under the cowl. The blood in him seemed to leap and fall back, changing to lead. Romulan had the impulse to run away, which in the face of no other enemy, in that hour, would he have entertained or yielded to. But this, this was beyond his ability to endure. The rider halted now, and was dismounting, pushing back, as he did so, the hood of his cloak. From under it the dark hair was drawn, matte as ebony, with a polish from the sun's fire. The empirical features, handsome and enclosed, the eyes like burnished liquid in the dry flesh skillfully chiseled by its slender lines of time and character. The face of thought and care and discipline, and doubt. The face of his father.

But there was nowhere to run to in the altered world. This was all that remained to Romulan, this final beating, this Ultima Thule of bitterness. He put his hands behind him then and gripped the upright of the oratory door, grinding palms and nails against the stonework. It was, under this onslaught, the only means of balance he could devise.

On the slope, the other rider had drawn rein. Both horses, the proud and the pack beast, were peaceably investigating the turf. Valentius walked forward, and stopped near to the wooden post with the golden wheel, looking at nothing but his son. Neither spoke. Overhead birds were fluting as they flew excitedly across the brilliant ether. The sun was beginning, very delicately, to release its colors.

Valentius said, "To forestall your question, I have been told of everything, and how to find you out, by two informants. One message from Estemba, and one, to my surprise, from the Rocca Tower. Of the two, the latter was the least accurate. Chesarius deduced you would go back to Marivero for sanctuary. Benevolo D'Estemba, it seems, knew your mind like his book."

The voice was articulate and level. It did not accuse, or seek to dismay. It held no threat of anything. It was not obvious what it cost Valentius to talk in such a way, fastidious and sober, everything held still for the sake of the other, who plainly only kept himself still by an effort of supreme defiance, that just as plainly could not long be maintained. And after the few concise sentences were uttered, the stoical ability to resume silence also, maybe, cost as much, or more.

After a scatter of moments, Romulan drew a breath and said, "You say you were told everything. Do you include my marriage to Iuletta Chenti?"

Valentius inclined his head. "That, and all the rest. Benevolo and Chesarius both deemed it sensible to betray you to me, under these circumstances. You should not blame them for that. They were right in what they did."

Romulan drew another breath.

"Well, I wait," he said. Valentius did not ask him what he waited for, so drawing in the air again, Romulan informed him: "I wait to be chastised, sir. I wait for your condemnation of my idiocy. Your catalogue of my blunders and my rashness. Your verdict on my crimes. Your rage, your contempt, your curse to damn me, my disinheritance." This voice, too, grappled by iron, as the hands grappled the stone at his back, shook only at the ends of breath, and was reinforced as breath was drawn in again. To breathe was patently an act of will, each time more was taken than was needed, and yet found to be inadequate. "For once," Romulan said, "I deserve every harsh thing you can say of me. But what comes after? Will you send me back to the Duke?"

Valentius swore then, sharply and briefly, his control going, then picked mercilessly up again. But the language of the Bhorga from his father's lips was so novel a thing, Romulan laughed.

"Dear me," Romulan said, "worst of all my execrable failings, to bring you, sir, to such a display." And choked on the last word, hearing Mercurio's voice come through his own. Everything then was breaking into pieces about him and he could not suffer it before his father, as he could not remain comfortably physically naked before him. Romulan let go of the upright, and turning, smashed his right fist, the hand which had held the sword, into the rough stone of the arch. The hand, stunned and bleeding, rebounded. He allowed it to fall to his side, and drank up the pain that gradually burned from it, putting this now between himself and the unendurable adversary.

Again, a space. And then again Valentius spoke to him, as if there had been no interruption of any sort.

"Contrary to your view of me, I'm not a man who hands over his only son to the rabble."

"Oh," Romulan said beautifully, "then in one instance at least, Father, you are unlike God."

Blood came from the sun now. Appropriately, to end this day of blood, the sunset would be steeped in it. A wind, harbinger of sunfall, rose abruptly from the hills, and shook their mantles and their trees, and the piled cloth of disguise lowered from the oratory. It caught the sun-wheel, too, and whirled it round. Romulan stared at the glancing lights, and the pain in his hand began to ebb away becoming one with the wheel's faint whistling. Until it did not matter.

"Listen to me," Valentius said. The tone remained quiet, but his face, in the gathering red shadow, had despaired. "We have ill-understood each other, and so come to this pass, and now is no time to remedy that. If I ask you to trust me, you will not. If I ask you to obey me you will refuse. Where am I to turn, then, when I would help you? No, your marriage does not please me, but it's done, and I prefer the honor of it to the deed of some greedy raping lout I thought you set on becoming. And no, Flavian Estemba was no friend I'd beg Heaven for you to have, but you clove to him in loyalty if you gave me none. I know you would not cause his murder, and I know you would take steel to the one who did. And if I'm to choose between Leopardo Chenti's death and yours, then I thank God you hacked him even in mincemeat, if you live. There's more. What is the purpose of saying it? I would have sent you to Lombardhia to keep you from all this, and now the preparations—so far advanced—will see you safe there. None came after us. But who knows if someone else, not your friend, will guess where you might be. Take my horse then. He's fresh. Doro will ride with you. By midnight you will be across the boundary of the Duca's lands. There, none of his laws or Verensa's quarrels can touch you."

And then, once more, patiently Valentius waited, leaving the silence for his son to fill. But Romulan now said nothing, merely staring on and on at the wheel of ruddy metal that spun and slowed, spun and slowed, on the wooden post.

Valentius turned a little way, noting Doro and the three horses, motionless as the trees between the sunset wind, moving with it as the trees did, the manes, the servant's cloak, stirring. The sky was deeper now, scorched out, the color of old gilding, and of smoke in the east. A bizarre light lay on everything, even in shadow, where the darkness seemed to glow.

Valentius considered. He might walk to Romulan, lash out

and render him senseless, then carry him to the horse and send him away in such fashion. But he must recollect, his son was fighter and swordsman. He had killed Leopardo Chenti, reckoned unkillable. He might not be so easy to dispatch.

So Valentius stood idly, unable to bring himself to any further effort. His thoughts went back and back, knowing well how to wound him, showing him, what he had always known, the limitless failure of his dealings with this son, the masculine image of Valentina the beloved and the forfeited. Valentius was aware how love and fear had marked him. But for the first time, reading the written messages, Chesarius', Benevolo's, papers which could strike like knives, Valentius had allowed himself to confront his own knowledge of himself. He came then to the inner page which read: I gave him nothing, afraid to give it, and now he will take nothing from me. Everything of consequence in Romulan's life had been conducted without Valentius' participation. Yet Valentius might have been a sharer, he might have risked the sharing in the face of death, that ondrawing shadow of night which now hung so close on land and soul. Who could escape? To waste life was surely worse. But, no remedy now, no remedy and no way to help. Damn this boy, what did Valentius care what he had done, who wed, who harmed, who slain. Romulan was the child of his body, the last emblem of love which was left. And Valentina. Had she, some starry microcosm beyond the earth, beheld all this, these barren years, and condemned him?

Valentius' mind, now, was fluid, flowing. But the sinews of his emotions were stiff, were mortised up. He could not move. And the wheel, making its curious little noise, spun and slowed. Spun and slowed.

Romulan said something then, ironically jarring him.

"If I run, what of Iulet?"

Valentius swept his mind of its litter and said,

"She is your wife. I will approach Chenti. It must be done with care, for I think we shall be at feud over this, though Chesarius has hinted at some bargaining. Iuletta, through you, has my name now, and can live, if she wishes, under my protection. Till you may return."

"May *return*?" Romulan's spirit re-entered his face, glaring and abstracted in the fiery shade, an angel from the Inferno.

Valentius, having caught the errant attention, said quickly, "Chesarius thinks Chenti can be bought, and offers to do it. The Duke, it seems, will consent if Chenti does, to pardon

you as the valued avenger of ducal kindred. Then you will
come back unstained, no doubt for some small extra fee.
There are Levantine interests of the Montargos that have always charmed the Duke."

"You'd do this."

"I'd do this."

"And Iuletta—my—wife—"

"And Iuletta your wife is now my daughter, by laws both
phlegmatic and divine. My roof is therefore hers also. But
first, you will go to Lombardhia. Nothing is settled yet. I will
get you word when and how I can."

Romulan took a step forward, but his eyes had widened,
lost the place and the moment, looking into a light as prepos-
terously brilliant as the sun—the sorcerous mirror of hope.
Which all at once dashed itself in fragments as Valentius
said:

"It seems you're going then, after all, where I send you."

He said it lightly, which also cost him something. He said
it in an aching relief. He did not know the likeness of these
words to the words Mercurio murmured, his golden head half
on Benevolo's arm, half in the dust, and the blood running
like a costly dye from his body. *It seems I'm going, after all,
where you sent me.* To Hell, where you sent me, to Hell,
your sword the key in the gate of it, your wretched game,
your gaming foolishness, the means. The price of love is
death. My love, my death. The bitter of farewell, my dear,
which bitterness is yours, for I am beyond all farewells. I am
with the worms.

The words seemed spoken in Romulan's brain. He heard
them out. And then the control by which he had somehow
held himself, its links weakened by the instant of hope, gave
way. Romulan turned, for there was no hope, could be no
hope, but there was death and there was despair, and an enemy at his back. To keep private from this enemy the agony
that now rose up in him again, like the breath he could only
snatch at, was impossible. To conceal his face was all he
could attain.

He did not find the wall until he fell against it. The landscape swam and roiled like a great ship, like the Argo herself,
nominatrix of his House. The storm broke from his brain and
through his eyes. The grief would itself now take the world
away from him and deliver him to darkness, and he was glad
of it.

Valentius stood and saw this dark beast lay hold on his son, not knowing its impetus, while knowing its cause. The father, whose emotions remained locked away, was startled and appalled, was moved, was reduced, put at a loss. Not since childhood had Romulan ever wept in Valentius' sight or hearing. And childhood's impassioned anguish—one could not compare those uncomplex laments to this stifled and tormented paroxysm that drove all the young man's body against the ungiving stone, and in stages down it, a thing that took breath and sight, that could deprive of sense and even consciousness.

Perhaps she reached out to him then, his Valentina, from whatever ethereal limbo she inhabited. Or perhaps it was that aspect of herself which had remained caught within him, undying, unrecognized. Valentius stepped free of himself. With an awkwardness that was not physical, nor mental, and which, whatever it was, he ignored, he went to Romulan and firmly pried him from the wall and from his knees, and lifting and supporting his son, held him in his arms, as he had not done since he was a child of six.

Romulan made no physical struggle; he was beyond it, hardly aware of anything. Yet the support, as he lay against and within it, caused him to make, through the harrowing spasms, some vague lost protest, wordless, indecipherable, grasped in a second.

"No shame to weep," Valentius Montargo said. "Shame would be ashamed to shame a man for weeping, in this world." He found then he could bring himself to touch the boy's hair, which was like his mother's, a shade stronger, coarser, the hair of a man. He caressed the hair, digging his fingers deeply to the skull beneath in hypnotic circling motions, as he would soothe a child, a dog, anything which came to him in its pain or distress to be healed, anything which he was not afraid to mark by his affection, lest death draw it from him. A second time. "When she died, your mother, I wept for her most nights of a year. I'd weep for her still, but the eyes grow chary of crying for what cannot be undone. You will find it so. We can bear what we must. But not yet. Not yet."

The claws of grief let Romulan go suddenly, as before. Then, coming back to himself, he found he was not stretched out on the ground, but inside the walls of a safety he had known only with one, and glimpsed only with another, and never dreamed to find as he found it, here.

Embarrassed yet consoled, consoled and warmed as if by

wine, he moved back from Valentius' support, and looked at him.

Valentius smiled, himself drained and emptied. There was no victory in truth.

"The sun is almost out," Valentius said. "And the horse is waiting. Doro has a cloak for you. I'll take the gelding back to Verensa."

"They'll have shut the gates," Romulan said, expressionless.

"They will, however, reopen one at sight of a gold coin."

"For God's sake, go carefully," Romulan said.

"And you, go more carefully even than I."

Romulan turned then and ran toward the slope. Halfway up it he checked, and swung about. He looked back toward the oratory where, under the now all-blood-red sky, his father stood watching him.

"Run, boy!" Valentius shouted, his voice rising clear through the dark on the ground. "Run for Lombardhia." And softly, as Romulan, turning about again with one momentarily upflung arm, obeyed him: "And live long, and let God guard you, my only son."

Under the sky of Leopardo's blood, Electra Chenti walked through the streets to the Rocca.

She walked in the torn net of her bloodstained dress, the embroidered camisola that in its turn bore the brown stains of human blood which was dry. She walked in the ribbons of her torn hair, a veil dropped over it like a fall of blackish reddish soot. She walked with the scratches staring on her cheeks and throat, as the women had walked of old, who mourned, and she walked barefoot. And from this madness her eyes looked forth, her sane, inclement eyes.

Lord Chenti, expected home that afternoon or evening, prepared for even in the midst of catastrophe, had not yet come. Nor had word come of any captured, any sentenced, or of the Duke's ruling on events. The bell had stopped tolling. In the lower town, the plague seethed, mostly forgotten.

The band of Chenti cousins, coming home to their lodges or to the Tower and informed of everything, stood about stricken by uncanny fears. Some sought out Gulio. They demanded his account. They cross-questioned him, they screamed at him.

Removed now to a more suitable chamber, washed and bound and dressed in new linen, unflawed damask, the sleeves of the doublet correctly tied, fenced in by candles, a priest chanting, the incense streaming by, the body of Leopardo Chenti lay on a draperied table, stretched for inspection. The eyes were sealed now, the hands lax on a prayer book of bossed gold. No wound visible. Irreproachable. The kindred filed in and out. Women fainted. Men swore oaths. The priests replaced each other, and the censers swung.

As the sky reddened, and reddened on its redness, when Chenti still had not come home, when word still went unpublished as to ducal decree, Electra came from her apartments, unaltered in her rags and tatters. In the hall some of the male kindred had gathered, drinking, arguing. They fell silent as she entered like a dreadful ghost among them.

"The Duke does not speak," she said. "I shall go to him, as I am." She did not say: I shall ask for blood. She said: "I shall ask for justice."

A few voices, drunkenly upraised, attempted dissuasion.

"No," she said. "The Duca pays no attention to the strength of this House, to all its fine young men." (They withered at her unstressed, implicit scorn.) "My lord is from home. Let us see what one frail woman can do."

Then, she walked from the hall, and so from the house, the guards by the entrance gaping at her.

Men decided she must not proceed alone. Their pride was stirred up, the wine aided in that. They called for torches and for their servants, and went out with their swords.

So she walked, and they walked behind her, some thirty-five to forty men spread on the streets, crimson clad, wearing black linen for mourning, servants and masters, and the torches trailing greenish-yellow over the darkening blood-cast sky, against the massive walls, the slanting stairs, beyond which the myriad towers rose and ever rose. Groups craned out of windows where the lamps were just now blushing up, women leaned down, and other men pressed back into doorways and under archways. *"The Chentis are on the street." "The cat-pack is out for Montargo blood."* Armored in its own pageant, the procession did not speak, save with the slide and chink of swords as it strode, and with its shadows thrown boundlessly before and behind it as the torches dipped and changed hands. And before them all, the woman walking, Lady Death.

They came to the Rocca, and the ascent to the doors was blocked by guards, as they might have expected. Their business with the Duke was inquired after, and their business with the Duke was stated. This business being relayed within, the Duke slammed his hand flat down on the table and gained his feet with two or three choice blasphemies.

"You see how it runs, Chesarius? They petition me, and half the town has seen them."

"Perhaps you might convince Verensa," Chesarius coldly said. "They have come personally to entreat your pardon for Romulan Montargo."

Obliged by arcane courtesies, the Duke let the woman into the Chitadella, but with two only of her male kin to support her, and lacking their weapons. He received them in the hall, whose walls of dressed stone striped with the gleaming of swords and draped only by the ringed sigil banners, intimated the fortress and its strength.

Standing on the dais, he let them approach him, and cursed under his breath this harpy Electra Chenti, mourning publicly like her namesake, forcing his hand now, where he had not wished to be forced.

"Well, lady," he said to her, however, "we bow to your bereavement. To lose the one that stood in place of a son to you, and to your lord, that is a desolation indeed."

"Then recompense us, Prince," she said.

"Where's your husband?" the Duca said.

"Delayed on the road, or he would plead here in my stead."

(And that I doubt, madama. And surely, if in your stead, not in your state.)

"Well, what's your suit?"

"The law of God. An eye for an eye."

The Duke, annoyed, could not resist.

"Whose eye, then, my donna, has been put out?"

He was not prepared for her reaction.

"The eye of my heart, my brother's son, my nephew, my flesh, my blood, my life!" And she began to rend herself again, in front of him, filling him with a horror of the degeneracy of women, their primaeval wildness, their ability to rush beyond reason and overthrow the tenets of good policy.

"Hold her from herself!" he roared at the two dumbfounded men by her sides. With some difficulty, they did so. "Madama," he said to her, meeting her evil eyes, "to mourn is your right. To take leave of your senses in my hall is frank bad manners. If you ask me for the death of Romulan Montargo—"

"I do not ask," she cried, "I do not ask it. I demand it. The House of Chenti," she said, "demands it."

"*If*," the Duca repeated woodenly, "you ask for Romulan Montargo's death, you may go home well satisfied. I, too, have lost kindred at the villain's hands." He sighed. He scowled at her, at the wickedness looking from her face as if around a narrow door. "Go to your house, lady. There's plague abroad, which your gathering may well have helped to spread. When taken, the Montargo's soul will be shifted by means of a strangler's noose.

"Words to this effect shall be published in the town at sunrise tomorrow."

Of all the Chentis, Gulio was perhaps the last to hear this joyful news. By then, he had news of his own, which, ultimately, he prudently did not disclose.

He had grown very drunk as the day wore on, and by the time the last stains of bloody mulberry and bloodiest blood had left the sky, he was drunk enough to be brave. The taunts and insinuations of his fellows had disturbed him. Leopardo's death disturbed him. He had been too afraid to pay his respects to the corpse. Some superstitious vision of the body sitting up, pointing at him and calling him a coward, as other cousins had now called him frequently, made Gulio giggle and writhe. In his innermost self, Gulio was thankful for 'Pardo's death, as all of them were most certainly thankful. And yet, with that warped and envenomed presence had passed also a brightness and a glamour from the Tower. As darkness fell, they each cast about themselves for some means to simulate a light.

To Gulio's unease had been added one other mite. The bothersome story the Leopard had rendered him before the fatal meeting in the square. Lord Chenti's wife, 'Pardo had said, had lain with another man. This tale had mingled, in Gulio's muddled intelligence, with 'Pardo's constant harping on Iuletta and Romulan Montargo playing the beast with two backs. The drunker Gulio grew, the more it seemed the Montargo had been creeping about in the house all night and night after night, shinning up creepers and over balustrades to get in. Lying now in the mother's bed and now in the daughter's. At some point then, a fearsome plan came to Gulio, as it seemed to him worthy of Leopardo himself.

In the first darkness, therefore, Gulio left the house of his ancestors (in this way, missing also a messenger from Padova to announce Lord Chenti's further delay), and rambled through the thoroughfares toward the mansion of the Montargos. As with several of the older towers, the outer doors were not externally guarded. Tonight, the lamps on their posts were also dead.

Gulio's scheme was uncomplex. Taking his dagger, he would scratch up a message on those ancient doors, perhaps in rhyme. He had been struggling with his poetry all the way; it concerned fornication, the stabbing of friends one way and maidens another, and Gulio wished to have it right before he began work.

To consider, he leaned in a nearby doorway, his bleared eyes on the black sky and slipping constantly off it.

When the horse and rider came leisurely clopping along the street, Gulio was no more than temporarily irritated—until a window shutter, thrown open suddenly in an adjacent building, tossed a bolt of rekindled day across the night. The mounted man passed through it, and Gulio clutched the hilt of his dagger to his mouth to keep from crying out. Cloaked in dun color, the rider might not be known, but the horse Gulio well remembered, the black gelding Romulan Montargo had ridden into the square. Was it conceivable? The murderer had flown Verensa and *returned*. Why not? Maybe, the most clever ruse of all, for who would think of it? Gulio drew himself together, ready to totter back to Chenti with these tidings, when a memory of all he had been named for smote him. It was so, he had left Leopardo alone with the Montargo, and 'Pardo had been decimated and the decimater escaped. And now—

The man had dismounted, a little heavily, exhausted no doubt, as the horse seemed to be. Leading it, he turned aside toward the stable gate, and in a moment would be knocking there for the grooms.

—And now the coward might become the avenger.

Drunken and brave and unable to plan this any better than his poetry, Gulio floundered from the shade of the door-mouth. He did not ponder on this act, which, at midnight, would pull him down with all its weight of terror and responsibility. No. The dagger was ready in his hand, and the back of Romulan Montargo before him. To bring these two entities together was but too simple.

With a silly little squeak, Gulio struck.

He had, at least, the wit to pull the dagger free as the man, without a sound, sank away from him. That, and the wit, now, to run. And later the wit to keep his own counsel. Although it was not until midnight that Gulio learned, from various uproars, that it was not the son but the father he had slain.

Valentius had been musing as he walked the horse toward the walls of home, on his wife, and on his son. Above, upstretched, the grim and glorious stones of the past. But his reverie was not with these. Nor was it gladsome, yet sufficiently sweet, and lit by a strange wonderment. So it was the youth left in him and not increeping age, and not death, that filled his mind as the short blade slammed against his heart. By mere chance, Gulio's stroke was pristine and exact. To Valentius, the night came sudden and kind. There was time only for the puzzled whisper: what is *this*? And then only the soft hair of night to fold and to catch him. He was dead, like a leaf, before his body reached the ground.

Having kept by, but not on, the Padova road, to avoid unwelcome meetings, next cutting across it where the track led southwest that would take them, at length, to the Lombardhi highway, the two riders made fair speed, the pack horse running ably behind.

The sunset gradually went out before and to the left of them; a Hellish afterglow persisted two or three miles and then was raked away. About half an hour after, Romulan felt a sensation like a blow upon his back, and turned to see what might have caused it, discovering nothing had. Another mile went by, and he brought his horse to a standstill without explanation, dismounted, and going to the roadside, threw up. When this happened again half a mile farther on, having crawled aside a little, he found himself too weak to return to the road.

Presently the servant, Doro, also dismounted and came over to him.

"I asked the priest for poison," Romulan said. "It seems he gave it me."

Doro bent and touched his forehead. Then straightened up and stood there looking down at him, the stars fiercely enameled behind his head. Doro, a few years Romulan's senior, had the face of a skinny clever baby, which now mildly frowned.

"Not poison," he said. "I think you have the plague."

Galvanized by incoherent automatic fear, Romulan came after all unevenly to his feet. "*What?*"

"The Summer Sickness. No, sir. There's no call for undue misgiving. You're young and healthy and can cheat the thing,

with proper care. But we must get to Lombardhia quickly.
Your hours in a saddle are rationed."

"Plague," said Romulan. He looked at Doro, who had
reached out to steady him. "Are you not afraid to take it,
too?"

"No, sir. I caught the ailment four years ago, and lived.
And so will you."

Romulan half smiled as, his head reeling, he pulled himself
back on to the horse, knowing, as Doro had told him, there
was no margin in this land to be ill. At some point he had
been ready, it seemed, for any death. But not this one, this
loathsome devil for centuries on the back of man, not this.

The night began to come and go, but he clung grimly to
the horse. When he vomited again, he somehow kept in the
saddle to do it.

By the time they reached the highway, he did not care very
much any more if he died or not.

Somewhere after that, under the overhang of a cypress tree
whose echoing scent briefly refreshed him, Doro got him off
the horse one way and loaded him back across it another,
and tied him there. This was a punishment beyond any he
had foretold, but the fever was already high, and soon he was
meshed in it, and all things else were gone.

SEVENTEEN

Within half a day of each other, inside the shadows of the Basilica, candles had flickered on an unlocking of two fragile gilded gates, and on the opening of two tall architectural tombs. Twice, men had gone up and a long shape had been offered, and had been devoured. Each tomb closed its jaws upon its dead, possessively. The banners were thrown like a coverlet across the marble, blue, and brass: Montargo, Estemba. The two gilded gates were locked again, the two separate groups of the living stole away. Later, a sleet-white Eros would come to mourn above Flavian Estemba, a pagan boy tactfully ignored, since he had wings and might well be only an angel. Above Valentius Montargo merely the dusts of the Basilica to gather, and to lie, and by his side the grey petals of the woman he had loved. But, what do the dead care for these things, the couch, the monument, the requiem? These are the toys by which the quick may comfort themselves. Clad for death as if for a wedding, they lay, unseen, the finery withering, the tactile flesh becoming nothing but foul air. Only the bones remaining, which could not any more see or think or laugh or sing or love.

Relinquish to the dark what the dark has taken. It will have all.

Outside, in the down-sloping death-garden, amid the trees of death, the mausoleum of the Chentis, delayed for Lord Chenti's order, had also cracked wide, to take Leopardo in. Thereafter they would mount guard for him three nights, encrimsoned men standing with their black linen and spurling torches.

Lord Chenti had come home behind a message, lagging either on his business at Padova, or his other business, come home some days late and so into discomfort. And sanctioning the opening of the vault, ordered the mounting of the guard, post internment, for Leopardo. Burial must be hasty in summer, and this was no show of honor to the dead, but of a Tower's strength and pride. Besides, in the tumult which had progressed, in all things but this, apparently beyond the House's master, Chenti had required to do something. Or be left behind.

Rumors ran in Verensa, lay down exhausted, started up again. Montargo had persuaded the Duca, by means of a bribe, to permit the escape of the heir, Romulan, from under the very hooves of the ducal guards. Ten Chentis had, in return, awaited Valentius at his own gate and cut him down. The old man who ruled the Estemba Tower, bereft now of his only surviving son, had resorted to witchcraft, and a woman in grey weeds stalked a cauldron, so the plague stole into Montargo. Many were sick of it there. But then, there were other Houses of the Higher Town which had also let that enemy inside their doors. It was no great mystery or magic, when their sons had so often frequented the Bhorgabba, where now plague ran like the hunted thing it was, biting as it passed.

Sana Verensa's Summer Sickness, not one of the mighty pestilences, but a little sister. High fever, an inflammation of glands and intestines, which produced vomiting, cramps, muscular anguish, and sometimes spasms resembling a fit. But these things would, having ascended to a crisis on the second, third or fourth day, die suddenly down. The fever broke and reason came back, hobbling and very tired. To survive the crisis strength was needful, though not always health. Sometimes the chronically sick recovered, their bodies accustomed to the long battle with illness, fighting as a matter of course, and shook off the ailment swiftly. It was often the sound whose constitutions, unused to war, surrendered the flesh in despair. Indeed, despair was the worst aspect of the disease, for it seemed intrinsic, a physical rather than a spiritual symptom. In the debility of the aftermath, when the dangerous fever had broken and the pain left behind begun to lessen, all wish for life seemed to have been burned away. The victim, who now had every hope of recovery, would refuse to take nourishment, would weep, would rise and stumble mindlessly about, as if searching for some exit. Some even forced the door, running after Death and catching his sleeve, by means of knives unwisely left out, and high windows.

It was rumored, with speculation, that the solitary, legal,

fair and nubile daughter of Lord Chenti had herself contracted the plague, and was set to die of it.

The morning after her mother had walked barefoot and terrible as a Fury to the Chitadella, Iuletta was found by one of her frightened maids, neither waking nor sleeping but wracked by heat and delirium in her narrow bed.

By the time Lord Chenti had ridden in through his gate and found the house to be not his own, but a variety of Purgatory, suitably peopled by wailing lunatics and shrieking demons, a physician from the Basilica college was in attendance. And by the time Chenti, in some horror, had cornered the physician, the man was able to say, "No, my lord, it's not plague. The fever is already diminishing and will demand no crisis. There are none of the other tendencies which we observe with the sickness." And pausing, noted the father's great concern, largely, one supposed, bound up with his hopes for the Belmorio match—already shaking from the slur of feud-murder following Valentius Montargo's death. "She will live, sir, I promise you," said the physician. "It is some maiden's humor. Perhaps brought on by fear for her marriage. Probably she is already attached to the young man and overly concerned, misunderstanding your own finesse, sir, in dealing with foolish gossip." And then, since Chenti lowered, "I myself will attend her, my lord, and see her returned to the full bloom of her health and beauty." (There would be gold in this if one were provident.)

A full hour after, having visited his nephew's corpse, now due for burial on the morrow, and already tinged by the unmistakable evidence of souring preservatives, its features subtly altered, its form heavy as dough, Chenti went to his wife.

She sat bolt upright in the anteroom of their chamber, not a hair today out of place. Her red gown was frankly as black as her linen. Her face bore no marks of tears, only the fading scratches her nails had made there. Her hands were crossed together in her lap.

"Did you not know, mistress," he said to her as he came in, "your daughter was sick?"

"I knew. It has been seen to."

"And you. What am I to think of you?"

"Whatever most pleases you, my lord."

"Please me? I'm not pleased to hear you walked the length of the town, screeching like a trull."

"There was no screeching done. Some thirty of our kin

walked with me. I went to ask the Duke for justice, for the death of the Montargo who slew my brother's son."

"Why should that trouble you? You never liked the boy."

"I was," she said, "disturbed for your honor, my lord. The honor of the Chenti Tower."

"It seems to me, Wife," he said, "you take more care for the dead than the living. Some word must be sent to Belmorio. What did the Duca say to you?"

"What you have already been told he said. He promised us the Montargo's death."

Chenti crossed the room. He caught Electra by her arm, with the added roughness of unfamiliarity, for he did not often touch her. "Was it *your* fancy to have Valentius killed on the street?"

She looked at him with her reptilian eyes.

"Mine?" The contempt in her white face, under its delicate embroidery of wounds, infuriated and dismayed him. "Valentius was nothing to me. It is the son's blood I would have."

"And why this damned tearing at your skin, woman?"

"To mark my grief," she said. "You know from past experience, gentle husband, I am unable to shed tears."

"God pardon me. Jesus and the Host of Heaven, forgive me," said Cornelia, over and over. "My baby's young and blameless. I should have restrained her, poor willful girl. My fault, Lord, mine. And," Cornelia added, with a sad slyness, "rather you should strike down me, in my sins, than this lovely child." Hoping by this means to suggest her virtue, and so gain reprieve for both.

A reprieve was gained. Whether due to Cornelia's prayers and exclamations, or to the physician's interesting physic—myrrh and saffron mixed with beeswax and burning day long in the room, at which one sneezed, vinegar dashed on the floor, in which one slid, plasters of powdered jacinth and thin honey applied to the patient's forehead and heart, through which one grew sticky. A few drops of blood were also let. The doctor, anxious to obtain his fee, gave of his money's worth.

Beyond the chamber, the Tower arose to bury its dead with brazen noises, then sank to its mourning, modestly. Word was sent to the Rocca, and to the Belmorio Tower. In each instance forebearing answers had come back. Satisfied, if not content, Chenti visited his daughter's sick room daily, determined on bludgeoning her toward health. The fever had passed, leaving only a weakness behind it. In reply to his jolly tirades there came her dutiful, "Yes, sir," soft as a feather stirring in the pillows. Pale and still though she was, Chenti was pleased to see she had not lost her looks. Cornelia he roused with verbal thumpings. "Cheer up! Let her see smiling faces! We'll have her wed presently, and then more of these fadings. Tell her, nurse, if she rallies, she shall yet have her ginger-haired knight. That will liven her."

When the master of the house was gone and the physician, and the scared maid—one of two Cornelia had sworn, by hideous vows, to secrecy—Cornelia leaned over the narrow bed. Iuletta, stranded on the sheets, gazed at her.

"You see how it is," the nurse said, bracingly. "He will have you wed."

Iuletta sighed. She gazed away and at her own hands, empty now of all rings, and lightly entwined on a small wooden doll. She had cried for the doll by name in her illness—"Ginevra! Bring me Ginevra!" and then cried over the doll and hugged it when, unearthed from a box, much the worse for neglect, it had been brought. Now the doll again meant nothing, only somewhere to rest her weary woman's hands which had clasped and comforted a living man.

"I dreamed," Iuletta said, in her faint clear voice. "I saw my love, and he was dead."

Cornelia crossed herself. She also sighed, and a minor gale gathered the bed hangings and let them go.

"Kitten, you dreamed very well. He is dead. To you, for-ever, he is. He must dwell in exile. If any of this House came on him, they'd murder him for sure. To slay that fine young gentleman your cousin—"

"It was a dark place," Iuletta said. "Or else it was night. I saw him. I remember how he lay, with his head turned on his shoulder, and his beautiful hair spreading."

"Think him dead," said Cornelia. "How can you live, oth-erwise? Look at what hedges you round. Your family, your father's adamant will—a girl is only goods for market. And your Troian, it seems, is still eager enough to buy. Hot as his hair, to have you. All this, and are you to stand against it, one hapless maid? Give in, and prettily accept. What else can you do?"

"To accept," said Iuletta slowly, her lids downcast, "is to be damned. I am already married."

"Perhaps not. Dreams may be true augeries. And will not God forgive you, placed as you are? Does his canon not or-

der you to obey your parents? Obey, then, think yourself a
widow, marry a second time. Belmorio will make you a fine
husband. Better than this other wretch, who brings you only
misery."

"He sent me no word."

"No, he dared not. Nor will he. Think him dead, my catling. And take the other."

"If not one, then another," Iuletta said. Tears moved quietly down her cheeks.

Cornelia snuffled. Speaking harshly of Romulan to galva-
nize her charge, she felt a pang of guilt. Romulan had been
charitable to her. She did not any more believe he had killed
his friend, some nagging doubt informed her the magnificent
Leopardo was to blame, for everything. But, expediently loyal
to the Chentis, she would not house this thought, and certainly never give it voice. Iuletta must learn similar tactics.
With a heavy blitheness, Cornelia began to describe the joys
of a wife in the Belmorio Tower. As she did so, she saw her
child, this daughter of her love if not her womb, burdened by
the dark, dull Belmorio green, (like cabbages), hung with
glittering chains, swollen big with infants, or shrinking shallow and mean without, as Electra did. Here was a wife's lot.
How was it that, seeing Iuletta with Romulan Montargo,
nothing of this had suggested itself? A red rose and a blue
sky meeting in laughter and sweet pain. The nurse felt again
the strange stabbing in her breast that had come as she
watched them together, like two severed halves of a perfect
whole, mending.

When at length Cornelia ran out of floral phrases, she realized Iuletta, her tears still luminous, had fallen asleep.

With a weighted heart, Cornelia rose. How malleable were
the sick. One might warm and mould them to anything, like
wax. Cooling, they kept the shape, whether they would or no.

For Iuletta, asleep in sorrow and her will quiescent, her
mind had already turned from love to resignation. The fever
had taken from her what little rigid and pathetic faith she
had had. Heaven was envious. It had seen her bliss and torn
it from her grasp. She had scarcely wept, even, her tears were
from lassitude more than distress. Her world had grown grey.
If he had loved her, would he not have kept himself from the
fight? Would he not, having fought, somehow have made
provision for her—would he not have sent word to her, as before, sorcerously, by a dove, or a dream. But her dream had
shown his death. Yes, he was dead to her, for he did not love

her, after all. He had allowed all these things of blood and horror to step between them. Seducer, fair bankrupt, false friend. She was alone. She must fend for herself.

So, in this dreary mind, she slept. And so she woke to the same desert and the same resolve. And so, two days after the burial of her cousin she found herself, clothed first in perfumed water and then in soft garments of dark mourning darted with asphodel, her colorless face like a white candleflame between the ropes of naturally mourning hair, her eyes the blue of irises and certain stars and dusks and oceanic minerals and all fearless and poignantly and heartbreakingly blue things, awaiting the visit of her betrothed, Troian Belmorio.

The last occasion of their meeting had been at their betrothal feast, (could it have been only seven nights before?) A crowd had surrounded them, quite properly. Now it was equally seemly that only one of the tiniest of Iuletta's maids, tucked in a corner of a decorously gilded and frescoed room, should leave the rest of the space free for Belmorio. It was Lord Chenti's courtesy (and guile), and ham-fisted as ever.

But Troian noticed nothing of that. He saw only the girl seated at the room's center on a small velvet chair.

The red-haired young man in his cabbage-green satins paneled by cloth-of-gold, knew well enough the politics of his wedding. He had, at the beginning, been prepared to join for commerce and bed for delight elsewhere, providing the girl was not an eyesore. But the girl had been very far from an eyesore, and his blood was up for her from the first sight. Then came the feast, and then came interruptions. Verensa had been generally placid some while, her feuding confined to scraps, the dead unlucky underlings. Three men of note, the kingpins of their Houses, dead in one day—that was like the long-ago years of bloody feuding that had stripped half the towers of their heirs. Troian had been a child then. A man now, with mercantile awareness, he saw the upsurge of strife with misgiving. To exercise in a duel was one thing, to be set on and die at one's door, another entirely. When the bloodstained name-calling had hit Chenti, threatening his marriage, Troian had been doubly aggrieved. His father was treated to a rampaging diatribe and sat amazed, unused to such tactics from his dutiful son. Then the way was smoothed, the wedding secure again, unless some Chenti fool stabbed another of the Montargos in full view of the Rocca. But from what one heard, half the Montargo Tower lay sick of plague,

too reduced even to fight over leadership with its lord buried
and the heir gone under sentence of the garotta.

On his way to this room Troian had barely been able to be
polite, while Lord Chenti's fussings delayed him. Entering the
room, seeing Iuletta, all Troian's rush left him and he hesitated, as if he must walk over eggshell to reach her.

She had been ill, not the Sickness, thank God, but sick
enough. They said that was lamenting for her cousin. They
hinted it was also her fear of losing Troian. He knew himself
a little, aware of the fine figure he could cut. Flattered, yet he
had quite easily believed them. Keyed up, he looked for her
responsive tumult, and so interpreted her desire for him from
the nervous trembling he saw in her hands and eyelids. But
she was like a shadow. How ill she must have been, how ex-
quisitely and beautifully ill. For the illness had left her behind it, fragile as a crystal shard. And when she raised her
eyes to his, he saw the entreaty in them, which was genuine
enough, through all their blinding color.

He dropped to one knee, prince of manners as he had
trained himself, and took her hands, careful not to break the
glass.

"How have I lived," he said, "so long without you?"

At these words she began to cry, soundlessly and artistically. It seemed quite fitting. Her tears said to him: *I, too,
have suffered, deprived of you.*

"You have not changed to me, then?" he said.

And when she lowered her eyes, took it for bashfulness:
How can you doubt me?

He sat then at her feet, and talked to her, to entertain her
and make her happy, of himself. His interview had been limited, for reasons of propriety, and this had been made plain
to him. And so he rendered all he could, before he must go
away, to stay her. He knew she listened, spellbound, and he
too, as he spoke, was spellbound by her loveliness and her
grace. When her eyes came to him he smiled to encourage
them, and left his history to remind her of her beauty with
courtly remarks. Oh, the love he saw in her eyes, the melting
tenderness. And, since her weeping had ceased, he knew he
had lifted her up, renovated her by his presence. And in turn
her dependence upon him made his own eyes smart with sudden tears. It was in his heart to protect her all his life, and
that he could never grow bored with her as with other
women. And though, when at last he said to her, teasing her,
hoping for her blush, "Say, then, Iuletta, that you'll be glad

to live with me. Let me hear you say it," she did not blush,
she did at least softly but unfalteringly answer: "I shall be
glad." Then she reached out and brushed his hair gently from
his forehead with her hand, surprising him, for the gesture
was like that of a woman much older, a woman who had
known the company of men, who had borne sons.

"You know I'll cherish you," he said. "You'll be a flower
to me always in bloom."

Her eyes were tender still, melting still. He saw the con-
sistency of her look, but not its cause. He did not comprehend her eyes were full of pity.

Do this, and she was damned. But that did not matter. Do
this, and she denied forever the love she had yearned for and
so briefly known.

"The shoe on your foot," he said, "the glove on your hand.
Your slave, lady."

"And I," she said, "your grateful wife."

Coming back from the depth of some great night, he did
not know the rafters above him were rafters in Lombardhia,
of a little deserted house by the wayside. Nor did he truly
know that the face in the low candlelight was that of Doro,
worn but smiling at him. But he drank what he was offered
to drink, and feeling the spears of pain go through his body,
sank back, and remembered the dream he had had, aloud.

"I thought I was dying," Romulan Montargo murmured,
"and then dead. And someone had tied me to my bier,
strapped me to the slab in the tomb."

"A necessity I regret," said Doro, "but there's sometimes a
fit comes in the delirium. I took no chances of your lordship
rolling on this dirty floor. But you're free of straps now. The
fever's broken."

Romulan hardly heard him.

"I was dead," he murmured, "and thought I should never
see the sky or the world again. And then the tomb was
opened, and Iuletta came into it, stooping a little, I remember, under the low lintel of the vault."

Doro sat patiently and listened, holding the partly tasted
cup in his hands. The inn nearby had been good to them,
putting out provisions on the ground, and a bowl of vinegar
and balsamum in which to drop payment, not grudging them
their refuge providing they kept alone until the infection
passed.

Romulan's eyes were almost closed. He was drowsy, as yet, and peaceful.

"But here is the strangeness. She did not mourn me. She drew my corpse into her arms as I lay there, and kissed me over and over. And I felt the warmth of her lips and her hands, and I began to breathe. Her kisses gave me back my life, for I revived, like Lazarus. Iulet," he said, and now his eyes fell shut, his head turning on his shoulder and the black hair spreading on the straw pillow. "My love," he said, and slept.

EIGHTEEN

Over the corpses of the dead, after all, a marriage was to be made, celebrated, consummated. The girl's father was eager to hurry matters, lest the feud flare up and muddy the waters again. The groom was eager for the same reason. Other parties proved accommodating. A date was fixed, somewhat precipitate. There would be those who would say the betrothed pair had sinned and were wary of results. Pure in their innocence of immoral conduct, however, the bridal couple walked demurely together, had brimming cups raised to them and sweetmeats showered over them, and astrological charts drawn up for them, and sat in rose arbors as preliminary sketches were organized for a classical nuptial canvas, the usual one: Venus and Mars.

There seemed a gentleness about them, which was admired. The young man restrained and courteous in his obvious ardor. The maiden docile yet receptive. They endured together the jests, the homilies, the ribaldry. The holy instructions. The droppings of the peacocks which the artist had wished to draw in situ. It was decided that Iuletta and Troian looked well together, and would breed pretty children. He played and sang to her. They sang duets. Though always well-mannered, his hands and his lips could not keep from her. And when the long merry-makings of their families sailed like lighted boats past midnight, and propriety winked, it was perceived how the girl seemed glad enough to lean in the circle of his arm.

"Just so," Cornelia said, cordial and gladsome, doubt broomed away. "He is a fine young Mars and no mistake. There's no bad stroke in catching him. A handsome fish on your line, miss." Low voiced lessons followed in the faking of virginity. "I doubt you're breached enough after one night, even with him you had, that you cannot offer the gentleman a little proper difficulty."

Iuletta said nothing. Her skin since she had been ill was

like milk-crystal, clear enough, it seemed, to look through at the shadow of the bones. The faint pale hollowing under her eyes did not quite go away, despite herbal and cosmetic applications. Yet she was more beautiful than ever, so everyone declared. Love's anxiety, merely, troubled her, and she would soon be wedded and free of that.

A month, a fraction more, was folded away in dust behind the tracks Leopardo's pall bearers had made to the Basilica. The heat of summer, having reached its peak, nested there, the dove on the mountaintop, softened and loving. The season of fruits drew in, the air was scented with fast-ripening peaches, apricots, berries. The Sickness, in its turn, had died and was, in the way of dark things, not talked of any more. The nights, like the trees, ripened with fruits of silver.

And each one of those nights that she was alone, remembering his words to her: "The sky is prayer enough—so full of stars," prayerlessly and quietly, Iuletta Chenti wept, knowing her love, her only love, had forgotten her.

Not knowing the dragging lethargy she felt so often pull her down was all his, that the fever, going from him, as often happened with the healthy ones, had left not much of him in its wake. That he must grow back upon his own bones, like a stricken tree, young enough to accomplish it, but in peril, never quite safe, except in his servant's careful adequate nursing. She did not know that his dreams—trusting, yearning— were all of her, as hers, bitter and desolate, were all of him. Romulan her lover, and before God her husband. She thought him laughing in some tavern, blessed in his freedom from her. She had not known him long enough to be able to believe, in adversity and blindness, that he loved her still. She had known him only with heart and soul, and when they spoke to her now, telling her her grave error, she would not listen. Belmorio was her solitary hope in her abandonment. She must deny her soul and her heart. There was no other way. And she was glad of Troian's protection, glad of the kind and fascinated hand, the caressing mouth, the strong arm to lean upon. It was all she was to have, now, of love. So the world was.

To her confessor she awarded nothing of her ultimate damning crime. For unlike Belmorio, God offered no supporting arm, and no promise of shelter. And she had ceased to credit angels.

Ten mounted Chenti guardsmen trotted at the head, in

crimson flecked with gilt, spread two by two, five times. After them, the two banner bearers, carrying the armorial standard, bleeding bullion, with the liopard in gold, and Lord Chenti's personal escutcheon. After these came five minstrels, valiantly blowing, twanging and thumping. After *these* came ten picked Chenti kinsmen, garlanded and red as roses, with not a hint of mourning, and ten garlanded ladies in spotless white. Behind *those*, two girls in apple-pink on little white mules, and then a palancina tied over with ribbons and with up-looped curtains of gold tissue. Servants in gold balanced the litter's poles. The bride was just visible, like a bird of paradise in a cage. Directly behind rode Lord Chenti, his attendants, a horde of cousins. Another litter of darkest mulberry contained the bride's mother. Out-rider to the litter, also wreathed in flowers and grimly smiling, rode one of Lord Chenti's bastards, officially a nephew, got on a brother's wife. The position, which should have been Leopardo's, was significant, and perhaps unpleasant to the woman in the mulberry palancina, who kept her curtains closed. The procession ended with fifteen Chenti guard, three abreast, five times.

Somehow contriving to enter the Basilica square from another angle, the Belmorio procession was just a touch, tactfully yet undeniably, larger. Three banner-bearers paraded the Belmorian sigil, the personal sigil of the lord, and a glove on a damson ground for the lady, by birth a Retzi. The banner of the Ducal House came at some juncture in the display, where Chesarius rode with his attendants, the witness from the Chitadella, his cloth-of-gold barely yet just outshone by the bridegroom's. Pages in pale green satin were already throwing candies and small money to the populace. Twenty musicians hooted and piped. The guards were thick and green as gilded grass blades.

Cherry preserve and angelica, the two colored assemblages presently drew up equidistant from each other and the Basilica steps.

The mass of people in the square applauded, as skirts and mantles stirred like wings in a partial dismounting, and the clash of the two musics thankfully ceased.

The doors of the Basilica stood wide. Approaching from the right, the groom's party reached them first. You could notice the bridegroom from the farthest edge of the square, a figment of the sun itself in his cloth-of-gold the doublet of which had been pleated to tightness and seamed on the pleats, and these seams then sewn with green dove-tails of polished beryls. His linen remained white, but splashed by a fine spray of emeralds. Over all this, his hair was alight and blazing, with the wreath of myrtle leaves and roses lying on it as if placed there to burn. His handsome face was flushed by the early morning wine and the triumph of desire to come. He had eyes only for the bright litter and what would emerge from it. One of his two gentlemen attendants, implacably decorous, inclined his head slightly toward the other, to catch the whisper: "I think we are watching Jacob, after his fourteen years' wait."

The crimson party shortly reached the top of the steps. There was a flourish of satins and jewelry as the bride was put down and aided from her enclosure. Iuletta Chenti, on the arms of her father and her legal cousin of the grim smile, was lifted into the sunlight.

Observing him slyly, his own closest generative cousin, witness for the Belmorio side, saw Troian's face had now paled. Jealously, the closest generative cousin acknowledged why.

Iuletta Chenti, outlined by noon on a lavender sky deliriously hazed with dust, was already like a painting. From her wreath of white roses a white lace veil with a telling stitchery of gold fountained down her back. Her black hair had been mingled with gold, and a heavy golden necklace of Eastern design lay on her breast. In the Eastern manner, also, the single huge drop pearl, with its unusual lilac orient, depending on her forehead. The crimson silk gown gave the impression of translucence, like wine. The camisola had nectarines done in garnets. So much, all this, and her beauty overwhelming it, her beauty so much more.

Exquisite, too lovely to see or to touch. And as she came toward him, led by her father beneath the carvings and the angels over the porch, Troian Belmorio (even he), knew a moment of doubt.

But his own father amiably nudged him. They walked, and met the Chentis at the door.

As once before, the hands of bride and groom were drawn up and linked. Given to each other, they stood looking at each other, as if surprised. While vaguely, far off, the crowd congratulated this move, as all others.

Iuletta, meeting his eyes now, had discovered his paleness, and, as their fathers placed their palms together, she had felt his hand's dry tension, and its disbelief. She saw at last that, however selfishly or fleetingly, Troian had brought himself to love her.

And then, looking involuntarily beyond him, she saw Chesarius the brother of the Duke, the witness of her wedding at Marivero.

Her shock was so enormous that it did not outwardly show itself, and if Troian felt her fingers turn icy cold, his powers of logic were not, in that instant, at their most infallible. Her lids had been immediately lowered; they gave the impression of shyness, not the shutters flung closed over turmoil, which they had become.

She had not guessed, in her remotest dismay, that Chesarius would be the ducal witness at her second wedding, as at the first. Her fear and misery had been throughout spiritual or carnal—never practical. After her initial reminder to the nurse that her first marriage had been overseen by outsiders, Iuletta had mostly forgotten it. While silence on the part of those who might undo her current match, led her to think, if and when she did so, that the witnesses would never speak. (Plague, so rife in the Montargo Tower, could have dispatched the witness there. The boy called Benevolo was only a child. And the Rocca Tower was prudent: perhaps a gift might later be sent to the Duca's brother, cajoled from her new husband's purse—Cornelia's verdict and notions, which had been the more confidently relayed to Iulet as time elapsed without betrayal.)

Now reliance upon abstraction had brought the false bride to this pass. Was betrayal imminent? The face of the grave young man above his scarlet and gold offered nothing, neither threat nor reassurance. It was probably not his express wish to be here. Probably not his express intention to strip her infamy naked in the midst of the church—

Iuletta could not bring herself to look at him again, and now in any case they were walking into the cool white cave of the Basilica, between the stacked marble of the pillars, through the drenchings of spangled dust.

(She could not even ask God what she should do.)

If Chesarius spoke out, her shame, her horror, would surely be insurmountable. She beheld it all in a dazzle of foretelling. The astounded face of the priest, the detonation of rage that was her father, the Belmorios leaning together as if stunned, defensive, malicious, incredulous. And Troian, his shame perhaps vaster and less tolerable even than her own, staring at her, now white, now red, at a standstill between the conflicting tides of fury, embarrassed hurt, tripped and sprawling pride.

They saluted the High Altar, and went by. Flowers of light from the round window filled the air, staining her gown, the floor. The petals fell away. There were smoke and frankincense and candles. They had entered the capella.

Lilies and roses currently screened the rapt faces of the blessed, the controlled unhappiness of the wriggling damned. Yet here she had stood with Romulan, by that pillar, before that altar. And known that an abyss wider than infinity had come between them.

The chapel was filled. Beside herself, fifteen essential persons occupied the space. Lord and Lady Chenti. The parental Belmorios. The golden groom. Iuletta's two garlanded attendants in their dresses of pink sunshine. Troian's garlanded gentlemen in their clear glassy green. The Belmorio witness, the cousin, envious and haughty. The "cousin" witness from the Chenti Tower, no longer smiling, gnawing his mouth. The priest and his assistant benignly stationed at the altar. One gentleman in scarlet attending on . . . Chesarius.

Iuletta did not look at them. She did not, as for a wild moment she was tempted to do, glance in appeal toward her mother. Her mother was a hollow vessel, a mask, from skull to foot. Her mother mourned Leopardo in hidden, indefinable ways Iuletta had, sensitive herself beyond endurance, interpreted. Iuletta had at last fathomed, wrongly, Electra Chenti's soul. She had wished for a son. Leopardo had been that son's image but not the truth, and so she had reviled him. But Iuletta, the female reality, she hated.

Neither her God nor her mother would assist her. Nor her beloved, who loved her not. Only the one she cheated, dishonorably and foully cheated, who, handfasted with her, now knelt with her in obedience to the motions of the priest.

So she had knelt to be blessed, in Marivero.

Her heart quickened, and the golden necklace weighed at her throat like lead.

The light rain of the holy water was scattered upon them. It should sting and burn and scar her for her sin. But no, soft as dew, the water kissed her flesh. Could she not die now? She should have died. Should not have come to this shame. A sharp knife would have ended her confusion. She had leaned at her colored window and cried salt tears, could she not have cried salt blood?

But she would not die. God would not strike her down. God would not oblige.

Troian Belmorio's hand, firm and tender, led her now toward the altar.

"Lord, have mercy on us. Christ, have mercy on us."

The Mass was beginning, the short Mass suitable to the impatience of the ceremonies of love. Through the smoke and the incense, she watched the wafer of Body elevated above the chalice of Blood.

Surely he must speak now? Surely Chesarius, his duty and his knowledge on him heavier than her leaden collar, bound by nothing but the peril to his soul and his anger at her harlotry—surely he must cry out against her—now—*now*—

Romulan. . . . *Let me die. Let me die now before he speaks.*

She could not even faint. Could not even loosen her joints sufficiently to fall down. The powder of dead flesh on her tongue, the taste of blood in her mouth. It should have choked her. It had not.

The Mass, its banquet partaken of, was concluded.

The phrases of the wedding were commencing. The priest was speaking of grace and the duality of man with woman that was the decree and gift of Heaven. And then, turning to Troian, the first of the momentous questions was being asked of him.

And Chesarius had not shouted, had not even stepped deliberately forward and interrupted the priest with a frowning shake of the head. Chesarius had done nothing. And suddenly, her senses swimming in a dreadful sickness that would not allow her to swoon, she knew Chesarius would not speak at all. His reasons, base or sympathetic, she could not devine. Perhaps he pitied her as she had pitied herself, the easement and discard of a murderer. That he was here was possibly, after all, intentional, his purpose to demonstrate his discretion publicly. No, he did not mean to reveal her treachery. Her conviction was utter. She was secure.

(Troian answered the priest's inquiry, slowly and carefully, his voice almost beautiful in the silent timeless chapel.)

And Iuletta knew, as utterly in that moment, that she had relied upon Chesarius' betrayal.

And if not betrayal here, today, betrayal sooner, during the days and days of preparation. When she was hailed and toasted, when she was sketched in the arbor, when the love songs had lingered with the candles and she had lain on Troian's

arm. All that while, she had expected the shouting voice—
Chesarius, Luca Montargo, Benevola Montargo D'Estemba.
Even Mercurio rising from the tomb to point at her, his
glamour only a little dimmed by death, laughing, cruel and
kind: "And may I hope to see you again at Susina's brothel?
And may I remind you, my donna, you are already wed?"
Yes, she had awaited them, her betrayers, quick or dead.
Each time Cornelia had prattled, soothing her—no one will
speak—Iuletta had known this was not so. She had known it
with such certainty she did not distinguish it and remained in
ignorance of her knowledge. For she had been *assured* of betrayal. For she had needed, trusted in, *desired* betrayal.

Which now was denied.

She saw the priest's face with its solemn smile turn to her,
and the lips parting.

"And will you, Iuletta Chenti, uphold the honor and fidel-
ity of this House?"

So simple, the answer: *I will*.

The silence spread, like something viscous spilled, between
them all.

The priest, solicitous of timidity, repeated his question
more firmly.

"And will you, Iuletta Chenti, uphold the honor and fidel-
ity of this House?"

The silence spread. She sensed Troian half turning to her.
She heard the pale rustlings of movements, gowns and
mantles and veils disturbed. A clink of gems. A mutter. The
face of the priest was concerned. Must he repeat the words
once more?

Iuletta drew her hand from Troian Belmorio's. Another
traitor had after all been available.

"Father, I am unable to marry this man."

Still the silence. She would have anticipated a reaction of
noise. But no, no noise at all now. She felt herself enclosed,
separated. The capella was far away, and the people in it.
She did not have to be afraid. She was old, and like
Daphnea, was petrifying inside a shell of bark.

"I cannot marry him," she said, "for I'm wed to another."

Then, the noise came. Her father, of course, bellowing like
a bull. She did not cower from the voice, nor the brutal steps,
and when the hand seized her arm in the gentle smoke, she
did not flinch.

"What are you saying, girl? Eh? Answer me! Did I hear

you rightly? Eh? Answer or you'll feel the weight of my hand."

The priest remonstrated. Troian, she supposed, could not at this point speak.

Chenti paid no heed to the priest. He shook her. She saw only boiling redness where he stood.

"I am married," she said.

He thundered. "Married? Damnable hussy, you're mad not married. Where did I get you? Dishonor me, you thankless jade, before my friends—" and in the middle of the tirade, ridiculously, macabrely, he was bowing to them, trying to restore himself, though beyond self-governance—"Forgive my chagrin, sirs. This girl of mine is playing the goose with us. Are you not, Iuletta? Come, let's hear the truth."

"You have had the truth."

His fingers seemed to meet through her arm. She could no longer see him, for she had closed her eyes. The darkness would protect her.

"Tell me his name then!" The man who held her roared. "Bring it up like vomit, you slut. Who are you wed to?"

She found then she could not speak the name. Not from fear, but because it was, even yet, so precious to her. The two words *Romulan Montargo* were beautiful, as her love had been. She could not form the syllables and give them over to this rampaging beast.

She heard the rasp of fabric then, and knew her father had thrown up his arm to hit her violently, before the priest, the altar, the wedding party, the blessed and the damned. He was very strong. The blow might break her neck. She waited, unable to move in his grasp, but the blast of skin, muscle and bone did not reach her. Instead she heard a strange grunting, and then the awful grasp of fingers was prized from her arm. Astonished, her eyes flew open.

Chesarius, the ducal kin, was lowering both Lord Chenti's arms to his sides, with the deceptive smoothness of great physical control.

"No, sir," Chesarius said, "there's no need to beat her." His voice was entirely level. But in it, conceivably, was the idea of a man who had grown tired of animal force, injustice and the death of friends.

Chenti mouthed. Some of the words were audible, others not.

Chesarius said: "I will tell you his name myself, sir, since it's gone so far. Your daughter is wedded to Romulan Montargo, dead Valentius' heir. I know this, for I was their witness, along with two or three others whose names I do not think you require. The marriage was legal and honorable, before men and before God. It was to have been revealed the next evening, and would have been, and compensation made where it was necessary, if," Chesarius paused. He said stiffly, "if there had been no bloodshed that day and two Houses brought low for it. Iuletta," he said, "you need not have spoken because of me."

She saw something of his face, mostly the serious eyes. She wished to say that this she knew, and that it was her own self which had driven her to speak. But she could no longer, it seemed, find words for anything.

Chesarius glanced at the priest.

"Yes, Father. You may expect me at the confessional. And my gratitude for absolution, in whatever form of penance you impose."

Iuletta, following his gaze, found, accidentally, Troian Belmorio.

Again, she was impelled to vocalize. Again, she could not. What remained for her to say?

His color was high, as if with fever, or as if he had been slashed across either cheek. His mouth was slightly open, and he breathed through it, very fast. His eyes were black with anguish, each of the agonies she had predicted for him. Humiliated and robbed, his new love stabbed in the heart, his pride in rags, Troian Belmorio stared at her, as he had stared from the moment she failed in her responses. Somewhere in his face, a very young boy pleaded with her to admit she lied. Beside the boy, the inevitable man, snarling, knew she did not.

It seemed that still he could not speak any more than she. Gestures must speak instead. And quickly then he pulled the bridal wreath unburned out of the flames of his hair, and tore it across and threw it, now two handfuls of mashed leaves and weeping roses, at the hem of her dress. After which he turned, and staying for no one, strode out of the chapel and away through the Basilica toward the doors, the steps, the square where the processions waited to sing and be merry, and the crowd to call and praise and hold out its paws for coins. In a second, with a muffled curse, tearing off his own wreath, Troian's cousin ran after him.

Old Belmorio, his face rewoven by disgust and bewilderment, hesitated only a few moments longer. He swept the

Chenti party with one look, and said, with a single cold nod to Chenti's Lord, "I shall expect your messenger," gave his Retzi wife his arm and stalked in the wake of his son; the two gentlemen attendants, still unfortunately garlanded, hastening to follow.

The two maiden attendants of Iuletta were softly crying, huddling together, alike in pink and tears.

Chesarius bowed to Lord Chenti.

"If you're wise, my lord, you'll keep your kin here till I can fetch some men from the Chitadella to clear the square."

Chenti drew in a thick labored breath.

"You knew of all this?"

"Yes, my lord, as I told you. But I hardly think you'll raise your arm to *me*."

Chenti balked. He shifted and plucked at his mantle.

"You misunderstand me, sir. I'm the Duke's loyal admirer."

"So are we all. He has admirable qualities, as your lady could attest, after her walk to the Rocca. Could you not, madama? But then my brother, sir, hates to see a woman physically abused. I am sure you will remember this, when alone with your daughter."

Chesarius and his gentleman went away. Next, the priest and his assistant, who the bastard Chenti "cousin" caught by a pillar, and presumably pressed money upon.

Chenti paced about, looking at none of them, till abruptly he ordered the bastard to collect his horse from its station under the steps and bring it to him in the alley that ran behind the graveyard. The bastard hastened to comply.

"I'll be damned if I'll wait in this soured slop," Chenti said to his wife. He examined her, and said, "*Your* work, you bitch. I might have known your fruit would be rotten."

Electra said nothing. Shouldering clumsily by the columns, Chenti went out, and so through the side-door that lovers used for trysts, along the cloister and down among the trees of death.

The two bridesmaids had crept on to a distant bench to cry when Electra rose and went to her daughter. Iuletta had not moved since Belmorio had cast the garland at her. In her flawless bridal finery she stood there, having brought chaos to everything else, herself apparently untouched.

When Electra stood before her, their likeness and their unlikeness, both, were disconcerting. The black hair, the slender shapely form. Yet hyacinth hair in one, dragon's blood in the other, and the one figure like a flower stem and the other figure like a bone. The faces were unmatched. The younger peerlessly beautiful, lowered, unreadable. The older face like a carving, with a snake behind it.

"Well, my child," Electra said, "look up, and get my news."

Iuletta, slowly, lifted her head. And Electra struck her, once, with a flat thin sound like a snapping blade.

"I doubt Chesarius will deny you one blow from your mother's correcting palm," Electra said. "The rest is soon given you. Listen carefully. You have wed the enemy of the Chenti Tower, the butcher of your cousin Leopardo, my brother's son, my nephew, who—even dead—is worth a score of you. What should I do then? The villain, your husband, murderer of my kindred, has vanished and I do not know his land or his lodging, nor could I come at him there. But take heed, for this will interest you. I'll set those to watch you that you cannot see, and if you see, cannot elude. And if your bedmate risks justice to find you here, or anywhere, or gets you word, or should you move to join him, I shall know of it, and how to come at him. And then I'll send another shall meet your love, your darling. Another who will embrace him with knives, kiss him with poisons, put him to bed in a grave. Do you believe me, Iuletta?"

"Yes, madama. But he's gone and will not come back to me." And, having regained the means of speech, Iuletta met the black insomniac eyes with her own, wondering and blue and deep, and older far than Electra Chenti's. "He has abandoned me, Mother. And now I thank God, my soul upon its knees, that he has."

NINETEEN

Lord Chenti had laid his anger to one side. Admittedly, laid it aside where it was still visible, and where he might swiftly pick it up again without fumbling for it, but so much was to the good. (A man of strong principles and political ability, beset by the idiocy of the females under his sway— Sweet Jesus, he had restrained himself where another would have used his rights to work havoc. He had been uncommonly lenient. Well, perhaps that also was to the good. He was a worldly and a cunning diplomat, who might yet wrest harmony from disorder.) So, clad in the under-mantle of the stern interrogator, he stood before the pink trees of his daughter's bedchamber, unsuitably framed by foliage, birds and fruit, bending on the girl his most awful look, and with it the full weight of his patriarchal majesty, quite unaware of the grotesque and horrifically laughable figure he cut. Perfectly aware of the extent of his God-dictated jurisdiction.

Iuletta sat, straightbacked and tearless, on a small brocade stool. In the corner, a pile of heaving clothes, the nurse rocked and cried and patted herself. Chenti was suspicious of Cornelia. He had been asking questions, his voice, the petrified voices of others, surging up and down the Tower like winds. He perceived now the damned marriage had been effected on the night Cornelia and her charge strayed afield to a priest's oratory and did not return till morning. That anyone would countenance such a pack of nonsense—if he had been home, things would have been ordered differently. But was a man to have no pleasure? He had thought them obedient and virtuous. And his fish-jelly of a wife—He had thought her at least vigilant.

Part of the matter had already been dissected, and found lamentably sound. The priest at Marivero was real, and not some excommunicate or stooge procured by the Montargos.

"And now you'll tell me," Lord Chenti said, "whether or not we may send to his Holiness at Roma for an annulment."

In the corner bawdy Cornelia choked on her tears, gazing at him aghast.

Iuletta did not even blush, though her eyes never left the ground.

"If you ask me, sir, if we are man and wife, we are."

"He had you then. Consummation. And no doubt the lock's broken wide."

"Oh!" Cornelia said.

"And since you're broken," went on Chenti, loudly, "are you filled? Are you bulging with his monster?"

"My lord!" Cornelia cried.

"Hold your tongue you bloody gossiping meddler. Do you think I will have missed who aided the fool in her foolery? Count your hours in this house, you splattering hag. They're done."

Cornelia collapsed.

Iuletta said softly and distinctly:

"You're mistaken, my lord. My nurse knew nothing of what I did."

"And the sun sets in the east. Her daughter's a whore. She'd make you another, and has done it. *Be silent!*" he thundered, and Cornelia was silent. Chenti dropped the edge of his anger again. Breathing like an engine, through his mouth, he said, "Look up, you slattern, and answer yes or no to what I asked."

And Iuletta raised her eyes, which seemed pale now, but steady, as steady as the eyes of one blind.

"No, my lord."

Chenti breathed. "You'd swear that?"

"I will swear to it."

Chenti took a turn between the park of painted trees, swiveled and faced her again. "This husband who is unable to prime you with child, this slayer of your kindred. Where is he?"

"I do not know."

"Your mother thinks you do."

"My mother hopes I do, so she may find him through me and have him killed."

"And what do you dream *I* want him for? To smack kisses on his forehead? I will have him—accommodated. Your marriage shall be annulled, one way or another."

"I know nothing of where he is."

"A charming knight. Takes your treasure then leaves you, worthless to me, on my hands. Well. A search can be made.

And when he's found, he's dead. Think him so from this instant. And now, attend to me. You have brought a rain of mud on this House, on the name and emblem of the Chentis. When I heard you speak in the chapel, I wished the earth had swallowed you and I'd never had a daughter. Do you listen?"

"Yes, my lord. I am sorry that I grieved you."

"*Grief.* Grief, you say?" The rage was lifted and shaken, incarnadine, smoking. "Shut your mouth and keep it so. Do as you're bid if you would be mine and no grief—*grief* by the howling stars—no grief to me. I'll tell you what you will do. You will write to Troian Belmorio. You will say you lied in the capella. That you lied from shame and terror, and out of the great love you bear for him, for Troian, that you could not contemplate his wrath, and his dishonor. You will explain the cause: that the Montargo devil forced you. Forced you, lady. No wedding, no consummation. A rape," Chenti straightened himself, glaring into his daughter's white and slowly comprehending dismay. "The letter will be conveyed secretly. A bribe will ensure Red-hair alone gets hold of it. The ninny is besotted with you. By the Christ, I thought he'd drop in a swound when you refused him. He will, like the numbskull he is, choose to overlook your defilement, and will persuade Belmorio Primo to back him. Doubtless, they'll want proof you'll not saddle them with a bastard, but you say you can supply them that. We shall have the wedding over again, and you, my lady, will go to it consenting. Forget the sin. By the time the ring's on your finger, Romulan Montargo will be dead." Chenti balanced, his thumbs hooked in his jeweled belt. Now a certain smugness augmented the interrogator. His own cleverness pleased him. Finally he said to her staring blind eyes, "Get on your knees, then, and thank me. You'll cost me a fortune in bribes. Even bloody Chesarius must be gifted. You slut, you should be rejoicing your father is so careful of you."

Iuletta rose.

"My lord," she said. "I cannot—do this."

"Cannot?" he said, and his red face solidified and filled with darker red, though still his voice was human. "You'll do as I tell you."

She took in one long breath and the golden necklace that was yet on her breast fanned and glittered. So much breath for one small word.

"No."

And Chenti drew back to him the garment of fury and

swathed himself therein. His voice ascended, shaking and foaming, and the spit flew from his lips.

"*No? No?*"

Cornelia, her hand to her mouth, stumbled up from her corner and her collapse. She saw fresh homicide, Iuletta its victim.

"*No?* What use then are you? For what have I nurtured you all these years, you parasite?" Chenti began to move forward in slow terrible strides, his hands two swollen fists. "To be the sport of my enemies? Ah? Ah? Do you reckon I must support another man's wife? Feed the beast, clothe it? Keep another man's heifer in grazing, eh? I am to do that?" Iuletta stood motionless before him. She did not look afraid, though probably she was. And her lack of fear inflamed him further. "You've had your share of my bounty," he shouted. "I fed you up to be a present for my friend. But you prefer to carve for yourself. Carve then, you damnable little whore—" and one great hand whirled upward.

Cornelia rushed and caught the hand, and hung on it.

Chenti's voice was now that of a beast. Braying, he tried to heave her away, but her bulk anchored her, could not be budged.

"No, my lord. My lord! She's sick, sir. She's stupid, sir. No sir! Pardon her—be gentle—"

"Off, you fat mutton," he cried, and the other hand came down on Cornelia, in a thud of heavy flesh and heavy materials and with one tiny wounded cry.

Iuletta came alive. She ran to him and stood between her father and the nurse, just as the nurse had come between herself and him.

Her eyes were frightened, at last, confused and afraid, the eyes of the child who, scarcely more than a month ago, she had been. Perhaps it was this that saved her from his fists, this sign and homage of fear. Or maybe the sheer murder of the bestial force had spent itself. Nevertheless, he turned from his daughter, and reaching up he ripped down the gleaming curtains of her bed. And next, walking steadfastly from place to place, he attended to her woman's playthings; her books were flung about, her mandolin taken down and smashed, her jewels scattered and trodden on. "*So*," he ranted methodically, smiling, the sweat and the spit bubbling from him, "*thus*," he said. "All this I lavished on you. No more."

Iuletta stooped to the nurse, who nodded and sat up huffing and puffing, trying to reassure her. And Lord Chenti, like a mischievous, malevolent small boy, flung a vial of scent at them which, breaking on the tessellations a foot away, strewed the skirts of both the women's gowns and Iuletta's hair with chips of pottery and drops of heady perfume.

When he was done, he stood, shredding the parchment of one last book in his hands.

"Well," he said. "Where will you go now?"

Iuletta, kneeling by her nurse, dropped her head, and the black splashed tresses hid her.

"You'll not stay in this house," Lord Chenti said. "What is mine obeys me and stays here. You're different. Out, then. Out with the whore-spawner on the floor. In the clothes you stand in, nothing more. You may both go free of the Chenti Tower."

Cornelia made a sound, and he bayed at her a long salivating jumble of profanities. Then, satisfied in his rank dissatisfaction, Lord Chenti turned and went to the inner door.

"Be away before sunset," he said. "Go," he said, "dirty hag, to your daughter's nunnery. And take your new little nun with you."

After the door had crashed shut, Cornelia and Iuletta remained for some minutes as they were, seated and kneeling amid the carnage and the reeking scent.

Eventually Cornelia spoke.

"He has a powerful arm, your father. But I'm not badly maimed. A bruise or two. It will mend. But you. . . . Give him an hour to cool, and then go to him, on your hands and knees, crawling on your belly if you must."

Iuletta came to her feet. She walked away through the rubble, and glancing down, the pools of perfume reminded her of rain water spilled there from a young man's mantle.

"I would rather," Iuletta said, "die than give in to him."

"But you needs must. Oh, dear Lord, what else can you do?"

"As he said."

"But he meant nothing of that."

"Do you think not?"

"For myself—why, I believe he did mean it. Despite the years I've served this House. But if you—"

"Even to save your place in the Tower, I could not. I am sorry. Truly so."

Iuletta had reached the window of colored panes. She leaned on it. The heat of afternoon glowed in it, it was not refreshing, but she could not now move away. For some reason, the window had always been her refuge. The symbol of an exit, closed by glass.

"You're a fool, girl," Cornelia said. There was no spring to her scolding. Her voice was a flat instrument. "What will become of you?"

"Am I to care for that? I had my day and my night of joy. Some do not get so much."

Cornelia, unseen, touched at her shoulder. It was quite numb from the blow. If it had reached her heart, it might have killed her. But no, her heart had been reached.

For her era, she was old. Old and cumbersome and fat, used to sweet living and soft beds, to a boy carrying her parasol, and a guard to ride behind her when she stirred far abroad. Used to good wine, and a provision for the unthinkable unavoidable future. If Iuletta had gone to the Belmorio Tower, Cornelia would have kept her place here, honored, at least not spurned. And when Iuletta was brought to childbirth, perhaps she would have sent for her canny nurse, asked her advice again, begged her sympathy. And the children, why they might have been as fair as—

But now, disgrace and poverty. And for sure, as the tyrant said, nowhere to fall save in the Bhorgabba, and on the hard daughter, kind enough when the visits were infrequent, but now, a provider?

Cornelia did not weep any more. So life was, and the world. And mortals, poor worms, slithering hopelessly toward the fiery pit in an effort to keep warm.

Now, at the window glass, Iuletta did weep. A strange and dreadful elation moved within her, like broken ice. She had lost everything, but not, in the end, the value of her love. That, even though Romulan had betrayed it, she had kept. And now, in despairing triumph, she knew she would have died indeed rather than leave go.

In the hour before sunset, Susina's merry house of boys and girls was generally tight-shut and bolted, its shutters clamped, baking like sugared bread in the sun. On the far side of it, the market tirelessly unwound its noises raucous and enterprising, its aromas delicious and repulsive, until dusk put paid to another day's commerce. Then, beneath the light of torches, or in pure shadow, other creatures plied their business there, more softly, while the pleasure houses all about flung wide their windows and put out their banners of lampshine and enticement. There were, of course, those of the trade who worked by day, and those who worked both by day and by night. Susina's house, being of high repute and buoyant with good custom, kept to its limited hours diligently and with pride. Susina's charges, well-fed, well-clad, well-doctored, lived often quite long enough to retire in comfort, if no longer in faultless beauty.

This late afternoon, the mistress of the establishment was seated in her garden-courtyard, already in a puce regalia with flauntings of vermilion, but her feet in battered slippers propped on the low table in company with the dish of figs and apricots and the wine jar. On Susina's right, a faun of dull marble leaned to her solicitously, offering marble grapes. On her left stood the cinnamon-skinned male child, slave from the East and great curiosity of the house, who fanned her with an oriental plume. The sumptuous odor of the courtyard trees was a decided protection against market smells. The trees also caught the sunlight in their net and hung it between their branches like an awning, tinting everything below with golden shade, the dish of fruit, the woman's hair, the boy, the marble faun. The other statuary glimpsed amber through the leaves, and the old walls glowed almost red. Here and there a stone or a leaf seemed burning, and in the wine jar a gold fish blazed as it drowned, until the sun should shift again.

From the market, over the roof and down the wall, came the distant difficult sounds of a bullock cart. Susina, recalled, raised her eyes and duly noted that behind the inward-facing glass of the upper floor there were now vague stirrings like those of insects in honey. Her protégées were waking and preparing themselves. Lazily, time was in hand.

And when the girl came running out to say the street door was knocked upon, she was imperiously instructed that the too-early guest be sent away.

"But it is two ladies, Maestra!"

The Maestra knew at once, by some unexplained inner means, that one of these was her mother. Uneasily, Susina took her feet from the table and arose.

"Let them come through," she said, and drained her cup.

The two women, who had stood gazing at the naughty frescoes in the anteroom (based upon hardly naughtier ones at Pompeia), presently arrived in the outdoors balm of screened sunlight, and halted. The girl who had let them in hurried away at her mistress's nod to fetch more wine cups. The Eastern boy and the marble faun remained unmoved.

Susina widened charcoaled eyes.

She had expected Cornelia, on this unlooked-for visit, to be
accompanied by some serving-maid, who perhaps wished to
exchange service of one sort for service of another—Cornelia
had once or twice brought the willing who had asked to be
interviewed here. But, under the sepia outer vestments and
the smoky veil, Susina perceived, for the second time, Iuletta
Chenti.

The first occasion Iuletta had been sprung on her, the
worldly daughter had quailed at her mother's stupidity. To
bring a virgin of high-birth to the stew-house . . . ! The
mother's motives—that her charge must go with her at that
time, and she craved to meet her daughter. . . . Susina
doubted, even somewhat divined some other inner reason of
Cornelia's that had to do with showing true daughter to sur-
rogate daughter and vice versa. Yet none of this had angered,
even it had intrigued. Susina, who had learned to be respect-
fully and cordially easy with the aristocracy, had managed
well enough. Now she was frankly shocked. Once was in-
triguement and risk sufficient. However, rather than burst out
in irritated remonstrance, the young woman bowed, after the
Eastern fashion, rather aware as she did so of her breast tips,
peeping over their ledge like eager birds. For this end her
gown was designed, but in the sight of the pure, one thought
of such things.

Through the syrupy light, she had not properly taken in
the color of her mother's face, even out of its veiling. Then
Cornelia, not approaching her, said flatly:

"I'm cast forth, and my nurseling with me. Let me sit
down. My heart is bleeding or weeping, I know not which."

"Sit," said the Maestra, and herself also sat, somewhat suddenly, again on her bench, under the bending of the faun.

Iuletta, in her disguise, stood on like a ghost.

"Pardon me, my lady. Please be seated," Susina said.

"You are kind," the girl replied. It had a strange wealth of
meaning, that little phrase, as if to be shown any such
kindness was astonishing at this season. But she sat and removed her veil, and Susina was put in mind of a dancer. The
grace was exquisite, just like the girl herself. Susina had
heeded as much before. She had no envy, the whore-mistress.
To her, Iuletta was like a star, rarefied and alien, the denizen
of another world, foreign as the pretty boy from Inde. (Who
had himself taken notice. Susina sent him on an errand at

once.) Thankfully, the servant came back then with the wine
cups, which were soon disposed and seen to.

Cornelia gulped, her throat parched by the daunting journey they had undertaken from the Higher Town to the Lower
in the westering glare of day. Pinched, prodded-at, awarded
cat-calls every inch of the way—so it had seemed to her.
They had no man to protect them, no litter to shield them, no
servant to show their rank and repel casual boarders. In their
chameleon drapes, alone, they might be anyone's prey. ("The
clothes you stand in, nothing more," the devil had said to
them—not even the rich bridal gown at that, for it had been
changed. Even the concealment of cloaks he would have denied. And Iuletta would have obeyed, scorning to take any
further charity from the Chenti Tower. Cornelia had insist-
ed.) In her soul, she knew all they did was insanity. They
should have waited. He would have cooled, the old pig, the
hog, the brute. But no. Iuletta, proud and white, stalked from
the house. Away from her childhood and her help and her
hope, and the nurse must follow. And as they crossed the
edge of the square under the Basilica, Iuletta had paused,
pointed at the fountain, and remarked: "See, a grey cat. My
sorrow's omen." Reaching the door of the bawdy-house, Cornelia was ready to sink. Heat and distress, dejection and frus-
trated choler. And now here, what?

"Well, Mother," Susina said at last, once more downing
her cup, "you do surprise me. You do set me whirling. *Cast
forth.*"

"Like emptyings," said Cornelia. Her heart thudded; her
arm ached and tingled where she had received the blow that
had still come to her heart.

"Why?" not unreasonably said Susina.

(Two girls about early in Hellish cochineal and angelic
blue caught the Maestra's warning eye, and withdrew into the
house again.)

Cornelia took breath, but only sighed.

It was Iuletta Chenti who spoke.

"I was secretly wedded to one of the Montargo Tower. I
should have married Troian Belmorio. My father would force
me to it still and I will not be forced."

Susina loosened her eyes, which had seemed for an instant
about to pop.

"And your husband?"

"Romulan Montargo. Under sentence of death, he has fled
for his life."

"Hah!" exclaimed Susina, and compressed her lips. Some
gossip reached her, though clear news of the debacle at the
Basilica earlier that day had not, as yet—certain persons having been exercised to mask it. Of the deaths of Leopardo
Chenti, Valentius Montargo and Flavian Estemba she was
well-informed. In her way, she had grieved for the last of
these. Physical glamour she admired, and an open purse like-
wise. Mercurio, on his rare visitations, had been generous
and, if she dared to admit it, for she did not often indulge
sentiment, a delightful patron of the wares of the house, so-
phisticated, gentle. His death had incensed her, briefly, for
she did not often either indulge her rage. Men fought and
died all the time. Montargo Primo she had not known. Of
Leopardo she had been greatly unenamored. At no stage had
Susina credited the rumor Romulan had slain Flavian Es-
tamba. She, like a number of others, sussed where to allocate
blame.

"Your husband then," said Susina, with some care, "will
send for you?"

"My husband, I think, has no wish for me."

Susina considered. She remembered Romulan, the straight
limbs and teeth, the woman's eyes of him, the man's arrogance. The sheer male beauty, so similar to, as she came to
dwell on it, this feminine beauty before her now.

"Maybe you're mistaken, lady," Susina observed. "But until
you know, what do you plan?"

"Not to impose upon you," Iuletta said. She came to her
feet and walked to Susina, so the Maestra felt obliged to get
up again in her turn. "I have no jewels which are not
Chenti's, save this ring. This is mine. He—my husband—gave
it me. Let me give it to you. It's gold. It will pay for my keep
a little while, and then I shall have found some transport
from the town."

"Where will you go?" Susina asked, struck by this senseless
courage and this silly, awe-inspiring independence. Neither
had been noticeable upon the other visit. Such did men bring
women to by their loss, great weakness or great self-reliance.

"To the only place which will consent to house me. Some
sisterhood. I shall become Christ's bride. A suora."

Before she could restrain herself, Susina laughed.

"*You*, lady?" she said. "I fear you're made for the world."

"So are we all," Iuletta said, "but I think the world is too
cruel for me."

She held out the wedding ring and Susina withdrew a step.

"I'd get ill-luck, taking that from you, little wife."

"I have nothing else."

"Then keep it. You're my mother's child, more than I ever was. You had her milk, not I. I will not call you 'sister,' in case you spit on me. But you can lodge here awhile gratis, as she will, the old puss."

On her bench, Cornelia was partaking of her third cup, and more cheerful for it. It was a fact, she knew Iulet far better than she knew this puce and vermilion plum of hers. Susina had made her own way. Judging by the courtyard and the house and the wine, a primrose path indeed. And if Hellfire was at the end of it, then so it was for many others.

"She's happy enough," Susina said. "What I'll do with her, Jesus and his saints alone know. I must beware. She could no doubt run the place better than I." Iuletta dropped her eyes, and Susina concluded she offended her. "Excuse my chatter, my donna. I mean you no harm."

But Iuletta softly said,

"It was here I saw him first."

Arrested, Susina poised, her eyes flying to the stair, the balustrade, the windows of the mezzanine floor above.

"So you did. He wounded by some scoundrel's sword—and you wounded by the blind child's arrow."

One thing was certain. Iuletta Chenti, even had she wished it, entreated it, and even might it have been safely done, would never make a whore. With one she loved she would be fire and flower and flood. But with any other, worthless, cold and useless. The Belmorio had missed a sad disappointment there. Besides, this beauty was too much. It was to be worshipped, not tumbled, or if tumbled, only by its equal. Brother and sister, Romulan and Iulet. Some hereditary trick, of course, from the cross-breeding of the aristocratic towers. Somewhere in their ancestors' past, the blood line must have been one.

Poor Mercurio, caught between such grinding stones. Belmorio, too. Even Leopardo now she could almost pity. For there was some traffic of destiny here, an astrologer or witch would see it in a second.

"I think, little donna," said Susina, "you should not despair quite yet." And in her practical way Susina was pleased, saddled with the mother, too, though she seemed to be. Romulan was now Montargo's heir, and one day might get his pardon—and be grateful to those who aided his loveling.

But then Iuletta looked at her again with adult eyes, chill and sure.

"Thank you for your kindness. But he will not return. That is death to him. Nor send me word—that would be death, too. Besides, I think he is happy to be free of me. He was not my bird to keep in a cage. I want nothing of this world anymore. I shall be a nun."

And she placed the ring quietly in Susina's open hand, and went silently back to her seat.

Then Susina perceived in her, not grace, but death, and crossed herself, unseen, over her half-bared breasts.

The sunset was soft. Milk mingled with the blue. The trees, the towers, held the sun to the horizon. Then began to let it go.

Electra Chenti, in the etiolated shadows, walked from the capella and waited, the Basilica before her, her attendants at her back. Her lord had sent her on his business here: "Go pray," he had said. "And slip this purse to the priests." She had done his command, of course, without fuss. Cold enough to burn, she was yet his dutiful wife.

He, for his part, had told her of Iuletta's flight. Plainly, he had not expected his child to act in such a manner. Going to the chamber of painted trees an hour after their confrontation, he had reckoned to find the girl amid the broken furnishings, screeching in a deluge of tears—*I will do anything, only do not send me away*. Instead, away she was. And the debris left on the floor, and her garments in their chests, and her gems, just as he had instructed. Flummoxed, he explained to himself how things were. He saw he should not have been quite so harsh. She had taken him at his word and deemed his forgiveness a goal impossible, whatever she promised. Well, let her tremble, then. Doubtless the fat jabberd had found them some lodging in the mercantile quarter. Tomorrow he would send one to seek them. The girl would be yet the more willing to accede after a night of poor food and fleas. (He had not read the eyes of his wife, which judged the outcome of his deeds and knew him a fool, and displayed their knowledge. He did not desire to realize he had earned defiance, and so caused the vast dislocation he had, or that in doing it he had also disturbed Electra's voiceless, sinuous plans.)

Electra. Her wifely duty done, she had halted, staring through her veil and between the columns. Her eyes had found one of the subsidiary caves where, behind their gilded palisades, stood the tombs of the mighty Houses who had held to Verensa the longest.

"Who is that?" she presently inquired.

A girl dipped her head.

"I do not know, madama. He is unseemly."

"The name of the tomb? Is it Estemba?"

"Yes, madama."

"Go ahead of me," Electra said. And when they had done so, she walked slowly, her raven's gown sweeping the dusts and the dried petals after it along the floor, toward the tomb, its lifeless mourning Eros above it, its living mourning Eros below.

Electra's mind did not move necessarily with logic. It moved with instinctual aptness, like the gathering and darting of a serpent. She had always had, too, where the world and custom permitted it, a serpent's near-perfect timing.

She stood perhaps half a minute beside the rail, and then she said, "You are lamenting with a great noise. Is it for Flavian Estemba? Beating your head on the marble, I assure you, will not appease him. You need another's blood for that."

Hearing her voice, registering that it was directed at him, the young man—whose tower had suitably clad him from birth in mourning black—fell silent, but did not turn.

"Oh, yes," she said then. "I understand your grief. I, too, have lost one dear to me. And at the same hands."

The figure clinging to the tomb stiffened. Inaudibly, the two words came, but they could only be the words they were, the name:

"*Romulan Montargo.*"

"Yes," Electra said. "That traitor villain. My nephew he has slain. He has disgraced my daughter."

Saffiro Vespelli moved about and laid his shoulders against the tomb of the Estembas. White Eros and black. The shadows were kind and hid his face.

"Their feud was old, was dead," he said to her, or through her. "Montargo, Estemba. And then he turned on him. As a dog will. Turned on him and slew him. And Mercurio had nothing to defend himself but the bronze sword I gave him as a gift, a jest—God forgive me. My fault, mine." He covered his face with one hand. The other would not let go of the tomb. Bowed in this way, slim and black-haired, he looked like Romulan. "I will kill myself. I'll damn myself. I'll be damned with him."

"While the murderer lives," said Electra, weightless as a silk glove falling at his feet.

Initially he made no move, and then, he picked it up, that glove.

"Do you ask me for vengeance?" he said, and for the first he looked at her and saw her through the gauze veil. "Lady Chenti—" he said. And startled for a moment beyond himself, "Your daughter—I know her married to Montargo—"

That he too had been one of the witnesses did not concern Electra. "My daughter has confessed her liaison and my lord has thrown her from the house. He has been poorly advised in this. Her nurse, a coarse sloven, has taken her to shelter, I would suppose at her own daughter's warren in the Bhorgabba. I entreat," said Electra stilly, "that you tell no one this disgraceful thing."

He peered at her from the abyss of his misery, uncertain.

"You would have it secret— Then why tell me?"

"To help you to justice."

"Justice does not live. A Montargo killed it."

"Then kill the Montargo."

"What?" he said.

"Avenge," she said, "my loss, and yours."

Scenting her deviousness, but beyond dealing with it, or resisting, he said, "Tell me where to find the murderer and I'll see to it. Do you know?"

"Not yet."

"Then you play with me."

"I have offered you the game."

"Where is it?"

"In this: Discover my daughter and you discover the Montargo."

Saffiro made a wild dismissive gesture.

"Romulan Montargo ran from the town."

"Do you believe," she said, "he'll not come back? He is alive. He thinks himself clever. No one can take him. He is hot for her. He'll come back, or send one to fetch her. You have only to watch her to see it. Then you may take him, or follow her and reach him and do as you wish, less mercifully than the strangler's noose."

"By the Christ," Saffiro said. "Can it be so simple?"

"Yes."

"Where," he said. He faltered, and leaned on the tomb

again as if to draw strength from it. "Where is your daughter?"

"You must find the sty; I cannot track the Bhorga. The old woman's whelp is named Susina, and her palace of entertainment, so I understand, somewhat talked of."

"I'll find it then, and watch. And when he comes, or if she goes to him, I'll be ready—Your daughter will mourn, too, madama."

"My daughter is nothing. Only the sweet in the trap."

He did not seem ready to leave the tomb, nor she to go away. They were strangers to each other, now inexorably bound.

"I must have," she said at length, still in that unemphatic pallid voice, "some token from you that you will do this thing."

"Trust me."

"No," she said. "Come to the High Altar and swear."

In his whiteness, he whitened.

"How can I swear to commit sin on the Name of God?"

"Swear only that you spoke the truth and will abide by it. Swear by Sana Vera, or I shall doubt you."

He flared suddenly.

"Is your doubt to trouble me?"

She smiled. They were strangers, but she knew him, or enough of him.

"I'm not afraid of Godless things. For this I would work a curse on you. My nephew thought me a sorceress. Come. Swear. Swear at least to find him and tell me of it. I will kill him myself, the butcher of your friend. *I* will do it."

He remembered stories he had not fully listened to in his frenzy. How this woman had walked barefoot to the Chitadella to beg Romulan's death. How she had ululated like a beast over the bloody corpse of mad Leopardo.

Saffiro wished she had not come on him. He wished the hedge of his brothers had been about him. But he was alone in his wretchedness, had been so since Marivero, and now he must manage a death. . . . Her face was contemptuous and maleficent, and he began to fear her, and all those past events which had driven him to this place and which her lustreless veiled eyes seemed to decipher.

And again he saw the child running into the Vespelli Tower, shouting: "Estemba Uno is dead!" One of Saffiro's brothers, he recalled, had applauded the tidings. While the sky fell in the courtyard.

She would not go away. He must swear her oath or she would not leave him by the tomb. He must.

He came abruptly from the gate in the railing—which he had bribed the priest to unlock for him. He went by her. He found himself running, and remembered running downhill toward the darkened inn, the wine, the jokes, and the awful bed that did not matter. A guide in darkness. Glad, afraid. Alone.

He raced to the altar and slashed down his fist on it.

What was God? To kill Romulan, should that not be the only answer, the classical ideal perpetuated to its essential climax? To kill Judas, surely that had been blessed.

"I swear it," he whispered. And he felt there was no God, as Mercurio, somewhere in the night, had maybe suggested, and maybe in his sleep. "I swear!" he shouted, and the Basilica boomed with his voice. Saffiro lifted his head in the dizzy horrible glory of it and heard only his shout, like the clamor of a bell.

When he looked down again, shuddering, the woman had gone away.

TWENTY

The lodging in Manta Sebastia looked out to one side on a square with a church in it, on the other to a small yard with a well and a pomegranate tree. The church, pilasters, grills, and greenish windows, was sinking backward now into the darkness. In the yard a bird sang, giving the tree a voice. Five minutes before, a boy had been let in to see to the candles, and was now let out. When he had gone, Doro said,

"I went also to the school again. Neither had any letter gone there. They looked for you still and were sorry to be told you would not be coming. But from your father, not a word."

"Then again, he had arranged my lodging here, and would have sent any messenger here."

"And then *again*, where is that devil I paid your gold to?"

"Carousing well on it, somewhere."

"Sir, bid me go myself."

"Or I—"

"I," said Doro, "am only a servant of the House. Who'll challenge me? For you—there's been no word, either, of the Duke's pardon. It might well be a death sentence. That could explain his lordship's silence."

"My father," Romulan said, and broke off.

He watched the church dissolving as if under the sea, and thought of Valentius, disturbed, flushing even at the memory with self-consciousness. His stern ungiving bloody father—who had held him, who had promised him Iuletta's safety. Who, perhaps more than everything, had been prepared at last to take Romulan even in sin and dishonor as his son. And then—to be ill and get no word. To recover and get no word. To ride here to the town in the hopes of word being here ahead of him—and get no word. To ponder then if the plague which had fastened on him had fastened also—perfidious irony—on his father, contaminating him in that parental embrace so long omitted. Then Doro's "No, sir. Your father had the fever, too, when he was a boy, And got free of the sickness more swiftly than you." (By which you saw your servant knew more of your father than you yourself.) It was Romulan's remorse and grief that had made his recovery sluggish. This Doro hinted, trying to chivvy the young man from the inevitable depression that followed on the illness. It was, in fact, the worry that began over the absence of any whisper from Verensa that finally thrust Romulan back to health. With Doro he began to walk about Manta Sebastia, concern and nerves needing some outlet. A couple of times, growing faint in the street and leaning on Doro or a wall, the cooing of nearby women over his handsomeness and deathlike pallor had him grinding his teeth and briskly striding on, his head whirling and his pulse gone mad. It offended Romulan to be ill. Eventually, his unwelcome drove the demon away. And then there was only the worry left to plague him.

More than a month had gone by without a letter from the Montargo Tower. His father had a choice of destinations to which he might send one. The proposed school with its square grey courtyards and perambulating debating scholars. The church close by, where the priests, for a voluntary sum, would retain messages written and verbal until the recipients might arrive. Or the lodging, some years ago a wealthy merchant's house, and well-known being near the citadel.

Eleven days before, Doro had happened on a man in a tavern with some transaction due in Sana Verensa. Romulan had accordingly authorized Doro to pay this migrant to inquire after the Montargos, and bring back his results—either letters from Valentius or at least some picture of events. A further payment had been promised on his return, but the return had failed to occur. Even allowing for the duration of the fellow's personal business, he should by now have sought them out. That he had not merely proved that thieves would hire out on cheaper rates than honest men. Content with what they had already given him, he had not bothered to earn it, or the rest.

One last foray to the college-school and the adjacent church, one last interrogation of the various servants about the lodging, and the sequence had ended. By the hour the candles came to be lit, only one course remained, and this Doro had put forth.

If Romulan smarted that he himself must stay in Lombardhia, there was no remedy. To go back in blindness, perhaps under death sentence, and doubtless with a Chenti or two ripe to try for him—that was the way of a fool. And he had learned that foolishness was permissible only when nothing else but one's own life was dependent on it. She—his wife—was now reliant on the surety that he live. Maybe, his father, too. Maybe even that progression of forebears of whose role in his existence he had always been reluctantly aware. The last direct heir of his line, after Valentius. With Iuletta, that line could continue, his debt to the past, if debt there was, set straight. Iuletta, his wife. It was feasible (though it would be also incredible, astonishing) that already, between them, they had begun the continuance.

His wife. His father. The hill-held town—sharp with dawn, shadow-struck by day, biscuit-colored in the closing light— Verensa as he remembered it, the dust blooming, the towers rising like slender rocks, indigenous and natural. His birthplace, the backdrop to almost all the occasions of all his years, till now. Till now. Miles off. Severed from sight and knowledge—and from all news.

"Doro," he said then, "can you start at first light?"

Doro grinned.

"I should be back inside two days."

"Do be. Or I'll ride after you, and damn Chenti and damn the Rocca."

Night clung, soaked into every stone, would stay forever—then stirred, debated with itself, rose like mist and followed yesterday's sun into the west. In the east, the new sun, which so constantly encircled the earth, or which the earth encircled—though never in the hearing of his Holiness—came up like a paper lantern on fire. The gates of Manta Sebastia were opened, and a single rider trotted forth and broke into a gallop on the sun-shot road.

The sky swept up into blue, and the dry extending land spread away, showing itself to Doro. Who, as he rode, spared scarcely a glance for it. Now and then a farm, with its pebbled russet roof, or trees pouring shade like water over the road, caught his physical attention, or the cry of some bird, floating toward the lakelike plains of distance, might alert his ears. His mind was elsewhere than the tawny landscape, its architecture and its verdure. Planning ahead toward the little river, and the highway's end, beyond that to the best speed he could win on the track, and the nicer speed on the Padova road, where he might expect to be before noon.

Too prosaic to experience foreboding, Doro was, nevertheless, in a stern mood.

Eight miles from the river, as the day was climbing into its apex of heat and lustre, Doro watered the horse at a pool below a rough and ragged village. Earlier, he had passed the inn which had given them food when Romulan lay sick. Someone had called a greeting to Doro, but he had not acknowledged it.

In sight of the river, by a line of trees resembling green swords, Doro's horse missed its footing once, like a drunkard, and went lame.

Opening, broadening like a rose, the day, containing within it, as flies in amber, horses which went lame, greetings unanswered, towns of churches and towers. Containing with the rapid, unwilling prayer of the blue-eyed young man on his knees in the deep nave of San Bebastianus, the vixens' cry: "Love for copper, love for gold!" from a lane between two brothels miles and miles away. And an unsleeping girl in a cochineal camisola poorly matched with the terracotta urn of basil at her elbow, leaning from her window slit, conversing with a young man, duncloaked, hooded and almost faceless, in the street below. A young man obviously a gentleman from the Higher Town, who claimed to be too poor to visit her tonight, yet asked questions all about the house and what girls Maestra Susina kept. A young man who embroidered his questions with wishes to be a glove on her hand or the linen next her breast, phrases got out with a desperate gallant insincerity that intrigued her. But in the end, when she went in and closed her shutters for fear of a noon-day blistering, it was a boy from the kitchen told Saffiro Vespelli of the black-haired angel and her fat wardress in the little room on the mezzanine.

Others, plumbing the depths of the merchant quarter for Cornelia, lacked success. Lord Chenti, by this night's sunfall, would be in a new rage, alarmed, recanting, tearing up in one hand a letter (seven words) come from Troian Belmorio in response to a tentative message and a lavish gift: *Sir, your daughter is dead to me.* Strangling in the other Cornelia's imagined neck. It was that gargantua who had coerced Iuletta into flight. Were they with the priest again? Which priest had it been? No, but that had been a lie. There was no priest, no oratory. Damn that fat slab of haggery. She had caused it all. That and the villainous Montargos, against whom he himself felt ready to take sword. That Cornelia might have fled to her daughter did not enter Chenti's pulsing brain, despite his jibe to that effect. To his idea, the nurse's child—Suzanna?— being a prostitute, was therefore mere flotsam, if not already deceased—as being in which state Cornelia, in the higher company of the Tower, had always referred to her. A rich whore with a house of her own did not fit with Chenti's vision, and he had never been informed otherwise. Nor did he even consider that Cornelia, in her feckless abduction of Iulet, would have taken her to such a refuge. So, in the amber of the day, richening now, its resin solidifying about them all, Chenti trumpeted and schemed and made vows, not knowing himself a mere trapped fly along with all the others.

And in the wine-amber, Lady Chenti, bolt upright in her seat, her unblinking lizard eyes on nothing but some thought inside them, her hands snapped shut upon a pendant of gold, which, like her eyes, hid what it held: a lock of a dead man's hair, glued by old blood. And in the room on the mezzanine, Cornelia snoring close by, Iulet Chenti, in the self-same position as her mother by some freak of genetic telepathy. Iulet bolt upright, her eyes wide, her hands tight upon the nothing which was all now she had left. And a scatter of walls away, Saffiro, drowsy and sick with heat and the Bhorga smells, and with a dream to kill or to die.

To die and be dead. Mercurio in his tomb, Valentius in his. Leopardo (who could have enlightened Lord Chenti in the matter of Susina) in the marble mausoleum of the Gatta-pulettas, and no longer informative. Troian on the brown hill, indulging in a vicious hunt, one cheek already bruised from a play fight of buffets with a friend, and the friend carried home, wrapping himself in the warmth of angry things. Troian who had drunk down the seeds of misogyny and who, tonight, would rape a girl in Marivero, telling her that he liked her resistance.

While Luca Montargo, the third witness at the ill-starred wedding, yellow as his fiendish horse, though not now from debauch but from a brush with the plague that had lodged that month in the Montargo Tower, dwelled with post-maledic despair on the futility of all things. But mostly the Argo fountain in the rectangular courtyard. And as he stared with positive hatred at the late afternoon light shuffled on and off the shining verdigris sail, he heard knocking on the stable entry, and, hating that too, walked through under the pile of the second floor veranda where the pigeons hatefully put-tered, in time to hear a groom shouting for the visitor's name and intention.

A name came in over the wall. The two Montargo guards loosened their stance, recognizing it. The groom shouted: "We have had the Summer Sickness here."

"So have I," called Doro. And swore at them until the gate was opened.

The servant rode in on a scarecrow horse, both of them white with dust as if oiled and dipped in flour. Sliding from the saddle, the man stood in the yard, perhaps seeking evidence of neglect, perhaps scenting dolor and confusion. But Doro, worn out by walking, by bartering for a horse, by nearly coming to blows over a horse, by hard riding on a thing ill-fed and untrained and disobedient and probably not a horse at all, required mostly a drink of wine and a catholic admittance to Valentius' study. What he received, however, was Luca's imperious cry across the cobbles: "Where have you left Montargo Uno?"

Doro looked, bowed staccato, and replied:

"Where my lord his father had me conduct him. And where," said Doro generally, "is Lord Valentius?"

There was a silence. Then Luca told him where Valentius was.

"Oh God and burning Hell," said Doro. And after that nothing for some while.

At length, unasked, one of the guards informed Doro of the circumstances of death, and who at present held authority in the Tower—on the heir's behalf.

Then Doro came over to Luca, bowed more adequately and said, "Sir, is the Lady Iuletta here?"

There followed a form of verbal and hierarchical chaos. Luca privy to one outdated set of secrets, and unwilling to admit as much to an underling. Doro privy to another set more current, and growing too impatient to reveal them. Both additionally hampered by something neither of them knew: the actual incidents that made up Iuletta's second wedding. Rumor there had been effectively trammelled. The story ran that the lady, still weak from her illness, had faded away in the capella. The ceremony was therefore postponed until her full recovery. But subsidiary rumors sprang from this story like young leaves. Troian had refused the girl at the last instant, having found some impediment or imperfection. Chenti Primo had cancelled the match, having been slandered by Old Belmorio in the Basilica. It was, though, fairly agreed that Iuletta was once more sick unto death in her father's house. Mostly these last snippets were not offered by Luca, who presently turned on his shoe heels and went off, having informed Doro only that Iuletta Chenti was expiring of plague in the Chenti Tower.

Doro bolstered this by a round of: "Is it so?" "Yes, so it is," with the three grooms now out in the yard and the Montargo guardsmen. He got it down with the aid of two cups of wine. Then he managed to obtain a real horse, folded himself more firmly in his drab cloak, and rode out again—in the direction of the Cat Tower of Chenti-Gattapuletta.

Prosaic Doro was, but not dull. Five years behind him, Doro had seen Valentius' son grow up in Montargo, robbed first of the smoothing influence of a dead mother, and then of the directive comfort of the living love-dead father. Doro knew. He had watched from a slope the scene between father and son, and cursed softly with relief at it. Now to tell Romulan Valentius was slain, stabbed in the back by the kinfolk of Romulan's wife. And to conclude by telling, as maybe he would have to, that the seemingly beautiful winsome bride Romulan had called to in his delirium, was also dead. . . . Doro would not shirk, but he could guess what would come after, the unravelling of all those fragile threads that bound together brain and heart and soul and flesh.

The day was shortening even now and Doro tired to his very blood. But he must get to Chenti and find out, how carefully, all he could. For if she died, he must know. He could only hope Romulan would not cleave to his threat to come after him, if return were tardy.

Smitten sideways by sun, all the towers looked out of true and ready to crash in the streets. These towers. Would they still stand in a hundred years, or in four hundred? And if they did, would men still be at feud, still killing one another? Or would the earth have grown so sad by then that she would wither like a vine? Or would the terror and sorrow finally drive men to fight within themselves, to free themselves of themselves, to change as never in all the centuries since the Garden?

Strange thoughts for Doro. Something from the wine and his tiredness.

But already the gold-plated lion-leopard gleamed overhead and before him like a spangle, and his own world blotted out the future.

The amber turned black after an intercession of purple. The flies, still captive, continued their operations.

At Susina's house, the guests were more numerous and less known tonight than usual. Not necessarily a useful factor under the circumstances. For though the door to the small apartment on the mezzanine had been firmly locked from within, once or twice it had been hammered on. The first time, Cornelia's startled cry had boosted the casual to the intent. With yodelings and kicks at the woodwork, five gentlemen had laid siege to the door—"Ho! There's a plump chicken in here, not too young a one either. Glad for attention at bargain rates." Susina had been forced to call upon assistance from her three courteous and large-thewed houseguards. Even when the riot was dispersed, unfortunate attention had been drawn to the door and the fundamental evidence that it was locked.

"Come now, Susina. Who's hidden away in the chamber?"

"My mother, sir," Susina had answered.

Her wit had been hailed, but she had not been believed. However, settling on more available fare, most of the guests had presently gone off to their pleasures. A succeeding batch sat drinking in the courtyard rather longer, but inevitably at last, a drunk patron careering up the stair with his choice, awarded the locked door a playful blow. Now, Cornelia was too wise to give tongue. But nevertheless, the guest, with the idée fixe of the sozzled: "Why lock this door, dearest Susina? Open it. It is the room I most desire to lie in." And "Now, Susina of Susinas, open or I will burst the timbers."

When this powder keg had been dampened (with grape-juice improved by storage), Susina took stock. Four guests yet lingered in the court, but they were docile patrons, well known. A fifth man lay asleep on a bench and should be no trouble, having already paid much for little. It was the sixth visitor who began to concern her. He had come in behind the first three customers, and sat over his wine, grudging of coins but engaging now and then in fierce conversations with her girls. Of these the girls reported only that he was more bothered by who worked at the house than interested in employing their services. And he, too, it now seemed, had grown obsessed by the locked door, for he had begun to watch it steadfastly.

"Well, sir," Susina said, going over to him and replenishing his wine herself with the gracious bow that trickled her nipples over the rim of her dress. "Well, but we do not seem

able to please you. Have you seen nothing to your taste?
There are certain others I may show you. We do, I assure
you, understand also the Eastern fashion here. Or you have,
perhaps, special requirements. If you could bring yourself to
intimation—"

"I heard," said the young man, an aristocrat, aggressive,
familiarly though unfriendly drunk, "I heard you have a new
whore."

"You refer to Cassia? I regret she is at a supper tonight."

"Not any Cassia."

"I have," Susina said, "three most alluring boys, who—"

"Not a—a *boy*. A girl. A girl from a tower. A kitten of a
girl. Guess who I mean? Behind that bloody door which
screams, perhaps."

Susina was perturbed. She did not wish to set her private
guard on this one. The cloak had slipped somewhat and she
glimpsed jewelwork. His rings were spectacular and he was
foolish to flaunt so many in the Bhorga.

"Handsome lord," said Susina, "we have no noble ladies
here engaged secretly in the trade, as some other houses of
joy boast that they do. If that's your hope, you'll have to seek
elsewhere."

And at that he came to his feet and seized her wrist. There
was a dagger in the ringed fingers now, pressing its point in
the mound of her breast. The last awake customers held their
breath, and so did she. He was tipsy enough, and for some
reason disturbed enough, to scar her nastily if she shouted for
her guard, or even if she did not. Susina lifted her hand quietly to brush his lips, as if toying with him, and drove one of
her own rings hard up into the base of his nose. He staggered
back, of course, in agony, blinded by tears, and the knife
clattering on the ground. Then, she called her guard, and
calmly she told him, for she was strident only in jest, that he
might expect to be unwelcome at her house henceforth. Her
men were also quite courteous with him, and only laid him
on the street, he choking with pain and humiliated emotion.
After the door shut, he crouched by the wall until his head
began to breathe and see again.

Saffiro knew that, as in the past, he had misjudged his target and his road. *Fool*. Why had he gone inside the place?
Why? Because in some manner he had wished to terrorize the
girl he now knew for certain was concealed there. Because he
had seen her a bride, and other things had followed that
seeing, making him superstitious about her. Because her lover

had murdered his friend. Yes, he had wished to behold Iuletta Chenti Montargo with anguish in her eyes. He would behold it. But not yet—

The tears of agony threatened to become the deluge of lamentation. Saffiro visualized himself, half lying in the dirt by the wall, the jape of harlots, ineffectual and afraid. There were Florias roaming the Bhorgabba in a pack tonight. And Malaghelas, too. And he alone, sent here by that witch of the Cat Tower. Yes, fool, fool as his brothers constantly assured him. Even if the Montargo were to come this very hour, how would Saffiro cope with him? Romulan had killed Leopardo—that had been a feat. To kill Mercurio no less, except it had been managed with steel against a man armed simply and unknowingly with bronze.

With bronze.

Like a shadow, Saffiro moved himself upward and leaned by the wall. Above him, a shutter slammed open and broken pieces of light fell on the street. A girl laughed, frivolously, falsely.

He heard the sound with contempt, dismissed it. He would wait. He would spy. Shame did not matter, nor his enemies on the streets, nor Romulan's prowess as a swordsman, nor who had asked him to do this and told him the means. Bronze—this must pay for that.

Susina, looking through the chink in the shutter of an unlighted room, noted the leaning shadow. Then she turned and made her way to the mezzanine. The courtyard was once more vacant, save for the peaceful sleeper, and knocking mildly on the locked door, she named herself and was let inside.

The situation within remained as she had previously left it. No hours seemed to have elapsed. Cornelia with the key, and clucking over a cup of wine. Iuletta straight-backed as a pin on her chair.

There were pointless preliminaries. One felt one must insert them, for the girl's sake. Her strength was appalling, it would not break or melt, she clearly could not give way.

The stupid chattering of courtesies done, Susina announced,

"There is one I've had put out on the street, who knows you are here, Donna Iuletta. This is not a servant, or anyone's hireling. He's a lord of the Higher Town, and I hazard from the device I glimpsed, a Vespelli. His grudge against you I cannot surmise. Perhaps he's a friend of Troian Belmorio's. I'm assured he wishes you harm. And he watches, I believe, to keep track of what you do."

Iuletta said tonelessly, "My mother promised me this. He will be awaiting my flight with Romulan. But he will need to wait until time's ending."

"There," said Cornelia automatically, and hiccupped.

"So soon," Iuletta said to Susina. "My stay here brings you inconvenience."

"It is you, lady, I fear for," said Susina. "This world is cruel, as you've said. This world bites."

"I have thought of a method," said Iuletta. (One wished she would sob or shriek or fly into a passion—those tantrums Cornelia had described of her charge's childhood and recent adolescence. This other thing, this death that lived—) "I'll send word to that priest, Fra Laurus. He's disinterested. He has no care for the woes and status of the towers—this is all I have ever heard of him, that he treats men and women like game pieces, either he or God to move them, and they mean as little to him. But I think he will advise me on how I may present myself to a sheltering and concealing sisterhood, and how I may journey there privately. I must beg a favor of you."

"What would it be?" said Susina with caution.

"Someone must take the priest a letter. Someone who goes in and out, that the man who watches will not notice him particularly. And, if you will grant me this too, one who cannot read."

"Easily done. I'm the only one in the house can read, and am no scholar. But to be extra sure, you may send it by Balshaza."

"That is the pagan boy," said Cornelia. "The brown boy from the spice lands. No, he'll not read it. Magnificent Christ. But you should not consider this. A nunnery? A poppy like my Iulet to be a nun?"

Iuletta paid no heed. And Cornelia fell suddenly dumb, and drank more wine.

Iuletta said, "If it were written tonight, he might take it tomorrow?"

"If written tonight, he might take it tonight. There is a stable nearby which will supply a mule, and we can gift the gate guards. Like my girls, hermit priests rarely sleep, they pray all through the dark."

"I have no money."

"The ring you gave me will see to it, my donna. There's

another way from the house also. A cellar, and a route I'll describe no further, but the boy knows it. It's been a fortunate road for one or two whose unfriends sat down at the door."

"It seems I put you to too much use."

"None at all. But lady, I'd ask you to consider. You were meant, you'll pardon me, to be neither bawd nor vestal."

"Then," said Iuletta, "you must tell God this is the case. The error in this is not mine."

Susina shut her lips together. The slap was restrained but decided. The stiff-backed fifteen-year-old woman on the chair was older far than Susina's twenty-three years, and sense was not to be wheedled or shaken into her. She would make a horribly correct suora, in the living death of piety. And with every orison, she would curse God.

"Come, guzzler," said Susina to her mother, laying a kind keen hand on her arm. "Bring your wine and come and talk with me. Let your lady be to pen her letter. I'll send a girl with ink and paper and fresh candles."

Iuletta thanked her, and Cornelia mumbled and was taken away.

Soon the girl came in with the ink-horn from Susina's wayward accountings, and with some sheets of grainy yellow paper. When the girl had gone, Iuletta rose and once more locked the door.

Through the sturdy walls about her came dim noises. They, and their derivation, did not offend her. Creature of spirit and physical essence that she was, only the imposed law of others had formed her moral code, and that with surprising superficiality. Iuletta had a capacity for great liberation. She might have committed acts of enormous immoderation, even crimes of extreme violence—if her life had led her in the way of them. She was, basically, a child of the wood, one of those maidens who in mythos, wreathed with ivy and bearing a staff crowned by a pinecone, had danced over mountains and seas after a god both beautiful and mad. Able to love beyond reason, able to slay, to tear in fragments, with the panther and the she-wolf, perhaps not her lover or her children, but decidedly herself.

She wrote with little hesitation, neatly and prettily as she had been tutored to do. Romulan had spoken to her of Laurus, during their solitary night of privacy and joining. Of the dove messenger, of the magician's insularium with its forbidden treasures, and its alembics, potions, spell books. And

Cornelia's words had also lodged: *A strange man. Will take no payment. He takes no care of what we do—we may do anything.* Yet, more than all this, it was the child of the wood in her that instinctively approached the weird priest. Oblique recognized oblique. And all her shrinking, and any inclination in her to preserve, these had perished. In some respects, she had forced herself to a train of thought, and could no longer get free. But in others, she only proceeded now as always, precipitate, yet with a true and proper motion, like that of a falling star.

About half an hour later, another delicate rap on the door. The letter was ready and was given over to the girl, and then, at the foot of the pitted stairway among the apricots, to the Indian boy.

No one was abroad, the thrifty customers away, the generous or lusty ensconced for the night. She should beware of thirsty wanderers, but did not. She stood at the balustrade, from which position she had first looked down and seen Romulan borne to her on the arms of a man now dead.

His skin seeming almost blue, the phantasmal boy flickered, now lit, now snuffed, between the lamps and the garden trees, and was gone. Thankfully illiterate Cornelia would have supplied directions. The boy, who appeared like a jewel of the night, could not fear the night, or that he might be lost in it, and had no doubt often traversed darkness and even countryside. (She wondered suddenly, inconsequently, that he had never used such a jaunt to run away. Perhaps now— No.) No. Before midnight, Laurus would have her question in his hands. Perhaps he would send an answer with the boy. Perhaps a dove would bring it. Or a crow.

The letter read:

Pious Father, grant me the blessing of your attention for the length of this. I would speak to you of a woman who has lost all her substance in the world. Her family have disowned her, she is penniless and must live upon the charity of acquaintances. All this, due to her marrying the only one who, in this world, or in any world, she might love, as love is. As may be believed, the man, her husband, has grown impatient at the toils their hasty marriage has entailed, and has abandoned her. She places on him no censure in this, but would wish him to be free of her, if only in freedom can he regain his happiness. Lastly, his enemies steal about her, spying upon her, thinking that he will return to her and so fall in their vengeful hands. Thus, even the hope of his arrival she may not entertain, nor thinks it likely to occur. But it is to her an unwarranted burden. It is salt in the wounds she bears. She therefore would beg from you a way to her release from prison. By prison, I mean her life. This is counted a sin, mystic father, but it seems to her there is no other formula. She must live a wasted span in misery, a trial and danger to those about her and a cause of anguish to the one she loves before all others, including even God. Or she may leave the earthly state at once, and this she purposes. Her only reason, therefore, in writing to you, sir, is to ask that in your pity you will condone and facilitate her sin. You are wise with herbs and medicines. Will you prepare for this woman, and send to her through one—the best able to effect the matter— a draught to end her unhappiness without further pain? This she entreats, partly that her death may appear ordinary and her friends be protected from false accusation. But also since, being a woman, she is much afraid of being hurt. Should you, in your magnitude, comply, pray send the elixir in a packet as if with a letter—for both your safety and her own. If you should refuse your help, which may well be your disposition (as she can offer neither a fee, nor a reward for your work in Heaven), she assures you your abstinence will not prevent her death. She will utilize what other means there may be, and swiftly. Again, at the finish as throughout, she begs your indulgence of this dismal request. She has ceased to credit damnation, and seeks only peace. Therefore, regard any help you may give her as only that. For she does not believe she shall be damned, but only dead, and that is what she most wishes for.

So much she swears then, upon her own soul, if such she has, and if not then upon her life while she lives and while she is

Iuletta Montargo de Chenti.

Cornelia, carousing below, did not come back to the chamber, and Iuletta lay down unsleeping on the wide bed, and began to nerve herself already for the refusal. Having sworn to die, and refused her means, she must go quickly, or perhaps be prevented. There were other modes. She did not think of them quite yet.

That the priest would deny her departure seemed one instant definite, and the next insupportable. But, by his leave or without it, depart she would.

She pictured Romulan sometimes. Her death would be broadcast, and he would hear of it. There would be guilt in that, maybe, but not for long. He would know himself unfettered. The stigma fate had cast on them would be done. She beheld his face bending to hers in the dark, the face of an angel, the beautiful god she had followed, over hills, over seas.

And then perhaps she slept, for all at once the knock came on the door, light now almost as air, yet her awareness sounding at it like a chord of music inside her.

When she opened the door, no one was there. But lying on this threshold, as once a broken dove had lain on another, there was a packet sealed by wax. She took it up, looking as she did so across the garden-court. Only the statuary regarded her. It was very dark, and early—cool and aromatic, and for a moment she felt life surge up inside her, but then she went in and shut the door, no longer turning the key.

Cornelia would mourn, would run with tears. But that must not dissuade her. No other would mourn at all, and that must not dissuade her, either.

She broke the seal and thought: *It is empty*—and then the tiny opaque phial lay in her hand.

That her death should be so small she might hold it in her hand—

There was nothing written on the paper, no reassurance, no avowal. Of course, how should he incriminate himself. But then, finding the paper, they would think he had refused that other help she had pretended to ask of him—her way to a sisterhood—and this would reflect poorly on him. But she must no longer care for the living she would leave behind.

She touched the phial. It felt very cold. Could it be it was not poison, but some eccentric potion or drug, or even water suitably tinctured? But no. She would wake, or vomit, or merely tremble and remain, and then she would cry out against him. There was no cunning in that. Either send, or refuse to send. He had sent. Unless—suppose there were dreadful pain in the phial? Suppose he sought to punish her for her blasphemy of suicide? Or suppose only he had no way to ensure the bane was bland. . . . Once more, no. He was a magician and could create magic. At worst, it would be a fast agent, or else she would have space to scream, perhaps reveal in her distress his hand in her death—yes, even if hurtful it would fly, it would race. She in its jaws.

She shut her eyes and saw Romulan inside her lids, clear as if painted there. She would never see him in the flesh again, and she had known it, somehow, the very morning that they parted at Marivero. Truly, she had known it then.

She drew the stopper from the phial. There was no odor, but she grew dizzy, which might be the potency of its fumes, or only her nervousness.

She would have died for him. Did die for him. It was this simple. While she could procrastinate, she had been able to face her empty life. As a vision it was bearable. But the spy had forced her hand too soon. She could no longer put off tomorrow. And coming to it, she found she could not bear it at all. Her childish avowals—"I will die if he does not love me"—they had come true.

She heard then, suddenly, as once Romulan has heard it, the bright plain note of a footstep on the stair. And so it must be now, at once.

She flung wide the window and put the phial to her mouth and drank the liquid in a gasp that left her breathless and afraid. But she threw the phial away into the dark, to safeguard the magician, before she moved her hands to her throat, her breast; waiting, listening for pain to begin.

But there was no pain. She felt an innocent faint numbness, not unpleasant, like the serene detachment that came prior to sleep, and she walked slowly to the bed once more, and lay down on it.

The steps had ended on the stair. After all, it was probably only one of the lovers strayed from his couch to ease himself or to fetch more wine. Or a late visitor, dallying. There came a far-off mutter of voices. She heard them, understanding nothing of what they said, uncaring, for they were no longer of her world.

Abruptly then, but without discomfort, her soul rose out of her body. She felt it lift and hover. A sensation of utter quietness, the very sensation she had desired, came to her. Death approached, not black, but of the most variable flowing whiteness, like a cloud, and she rose into it and he took her in his arms. "Sleep well, my child," he said.

It seemed to her she knew the voice from long ago, that of one who had been gentle to her. And she smiled as she died.

This was how she was found, less than a minute after, by those who came into the chamber, already icy cold and her limbs stiffening, but her face smiling and beautiful. It was for this reason that so many attempts were made to rouse her. It was difficult to accept something so lovely and so gladsome could be dead.

Doro, who had only glimpsed her, was of this mind. But presently, when they left off their ministrations, he did not want to look at her again.

He had come on a page near one of the Chenti lodges, Pieto by name, who had told him, between upset, spite, and a well-advanced cupidity, all one might need to know. Even the location of Susina's house came out, for though never having visited, Pieto had overheard a great deal in his short years with Cornelia.

Coming into the brothel with other guests, Doro had paid out coins in order to get good will. But before Susina should be free enough of her patrons for him to speak to her in a way not guaranteed to make a spectacle, he had fallen inevitably asleep. Nothing had penetrated to him then, until hours later someone slipping like a ghost through the courtyard had somehow woken him as a louder noise would not have done. Then had come an astonishing stroke of what he took to be luck.

The boy flitted up to the mezzanine floor, rapped on a door, left something by it, and stole away. Not long after, the door was opened and out came a girl to take the package up, and then to stand for a moment, before returning inside the room.

The most obvious thing about the girl, seen over distance and between the foliage which had also handily masked him, was her glory of black hair, shining and shimmering from the light behind her. Romulan, and not only in fever, had described Iuletta. From that hair alone, Doro became convinced that this was the lady he sought, seeming at first never to be found, and yet here before him, close as the sweet fruit on the trees.

He meant not to startle her, and went up stealthily, considering his approach. Then another girl, one of the furnishings of the house, appeared as he reached the top step and asked him his needs. He had requested Susina, then, rather than explain superfluously to the wrong ears.

When Susina came, clad in a robe of flames and sunsets, her hair a nest wanting only unhouse-proud birds, she heard him through and nodded, without protest, as if indeed she had expected him momently.

Then they knocked, had no answer, and opened the door. And so he saw the most beautiful human thing he had ever set eyes on, lying in the fabulous night river of her hair, dead as a year-old corpse pulled up from the ground.

PART FOUR:

The Gate

TWENTY-ONE

"She was so fair
"Death fell in love with her—"

The bridal procession moved slowly, and dark as a thunder cloud, along the streets. Clad in crimsons dulled to black, linen that was black, silver for gold. Foremost, the drummers, beating with long-paced blows, the rhythm of the advance. After the drummers, the gentlemen and the ladies of the Chenti kindred; scores of them had come, this time, to celebrate her wedding. And not a horse anywhere, each man, each woman, walking in the early morning that already burned their bowed necks, in the dust that already bloomed their garments. There were twenty attendants for the bride. They were wreathed in roses which had been dyed jet-black; dyed and dying of the poison, like crisp black papers on all this sunlit young girls' hair. This living hair.

The musicians sang to the beat of the drums, and the horns came in crying, and the toiling violas throbbed out their somber notes, and somewhere there was scattered the rill of a lute. The lutes of boys' voices followed.

The bride herself lay on her open bier, dressed in her bridal finery, her hands folded like gloves on a jeweled crucifix and a silver rose. How beautiful she was, the skeins of her hair combed about her—this hair, quite dead.

Fifteen years of age, a few days loving and loved. Ended now, to be packed away now into a chest of stone until the last trump.

This wedding was more vivid than either of her others. This third wedding, the true wedding. The show, of course, was the tragic whimsicality of a father who had lost his only daughter. (Indeed, Lord Chenti, whimsical, was seldom to be thwarted.)

Iuletta. Iuletta Chenti.

She was so fair
Death fell in love with her,
That loathsome paramour.
He'll keep her sure,
He'll keep her close and dear,
And love her evermore.

Come strew your roses for this bride
Veiled in white flesh, which Death will draw aside.

The song, being sad, caused some of the children who sang
it to shed tears. But it was the music which moved them, not
the girl lying on the shoulder-borne bier, above and behind
their heads. Those who stood on the sloping street, or craned
from balconies and windows, sometimes wept too, touched by
the idea of her beauty and her youth, and the dire stories that
she had died of shame and dishonor. Vicarious pain, poi-
gnant, and safe.

Past the piled library and the college, the procession slid
inexorably on toward the Basilica square. This, a walk of five
minutes, and to a running man, pursued by the sword of an
enemy, a race of two. For the procession a road requiring the
half of one hour.

"Come strew your roses for this bride

"Veiled in white flesh—"

But spilling at last, like the Chenti Tower's black blood,
across the square—

"—which death will draw aside."

On the steps of the Basilica, twenty tapers were ignited,
shielded, carried up out of the glare of day and brought like
splinters of the sun into the nave.

So, lit by fireflies, the bride lay still, while the responses
were spoken over her under the lacework dream-lights of the
windows.

How lovely, how not remotely dead. . . .

A day had elapsed since they had found her. There had
been a great deal to do, messengers to send, a means of
discreet conveyancing to be devised. Rumors to be killed, or
birthed. Lamentation to be made loud as fury. A day, a
night, at this season of heat, when a day might prove too
long. (Leopardo, sunken and discolored like a fermenting
cheese—) But she, this last legal daughter of the Tower of
the Cat, she had remained exquisite, her lips still delicately
flushed with rose, her eyelids with the blue of the iris. Even

her nails, flawless ovals like mother-of-pearl. One expected any moment that she would draw sudden breath, would wake—

Iuletta.

The responses were done, and the other rites. Despite the rumor briefly current in the world of the town, she could be no suicide, this service her proof: she lay without a mark upon her. She had died of a broken heart.

The procession stirred. It took her up again, and moved away through the misty auroras of the windows, away through a remote and echoing door, and presently out again, not into the sunlight now, but into the hanging shade of cypresses.

This was the way Leopardo had come. This was the way all the Chentis had, eventually, to come. To the mausoleum, framed by its clustered trees, inevitable before them all.

The carving of the stone uprights by the massive doors depicted the angels of the Resurrection of Souls. How blind and terrible their faces were, ruthless as only the faces of angels would ever dare to be. Strings struck like tinders. The boys' voices soared now to the descant, with an anguished pride.

> *Beauty so rare,*
> *A jewel in darkness' ear*
> *Did never burn so bright.*
> *To give him light*
> *Cold Death has brought her here—*
> *This palace of dim night.*
>
> *Come strew your roses; she's his wife.*
> *Sweet maid, you spurned your better suitor, Life.*

The music sobbed and faded. There was silence. Beyond the cypresses the sun flamed on, ignoring the funeral, not even decently veiling itself in a cloud.

The men who carried Iuletta's bier, dreadfully conscious of her lack of weight—which had seemed somehow to reproach them, resembling as it did the slightness of her years—moved forward once more as the great hollow doors, now unbarred, were dragged aside.

Without, the sun and the music of birds and the deep clear shadows of the trees. Within, the opaque dark, like loss of sight, and from its opening a whisper of some stench, not so much decay as atrophy. And into that hole, that negation of everything, this girl must be passed, set down, and then sealed in, and hastily abandoned. It seemed impossible. Would she not wake up and call aloud?

They entered the doorway of the tomb, and were inside.

This palace of dim night. It was like some Hellish dormitory. Between the thick archaic pillars that held up the roof, the marble slabs progressed in a horrible orderliness. And on each couch, something lay, something dead, long dead, its flesh gone from its bones, its bones parting from each other, so that in some cases they had rolled away and lay upon the floor. Close at hand here, though unlooked for, Leopardo rested; not much left now to please the eye in his lean young man's body. Aromatics burned, filling the close dead air with vapor—some had been sent in ahead of the party of internment, to perform this service for those who came after. Yet the cloy of perfume did nothing to dispel the underlying fragrance of the tomb. And the dust, which in here had become clotted and tangible, stirred and fluttered in vast nets, as if anxious that it should be disturbed.

A candle was once more lit, another and another. They feebly caught the light of gems that lay over the bones and under the dusts.

Those that carried her laid her on her allotted bed, and black roses showered down. In the deceptive candle-flicker, as in the nave of the Basilica, you might almost think you saw her eyelids quiver, the slightest dilation of the nostrils, the merest tremble of a pulse, for an instant, in the smooth vessel of the throat.

Someone spoke, hoarsely, appallingly.

"To this," the voice, masculine and unwieldy, thickened, and very loud: "To this my enemies have brought me."

Lord Chenti stood in the tomb, surfacing from its deadness like some enormous beast from a body of dank water.

"To *this*. All my hopes gone. Are they to thrive, these Montargos?"

No reply of any kind came to him. His people watched him intently, as the eyes of the gems in the tomb watched him. His face remained richly red, from grief or rage or drink, or from all three, unlike the blackened red of his mourning garments.

"What am I to do?" he said. "I have no son, now, to avenge me."

He turned and forced his way through the press, pushing out into the sunlight. He waited on the lawn, and those outside now watched him. His eyes were shot with blood, and wet. But it was not unmanly for a father to weep at the death of his only recognized child, his virtuous daughter, ruined by the treachery of his foes.

There were two stories current. The first was general to the streets. Its form was this: Young Montargo, he that was called Romulan—antique glorious name now despoiled—had, with others of his House, abducted Iuletta Chenti. In some hut on the hills, she had been forced into a profane parody of marriage, and thereafter forced more thoroughly. Released, she had concealed her wretchedness from fond parents and friends alike until, unable to bring dishonor on her betrothed, (Troian Belmorio), she had refused him at the very altar. And thereafter taken herself in her despair from the willing sanctuary of her House, to the domicile of a servant known from her childhood. And here, of her own honor's defilement, like chaste Lucrezia—though not blasphemously at her own hand—she had died.

This then should be the cause of feud between the Cat and the Ship until the stars went out. It was even supposed that Leopardo Chenti, standing as he did in lieu of any brother, for this reason sought out Romulan Montargo in the square, and there would have killed him, but for some trick—

The second story, offered about the towers, penetrated even to the Rocca, where Chesarius, hearing the *other* tale, had remarked: "It gives me to wish I might publish the truth on the walls." To which the Duke his brother had irritably rejoined: "There's trouble enough. Meddle, and I might see you banished, kinsman. I'm coming to just such a mood." The second tale, which did not assuage Chesarius' particular mood, nevertheless recounted the legality of the secret marriage, detailed Lord Chenti's justifiable wrath, and had Iuletta in misinterpreting flight at it, again to the obscure respectable home of some servant in the mercantile quarter. Where she had died of an ailment brought on and nourished by unhappiness, conceivably some delayed visitation of the plague. The irony being that the father's wrath had, of course, cooled. That he would, of course, have forgiven her. He was not monstrous. Certainly, he had threatened her with nothing, and did not cast out his own. Such a reflection upon him could be unbecoming. He had seen to it that such a reflection was amended.

He even believed it, now, as he stood in the sunlight. And something, perhaps the brilliance of the day, squeezed two shallow moistures between his lids. He was not to blame. He would have been lenient, beyond any leniency that laws moral or temporal would expect of him, magnanimous and clement to Iuletta's straying idiocy. The simpleton. Why had she died? Could she not have waited until his agents located her? Belmorio he could have managed, and the Montargo been managed, too, in some alleyway—well, but she had not waited. (And to perish in a *whorehouse*. For sure, he had warned that strumpet Suzanna from revelation, he had made sure of *her*. She knew how the world was, and would keep quiet.)

And here came the other bitch, out of the hole of the mausoleum. An error, in this. Why had he not been able to bury the mother in place of the child today, bony Electra, that unbending stick. Yet here she was, improperly dry-eyed. They had told him how she had howled like a she-wolf when the nephew was brought in, howled and ripped at herself, and walked to the Chitadella for justice. But for the fruit of her own womb—nothing.

He studied her, her colorless face expressionlessly fixed under its thunder of veiling. For the very first, something moved sluggishly at the bottom of his thoughts. Leopardo, the constant tormentor of Lord Chenti's frigid wife. And Electra, who had hated him, who never spoke of him without hate, *passionate* hate—Leopardo and Electra—

The last mourners had issued from the tomb. The doors ground shut and the cumbersome iron was let down to secure them. There was to be no honorary guard for a woman, who might have sinned, in one way or another. Let her lie now. Death was her husband. Death had taken all, her youth, her charm, her worth.

But Electra, Electra and Leopardo—

"My lord," she said, her little voice piercing through his brooding all too aptly, "I would be grateful to pray in the chapel. Will you permit me?"

"Why not," he said into an ear muffled by gauzes. "Why not? Who can you meet there, except the dead?"

Electra did not respond, save in her barren way to thank him. Nor did she consider his mouthed and uncouthly formed words, any more than she had considered the outburst, impotent, banal, in the mausoleum. As to whom she might meet in the capella, she understood quite well.

In the dimness of the chapel, her women left on the threshold, the priest gifted and dispatched, Electra halted, looking about her. No reverie passed through her skull as she did so. She was quite single-minded now, as always. Even the minutes spent in the Chenti tomb, so close to the remains of her lover, had not moved her. The dead had no interest for Electra. When she had screamed above Leopardo's corpse, it was the curtailment of her own life she worshipped, not his. Leopardo had cheated her, but in that he had been aided.

Initially, noting herself alone in the capella, she did not wonder if the one she expected would be strong enough to stay away. Her message to him had been succinct. The hour, the day, the circumstance and the place. Otherwise, she had neither signed the paper nor impressed her seal upon it. For its deliverance she had employed a man loitering on the street. She was, however, convinced the recipient would know who sent to him and why. Nor had she any grave doubts that he could keep away. Her power over Saffiro Vespelli, so swiftly and startlingly achieved, she had never questioned. She understood it by infallible instinct alone.

Presently she heard his step. He had come via the cloister and the side door, like a penitent or a lover. He saluted the alter, and stared at her.

"You are very kind to have attended me," she said.

He laughed melodramatically and shortly at this.

"Kind? And are you kind? Can I credit you her mother? Truly, she can have meant nothing to you."

"She meant something. She would have enabled me to gain justice. And still she may."

"How? She's dead, madama."

"So she is. And therefore, her dwelling is fixed, as at no other time."

"What?" Saffiro said. "You think he would come to her *tomb?*"

"I believe so."

"Risk his life only to make elegy over her—"

"Or worse, perhaps," she murmured. "If we are to attend certain stories rife in the town, the Montargo may be capable of any infamy against my daughter."

Saffiro scowled. He did not know why he had returned to confront her. Electra, at the roots of her unanalytical awareness, did know. So she held him as if in shackles.

"I do not suppose Romulan Montargo so base," Saffiro said.

"You suppose him base enough to slay his friend."

Saffiro flinched.

"That is my quarrel, not yours, my donna."

"Will you," she said dispassionately, "watch by the Chenti mausoleum? He will come at night, I think. And very soon. It must be soon. Someone will get word to him."

"I watch?" Saffiro assumed an arrogant stance. Too late. "You've had me skulking in the Bhorga, lady, to please you. Now I must lurk amid bones and stones, it seems."

"You no longer hanker after his death."

"I wonder that you do," said Saffiro, feeling himself clever, "with such fervor. You mourn your nephew with great zeal."

"Oh," she said, "but my mourning to yours, sir, is nothing. Your mourning of Flavian Estemba."

If she grasped the menace in her own words one could not be sure. But certainly Saffiro grasped it. He sidled back a step. He said, and his voice was no longer level: "I am a man, my donna. It is my right to avenge my friend."

"Avenge him then," she said. "Remember, you swore you would, upon the High Altar."

Saffiro shivered.

"One night then, I'll watch. Only one."

"One night and be cheated of vengeance? No, I do not think you so lax. You'll watch until recompensed."

He opened his mouth, faltered, and said nothing.

"I will," she said, "pray for your success."

"Pray then," he blurted. "But surely not to God—"

He turned and fled.

Above, the bell was ringing of death and burial, to speed him.

It could be heard across the whole town, the bell. Even in the court of the Belmorio Tower it could be heard, though dimly, as if it smote under ground.

And so Troian Belmorio, trapped by form inside the palace of his ancestors, prowled an open gallery above the court below, turning over in his hands that inaccurate pretty portrait of the girl he was to have wed, her death-knell in his ears. And when at last he flung the portrait down into the court, the sound of its breakage did nothing to ease him, or to stop the bell.

With the disappointed lover's egomania, he could not rid himself of the notion that he was responsible in some way for her fate. Should he have remained to comfort her, ignoring her fall from grace—for had he not seen by her eyes that she loved him, whatever misalliances had gone on elsewhere? The rejected suitor, he could not break the flowerless staff across his knee. He could hate all women but Iuletta, who must remain for him a cause of argument and doubt. No use to seek answers from her, and thus he would never know any undisputed fact he did not want to know. But nor could he grieve for her. It was beneath him, beyond him. Had he not sentenced her—*your daughter is dead to me.* To wake up sweating and shouting aloud in the depth of the night, his red hair wringing wet, these were the only outer signs of his inner turbulence.

Nor did they last very long.

This harsh lesson—an end to obsequie before even it had begun—Susina attempted to teach her mother, who had surprised her by seeming to need it. "Now then, it's past. Come, she's lost, and nothing will bring her back." (It might have been Cornelia herself talking so.) "She's in Heaven, and where nicer if she was good enough. Better than any husband on earth. Did you never see the picture of an angel?"

In her own mind, Susina was wary of the chances of Heaven for Iulet. With no means to be sure, yet sure she was that the girl had found a way to kill herself, either with help from the dubious hermit Laurus, or without. There were poisons which could remove without evidence. Their existence had been known of since classical times. If so it had been, then to some fiery pit with that silly girl, who should have waited but a few hours more to get glad tidings, just as Susina had advised her. Having hesitated in awe at the noble stubbornness of her guest, Cornelia's daughter had come at last instead to despise it. A stab of pity and regret made this emotion all the sterner. Where, after all, had been Iuletta's stamina, bravery or strength? Why, Susina had seen young girls, younger than this Chenti maiden, endure far worse, and cling to life, tenacious as a vine. Of course, they were not stars in the sky, their atmosphere was never rarefied. And yet. Not to be loved, what was that? One could live without love. A great many did so, and lived well.

Susina, finding her dead, had posthumously cursed Iuletta in her heart. Not only for her precipitate stupidity. The pale young man, the Montargo's servant, at her very elbow, who had come all the distance from Lombardhia to rescue his master's wife, and viewed in her place a corpse. No, not only for that, but for the damnable consequences which followed after: that butcher-like lord of the Cat tribe, foul-mouthed as any man Susina had met, who came crashing about her house, threatening her, and all her girls and boys, and with not even the charity to offer a bribe for a discretion she would, being prudent, have awarded him without one. Cornelia, at the onslaught of Lord Chenti, Susina had wisely hidden away. "My mother, my lord, is sick to death with distress. I will answer for her, and for myself. I can hold my tongue and so will she." "Ah, you poxy slattern!" he had bellowed. "Hold them so, or you'll find yourself in a nastier spot than this." And to speak of the Pox to her, in this clean house that was famous for its wholesomeness—It had given her a cautious satisfaction to hold her tongue also to him, on the subject of Romulan Montargo's servant, sent himself by the secret way to freedom. Nor for that matter had she told Cornelia. With her charge dead, there seemed little point.

Dear God, when they had lifted her up, white wisp of a thing, and so beautiful, and carried her out, wrapped like a bolster for disguise. A cut flower. *A fool.*

And thereafter Cornelia, sitting over the wine all night, no longer weeping now, all wept out, wrung of tears, cheery blasphemies instead spilling from her: "Yes, she would make some angel a fine wife, so she would. God pardon me for thinking of it." And never any suggestion that shrewd Cornelia, too, might have doubts of Iuletta's fitness for Paradise.

Yet Susina, even as she conspired to liven her, saw the beginnings of a strange and insidious thing, which soon she was to perceive continuously. How her buxom billowy mother seemed to shrink, wrung not only of tears, but most curiously of flesh. Inside a week, caverns would appear under the bold eyes; inside three, only the slack and the big veins would be left of the busy hands. The death of flesh. There would come to be death in the hair, too, first only a peeling of its tint, which all this while had stayed fair under the veiling, fair as the tresses of a girl, finer and brighter than Susina's own. Inside the year it would be thin and grey. There would set in a stiffness in one side, extending from the arm on which Lord Chenti had struck her. By the year's end Susina, exasperated, would see an old and withered lady, laughing in a reedy cackle a laugh that never rose higher than her lips, that never reached as low as her heart. It somehow seemed Cornelia no longer had the wit to make do.

And Susina, prosperous and tolerant as she had become, prosperously would tolerate this aged child, aware it was dependent on her charity as she, farmed out in infancy, had never been dependent on Cornelia. Another had drunk the milk of those breasts, due to be shriveled bags, another run to be hushed and caroled and made much of against that stalwart side, due to be a bundle of clothes growing too large for it. And the endless anecdotes of Iuletta's babyhood, these too Susina must then put up with: How she had fallen down, how she had got up again; her quaint sayings, her precocious deeds.

And a few years after, by Cornelia's own deathbed, Susina must hold the frightened and bewildered shrunken hand, and hear the poor pipe of her voice over and over inquiring, "Where is my poppy, my catling? Where is my young lady? She is a fine donna of the Belmorio Tower. Yes, I saw her wed. Her husband was a beauty of a man, his hair was black as a raven, and such a fine dancer's legs on him—But will she not come in and visit me, now I'm fallen so sick?"

And, "There, Mother," Susina would murmur, "you shall see her very soon." Wondering, half in cynicism, half in foreboding, if Lord Lucifer would grant them space to greet each other, before he roused up the fires.

TWENTY-TWO

It seemed to Doro, where he noticed it at all, that the weather was abnormally oppressive, as if every atom of the abundant summer was gathering to produce strange alcohols of itself. The fierce clarity of the morning had given way to a brown afternoon, hot sun and overcast combining in the sky. The wild orchards, which occasionally overhung the Padova road, were loaded with fruit, weighed down, and already falls of damsons and apples rolled in the grass generating a low heady fume and clouds of drunken bees which dismayed the horse.

The streets of Sana Verensa had been buzzing like the bees until the first hour of the afternoon. That was the effect of the lavish Chenti funeral. Doro, secreted in the Montargo Tower, had seen nothing of it, nor had wished to.

At first light yesterday, the woman Susina had gifted him space and privacy to leave the brothel, before summoning perforce the old red Gattapuletta Cat himself. Doro sought Montargo, and once back there had found, as he suspected, some necessary dealings to accomplish. An odd thing and no mistake, that he should end up compelled to steal the seal-ring of Valentius in order that Valentius' heir should have it. That, and certain strategic documents in a box in Montargo Primo's study—these items Doro was privy to, and these items he had determined to come away with. When asking failed, and reason, Doro had resorted to a sly maneuver or two and a picked lock. The dispirited officiousness and confusion in the Tower oppressed him, and he was glad to get away from it, going from the house meekly and rather unnoticeably, with Romulan's rightful property concealed in his cloak.

There could be no going back there for Romulan himself, so much was certain. There was little enough to go back to now, save an heir's duty to the frowning stones themselves.

Under the circumstances, such duty was worth nothing. To approach the gates of Montargo would be to incite death.

Fortunately, there were other places to which a son of the Montargo family could escape, with impunity and some wealth. The symbol of the ship was appropriate, for Valentius' shipping interests were sound and far-flung, and would provide a path of flight and ultimately a foreign haven. A haven secure in a manner Lombardhia could no longer be reckoned to be. Tower feuds at the pitch the escalating Chenti-Montargo war had now reached had been known to spread over ducal borders, and miles beyond.

These matters Doro would put to Romulan. Somehow, he would put them, and at some juncture. But first there would be other words he must say.

Beside him, the sagging trees; above, the sinking sky. Within him this burden of news, weighing him down unutterably, unavoidably.

His spirits were on the ground, scuffed by the hooves of his horse along with the dust and the fallen damsons. His only consolation had come to be the length of road and therefore of time that lay between him and his accounting to Romulan. That it grew shorter step by step he was only too conscious, and, ashamed, he had not so far allowed the horse to slow its pace.

Wanting to, probably, he had by now forgotten Romulan's vow to come after him, should he be late in his return to Manta Sebastia.

It was therefore with a woeful miscellany of feelings that Doro, less than a mile from the turning-off point of the road, glanced up and beheld another rider moving toward him in a whirlwind of coppery dust. Edging to the side of the thoroughfare to permit the other fellow free passage, asking himself vaguely who this could be, riding from the branching track that led eventually to Lombardhia, at the same instant totally and fatally informed of who it was and that the rider's business, current too quickly, was with him.

Shortly, even the radiation of the sun could no longer excuse Doro of recognition.

The horse was reined in a few feet away, and the unmistakable countenance was before him, and the blue eyes that seemed at first alive with anger.

"Doro! In the Name of God—"

"Yes, sir. I was delayed. I'm sorry. But you should not be here."

Romulan said nothing to this, and for a few moments then they sat their horses, facing each other through the settling dust, not speaking.

It began to come to Doro that Romulan's face had grown extraordinarily still, almost immobilized. The lips were sealed together and the eyes very wide, no longer angry, if they had ever been. Unlike the face, the hands on the reins were nervous and agitated. Doro began to see in this face, these hands, some dreadful indication of prior knowledge. And even as he thought this, Romulan said:

"Tell me what it is."

"There's no good way to tell it. The report is bad."

"I know that. Say it out."

"We had no letter from your father, sir, because he could send no letter. On the night you rode for Lombardhia, he was killed outside Montargo. A stabbing. It's supposed the Chentis are to blame." Doro paused. Romulan said nothing, did not look away. It was all too plain he was waiting to hear something further. "Another," Doro said, "another has also died."

It was so quiet, here on this stretch of the road. Bees still harvesting somewhere, and a bird singing, and now and then the tamp of the horses' hooves as they lifted them and set them down. But these sounds composed the quietness. They were not compatible with the speech that must continue to be pulled out, somehow, through his mouth.

And then Doro found he did not need to speak for a while.

"Iuletta," Romulan said. There was nothing in his voice at all. "You are contriving to tell me she's dead. Tell me how, then?"

Doro straightened.

"It's generally reckoned of—some illness."

"And the truth?"

"Perhaps, she may have taken poison."

Romulan looked away at last. He looked along the road, in the direction of the town, which was not visible from here, only the pastel umbras of its hills.

Doro said, "Chenti Primo would have her wed the Belmorio, and at the altar, so the story runs, she refused him. And the Chentis cast her out. She went with the old nurse, whose daughter is in trade in the Bhorgabba."

"A whore."

"Just so. But Iuletta was received honorably and discreetly there, and kept from the ways of the house. And there she was to wait until—but it seems—"

"It seems she was to wait for me and thought I had forsaken her," Romulan said gently. His eyes after all were lowered now, and his hands as immobile as his face had been. "Because I lay sick, and my father lay dead, and neither of us had therefore the means to send to her."

"It may have appeared so."

"It did appear so. It appears, too, she had but little faith in me. It appears she thought very little of me altogether." Something grated in the voice, and was gone. Almost idly, Romulan added, "Of course, it has been some while. I trusted her safe, did I not, safe in Montargo. But she, very likely, might have judged I was done with it all, the marriage, the compact of love. All of it. Yes." His hands lightly woke the reins. The horse began to move forward. "And my father, too," Romulan said. He was past Doro before Doro quite knew it, the horse trotting on along the Verensa road.

Doro set his own horse after it.

"My lord, there's nothing to be gained in Verensa. The Chentis are gluttonous to murder you, or if not the Duca has ruled—"

"I care nothing for the Duca. Less for the Chentis."

"The sentence either way is for your death."

"Less than for both of them, what may happen to myself. There is no one to need me living, now."

Doro said, riding beside him:

"The Lord Valentius sent you away to keep you unharmed. He died crediting this. If you could ask him now what he desired—"

"He would desire that I remain unharmed in Lombardhia."

"No. He would want you in better security than that." Calmly and sensibly, though it was not ethically at all the time, Doro began to broach the plan of escape, the seal ring and the documents, the shipmaster who should be employed, the vessel and the route. Next he moved to monetary concerns, mentioning bankers and how they might best be dealt with. Romulan listened. It was evident that he listened. Once or twice he nodded, and once he said, "Yes." Nevertheless, he continued to ride in the wrong direction. Eventually Doro produced the seal ring and extended it. Romulan, turning in the saddle, took the ring but did not draw it on to his finger, where indeed it might not have fitted, for Romulan's hands were of another mould than Valentius' had been, the articulate hands of a swordsman. This mark on him of what he was, this key almost to what had come about, checked

Doro even as Romulan checked, curling and uncurling his fingers about his father's ring. And they rode on, unhurriedly, toward Verensa. Which was death.

Finally Doro declaimed, in a tone of intense casualness, "If we turn the horses now, we should reach Manta before sunset."

"With ease," Romulan said. He rode on, playing with the ring, his eyes on the horizon of insubstantial hills.

"My lord," Doro said.

"Go back," Romulan said. "Go back without me. I'd not haul you after me into this." He fell silent, and Doro waited. After a minute, Romulan said to him, "There's nowhere in the whole world I wish to be, or to journey to. But this place I know. And they are there. Both of them. My father, and my wife."

"No, my lord," Doro said. "They are *not*."

"Religious pedantry. Very well. In the sky, then, my father in the cloud there, and Iuletta waiting to arise with the morning star."

"My lord—"

"I brought them this. Their deaths are on me, as Flavian's death is on me. And Leopardo's, for that matter."

Doro was repelled by the reasonable adult voice of the young man riding beside him. Doggedly he kept up, would not leave go. But there seemed nothing more to say for the present.

"Doro, return yourself to Manta."

"I was instructed to guard you and shall do so," Doro said after all, embarrassed.

"Oh, God." Romulan laughed very softly. He palmed Valentius' ring abruptly and put it away inside his doublet, which was of a dull, cold blue, nondescript on the streets of Manta Sebastia, but sufficient to kill him in Verensa, of course. "Would you believe me, Doro, if I told you that I knew, before you spoke of it, my father's death, and her's?"

"I saw that in your face."

"Did you? Yes, perhaps. Yesterday, in the black of the morning before the sun climbed—I woke suddenly, and knew her dead. I used that day in discussion with myself, scolding myself I was an idiot. And by the time they rang midnight from the citadel, I understood my father also—And so, today I came after you, and every beat of the beast's hooves was like the bell, the bloody death bell I heard when Mercurio died on my sword and when—" Romulan relinquished words, and as he did so the alternating light of the sky closed over. Across the amberous clouds there flickered a sheen of lightning and after a second or so the thunder tumbled down on the land, dry and sullen and strangely spent.

In the wake of the announcing storm, tossed coins of rain were broadcast on the dust. Doro caught at the bridle of Romulan's horse and tugged, trotting his own animal under a stand of trees beside the road. Romulan did not resist and his horse came willingly.

"Shelter from the weather," Doro said. It was a pretext, but it might serve, maybe.

The darkness seemed to fence them in under the trees, shadows unsnarling from their branches. The distant hills ran down into the rain.

Romulan sat motionless, watching the water slant beyond the enclosure, his hands loose, relaxed and elegant. In his handsomeness, the long black hair on his shoulders, his clothes fashionable, everything about him hinting at a paragon, he distressed Doro, for he was beyond him. In rank, in person, in all things. Such a being was not to be managed. Particularly now it had assumed this ghastly self-defeating strength.

Romulan seemed to guess some aspect of Doro's frustration. At length, Romulan indicated the rain. "You were looking for my tears," he said. "Well, you must make do with these. Let the sky weep for me, Doro. Now I can only weep blood."

The lightning came again, a broad flash, the progress of which might almost be examined. The thunder was tardy, some way away. The trees rattled above them. Soon the water would work through and there could be no more pretense for remaining stationary in this spot. The scents of the slaked dust, earthy and unexpected, filled the nostrils, seeming to bring a promise of some sort. But of what?

Doro began to speak, rapidly. He produced, one by one, every element of persuasion and logic and emotional coercion that he could lay hand to. The sentences were rough, and roughly cobbled together. If the arguments were flawless, he could not be certain Romulan paid heed. Yet, as previously, it seemed he listened, seriously and courteously, in a way Valentius had had, and Romulan himself never, never had, before today.

Romulan did indeed listen. The thick armor of acceptance was on him, and through it he could afford to hear even the most hurtful and energizing things, they did not really touch him, and it seemed that they never could touch him, or anything again. He was snared, too, by that bizarre disadvantage of the truly beautiful. He knew and did not know the picture he presented, that which brought him the violent responses of others, devotion or hatred, and which impaired the judgment of others more or less consistently. To himself he was himself, an inadequate machine that stumbled and cried out, and in this human condition, the reactions about him were a source of discomfort. Mercurio had spared him that, and with Iuletta had come a counterbalance, a mirror in which to see himself and also beyond himself. But no more.

How curious, that awakening yesterday, which had been, rather, like the descent into sleep, the extended sleep of oblivion. Where now was she, in perfect fact? In expurgation on some plain of the afterlife? Or in the Chenti sepulchre, which seemed to draw him helplessly toward itself, and for no purpose, none at all. For why pay calls upon the dead? Would they converse, would they stretch out their hands in welcome? Or did they peer in gratification through some trapdoor in the floor of Heaven?

For the first time, he found that he had sought perception beyond the grave, and was no longer assured of its character. Even Hell had become indefinite. Was he to think of Iuletta there, or anywhere, save where he had seen her, in the world of light and shade and flesh and breath and here and now? He was unable to visualize her in another form, and so could not visualize those extraterrestrial domains that might encompass her.

"With these papers, no one will gainsay you," Doro said.

Romulan nodded.

He recalled Mercurio's persuasions, drastic or mellifluous, brief or verbose, but always . . . persuasive. If Mercurio had lived, what would he say now? But if Mercurio had lived, now would not be now, but some other station on the highway of events. What was it the priest had said—*If you think so, then so it is for you.* The teaching of Christ, no less. *He that believes in me*—Ah, Laurus. If I could alter all this, by my belief. Oh, Laurus, I'd give up my soul—Romulan raised his head and felt the rain sprinkled through the trees mildly across his brow, his cheeks. Warm rain, warm as milk. When had he said those words? Before the Chenti betrothal feast, was it not?

Where was it Doro was talking of? The Levant. His proposed sanctuary. The cindery skies, the orange groves, the walled seaports pushed by their crumbling mountains into the ocean. Another world. And Verensa on her hills, never to see her towers again. And did that horrify him then? Verensa, where all his kin, of blood or heart, were changed into marble.

He had not slept last night, but paced about, and today he had been riding, and now he was all at once worn and weary, and to stop Doro prating he would do anything on earth.

"Yes, Doro," Romulan said. "Then we'll turn back to Lombardhia."

And Doro, naturally, stopped. And as naturally re-started in a low voice: "—To Lombardhia?"

"Why not? Let me defy my stars. Let me not die. What do I care where I go or where I'm to be? To bloody damnable and accursed Lombardhia. And to the Levant, or to the surface of the moon, if there's room for me to balance there. Yes, Doro. We'll ride to Manta and reach the gates before sunset."

Doro's horse started forward with a jerk, and then, shying wildly, pranced backwards. Romulan's horse shied at the exact and matching instant. As this occurred, Romulan became aware of a pale shimmer on the road some fifteen or sixteen paces away from them, a glare he had taken for rogue sunlight in the rain. Yet now the shimmer seemed to drift, pulsing, and as he gazed at it, harden into a coherent rounded image.

Romulan's horse brought up its head and neighed sharply, rolling its eyes, sweating with fear. There was a new aroma above the scent of the freshened soil, the laved path of the road, indescribable, yet peculiarly arid in the wetness.

"It moves," Doro said, rational and very quiet.

"Does it have a shape? It seems to me it does."

"Yes. The shape of an egg."

They held their horses as best they could, and the shining shape, which was like an egg, blew toward them. It whispered as it came, and Romulan felt all the hairs of his body shift. The horses pawed the ground. Was this some proof, some omen, of the existence of phenomenal things?

There began to be a shadow now, within the glowing egg, bisecting it. He remembered the golden ray which had bisected the silver crescent in the magician's insularium. Laurus. *Laurus.* Romulan leaned forward, staring, his breath and his

thought going together. For the magician-priest stood before
him on the road, rimmed by ovoid colorless fire.

"What is it?" Doro said.

"A man. The priest—" Romulan, forcing himself to answer, felt his strength flowing away into the sphere of light. It
drained him to fuel itself, oil for a lamp, no more.

Doro was crossing himself. Romulan laughed. He shouted,
breathless, across the road:

"Well, you're here. What do you want?"

He could see Laurus quite clearly now, the mantle, the
sunless skin, the orderly features. Even the glint of the crucifix on the breast. And the left hand uplifted, delivering one
single, minimal gesture, that of beckoning. Once only.

"What," Romulan said, "you would not have me rush to
safety? You'd have me tangled in the snares of my foes,
would you, sorcerer-priest?"

There was a sizzle like fat thrown on a fire. Something exploded, resembling cannon-shot in the distance.

Save for themselves and their trembling animals, the road
was empty.

Romulan swung himself from his horse, and commenced
the work of soothing it. His eyes were blank and oddly darkened as if from some drug, and as his hands moved, his face
grew still again, and uninhabited.

Doro was unsure what he himself had witnessed. He had
seen the glow, and in the glow a dark patch rather like the
contours of a man. But he would not have sworn to it, nor
to the presence of the occult. The weather might itself invent
weird creatures. He had heard tell of them, entities such as
those lights which danced on the masts of storm-running
ships. As for the priest, Laurus, there had been some sort of
hinted aversion to him at the brothel Doro had not liked.

"He sheltered me before," Romulan said. He was steady,
bemused but not alarmed, still insulated by his general state,
which Doro recognized. "Shelter, and foul medicine, for I
think he knew I had taken up with the plague. And then, he
predicted my father would come after me. What, by Christ,
does he want from me now?"

"Nothing," said Doro promptly. "Let's—"

"Something. Something his black magic wishes of me." Romulan suddenly turned, his body tensed, his arms outflung in
a ridiculous drama that was terrifying. "He's a necromancer,
Doro. Doro—can he raise the dead for me, do you hazard?"
And grinning, he turned back again. "Oh, Jesus," he said, "let

me see." And he was in the saddle in that insane showman's leap Flavian Estemba had taught him, and the horse was away, pelting down the road with him. Again, again, in the direction of Sana Verensa, her pitiless towers, and death.

To approach now from another quarter the hermit's oratory, which he had visited three times before, that was something, perhaps, to weaken the power of repeated things.

The horse was not overly tired, and fear had galvanized it. As he deserted him, however, poor Doro had seemed in difficulties with his own mount. And now they were left behind. A look past his shoulder awarded Romulan the vacant road, glittering as sun slit the cloud.

In the tumult of the ride there was a senseless exhilaration. Only arrival could end it, but ended it would be. For it was no more than some jest to think the hermit might rouse the dead. Had Romulan not, once before, suggested such a thing and mocked it? Why now then hurtle toward the place, his chances given to the winds, when one minute before he had decided to protect himself? Had there been real witchcraft performed on the road, not some dream or fantasy, and was it the spell which magnetized him?

Yes. The mirage had seemed real. The priest within the sphere of sheeny lightning, beckoning. And if Laurus could do such a thing as that—

Birds spiraled up from a ragged field and a spoke of sunlight broke, sheer and yellow, through the stalks and across the road. Impulsively, Romulan pulled the horse's head around and sent it in through the field, running diagonally now toward his destination. (Perhaps the oratory would not be there, gone up in the air as the birds had done, or slid down into Hell beneath.)

And he thought abruptly of galloping to Marivero, Iuletta on the gelding before him, and thrust the vision away. It had hurt him to think of her, the first time he had felt the pain of it. And now he urged the horse to greater speed, to leave the pain behind him for the birds to tear and destroy with their beaks.

The land already rose and fell, and soon, smashing through the tall grasses, half surprised, he drew the horse in hand above a rolling slope, and saw the stone pines grouped below him. Beyond them, the oratory, very small, only its topmost angle tinctured by the westering sun.

How brief the ride had been, or seemed to be. And now he

was here, and what should he do here? *Turn back*, Doro's voice said within him.

Not aware he did so, Romulan shook his head. Exhilaration had ceased.

He rode the horse at an amble down the slope, the grasses bending now away from them and springing up behind. The flowers that had filled the grass with fire were dead.

A little wind was turning the sun-wheel on the post and he heard it whining, dimly, but did not look to see, as he came up to the door. He tethered the horse, utilizing the bough of the pine tree, as always before. The mechanical slave failed to call out at him as he did this. And going to the door he found it would open.

When he entered the whitewashed drum of the building, it seemed to have faded and to have shrunk. There was something strangely lacking, as if a presence had been removed from it; removed as the cross with the ivory Christ, its solitary ornament, had been removed.

Romulan walked to the second door behind the altar. He had sought this hermitage three times. At the first a peevish cynical brat, the second, a ranting bully, the third, dying of grief and terror, crawling on his knees, plague on him and all the unbearable anguish of life itself. This fourth time he stood at the entrance of the magician's cell, what was he now? He considered himself, and found he no longer knew what or who he was, or what he might become. Seeing that he might presently be slain, perhaps this did not matter very much.

He drew the black curtain aside. As he raised his hand to knock on it, the second door opened.

Within, the cell was filled by daylight. Startled, Romulan glanced about, missing the source of the light entirely in his disorientation, then comprehending that a line of round-topped windows were revealed where only one was ever visible formerly. As the windows had appeared, so the sorcerous paraphernalia had disappeared. Not a map, not an astrolabe, not a point-toothed fish remained. Even the table was gone, the candle stands and the lamp. Even the stuffed dragon, the turtle on its eminence of impure jade. Only a phalanx of great chests towered along one wall.

The magio stood beside the chests, his hands folded before him.

Romulan Montargo gazed at him, an extended searching gaze, no more adolescent, no more merely askance or defiant.

After a moment, Romulan said, "Did I see what I reckoned I saw, on the Padova road?"

"If you saw anything which brought you here, then be assured, it found you at my will."

"Another boast? I'm to quake at your genius and your supernatural strength? I'm past such antics, spiritual Father."

"Attend. It's only this: I supposed you near and sent to summon you, if you would obey the summons. You have done so."

"How was it achieved?"

"By means of the mind, and the mind's capacity. This is superfluous to your needs, to know so much. A message has waited on you."

"From whom?"

"From one that you come back to mourn." The hands of Fra Laurus unfolded, and held out to him a leaf of paper.

Romulan came to it raging and at last afraid.

"*What*? Some ghost has come flapping in and wailed for pen and ink? Dare I read it?"

"Read. Though it will bring you no pleasure to do so. A necessary preface."

Romulan, hardly intending it, took the paper and looked down at it. He saw a delicate tracery of letters, never seen, known at once: the handwriting of Iuletta Chenti.

Pious Father, grant me the blessing of your attention for the length of this. I would speak to you of a woman who has lost all her substance in the world.

He read on. He held himself in a vise, and read it all. And when it was done, ocular ducts dryer than bones, hands steady, and voice unchanged, he lifted his eyes and met the remote intelligent eyes of his tormentor.

"Well," Romulan said. "I am astonished, sir, you invite me here to peruse this. Do you think yourself safe from me, now I know you were the agent of her death? Now I may wonder what agony she endured from your bungling potion, despite her pleas, or what pangs she suffers now, in the other world, for her craven suicide, which act you abetted so punctually. She was my wife, magician. You've stolen her from me like a robber. What are you? Not what you say, for sure. If you'd followed the injunctions of your calling, *false priest*, she would be here for me, still. Oh, she says not, but would she have dared some other method when she was so fearful of all means but this soft drowsy death she trusted you, you viper, to give her? *No.*" At each emphasis, his voice stumbled, and righted itself again swiftly. He saw the words dance on the paper, blacker than pitch: *Her husband has grown impatient . . . abandoned her. Only to be dead, that is what she most wishes for.* He hated her, he hated her feebleness and her lack of faith. She had deserved betrayal, then, since she had only looked for betrayal, and merited death by entreating it. Yet: "You foul devil of a priest, you *Laurus.* Tell me why I should not kill you as bloodily as I can devise and send you after her to suffer Hell as she now does? I'd say it was my right, to have vengeance for my wife. Since, but for you she would have *lived.*"

Fra Laurus refolded one hand, this time upon his golden crucifix.

"She lives."

The world grew motionless. Not a blade of grass, not a mote of dust could bend, or spin. The light curtaining the windows became darker, for the sun had hesitated in the sky, its effulgence faltering. Birds, deprived of volition, would be showering out of the air as the rain had done. The hills—

"She lives," Romulan said. He spoke from the midst of the stasis of all things, and now his words lay on the room, meaningless but unable to depart, and he must hear them forever, and know their absurdity forever.

"The rivers and the streams of life," Fra Laurus said, "when one is in accord with them, bear destiny faultlessly along those routes and toward those goals which provide harmony both in the spirit of the earth and in the soul of man. Anything which jars this harmony, anything which has no purpose in the wholeness of the scheme, may be controlled. At times one must not seek to intervene. At times, even, some tragic flaw may prove essential to the whole. At other times I will stretch out my hand. I once explained this to you, Romulan Montargo."

"She lives," Romulan said again, or else the words reiterated themselves.

"She lives. I had her letter, delivered to me in the depth of night. I foresaw her able to harm herself as she promised. She asked for poison. I sent her Curaris. What is Curaris? An elixir known to the Egeptsi, but believed, in origin, to have been brought aboard papyrus ships from the continent of Atlantus, of which your Plato will have informed you. Mixed with certain other juices, the cordial has this property, it will induce trance. The muscles grow quiescent, the limbs rigid. The heart beats at a rate no physician can detect, unless primed with the cause, not always then. To the recipient, it will seem to be a sleep. To the observer, no less than death." The priest's eyes looked down on him from their heights. "So she drank it, and so fell into this sleep, was taken for dead and interred in the Chenti tomb. As I judge the working of the medicine, she'll wake tonight."

The shadow of a bird went by each window in turn, and the world drew breath and lived again.

"I think I must be mad," Romulan said. "Madness like a contagion, had from you."

"No madness. She sleeps, is quick, and will wake up. Nor should she wake alone there."

"The mausoleum—she lies *there?*"

"Where else? They thought her well-qualified."

"Festering bones, and air like the strangler's noose—it would kill her in earnest to revive in such a spot. But then, she's dead. She's dead."

The priest began to stir. Over his head he drew the cowl of his robe. From the shadow that lay across the foremost chest, he took up a drapery, a priestly garment identical to his own.

"You know very well what you risk in entering the town, and in seeking the sepulchre of the Chentis, especially. Here is your disguise, since you thought to bring nothing for yourself."

Romulan made no move to take the robe. Ridiculously he caught himself listening, thinking to detect the blunted sound of hooves on grass—Doro riding down the slope to the oratory. But Doro was delayed. The horse, skittish with fear of the lightning's egg on the road, would not be managed, or had run away. Doro would not enter to add his commonplace sense to this senselessness.

"Come, then," the magician said. Leaving the chests, the down-burning sunlight and Romulan together, he had walked to the doorway, still carrying the second robe.

"Wait," Romulan burst out. "Wait, in God's name." And when Laurus took no notice and was gone, he said to the walls, "What am I to do?"

But as Laurus passed through into the landscape beyond the oratory door, his figure black and flat, soulless it seemed against the glow of westering light, Romulan came up behind him.

"Necromancer," he said, "do you not require your luminous scroll—the Book of the Dead?"

Laurus turned, faceless silhouette, and held out to him the

disguising robe. Romulan took it. "This is damnation," he said, and dressed himself, becoming thereby a hooded priest, darkened, silhouetted, and deprived of soul as Laurus was.

"It must be," Romulan said, "some disgusting ceremony you mean to attempt, must attempt, in order to call her back from the shadows. I'll tell you now, do anything that would sully her, and I'll kill you."

"There is no ceremony. You yourself can wake her, with a kiss. You absence was, according to her words, her reason for death. Your presence will ensure her life. You must be the first thing that she sees."

The priest began to climb away from the oratory. Romulan went after him. (The horse whickered as he passed it, thinking he came for it, falling quiet as he went on.) The hills were dappled with birdsong now, and rain hung sparkling on the grass. The scents of trees and plants were vibrant, and he recalled the perfume of her hair and skin. He sank on his knees in the grass, bowed to the soil, clutching it in his hands. He began to pray, but the prayers were uninspired, and as he prayed he almost wept, but his hurt and desperation could not sustain themselves. His passions had withered. When he pulled himself to his feet again, the priest was far ahead.

"Iuletta," Romulan said, thrusting on up the slope, regaining ground quickly.

Sleep not death. If she slept and lived—

There had been the fraction of an instant, long ago, when he had seen her stand between him and some abyss. Yet she had thrown herself into the abyss before him.

No. She did not live. Mercurio, Valentius, Iuletta, each was gone for good. This was merely some nightmare he must act out. Perhaps some further experiment which the monstrous sorcerer was intent upon. (The marriage of Sun and Moon, the illusion of gold, Hell, flaming inside a crystal.) The sun was going down. But they would reach the gates—Verensa's—before sunset.

As the ruby-red blaze diminished in the sky to a band, a ribbon, finally a thread, the garden of death turned black. The blind walls, pillars, porticos of its aristocratic mausoleums, which dominated the upland of the garden, became at first blocks of strident ebony on the ceiling of a lavender twilight, while downhill that lessening pool of scarlet bled away. Then, losing all contour and all pride with the light, they blended and embraced with the trees. As the fullness of the

dark dripped down, the graveyard grew ominous and impos-
ingly still. The perfume of growing things mingled with de-
caying stone and broken earth, and with some other
component, perhaps imagined, unique to its situation. Above,
the Basilica, a silvery diadem. Below, the sequined washes of
the Lower Town, the mercantile quarter, the Bhorga. And
floating far off in the air, like an island, the lamplit tops of
the eternal towers. Yet these things were alien, having no influence it seemed upon this silent bedchamber of the dead.

Wrapped in the stigma and mystery of the garden, Saffiro
Vespelli waited, leaning one shoulder on an upright of
marble, his head sunk forward, himself in a sort of sleep that
yet could partly hear and vaguely see, and hopelessly, tirelessly ponder.

Saffiro was exhausted and disillusioned. His personal feud
with the Montargo had begun both to appall and to bore him.
To avenge Mercurio Estemba was a pact with the antique
rulings of romance. It had no true substance. Its purpose had
been to assuage guilt and pain, and fear, that too. Its reality—these vigils, these seekings after an elusive villain who
would not come to him, stunned and destroyed the healing
force of Saffiro's hate, and left him to confront the dismay
within himself. That which he had sought to evade.

Here he stood now, upon this hillside burial mound,
charged with murderous waiting for one who, obviously, was
elsewhere. Romulan, his father's fortune doubtless now open
to him, might spend it over the whole earth. If he had loved
the girl enough to mourn for her, he would not risk mourning
at her tomb, that tomb now twenty short paces from where
Saffiro lurked like a cutthroat.

And for Flavian—did Flavian demand vengeance? (Flavian Estemba, perhaps not the superlative guide, the friend,
the brother, but one who would corrupt.)

Saffiro's inner voices now began to nag at him. If he were
free of this, might he not be free of all of it? No guilt, no lin-
gering alarm. All swept away with Mercurio by the cleansing
brooms of hours and days and months. Without this task
(imposed by Electra Chenti—do not think of her), perhaps
one could be permitted to forget the deed and what one had
learned, and what one owed . . . ? He reached for the
wineskin that leaned with him on the stonework porch of the
Retzis' monument, and drank. Rough wine from the Bhorga,
Flavian's choice.

Saffiro sighed, and then snatched back his breath, and held

it. For there was a movement through the garden, a rippling disturbance of darkness among the cypresses.

Almost involuntarily, setting down the wine, Saffiro's gloved hand crossed his body and fell upon the hilt of his sword. In the cool of night, sweat started on his forehead and his spine.

Then, like phantoms, but not like the one who had troubled his brain, two figures stepped out onto the turf before the Chenti mausoleum. Saffiro released his breath again in a noiseless curse. Two priests of some mundane order, plain to his night-vision by the outline of their habits and the ubiquitous cowls. It seemed they looked around them, and he wondered sardonically what their business might be, and reckoned almost at once on some illegality, a hunt for stray skulls or wild mandrakes, that might prove amusing to a hidden watcher.

Then his humor perished in amazement. Producing some instrument from his robes, one of the holy men smote violently on the iron bar across the doors of the tomb. Once, twice, three times, four. At the fifth blow, the obstruction gave way and clattered down. A thrust, and the nearer of the doors swung inwards.

Then came a hiatus, a murmur of voices—Saffiro could make out nothing, save that one man seemed younger than the other, and in anger. Suddenly, this younger, angry priest strode forward, into the violated sepulchre. His companion smoothly followed him, and the broken-in door swung out again to close, with a rough appearance of wholeness, against its fellow.

Saffiro's thoughts now babbled. He would have wished to silence them. Some spasm of pure knowledge had enveloped him. Even rogue priests, in search of remedial thigh-bones, did not crush in the doors of the tower-born dead. While the instrument of breakage had been a sword.

His hand locked on the hilt of his own blade, his heart pounding, Saffiro asked himself, (in hopes of a firm denial), if one of those who had entered the mausoleum was not in fact, after all, the very man he sought, Romulan Montargo.

TWENTY-THREE

In the blackness, the tomb smelled of cold iron, colder powders, leisurely decays. And under everything, incoherent foulness came and went, threatening but insubstantial. Having entered, Romulan stood to one side, allowing the sorcerer to come after him. Yet the eerie brushing by of the Fra Magio's long robe sent a chill across every inch of Romulan's skin. An insidious panic, that had nothing to do with his intellect or reason, or even with his emotion, had begun to grapple with him, when a light broke and rinsed away the dark.

He saw the interior of the tomb, then, its ranked pillars, its hard scrolled couches with their freight of bones, cobwebs and jewels. He saw it all and despised it all, as something noisome and obvious. The unsubtlety of death. And fear left him, his anger returned, and the awful limping sorrow that could seem to find no meaning for him.

"So the Chentis sleep, then," he said aloud. "The one I butchered, also, somewhere hereabouts. And where is *she*?"

"She is here."

The light had been made or conjured, and fixed on two slender candles now stuck by their own wax to a slab of stone. Romulan stared at them, and from them to the points of two narrow Eastern slippers of ivory satin crusted over by gold, and from these to the long folds of a wine-colored gown.

"There," he said, and found he could not move, either to advance or to turn away. Yet his eyes traveled on. They discovered shimmerings where the light now spilled and dusks where the shadow waited to return. They discovered the soft swell of the breast, where two hands lay on a silver flower. They discovered scatterings of black paper, the petals of uncanny charcoal roses, and one petal lying on the white marvellous curve above the edge of the gown, the fluted brim of the camisola. Garnets smouldered steadily. The black petal on the white surface of the breast (where once he had lain blinded as the fountains of life sprang from his loins to hers, their arms locked about each other as they drowned together), the black petal did not quiver, but stood like a blot, opaque, immobile. And now, the hair, hair blacker than the rose petals, brighter than the darkness. And so the slim arch of the neck, and so the sculpted chin, the chiseled underlip, blushed by some cosmetic—and so—and so—the straight line of the nose, the fragile plane of the cheek, the hollows where the lashes lay like black wings, the lids made of nacre, the brows of sooty feathers, the forehead of milk-white glass with a mauve pearl lying a little sideways on it, and the grape-bloom roots of the hair, and the hair again and the gold bees which held the chain of the pearl to the hair hardly shining, losing the light, and the black nothing beyond.

"You should approach, Romulan Montargo," Fra Laurus said.

Romulan felt the floor heaving under his feet and his eyes clouded over. He recalled the insularium, where first this oppression had fastened on him. He smelled death and rottenness, and needing to cry aloud, he shouted at the priest.

"I've seen her. Do what you have to. Try to bring her soul out of her mouth."

But: "Approach," the priest said again, and nothing else.

And Romulan, pushing the clinging cowl from his head, went forward, peculiarly compelled by the uninsistence of the voice.

Coming close, however, he did not look at her, dizzy, his sight dazzled by the candles, it was easy to see nothing of anything. Yet it seemed necessary to speak.

"I'm here. What next?"

"Take up her hand."

"She's wed to death. Is it honorable to touch another man's wife?" Romulan turned away.

The priest repeated, softly, "There is nothing to repel you. Take her hand."

So, he leaned and let his fingers close over hers, shutting his eyes as he did so, as a pain quite physical, grey and screaming, rose in his side, in his ribs, his heart; that was utterly non-physical, only the clamor of grief. And this went from him almost instantly, leaving him once more in the other state, through which he was able to endure all this.

"Notice," the priest's voice murmured, "the fingers are warm, and flexible."

Romulan held the hand of Iuletta. It did not seem warm to

him, but cool, waxy and immovable. Opening his eyes, he beheld her rings staring at him. They had sent her into the dark with riches, as befitted the legal child of a mighty House. He pictured Lord Chenti blustering, deciding her portion, that she should gleam to confront the quick. The pearl was exquisite and rare, they had given her that. Or was it the Belmorios' gift, maybe, before she humiliated them at the altar. The chain and its pearl, the gems on her dress. Her rings. Not his ring, of course, the marriage token. Who had had that? Maybe the whore-daughter in the Bhorga had filched it. For some reason, the pain struck at him again when he thought of this. He dropped her lifeless hand and straightened. She had no look of the grave, and no scent of it, either. Pure and delicious she lay stretched before him. Her face was cruel in its repose, for she seemed almost to be smiling.

He visualized her despair and her degradation, how she had penned the letter, waited for its reply. How she had uncorked the phial and drunk. He saw her suddenly in poisoned torture, writhing on some filthy brothel floor, alone, suffocating, blood running from her mouth. The smile could be the aftermath of some grimace, and misleading as to the nature of her death. He should turn back and wring the windpipe of this priest, this necromantic dabbler. Do it *now*. He did nothing.

It was a fragrance of cinnamon and incense which caused him at length to look about. A small cake of aromatics had been lighted and placed on the floor, a safeguard against the fetor of the tomb.

Romulan said, "I thought there would be some show by now. The scroll with the green figure on it. A raucous invocation. Is it blood you need? Use mine, all of it if you wish, for her sake. Only pardon me if I forget courtesy and laugh at you."

The priest stood across from him now, the other side of Iuletta's serene corpse. He observed her, no more than that, but intently, with great watchfulness.

Romulan's pulses hammered against his flesh. His entire body paused in terrified expectancy, a yearning dread, for some event he knew impossible.

Getting no answer to his challenge, he made a wild pass before the face of the priest, and when Laurus lifted his eyes to him, said: "I may kill you yet. Tell me the agenda of this rite, or it shall be now."

With simple logic the priest answered, "Your sword was broken on the door."

"Not my hands, however."

"And do you suppose yourself a match for me, Romulan Montargo?"

Romulan glared at him, into the composed face, the hermit's eyes gazing from their mountaintops. Something had caused the candles to flare up; the pallor of the magician's skin, so intensified, grew mask-like. It seemed then as if it might be, all of it, a mask, this face, this tonsured fashionable hair, the body—or at least the robe in which the body was concealed. Only the eyes looked through, to give away the nature of what had so sheltered itself.

Romulan, trying to fathom it, come on it, was abruptly half afraid. It was no fear he knew, nothing rational. It was unexplained. But surely, in that moment, he did judge himself less than this priest of darkness.

The young man lowered his gaze. Very civilly he said, "No match at all, of course. Accept that I am duly cowed." And regarded the girl's hands crossed on the silver rose. The pain had gone. He had no urge to lament. He did not know her, this was not Iulet.

"All that must be done," said the priest then, "is to wait patiently."

"Until she wakes."

"Exactly so."

"May I ask how long a wait? You see, Father, I've some business in the Levant."

"It seems to me it should be soon. The positive moment is unknown to me."

"Unknown?" Romulan glanced up. The blue eyes lilted, bowed. "But, omniscient Father, you seem to have a knowledge of all things. You seem to assume the role of God. Or would it be his rival in the cellerage?"

Romulan moved from the slab where the unrecognized maiden lay.

"And so," he said, "I will listen for your gladsome cry of triumph, outside, where the air is clean. Or else I may seek the covered cart you told me attends for you in the alley below the graveyard. May set it afire and send it running for the Bhorga. Rouse the town and lead the good people here to applaud your infallible art."

The priest stood beside the dead girl, bending a little toward her now, to lay two fingers against her temple.

Romulan wrenched open the doors of the tomb and went out into the freshness of the night.

The moon was rising, and as he leaned a second on the angels by the door, the melancholy light seemed to calm some vital nerve within him. He wished then, with a dreary desire like that of an old man, for a resting place.

But presently he left the unloving support of the angels. He began aimlessly to cross the stretch of land that divided this sepulchre from another that a stone glove wound with stone flowers identified with the Retzi family.

So, between two cypress trees, he met with Saffiro Vespelli.

Saffiro was very drunk; it had seemed needful to be. Drink if not hatred now kindled him, and drink seemed to become hatred as he saw again Romulan Montargo's exceptional face, garlanded in its black hair, above the blasphemously adopted habit.

"Now," said Saffiro precisely, and impressively swirled out his sword from its scabbard.

Romulan glanced at it. His appearance did not change.

"And what," he said, "is my quarrel with *you?*"

"Draw," said Saffiro, "and discover."

"Oh, pray tell me first."

"I mean to recompense one you killed."

"Leopardo Chenti."

"Not he. The one you claimed your friend. Mercurio Estemba."

Still Romulan remained, detached it seemed, uninterested.

"Chenti slew him, not I."

"Liar! Felon and traitor. Devil. Backstabber."

"So many titles," said Romulan.

"So many, and all vile. Each earns you death."

"Which I gather the Duke has decreed for me."

"No, the brink is nearer than that."

"Sir," Romulan said, with great gentleness, "if you would keep from cutting off your nose, or some other, conceivably more valuable part, you should refrain from waving your blade in the air like a daisy which, I assure you, it is not."

The inflexion, the pattern of the words, they were both Mercurio's. Romulan recognized it with a sullen shock, a numbed limb jarred. Saffiro recognized it with fury. He yelled like an enraged child:

"Draw! Fight me on this ground. Or I'll kill you as you killed him—empty-handed."

"Alas. I broke my sword on the door of the tomb."

"And yet more lies. Mercurio's sword was broken. Yours is not. Come," Saffiro said, his voice falling. "I will allow you space to catch your breath. No doubt you had some labor in the Chenti tomb, arranging the stiffened legs of your mistress with your companion's aid, so you might dance with her."

Romulan said, "Dance—"

"Dance the dance that's danced on the belly, or the back. The merry dance the lover returns for when his lady has no means to prevent him."

Saffiro panted, frowning, seeing a response at last. It was a sort of bewilderment only, yet, painted over by the low moon, it had a look of madness, too.

"And who helped you," Saffiro gabbled. "Your bastard cousin, that Benevola who *sings*? Dancing and singing. And did you enjoy her, your honey love, darling Iuletta?"

The face had continued to reveal such a scarcity of feeling Saffiro had missed it. When Romulan came toward him it was at a run. Somehow the wavering sword was beaten aside, away, and even as Saffiro peered after its flight, in disbelief, Romulan's hands had gripped him. Saffiro found himself wrenched excruciatingly from balance by his hair as the first blow thundered against him, seeming to shatter his rib cage.

Saffiro attempted retaliation, but his lashing fists and feet were deflected and submerged. He went down and felt the other come down on top of him like a springing lion. Blow on blow clove through him, so that his only defense became to roll and grunt, mutely asking the bombardment to end. This was not as he had planned.

Then he heard his own voice, like that of some other, begging for mercy, and shame made him weep, and still he could not silence himself. He did not know any longer what damage had been done to him. His face had lost its perfect fit upon his bones, he was bloody, and thought himself disfigured.

Then, quite suddenly, the beating stopped. Groaning, Saffiro crawled on his knees and lost the wine he had drunk so earnestly. The pain caused by this simple exercise brought him close to fainting and as he sank down again, a couple of kicks were delivered to his back.

He heard Romulan's feet go away, and the susurration of the long mantle, and then, with nauseous fear, heard them return. Something fell beside him on the rough lawn.

"Your brave steel, noble adversary," Romulan Montargo said.

Saffiro lay a long while, fully conscious now, knowing his enemy stood over him, not knowing what he should do. Eventually, there was an instruction.

"Take your useless sword," Romulan said, "and get up."

Saffiro, in abject abhorrence, reached out and gripped the flung-down blade. It rendered support as he strove to rise. Too soon he was what passed for upright, swaying, hunched forward from the anguish in his abused guts, staring through a visor of blood and bloody hair at the conquering knight he had meant, and sworn, to slay.

"You," Romulan said, "listen. Leopardo Chenti dispatched Flavian Estemba by thrusting him on the sword I held ready to defend myself from the Chentis. Iuletta Chenti lies undisturbed in the sepulchre. She was my wife. Now she is that thing which all of us shall be: carrion." Saffiro made a sound, swiftly choked off. Romulan observed him. A few thin lines from Saffiro's nails ran down the backs of his hands. Otherwise the fight had not marred him. But, like Saffiro, he wept. The tears were intermittent and he paid them no heed. He said, "I do not slaughter my friends, I do not violate my dead. And there is your sword, which you may swallow."

And then he went away across the lawn, not even, though Saffiro did not note this, in the direction of the Chenti mausoleum.

Bowed over, gasping, bleeding, almost witless, Saffiro tried to concentrate solely upon the weight and strength of the implement in his hand. Though, obediently, he had indeed listened, he had not altered his opinion. And so he swelled on his failure, sobbing with misery and disappointment in himself, until the wine, of which he had been despoiled, but which had yet left its rhythms in his brain, caused the sword to twitch and twist and seem to take on a life all its own.

At which, Saffiro looked at it, and from which he looked up and after the retreating shadow-shape of his foe.

The moon cut through the garden like a knife. It was like soft water on his wounds. Saffiro straightened, and breathed the moonlight. And felt his inner self revive in him.

He ran, now, and did not stumble, and if Romulan heard him, Romulan did not turn to see. So that a handful of yards from him, Saffiro raised the living thrumming sword, and called with savage joy.

"*Montargo!*"

And as Romulan hesitated and then came about to face him, Saffiro lunged. The sword drove forward like the beak

of a ravenous bird. There seemed no impediment. It was irresistible. Metal raced and vanished to a third of its length and
was drawn out again with a purple flash that spattered Saffiro's beaten hands with blood. Then he stood away to view,
from a proper vantage, Romulan Montargo's death.

The agony was beyond all agony, yet he had not cried out.
There seemed to have been no time. The light went from his
eyes and he saw it go, and Saffiro watched it go, each one on
either side of two darkening windowpanes of bluest glass.
Then the windows dulled.

Lying, as Saffiro had lain, he did not notice it as the blood-
smeared sword was wiped on his borrowed robe.

But Saffiro, very conscious of the Chenti tomb, had heard
the scrape of a door. He hastened away among the mausoleums and the heavy trees, the paean of his vengeance stifled in
his soul. For once, he had achieved something. And he was
drunk enough still, the doubt and creeping fright of the deed
had not yet come to him. Tomorrow he would regret it, its
method, and—at last—its impetus. Tomorrow in the physician's hands, temporarily disfigured but no more than that,
and somehow made aware by the simplicity of his injuries of
the unfittingness of himself for such a classic and enormous
role. He would regret, too, the unsigned letter he had flung to
the Chenti Tower as the bell struck for midnight.

But Electra, poised in a pool of lamplight, her black hair
down her spine like a coil of snakes, had scanned the curious
faded brownish ink once only before burning it, that solitary,
unambiguous sentence. Which she would nevertheless retain
forever in her shriveled heart.

*This I have written in the blood, washed from my hands,
of one who no longer lives.*

The priest had remained a moment, framed by the mausoleum doors. The night seemed empty of life, only a dim rustling went away across the garden that might be the passage
of some questing animal. The body of the man was not immediately visible, yet the priest seemed to descry it at once.
Presently he went across the lawn, and kneeling by the side
of Romulan Montargo, examined him with a light punctili-
ousness, then let him go.

The darkness on the ground canceled the face of the priest,
but rising and returning to the mausoleum, the moon caught
him. He was impassive. Death for Fra Laurus, seemingly, in
any form was minor, perhaps irrelevant.

Inside the tomb, the candles fluttered at the closing of the door, steadied, and burned on. As they did so, they struck a dark red spark among the garnets of Iuletta's bodice, a spark which went out, and then was struck again. Suddenly the black petal wavered and drifted from her breast.

Fra Laurus walked to the side of the death couch, and looked down on the girl who lay there, and who breathed, deeply and slowly, the heartbeat discernible in the column of her throat. After a few minutes, her eyelids swam upward, with a lazy dreaminess. The blue of the eyes, now revealed, brought a lawless splendor and vehemence to the exquisite face, but as yet they appeared to see nothing, or at least they did not ask what they saw.

"Now I fathom it," the priest said quietly, without inflection. "The Gemini. Twins of one essence. Each is the other."

At which the blue eyes drifted to him as mildly as the petal had drifted, unalarmed, yet to ask for sure.

"An alchemy," the priest said. And then, to the awakening girl, "Lie calmly. The circumstance is strange. You are not dead, but alive and in the mortal world."

"But—" the word was only a whisper. The vault of the tomb magnified it, made it audible. "I have died. I drank death. And then a shadow came and pierced me with a sword—the hurt, the hurt of it—"

Unafraid, the tiny whisper, but terror now beating in the startled eyes. And then the voice rising up whole and wild: *"What is this place?"*

"Fear nothing," Fra Laurus said, without compassion or unkindness, but with such authority that the eyes complied, and the lips, smoothing and growing still. "You will pay heed to me, and I shall lesson you. There's no danger. There is no punishment. But you will need great strength to encompass what this night sets on you."

TWENTY-FOUR

"Love leads here, then."

"Here? Where is this 'here' you speak of?"

"The land beyond the gorgeous gate. Open your eyes, and see."

"Yes—I see a sky, now. A sky the color of the palest reddest wine."

"Wine of roses. The pale red rose of love."

Truly, the sky was crimson, like a rose, nor was it the sky of sunset. The shade of it was uniform, only softer here and there where clouds sailed like bubbles. And high above, at the apex, the sun itself, its disc and its brilliance both misted over, like a rosy pearl.

His eyes ran downward, seeking the earth. And so he saw a palisade of extraordinary towers, higher than any he had ever known, some thin as needles, or looking to be, others not much broader, and some in silhouette against the blush of the sky, and some translucent like old glass, letting the rays of the sky sheer through them. And then his eyes reached a somber wall, and on the wall two jet-black urns. Between them, someone idly sat, watching him in return through the pomegranate air.

"Is it you?"

"I."

"Then I am—"

"In Hades, the country of lost souls. In Hell. In hereafter. Some condition not the one you left."

"I'm dead."

"Yes, child. My regrets, and welcome to the endless sunset of the damned."

A mandolin leaned by the wall, the yellowish white of aging ivory. Flavian Estemba, generally called Mercurio by those who had known him, was clad in the garments he had worn to the wedding at Marivero, the garments in which he had died in the Basilica square. Untarnished, immaculate, the brazen pineapples of the doublet. There was no mark to show where the sword had gone into him, or out.

Romulan glanced, half in foreboding, at his own apparel. The priest's robe, and under it the clothes he had ridden in from Lombardhia. The fabrics were untorn and unbloody. The wound—

"No, my dear," Mercurio said. "You're done with that. Let it go."

"Let it go then," Romulan said, and with an aching heaviness of the spirit, which now was all he was, he moved a short way along the terrace, and looked over.

This view he seemed at first familiar with. The downsurge of the ancient garden, a coalescence of alleys, walls, courtyards and streets. And there, the square of the Basilica itself. This was Verensa, a Verensa seethed at the bottom of a cup of wine, a Verensa oddly and subtly distorted. . . .

"Hell, then, is the town."

"Perhaps." Mercurio's voice was musical, exactly as remembered. "Perhaps, to another man, his birthplace and not ours. We see each through our own dark and misleading glass. Turn that way, and search for the Montargo Tower. Can you find it?"

Romulan turned and stared. The phantasmal parodies of a score of towers arose, but the one he sought eluded him. The stones of Montargo were absent. While in the Basilica square, now he swung back and searched in that direction, a building had sprung up, sable for the Basilica's whiteness, and many-tiered, like some temple of the antique East. Lights burned and coruscated there, as if a fire blazed within.

"What place is that?"

"The place to which we are invited for our entertainment."

Mercurio was already in the process of leaving the garden, swinging over a broken shoulder of the terrace and vanishing on to the path below. Half recollecting, Romulan tensed to hear the notes of the mandolin plinck upward in his wake, but they did not.

Nevertheless, as before, Romulan would follow, listlessly now. There was something in him which should clamor for questions to be answered, and was dumb. Nor did he feel any urge to resist those actions which this hinterland of the grave demanded. Even though to approach the burning palace might be to surrender himself to the fires of demons, who would then work out on him their reward for his earthly sins. Could it be Mercurio would lead him to that? Why not? Romulan experienced no trepidation, only a quantity of uncurious wonder.

His murderer's sword he could just envision, mostly the excruciation that had filled and then emptied him. And overlaid upon this sightless scene, the ghostly form of a girl who had been his lover, but no longer, for in this world love would not linger, having no purpose. Nor did it seem to him he could find her here. This Hell was not as he had ever been taught, or imagined—unless—was it that once before he had glimpsed such a thing, a microcosm inside a crystal? And could this still be so, for surely, beyond the towers the hills that went up were made of crystal, transparent and glittering, and beyond them, there was nothing but the red sky.

Mercurio walked a little before him. The grey-gold hair, the doublet, the mandolin (now cadaverous), hung from his shoulder—so much that was to be identified. And yet, if love were dead with the flesh, and kinship and friendship dead, this was a stranger he followed, possibly toward flames.

No fear touched Romulan, but he said, "The palace you'd visit. Whose, and what goes on there?"

"The shadow of a feast, and we the shadows that sit down to it. The lord of the palace is the Duca."

"The Duca."

"And who should be Duke here, do you suppose?"

Humanly—such idiosyncracies, maybe, were reluctant to fade—Romulan sneered. Arrogantly, he said,

"You'd drag me before Lucifer himself, then. I did not ask you, yet, if you forgave me my part in your death."

Flavian Estemba had reached the point on the descending path where a damson tree grew in Sana Verensa. One stood here also, but a dead tree, without fruit or leaves, a mere carving of branches. Under their edited shade Estemba turned to him unhurriedly.

"When I lived," Mercurio said, "I would have forgiven you anything that required my forgiveness. But I live no longer. Forgiveness, resentment, partiality and hate, all these devils of the flesh and brain are gone. For a while, one inquires after them, as of sick friends, one endeavors to perform their drama. But one tires. One rests."

"No appetite for vengeance, then?"

"No appetite of any sort. If that is retribution, then peace is our scourge."

"And is this the sum? The mortification of our humors under this rose of a sky, and nothing else?"

"Who knows, who knows? I thought you were done with questions."

"So I thought, too."

Romulan went forward, as if toward some painting or a statue, and looked into its face. The verity of all that Mercurio had said was there. The handsome countenance of his soul, so entirely resembling that of his earthly body, was yet unlike and very changed. There was such tranquility in it, such terminus. It had no inner light and hardly any outer expression. The madness, the quicksilver that had earned the name, these things were gone forever. Mercurio, but Mercurio no more.

And to this deadly complacence Romulan, too, would come. Already he had felt the lulling breath of it upon his awareness, a mild going out of all the coals and the lamps that were life. Must he fight the lethargy, or was it resistless as sleep?

Flavian nodded to him. As he moved on again, Romulan kept pace with his step. They went out of the garden, and walked between the strangely skeletal walls beyond, and behind them, the towers of Hell stretched up against the crystal hills. They had no emblems, those towers, no banners, and no windows, and their wonderful distinctness they owed to the lack of any dust.

As they arrived at the edge of the square, Romulan took note of the fountain. It did not play, while on the rim sat a black cat with eyes of carnelian; it did not run at their approach. And even as he beheld the cat, a beast also condemned to Hell, or else a figment of translated remembrance, a flight of dark doves burst from the highest tier of the blazing palace, like ashes from a brazier. The next moment, thunder rolled across and across the sky, and rain came down on the square. Each drop of rain was a drop of fire. They fell on his clothing, into his hair and on his hands, and every flame was warm as milk and dainty as a petal. And so he understood Hellfire did not, after all, have the means to burn.

In the rain, they climbed the long stair toward the vast double doors of the palace tower. The doors were bronze, and over them bronze creatures loomed on dragon wings: the angels of Hell, flung into the Pit, the Fall from Heaven that preceded the Fall of men. The doors opened the instant the stair top was achieved.

The briefest lobby, like a valve, gave on a banquet hall

(familiar, unfamiliar). There was an impression of walls that
flew ever upward into a ceiling of light. Out of the light, impressive swords hung down, their blades twelve feet or more
in length. Black vases tipped beneath out of which gushed
jets of fire. But, more bizarre than anything, the enormous
room was filled by people. Men and women in the multitudinous finery and colors of countless Houses circled about
each other, and posed, in chains and wreaths and knots.
Their appearance was unnaturally natural. They conversed,
and drank from goblets of the most lucent glass, they peram-
bulated with linked arms. The gowns of the women swept the
floor and their Eastern slippers peeped from under the hems.
The legs of the young men in the naked lustre of short doublet and moulded hose assumed their ritual lines of elegance
and display. There a rope of pearls toyed with, and there a
sweetmeat. And there a low reverberation of formal mirth
swelled and diminished. And there a woman passed, flirting a
fan of plumes.

Romulan looked along their ranks, and saw the hawklike
profile of a man who had died of a fever when Romulan
himself was twelve years of age. And not much distance
away another who had been killed at the height of Floria's
feud with the Lippis. The woman with the plumed fan turned
to Romulan, and inclined her head graciously, without interest. How had she perished, and what sin had earned her the
feasts and fires of Hell?

Wine stood on a table. He took up one of the peerless
goblets—glass sheer as air—and filled the bowl from a jug of
gold chased with silver. (The woman had looked away from
him, as women in the world had not been wont to do so
quickly.) He drank the crimson fluid from the glass. It
seemed real, full and heady, the juice of a vineyard.

"It tastes of wine."

Flavian glanced at him. The glance was very like the
woman's, courteous, barely seeing.

"And will taste of wine while you recall wine's taste."

"And to you?"

"Of nothing."

"And to me, tomorrow, of nothing?"

"But not tomorrow. Here, there's neither day nor night, no
yesterday, and no today."

Romulan lifted his brows, some joke almost on his lips—
stillborn. And soon the wine would die on his lips also.

He set down the goblet, and as he again began, involuntarily, to scrutinize the hall, a pair of long unblinking eyes echoed his scrutiny. But this apparition was too recent. Romulan gazed, lips parted, his hand moving of itself toward the dagger in his belt.

The sleeves were correctly tied now, the hair, like ginger spice, was groomed. This stylish parcel hesitated beside Romulan, and then made to go on.

"Wait." Romulan caught the flawless sleeve, and won back Leopardo Chenti's stare.

"What, sir, do you want of me?"

"I am your assassin. What do you want of *me?*"

"Take your hand from my arm."

"And my deathblow from your flesh? What if I cannot?"

Leopardo offered the slightest brushing with his fingers, and Romulan found his grasp had been suspended.

Betrayed by his own incorporeal form, Romulan said swiftly: "Think of your death, and remember who I am."

"I remember you. You're nothing to me."

"I sent you here."

"And someone has sent you."

"If I could, I'd pay him for it."

Leopardo's eyes poured into his. They had a terrible depth that told only of unoccupancy, Yet, for a second, the mouth was wry.

"There's no coin here, Romulan Montargo, to pay for anything. All is free. And all is worthless. Flourish in the bounty of the Duke."

Trumpets sounded from somewhere inside the seams of the tower. The crowd made a suitable respectful noise. Romulan was taken with a horrid desire to laugh. Here the old man came himself. Lucifer the Prince. But what else?

Romulan took heed across the distance, between the headdresses, the caps, the mantled curls, of an entry of cloth-of-gold and black, while the trumpets peeled themselves to nothing. But the assemblage, already swaying like a young forest, next uprooted itself and flowed to the tables. Romulan, borne with them, seated himself, and when he looked again, beheld the Duke far off from him, a manikin framed by a tall ebony chair. Which did not greatly matter, since he had been named already, and that in a tomb by night.

There was food on the tables. Romulan reached toward it and drew back his hand. He saw how the other feasters did not feast, toying now with bread and pearls and meat and fans alike. Beside him, to his left, a woman puzzled over a

jeweled book that had no words in it. To his right another cut
up a peach into a myriad slivers with a tiny knife. Flavian
Estemba was watching her. She was beautiful, yet there was
no fascination now in the eyes of one who had been so enamored of beauty. Across the room, Leopardo Chenti sat like a
figure of skillfully painted wax. Here, liking died, and hate
died, with the dead.

No, all questioning was done. To this Romulan had descended, to this painless Nemesis that would destroy him a
second time, melting away all that was within him, all that
had made him a man, able to love, to rage, to mourn, all that
had been himself.

Yet to this he had already turned, when alive, this dullness,
this refusal of anguish and hope alike. Unwilling to believe
some chance of happiness remained, incapable of summoning
the force of prayer, inciting death in the Basilica garden. Yes,
his sin, worse than all other sins, was that denial, and now
justice had discovered him.

A faint murmur was blossoming from the tables, thickening, becoming a cry.

With offended shock, Romulan interpreted it as a call for
the voice and mandolin of Flavian Estemba.

And Flavian was standing up, glancing about at them.

"Well," he said. "What would you have me sing?"

"A song, Mercurio!" someone shouted, loud as recollection,
and the formal mirth again started up.

"Oh, a song. I do not sing songs. I sing dreams, and they
are nothing. And since you'll have me sing nothing, I need
not sing at all."

The feasters in the hall answered with uproar, next with a
sudden silence, from which there came the Duca's voice like
a low far drumming.

"To sing, Flavian Estemba: I request it of you."

Flavian bowed to the ebony chair, with charm, without
mockery, with no edge at all.

"I ask a favor in return. My minstrel's fee."

"Sing, Orpheus. And ask what you want."

Flavian walked around the tables and between them, out
on to the fire-freckled space of the floor. As he did so, he un-
slung the ivory cadaver of the mandolin from his shoulder.

The hall remained silent, and at the announcing chord, no
fresh silence fell. Everyone of their faces was turned toward
Estemba like flowers toward the sun. But faces that were
void, faces that listened and heard nothing, as he had told

them, faces that dreamed the hollow dreams of those who did not sleep.

And Lucifer himself, his hands folded, his white and priestly brow bending, as if in concentration. . . . To rule such a kingdom, what could he be but a desert, like all the rest?

Then the song sank upward and gathered like black petals on the air.

> *Who can know where love will find us,*
> *Love far darker than the night,*
> *Love far colder than the snow—*
> *That has been both warm and bright—*
> *Sung in shadow, that was show;*
> *Bitter-tasting are you now,*
> *Music of sweet and delight.*

The last notes sighed from the mandolin and were gone. The promised nothingness contained the hall. There was no applause, and only the lifted heads were lowered, in homage or wretchedness or the awesome inadequacy of unfeeling.

"I deserve no reward," Flavian Estemba said. "But still I ask it."

The Hell-Priest, ensconced in his black frame, inclined the head that was no longer tonsured, and from which the malt-colored hair cascaded to a golden breast properly innocent of a crucifix.

"Ask."

"A gentleman feasts with you tonight, an acquaintance of mine, and recently married. He has looked around for his wife, Lord Duke, and not seen her. Though he's good reason to think her here."

"Mistaken reason. She lives."

And at the phrase, as when he had seen Leopardo, for a few moments Romulan thought himself, too, to be alive.

Throwing back his chair, he strode up the hall, under the fiery vases, past all the banks of the damned, and came to the place where Laurus reclined, who was Lucifer. But before Romulan could speak, Flavian Estemba spoke again from the center of the hall.

"My fee, then, my lord. They say the living necromancer can compel the dead to talk with him. Cannot the Master of the Underworld draw down the living to converse with the dead?"

Lucifer raised his hand, and everywhere flames shattered. Darkness smoked outward from the walls and from the ceiling which had been light. Here it seemed was the shadow, in which dead lovers sang the songs they had vaunted at the sun of the world. The shadow of impending night.

"I have summoned her," Lucifer said, "and she draws near. It is a dream she has, of nothing. See, where she comes."

And the shadow folded apart like a breaking bud and from it came a woman, blown on a black wind of hair. She was like a ghost, translucent, luminous, tinted by indefinite colors. Her eyes were open, and now and then they blinked with a glorious glimmering languidness. Otherwise, her face was quite as void as the faces of the dead themselves. And, as the wind that made no sound blew her hair, the long waves of her dress, about her, she herself stood in the heart of its energy, motionless.

Romulan stepped away from the black chair and the Archdemon. He moved toward the woman, hardly knowing that he did so, only that she drew closer to him. While at his back the priest said soberly: "The embodied fail to perceive the soil, even when most they look for it. Nor do they attend when most they entreat for chat. She'll neither hear nor see, so faithless are the living to the dead."

The hall was black now, all but the last flame of Iuletta, and there, as he went by, a man limned with her radiance, stepping aside as if in at a doorway, the mandolin on his shoulder bald-white a moment as a halved apple, before it turned away with him into the dark.

Alone, Romulan paused before the apparition of his wife.

"Bright angel," he said to her, to her living ghost, that could not hear him, "bright angel, see how you teach the torches, that they fail and fade in shame. Bright love, I shall forget as I forget the taste of wine, the perfume of the rose—" The words he took for courtliness, and somberly he let them come, before suddenly he knew how he spoke, and that the measure of this language, its stylized cadences, was that of a prayer. Living or dead, he had not brought himself to pray to God. But now he prayed to Iuletta. The pilgrim before the icon, he asked unreasonably—for what he did not know. Until at last he met again her eyes, and saw that they had widened, and that, despite the pronouncement of Laurus-Lucifer, as if through a kind of veil they seemed to look at him. Those eyes which were his own, his eyes in the face of Iulet, which now were two sapphire lamps seeking across a huge gulf of night or perhaps of black water, two stars, two shining fractures in a colossal gate.

"Iuletta Montargo de Chenti."

She turned, and faced the priest across the bare stone altar.

"No one," he said, "is there."

"I heard a sound."

"The mules have been loosed for the present from the cart and are grazing outside, with the mare from Lombardhia. At sunrise," Fra Laurus said, indicating the oratory's open door patched by night, foliage and stars, "the young servant of the Montargos will arrive. His horse, by dislodging him and running off on the Padova road, kept him from his attempt to follow Romulan Montargo. Now he sleeps in a wayside barn. Just before dawn he'll wake, and walk here across the hills. His name is Doro. You will find him bruised but astute."

"But if another should come—" she said.

"No other will come."

"Will you make it to be so?"

"I know it to be so."

Iuletta pressed her ringed fingers to her throat, as if to communicate with the pulse which beat there, quickly, steadily. She was drowsy still, not so much from the effects of the stuporous drug with which he had duped her, more from the glow of the candleflame at which he had persuaded her to stare, until it had seemed to burn into and become her spirit.

How strange, all this. To wake to life, too bewildered to be angry, and soon too much in awe of this magician to be so. And then, to gaze on fire, and after to be lifted from the couch of death, to be led and supported and shown death itself, lying on a lawn by night, under the cruelly constant moon, who would obscure nothing, not even the face which next Iuletta must lean close to see. To see Romulan, as she had never thought to see him again, and to see him not, for he was no longer at hand inside the glove of flesh. Yet, so at the very first she had witnessed him, carried up as if dead, offered before her like a sacrifice. His eyes seemed only sleeping now, as hers had been. Might she not waken him? How strange, how strange. Surely the most awful despair should have rushed her away with it, but had not. Quiet as the night, she bowed above him, quiet as the night she followed the tall priest when he took up Romulan from the ground and bore him to the little gate, the alleyway and the cart with its stoical mules. And, the dead concealed within the cart, and she

shawled over by some homely cloak that had the smell of
sage and straw, they rode through Sana Verensa, under the
high red windows of the towers, one tower with a huge cat
upon its topmost roof, by the pallor of the Emperor's Monument, to the gate and its fast rank bribery—and so into the
open land beyond.

Here was the route she was said to have taken on the eve
of her marriage to Romulan. In the cell of the hermit's oratory she had lain in the lie, when in reality she had lain in
the arms of her husband, between the posts of the inn bed
and the tumbled flowers and sheets. Now Romulan was to lie
here, in that liar's cell she had never visited, on the stone
floor of it, while moonlight poured over him once again from
round-topped windows. There had been chests here, too, but
they had gone away into the cart. The priest, his own haulier,
was a strong man, but perhaps the chests were unfilled. Now
the cell was totally the possession of her lover. Alone there he
lay, as he would lie alone forever. She looked to see, and saw
a haunting flame like a topaz on a candle. The flame stood
between her and the death of Romulan and her pitiless insurmountable agony, the blade in her breast that was the sword
of utter loss.

She knew it all, the magic potion that had played her
death, the slaughtering in earnest of her love. How long before the miniature flame would also die and she would know
her tragedy and go mad? But there were no words to ask the
wise and uncanny priest. And now, in any case, he spoke to
her.

"Come, Iuletta."

Dazedly, yet with a curious certainty, she went with him,
from the altar, into the cell. And beheld death again, before
the priest gestured her to look up.

Then, beautifully, and with the miraculous grace of the
magus, he beckoned, and a gentle light bloomed all about
them. It had no source, this light, and perhaps she imagined
it, or he gave her to imagine it.

Composed, in the aura of that which she had always intui-
tively credited—magic, the human psychosm, the majesty of
all gods and One—her lips curved as if with pleasure.

"In the myth of the Egepsti," the magician said to her,
"when Osirus perished at the hands of his red-haired enemy,
his wife, Isetta—whose name is not unlike your own—sought
his body and took it away with her to the swamps beside the
River Nilus. And here, by means of her sorcery, and through

the vitality of her love, she permitted him who was dead to live. Answer if you hear me, Iuletta Montargo de Chenti."

"I do hear, Father," Iuletta murmured.

"Then I will tell you of yourself. Heed me carefully. There is in you the Chaldean seed, the grain which is the root of Power. You have turned to the longing of the flesh, and so the seed will wither, but not yet. Still you are not all of the flesh, and these things which have seemed random chance to you have been the searchings of your essence, of your soul. Indeed it was you yourself, and not the harlot's herbal witchery, which brought this man to you. And now, if you will it, may bring him to you once again."

"But," Iuletta faltered, prettily, almost childishly. "But I can do nothing—"

"And do you," said Fra Laurus, "believe this?" Iuletta's eyes rose to his, stared, became two floods of seeing sightlessness. "Do you, who love, accept that your love is finished? Though the sword passed through his body a thousand times, do you believe in it?"

Iuletta lifted her hands to her face, and held her face between her hands, staring through the priest into the heart of the flame.

"No," she said. Her eyes returned, and leveled on his like two spears. "No, spiritual Father." And the flame dissolved in the bluest smoke, she let down her hands, her face grew stern, severe, losing all its beauty in a sudden transfiguration, dehumanized and limitless. "*No.*"

"Then," he said, "it is with you."

Her eyes blinded her, and when she saw again, the priest was gone.

Then, for several minutes, she became indeed a child. She ran to the door and found only the night, star-splashed and voiceless, and with the horse munching placidly nearby under the pines. The cart and the mules had departed, and when she ran out on to the grass, the moonlight pulled away the shade from the hills and showed that the priest was no longer anywhere among them.

So then she ran back into the oratory and fell down at the altar and sobbed and begged, until it came to her that her tears and prayers had no substance, that despair and agony had not yet seized on her. And then she got up, politely crossing herself before God, and walked back slowly to the door of the cell, forgetting Him.

There was no longer any illumination save that of the

moon. Its description of Romulan was so heartless and so bloodless. No store was to be set by it.

Iuletta's beauty, which had already returned, reflected up at her from the white face on the floor. So she kneeled at last, and kissed the mouth. There was no warmth in his lips, yet she kissed them again, and once again, and so her own warmth was imparted to them. At this, she took his hands and held them to her breast. As she did so, she felt the strangest tingling in her palms and fingers, as if some supernatural chemical had been absorbed there. She considered it, and then she received it into herself, and dismissed it immediately.

She had been dead, surely she had been, and now she lived. And Romulan, not her good angel, not her slave, nor her master (though she could remember this), but herself. And she was Romulan. Yes, she could sense him now, his eyes, her eyes, behind the wooden eyelids, looking back at her. And the colossal gate between them. But she would bring him back through the gate.

She called his name, very low. And once more. And once more. For, as with her kiss, it seemed to her the resonance of her voice could fill him, so he must give back some echo, as the wind or the sea sang in a shell, they said.

Later, her voice grew hoarse and dry with calling, became a whisper, and she no longer felt her hands, they had become his hands, or her body, for it had become his body. And as she breathed, she breathed for him.

The night gave up its light and the moon went away. The night was a score of nights, a world of nights. And eventually the night entered her mind, and she lay down beside Romulan and upon him, in his arms and he in hers, as once before. There was a distance now in the blackness beyond the windows, and the stars were out, having masked themselves humbly before the intimation of sunrise. Iuletta's heart beat slowly now, slowly, unevenly, but also swiftly, urgently. Her heart beat twice at every beat. Her heart, and the heart of Romulan, beating also, beneath her hand, her breast.

Without amazement, for she had known he lived, she drew away again and looked at him. The torn doublet and the shirt, disturbed by her hand, revealed a slender seemly scar, like a rivulet. Maybe such a scar was only the impress of some pleat or fold of cloth, or a strand of the coiling hair of the girl who leaned above him.

Her face was like the face of any woman who lives, and

description unwrites itself. As his eyes opened, lighting on her with, for the moment, no memory or demand, he smiled. He had found only what he had thought to find. He took her down into his arms once more, and they lay in silence and comfort together.

When the dawn broke, when the astute servant came, there would be means and human cunning enough to invent tales to shelter the truth, for others, for themselves. That, and the fury of the broken tomb, the rumor of death to leave behind, and all the wide world to fly to.

But for now they were only nameless lovers, and the shadow of the night had passed them by.

TANITH LEE

"Princess Royal of Heroic Fantasy and Goddess-Empress of the Hot Read."

—Village Voice (N.Y.C.)

Presenting C. J. CHERRYH